Prayer
to the
Eskimo Saints

To request permissions, contact the publisher at:
publishing@villagebooks.com

ISBN: 979-8-218-58021-6

Library of Congress Control Number: 2024927235

Edited by Nancy Tupper
Cover and book design by Jill Flores

Printed in the USA by IngramSpark

Village Books Publishing
1200 11th St.
Bellingham, WA, 98225
villagebooks.com

To all the Darcys

Prayer to the Eskimo Saints

Scott Swanson

I DON'T THINK WE EVER MADE LOVE in a bed. It was always outside, on the grass, in the leaves, with wildflowers blooming at eye level. First time we got naked, she was stretched out beside me, one knee cocked, drawn up on her elbows, her back arched high off the blanket. With her chin tucked down and tummy drawn flat, she watched my fingers drift over her skin, every sensation recorded on her lips, in the smile she couldn't contain. She was tanned all over from laying out in her yard, the tiny hairs on her tummy turned gold in the slanting afternoon light, the shadows of leaves like a leopard's skin across us both. My finger filled the diamond of her belly button, traced down around her stomach to the taut underside of her thigh. Sliding my hand up the length of her hip, over the swell of her bottom, I brushed the tickle spot at her waist, and she giggled. Dampness glistened along the curve of a breast, and when I leaned and blew cool air there, she caught her breath and pinned me with her eyes, so blue against white, white teeth against tan, her skin so smooth and her face so perfect I wanted to eat her, to absorb every inch of her, my beautiful gingerbread girl.

When finally we kissed, our legs slid together, winding slowly like the tendrils of a morning glory, like the dampened twists of platinum hair at Darcy's glistening temples. Our hips moved together as if they'd formed those shapes forever, the warmth of our bodies shocking, bone pressing soft against bone, muscle kneading muscle as we worked to smooth out every cleft and hollow that kept our skin apart.

Later, face to face and knee to thigh, I felt her breath upon my cheek as she talked about her father, studying the strands of gleaming hair caught in the corner of her mouth, the star shapes of her eyelashes when she cried. We could never get close enough. It was like we wanted to be inside each other, or maybe even *be* each other. I suppose that's the way love eventually goes wrong, when you see yourself in another person and don't like who they are.

Darcy's favorite color was red, her hair smelled like flowers, and she was fond of biting, but not too hard, just the tiniest crescents of fast-fading teeth marks, like wet tattoos on your skin. She liked eating wild strawberries, making dinosaur pancakes, and dancing alone without music. She always fell asleep when I read to her aloud, or when clutching my arm at the movies, staying up to all hours watching satellites and stars until dawn found us wrapped in a blanket. She didn't like perfume, and she rarely wore makeup, and would never, ever, let me enter her room. Some of my friends called her selfish, vain, caught up in her privileged life. But people just think that of beautiful young girls, and beautiful girls are the last ones to know what might actually be beautiful about them.

I can never breathe the scent of fresh-cut grass without thinking of her, never see a patch of dandelioned lawn without wanting to lie down on it, to look up at the clouds and reach out with my arms to see if some memory doesn't fall into them. I imagine her now leaning over me like that, her face a tide pool of cool blue shadow, star bursts of sunlight igniting her hair as she lowers her lips to my cheek. I cannot remember our last real kiss, though the taste of her mouth ever lingers.

PART
ONE

Chapter 1

FROM THE ROOF of the old Van Tassel apartments, you could look out over treetops to the Hudson River and the sinuous curve of the Tappan Zee Bridge, across to the cliffs of the Palisades and down to the skyscrapers in Manhattan. The gray stone turret of Brandywine Castle breached the green canopy of trees, a singular, solitary, fortress-like column where monks were once said to have lived. Encircled by pigeons like leaves in the wind, the pointed steeple of Saint Teresa's Church loomed above the edge of the building, tapered and armored in blue slate tiles, its gold cross lancing the clouds. Its bells had tolled the hour for as long as I'd lived, like a pulse I could feel in my wrist, peeling through the valley from hilltop to train tracks before fading out over the river.

Living with my mom in the red brick apartments, I had always walked to school, to Morse Elementary across the street, then Sleepy Hollow High School at the top of the hill. Shortcutting through the cellars and the laundry rooms, I'd resurface on Pocantico Street, its name derived from the slow green river once spanned by the Headless Horseman Bridge. Down in the playground on Beekman Avenue, Todd would be waiting on the swings, or under the marquee of the Strand Theater if it happened to be raining or snowing. Mouse struggled up from Barnhart Park with her ponderous armload of books, hooking up with Dionne at the top of Cortlandt Street where she'd hiked up the hill from the projects.

One side of the Avenue was fronted by trees overhanging the buckled sidewalks, a stacked-stone wall with a wrought iron fence defended by old men on benches. Across the street, on the merchant's side, we'd laugh and prance and walk backwards as we talked beneath colorful storefront awnings, shouting to friends in slow-moving cars who waved through opened windows. Hardware hung in the windows of Geldern's, salamis in Malandrino's Deli. Maguire's wrote its specials on butcher paper taped to the heavy glass door: pastrami, coleslaw, potato salad; corned beef on Saint Paddy's Day. Pete the Greek's sold beef and lamb gyros wrapped in aluminum foil, Mary Kay's lunch counter served ice cream sundaes with whipped cream six inches tall, poked full of cherries like a Christmas tree, tinseled with milk chocolate sprinkles. In junior high we'd all pack into Rosenbloom's and swipe corncob pipes from the rack, the sweet-smelling perfume of cherry-blend tobacco engulfing the block like high mass. One summer the rage was red-striped peashooters, a nickel a piece at Sol's. Navy beans littered the streets like ball bearings, cheap at a quarter a box.

Arriving at Rose's Corner Store, we'd chip in for a bottle of Coke, old Ollie sipping coffee on his stool by the register, the whole place reeking of Marlboros. Eric Neumann might dash in for Zig-Zags and Visine before heading off to class, his forest green Audi double parked in the street, its door left wide open in traffic. Pausing at the corner in their parents' new cars, the Manor kids waited for the stop light to change, the girls wiping fog where they'd breathed on the window to sneak a quick peek at Todd. Deloit's orange Mustang sat idling by the benches where the greaser kids palmed cigarettes, reliving the glory of years gone by before they all flunked out of school.

Climbing the grassy hill to the high school—everyone panting but Todd—he'd pose on the steps in his linebacker's stance and jab his thick finger in my chest. "Lunch at Malandrino's, and don't be late, or I'll kick your skinny Dutch ass." I'd smirk, and nod, the girls would laugh, and Todd would race off to the gym; Dionne to chorus; Mouse to math; and I would trudge off to the art room.

That's how it went, and that's how it had gone almost every day of my life, the people, the storefronts, the streets of my town like the Saturday morning cartoons: I'd seen the same episodes so many times I could mouth every word and *ka-bong!*, every sight, every sound and smell on the Avenue recalling the day just before, and the week before, and the year before that—every second since the death of my father.

I was never late for history class, where we studied every war but Vietnam, history confined to the long-dead past, never daring intrude on the present. Slouched by the window in the back of the room behind hulking Bosco Jones—Dionne's boyfriend and first negro captain of the football team—I could spy on the new girl undetected. Seated one row over and three desks up, she appeared unaware of my presence, freeing me to stare at the curve of her cheek, the silvery down on her neck. When she'd turn toward the window and the light caught her hair, each strand gleamed bright as a filament, her iris in profile a cat's eye marble, as blue and transparent as pool water.

Darcy sat with her long legs crossed and a bare foot bobbing, one loafer slipped off in the aisle. How I loved to study the arch of her foot, the way she unconsciously flexed it, the bones of her ankle, her elegant calf, the angular bend of her knee. Leaning forward just slightly she'd tug at her skirt, smoothing it over her hip, tapping her pencil on the tip of a tooth, the eraser as pink as her tongue. One day she pretended to drop that pencil, and bending to retrieve it she glanced down the aisle where I was too slow to react. Caught in the act, I struggled to smile, or do something less creepy with my face, and she winked at me through her curtain of hair before returning her attention to the chalkboard.

We never spoke until that spring when Dewey Arstahl, the art teacher, arranged a field trip to the Metropolitan Museum. Postponed since April due to the race riots in Newark and Harlem, the date was changed to May 13, my birthday. We were a mixed class of juniors: would-be writers, Kodak photographers, or anyone bookish or lazy enough to want to go to a museum. I'd known everyone on the bus since kindergarten, since Little League and Boy Scouts and stickball games at the playground. Everyone, that is, except Darcy Saint James, the prep school transfer student who walked up the aisle and sat down beside me in what was far from the only seat available.

"This is weird, huh?" she said without prologue, snuggling into the cushions. "It feels like grammar school, going to the big city."

Minutes must have passed before I spoke, and I heard myself say, "They took us to the Museum of Natural History, fifth, maybe sixth grade."

"We went to Saint Pat's. A mass by some Cardinal."

"That must have been cool," I stammered. "The spectacle."

Darcy shook her head. "Not really. It's no fun being Catholic."

Giving her silvery hair a toss, she adjusted the hem of her neckline. Her sundress was cotton, her loafers scuffed; she didn't look wealthy at all. "That's a new sweater," she was quick to observe, and pinched the blue wool of my sleeve.

Surprised that she'd noticed, my heart skipped a beat, and I ransacked my brain for a fitting reply. "It's a birthday present. From my mom," I added. "This is the first time I've worn it."

"Today? Today is your birthday?"

When I managed to nod, she wiggled in her seat, not one to conceal her excitement.

"Well, happy baby-day!" she squealed, this being the point where my mom or an aunt might have given me a kiss. Then she did kiss me, just a peck on the cheek that startled us both. "Thanks," I said, my face burning hot, so recently seared by her lips. "Thanks a lot."

"Soo," she exhaled, leaning back in her seat, "your name is Teal—a nice name, a duck's name. What else is interesting about you?"

There really was nothing interesting about me. I was an average kid, and I told her so.

"Hmmm," she *hmmed*, as if she knew better, "I heard your father died."

Shocked by the very mention of his name, I fumbled for a reply. It had been three years since my life had changed, in ways that I couldn't describe, and as much as I wanted to keep her talking, I didn't know what to say. "My dad was a cop," was all I came up with. "He died when I was twelve."

Pausing for a second to absorb this thought, as though trying it on for size, she said, "I'm trying to imagine how that must feel, your whole life turned upside down. See!" she exclaimed, when the moment had passed, "you're not so average after all!"

From what little I'd heard through the high school grapevine, Darcy Saint James had grown up in the Manor, briefly attended Saint Teresa's, but had since been living in private schools in New Hampshire, or maybe Vermont. Expelled from the last one, she was back at home and enrolled at Sleepy Hollow, her option of last resort.

"What about you?" I asked.

"Ohh," she sighed, "my parents are old. It's just a matter of time."

That wasn't really what I'd meant, but I let it go, looking to change the subject.

The bus was bouncing through the Bronx by then, through a minefield of steel plates and potholes. "Hey," I said, pointing out the window, "you ever been there?" Leaning with her shoulder pressed to mine, she strained to peer out the dirty window as we drove past Yankee Stadium, its name emblazoned in big blue letters across its curved façade.

"Nope," she said, "I've never been. Let's go sometime. Whaddya say?"

"Sure," I replied, trying to sound casual, swallowing the lump in my throat. "Why not?"

She smiled at me then, the narrowest crescent, and collapsed in her seat with her eyes closed. "Wake me up when we get there," she sighed, appearing to drift off to sleep.

Her impromptu nap lasted less than a minute, after which she began to tell me all about ducks, explaining how her family had a lake house somewhere, where she floated around in a boat, talking at length to a grumpy old man who eventually revealed all he knew about mallards, harlequins, and teals. I ended up telling her about going fishing with my dad and his brother, sleeping in tents on Army cots, getting up in the dark of morning. "And at dusk," I explained, "we'd cook hot dogs on sticks, holding them over the fire. My dad set our lawn chairs by the shore of the lake with our fishing poles propped against them, empty beer cans tied to their lines so they'd rattle on the rocks if we got a bite."

"You were drinking beer?"

"Not me, them, my dad and Uncle Walter. I was just a kid, before I ever tasted beer. I thought the world was perfect then, like nothing would ever change."

She looked at me then as though studying a painting, reading the look in my eyes. "That must have been fun," she said at length. "I want to go fishing, too."

"After the museum," I laughed. "And Yankee Stadium."

"Deal," she said, and held out her hand. When I took it in mine there was a static shock, and she snapped her hand back, giggling. "Once more," she said, and reached again, and our cool palms slid together, slowly, gently, hovering there for what seemed to me like minutes. I suppose I knew then that something would happen between us, something deep, and long, and bittersweet, the first of the *deals* and unspoken agreements that would haunt me the rest of my life. It was 1967, the Summer of Love, the summer that I loved, and was loved, more completely than I'd ever dreamed.

Chapter 2

THE METROPOLITAN MUSEUM took a bite out of Central Park a good city block in size, surrounded on three sides by luxuriant trees, the only building in Manhattan not hemmed in by concrete and glass. It felt like spring, the hazel wash of budding leaves softening the granite edges of things, alive with birds that chirped and flitted from branch to wooden bench. The wide stone stairway along Fifth Avenue bustled with visitors, groups and couples wandering lazily up and down or sitting on the steps smoking cigarettes, eating pretzels from the umbrellaed carts of sidewalk vendors. Fluted columns rose at the head of the stairs, stout as tree trunks beneath an ornate portico where pigeons cooed and long, silky banners furled green, purple, and gold.

A string of yellow school buses idled at the curb, frantic teachers waving their arms, shouting instructions as their students disembarked. We were probably the oldest kids there and in our coolness largely ignored the arrival of others, posing aloofly in the general vicinity of Mr. Arstahl while he and the bus driver pointed at each other's watches. Dewey was a large, gourd-shaped man with droopy gray eyes and a crew cut flat as an aircraft carrier. He wore a vest with a watch fob, and a tie clip that matched his gold cufflinks. He and the driver apparently approved of the time, and the driver returned to the empty bus and ground its gears away.

The other groups were mostly grade-schoolers toting paper lunch sacks, handmade name tags pinned to their sweaters. One was a class of very young Chinese girls in identical plaid skirts. With white wicker lunch boxes strapped to their backs and their black hair braided in pigtails, they giggled like the ringing of tiny bells, their cheeks so rosy and eyes so bright they might have been miniature clowns. A severe young woman, no less impeccably coiffed, signaled them to silence and ordered them to line up hand in hand and two abreast. They fell into formation with a practiced precision and at once marched off up the stairs, singing a cheerful, tinkling song in their lilting native tongue.

"Their voices are like flutes," said Darcy. "I wish we could take one home!"

"I'll speak to the bus driver," I joked, hoping to make her laugh.

We followed Dewey up the steps and through the heavy glass doors of the lobby. The cavernous chamber was taller than treetops, full of stone arches and the hollow refrain of a thousand cheerful voices. Silk banners hung in the mitered alcoves proclaiming the various shows, a chorus of bird song from dozens of sparrows echoing in the vaulted ceiling.

Dewey spoke to the garrulous ticket lady, who presented us each with a tin *MMA* button the size and shape of a nickel. Darcy asked for red but settled for pink. Mine was robin's egg blue. Helping me clip it to the neck of my sweater, her knuckles grazed my throat. She didn't appear to notice the contact, or accord it any significance, but I recorded our every encounter, each touch or overlong glance.

Gathered beside Michelangelo's *David*, in close enough proximity to warrant a bit of finger pointing, Darcy stared raptly at the nude sculpture and, after some moments, leaned in close and whispered, "He reminds me a little of you."

"I see what you mean," I had to agree. "But my *nose* is bigger."

Dewey gave me the evil eye and Darcy a little smile. When his attention returned to the rest of the class, I bent and whispered in Darcy's ear, "I think Dewey likes you."

"No," she replied, shaking her head. "I know when boys like me, and Mr. Arstahl doesn't. Not like that. I think he's homosexual."

Too stunned for words, I swallowed my tongue and stood watching Dewey drone on, searching for something—a sparkle in his eye, a lisp in his voice—to confirm what Darcy had told me.

"We have come here for *you*," Dewey was saying, "the art in this building is *yours*. That is the ultimate purpose of this trip, this pilgrimage, to avail you of this magnanimous gift." Warming to the subject, his expression grew thoughtful, his usually stoic demeanor turned mirthful.

"Tolstoy wrote a very long, very fussy essay called *What Is Art?* He was hardly the first to pose the question and will certainly not be the last. In a nutshell, he concluded that art is primarily *intent*, a motive within the artist to create something that contributes to the betterment, the nourishment of mankind. Or *humankind*, for all you women's libbers.

"I want you to be thinking about that as you absorb these magnificent paintings, and ask yourself if you can divine the artist's intent—if you think there was one—and whether it might be the kind that Tolstoy describes. Think also of how the masterpieces you see here are representative of an artist's life, their individual experience, and consider then whether art is confined only to the two-dimensional surface of a canvas.

"If Tolstoy is right, then the intent to create art, to revel in humanity, precedes the work itself, and therefore one's entire life is art, if informed by the desire to exalt in ourselves. And so, art students, whether or not you continue to draw, paint, write, or photograph, your lives can be lived with an artist's passion, experienced with an artist's sense of purpose and fulfillment, such that every deed and simple thought serves to celebrate us all."

I was oddly taken by what Dewey had said, and stared unabashedly at *David*, irrespective of his genitals. There was something naked about art itself, I thought, and the best art was the most naked, the most revealing of the artist, the artist as *all* people, marble penis not withstanding.

"Lunch at noon in the cafeteria," Dewey added, reminding me of Todd, and I wondered if Dewey would kick my ass if I dared to show up late. "Saddle up, people. Hold hands if you must. No singing."

Mr. Arstahl too had noted the march of the little Chinese girls, and everyone chuckled, pretending to appreciate his rare attempt at humor.

We scaled another flight of stairs to the second-floor galleries, sunlight pouring through the lobby windows, gleaming like chrome on the marble busts and ancient urns displayed there. A maze of galleries branched off at every turn, as cool and echoing as castle chambers. The first room we entered was full of canvases that stretched from floor to ceiling: Titian, Vermeer, Rembrandt Van Rijn, El Greco, and others I'd never heard of. Many of the paintings I recognized from books, and merging with the whispering knots of onlookers, we leaned in to read the name plates.

Darcy bent beside me, squinting to better see the deep blues and rich umbers swabbed on the monstrous canvases. "Was it just darker in those days," she whispered, "or did everyone paint by candlelight?"

"It was all about contrast," I sought to explain, "getting the tone just right." Pointing my finger, she followed its lead, sighting down the length of my arm. "See?" I elaborated, "Rembrandt's white collar, the pinkish glow of his cheek?"

Darcy's own rosy cheek was pressed to my bicep, the touch of it electric through my birthday sweater. Her bare arms were tanned in a sleeveless sundress patterned with tiny green flowers, the loop of her bra strap slipped down on one shoulder, as crimson as the blush on my face. "C'mon," she said, tugging at my sleeve, "it's way too crowded in here."

We made our escape without looking back, and I trailed her from room to room, our laughter deflected off the cool marble floors, returned by the towering ceilings. We jousted with knights in the great hall of armor, galloping the length of the room, walked like Egyptians with our elbows bent, and watusied to African drums. One entire wing appeared filled with Madonnas, the Holy Mother and her even Holier Child. Darcy posed beside them with her eyes cast down at a make-believe infant in her arms, a look of adoration on her angelic face, and I wondered if *she* was a virgin.

In the American wing we paused to rest in a canyon of landscape paintings, stopping at one in particular, a large, glowing canvas by an artist named Albert Bierstadt. "*The Rocky Mountains*," Darcy read from its brass name tag. "Wouldn't you love to live there?" she said, her blue eyes drifting over pink mountains, green forests, and gleaming waterfalls.

"Who wouldn't?" I replied.

"Woody Allen," she stated matter-of-factly. "He says driving in the country makes him vomit."

Sweeping an arm at the sprawling canvas, I said, "How could anyone *not* love this? Nature is the seed, the primordial source, the place where all art begins."

She shrugged. "Some people just have delicate stomachs. One time I threw up eating Pez."

It was quiet, lonely in the Asian Wing, as the delicate scrolls and ancient vases seemed to dictate. We were looking at one such timeless piece, a jade egg the size and shape of a football, into which a procession of tiny figures had been carved, spiraling up and around the polished surface of the stone. Their clothing and features were so meticulously sculpted, so perfectly scaled, that the egg itself was a portrait of patience and dedication, perhaps a lifetime of it, depicted in this journey of miniscule monks on a shiny green chunk of the earth.

"Can you see us in there?" Darcy asked, her finger poised on the glass. "It's like one of those hollow Easter egg things, the kind with the little round window."

We then heard a tiny titter of laughter and, turning, discovered a tidy row of bent heads lining one marble wall, blue plaid skirts and stark white stockings nearly phosphorescent in the dark. Appearing almost as part of the exhibit, the group of little Chinese girls sat each upon a wicker lunch box, hands gripping the ankles of their slender legs, foreheads pressed to their knees. The braids of their hair were as intricately woven as the ancient tapestries around them, the toes of their saddle shoes perfectly aligned, like the terra cotta roof tiles of a temple. Their teacher sat hunched on a nearby bench as though bowing to her disciples, her head bent low as she slashed at a notebook in mysterious Chinese characters.

At the end of the line one girl looked up, her cheeks as rosy as Rembrandt's brush, the tiniest stroke of a smile on her face as she dared to acknowledge our presence. We smiled, and waved, and the princess smiled back and blew us a kiss with one hand. Darcy pretended to catch it on her cheek, and the little girl blushed and giggled, prompting the teacher to glance up from her work, and her student to lower her head.

"She's the one," I whispered. "We'll hide her in a lunch box. The bus driver will never know."

"Speaking of lunch …" said Darcy.

"One more gallery," I insisted, inspired by the little girl's daring, "then, to the cafeteria."

I took her straight to the Impressionist wing—Monet, Manet, Renoir, Degas. I knew all the paintings from library books and purloined art magazines and led her directly to Van Gogh's *Cypress With a Star*.

"Vincent actually did paint by candlelight," I explained, "out in the wheat fields at night. He tied candles to the brim of his big straw hat in a halo of flickering flame. This one's my favorite. It reminds me of a place in the cemetery with the swirly trees and stars."

Darcy reached out to touch the canvas, eliciting a cough from the uniformed guard. "You can actually *feel* this painting," she whispered, "like your mind is a finger, exploring all the bumps! And this one!" she squealed, pulling me again by my sleeve, my sweater developing a pronounced handle. "I'm gonna decorate my bedroom like this!"

It was Vincent's room in the Yellow House at Arles, its walls sky blue, the bed bright orange and draped with a scarlet quilt, a yellow chair drawing one's eye toward the center where the window was limned in green light. "That's where he cut off his ear," I said, "after the fight with Gauguin. He was Tolstoy's artist if there was one."

"Do all artists have to be crazy?" she asked. "Do they all have to suffer like that?"

"They don't have to suffer, but crazy helps. At least be as goofy as mankind."

Making our way down the echoing stairway, I figured we were late for lunch. But there in the lobby, leaning against *David*, manifestly disinterested in male genitalia, was Jonah Gold, dressed in the same blue blazer and maroon tie he always wore, his signature attempt at prep school cachet. Waving us over, we joined him by the pedestal where he posed as casually as the famous sculpture itself.

"Teal," he nodded, glancing quickly at Darcy.

"I'm Darcy," she offered, extending her hand.

"I know," he said timidly. "I remember you from the Beach Club. You were a good swimmer, always diving off the raft."

"Where is everybody?" I asked. "Did we miss lunch?"

"They just went in. I never eat lunch. I save my lunch money for …. Say," he mumbled, nodding at Darcy, "is she cool?"

"Very."

"You get high?" he asked her.

"Sure," said Darcy, "of course."

Grinning, cackling, instantly animated, he said, "Far out! Let's go to the Pharaoh's Tomb. You can get lost in there." Striding off in that direction, he quickly turned and beckoned us to follow. "C'mon, man, this is the city. No one gives a fuck what you do."

The Tomb was in the wing opposite the cafeteria, beyond the grand staircase. A replica of the pyramid burial chamber of Tutankhamun, the display was a winding catacomb of alcoved passageways populated by elongated cat's heads and stick-figure hieroglyphs. There were mostly little kids inside, laughing, running, screaming through the tunnels, oblivious to the array of antiquities around them. The sarcophagus itself was in the center of the maze, a gold-painted capsule with the requisite Egyptian-style head at one end, over-sized clown's feet at the other. The head sported a traditional, striped *do-rag*, as Darcy called it, and a small goatee.

"I'm gonna grow a beard, man," Jonah said, slipping a pin joint from his billfold. Slender and yellow, it was curved like a scimitar, conformed to the shape of his ass. "I could, you know. My brother Silas grew one, and he's only two years older than me. His is kind of ratty, though. Mine would be much better."

He fired the doob, and the chamber filled quickly with the reek of pot smoke. Taking a toke, Jonah coughed it out and passed the joint to Darcy. She took a timid, tentative drag, her blue eyes focused on the glowing tip, then blew it all out in a plume of white smoke. Snagging the joint, I took a healthy hit. "Hold it in as long as you can," I explained, my jaw clenched tight as I spoke. Pointing the joint at Jonah, who was still choking, he waved it away. Darcy took another puff, a bigger one this time, and held it in as directed. Instantly her eyes began to water, and she passed it back to me. I took another puff, and by then Jonah had recovered enough to hazard a second toke.

"This is some heavy shit," he wheezed. "Acapulco Gold, man. I stole it from my brother."

"Levi?"

"Hell no, he's in Europe, conscientiously objecting to the draft."

I held up the butt, a tiny burnt stub the size of a match head. "You wanna save this roach?" I asked.

Jonah took it and popped it in his mouth, the way some people do. Wincing immediately, he tried to spit it out, but it stuck to his tongue and fizzled. He gulped just once, and swallowed.

"Fuck, man," he gasped, fingering his lip. "Whatcha do that for? It was still lit!"

Darcy started laughing, hugging herself with both arms. I laughed too, but not Jonah.

"How you feeling?" I asked her, figuring she'd never smoked pot before.

"Fine," she said. "Great!" and burst out laughing again.

Then Jonah laughed too. "Maybe its Panama Red," he said. "I suddenly can't remember! Teal, man," he added, "did I tell you I went to the March?"

"Yeah, you told me."

"What march?" said Darcy. "When?"

"In March, man. The March in March!" Jonah laughed, cracking himself up. "It was so cool! There were so many people, and everyone was chanting, like— *No more war! No more war!*

The cops were everywhere, but nobody cared, and everyone just kept on marching, tens of thousands of us!"

"In New York?"

"Of course New York! From Central Park to the United Nations! I saw Martin Luther King, man. He was so far-out! That guy is really cool!"

"I want to go to a march!" said Darcy. "Will there be another?"

"Fuck yeah! There'll be lots more, long as there's a war. Long as fucking LBJ is president!"

We heard voices then, adult voices heading toward the chamber, and we exited in the opposite direction, laughing to realize our smoke had filled the entire exhibit. Passing a museum guard hustling our way, we held our breath until safely around a corner.

"Off the pigs!" Jonah giggled, stumbling into the lobby.

The sunlight was blinding, and we paused to let our eyes adjust, certain that everyone knew we were stoned.

"I'm really hungry," said Jonah. "How about you?"

"Starving!" said Darcy. "Let's eat!"

Darcy nudged me as we passed Michelangelo's statue; *Dave*, she called him, making sure I noticed her give him a wink. Passing through arches on our way to the cafeteria, Jonah leading the way, Darcy grabbed my sleeve and pulled me toward an opening elevator door. "Going down," she said, punching a button, sealing our fate for the remainder of the day, as well as the rest of our lives.

"I just *have* to be outside," she exclaimed, exiting the building at basement level. Stepping out into brilliant sunshine, she spun on her heel with her arms flung wide, her hair like a chrome obelisk. "This is fantastic!" she laughed. "I can't believe I feel this good!"

I reached out to catch her when she wobbled like a top, and she tumbled into my arms. Her heart beat hard against the fabric of my sweater, and I breathed in the scent of her hair; the very first time I quaffed its bouquet, as heady and intoxicating as flowers.

Chapter 3

LEAVING THE BUILDING was riskier business than merely skipping lunch, and it gave me pause, if only briefly, as we wandered away from the museum, strolling aimlessly down a Central Park path through a lime green tunnel of trees. Broods of pigeons cooed along the cobblestones, gathered at the benches of brown-shoed old men who tossed out bread crumbs like alms. The birds barely moved as we waded through their midst, their feathers a rainbow of kaleidoscope hues, metallic and shiny in the sun. Posing with the statues in the *Wonderland* playground, Darcy was the image of *Alice*, her bare legs bronzed in her sheer cotton dress, her hair tumbled down on her shoulders. The little kids flocked to her, tugging at her arms, coaxing her to climb The Mad Hatter. "The *Madhatterhorn*!" she shouted, waving from the top, while I stood with my neck craned, holding her shoes. Standing by the aquarium at the Central Park Zoo, watching the seals as they dove from the rocks, she said, "How lucky are seals? Nothing to do but swim all day."

"So, you know Jonah, huh?" I asked, reminded of the Beach Club.

"Not that I remember."

"He remembers you, though. Probably happens a lot," I added. "Guys remember you; you don't remember them."

"Why's that?" she asked, instantly defensive.

"No reason," I backpedaled. "It's just, you know … you're beautiful."

An angry grimace transformed her face, looking as though she'd been slapped, and she stalked away without saying a word and headed for the "big cat" enclosure.

Racing to catch her, I tugged the door open, and we were swallowed in near total darkness. Darcy walked ahead of me with her arms held wide, gliding blind while our eyes adjusted. She stopped by a cage with a wild, musky odor, where a guttural breathing issued deep from within the stall.

"Hey," I said, easing up behind her, "I'm sorry if—"

"Shh," she admonished, reaching for my hand, holding it at the small of her back.

"*He* is beautiful," she whispered, peering through the shadows, leaning with her forehead to the bars. Sweater to sundress, and hand in hand, we waited for the tiger to resolve, its white chest emerging like the first evening star, the orange stripes bleeding through darkness. A pink tongue lolled through a rampart of fangs, heaving with the labor of breathing. Stretched out with his great head leveled at the world, he posed with the air of a sphinx, staring at us with predatory eyes, claws flexing with the patience of Pharaoh.

"Darcy," I whispered in the shell of her ear, "I would never say anything to hurt you."

"I know," she said, "it's not your fault. You'll get used to me after a while."

Parents with kids straggled noisily down the aisle, shrill little boys with their hands crooked like claws attempting to prompt a reaction. But the cats in their cages showed no sign of caring, inured to the antics of humans.

"I can't watch this," said Darcy, and was turning to leave when the great tiger issued a roar, an eloquent snarl of distinct displeasure as his object of desire departed. Frozen mid-step, she looked over her shoulder, submitting to the creature's demand. The growling subsided to a satiated purr and idled with the rumble of a race car.

"He wants me to stay," she said.

"Maybe he's hungry."

"You think he wants to eat me?"

"Understandable," I joked, instantly regretting my wit.

But Darcy just smiled and squeezed my hand. "Let's get a pretzel," she said.

Glancing at the tiger as we turned away, he'd resumed his diaphragmed mantra, his great chest heaving in the aftermath of lust, consumed by insatiable craving.

It was early enough that we could have turned back and made it in time for the bus. I pictured Mister Arstahl standing by the curb, checking his gold fobbed watch, Jonah describing the scene in the tomb to a circle of appreciative friends. The more I thought about it, the more anxious I became, yet more excited as well. Our story would grow into miniature legend if the cops were called into play, and even if they weren't, the rumors would persist, and Darcy and I would be outlaws. As the son of a cop and a registered nurse, I'd been brought up to honor the rules, but I saw no harm in what we were doing—exactly the opposite, in fact. These moments we stole were ours for the taking, belonging only to us. Or that's what I told myself, studying Darcy, who registered little concern. A veteran of prep schools and living with strangers, she was used to flaunting the rules—and getting caught at it, apparently. But I should at least give my mother a call; it's what she'd have done for me, was in fact what she always did, phoning from the hospital to say she'd be late, that she'd bring home a pizza for dinner.

These were the thoughts that swirled through my head as we wandered even farther from the bus, stretching my resolve into gossamer threads that gleamed like the strands of Darcy's long hair.

We bought hot pretzels at a vendor's cart with a yellow umbrella overhead, Darcy squeezing squiggles of mustard on hers, while I chose to eat mine plain. Souvenir vendors sold post cards and tee shirts emblazoned with New York icons: the Empire State Building, the Statue of Liberty, Andy Warhol lithographs. Portrait artists sat at their easels beneath the green awning of trees, scribbling away with charcoal and pencil while nannies rushed by pushing strollers. Most of the artists were pretty good, and most of their subjects impatient, little kids gnawing at oversized pretzels while pigeons pecked crumbs at their feet.

"So, you're an artist," Darcy said. "What do you like to paint?"

"Landscapes mostly. Flowers and trees. Impressionist kinds of stuff."

"So that's why you want to live in the mountains?"

"Who said that?"

"You did. Albert Bierstadt? *The Rocky Mountains?* You said you wanted to live there."

"I said *who wouldn't.*"

"But you do," she informed me. "That's why you paint landscapes. Artists paint what they see in their head, tucked in their hat like a candle. How about a hot dog?"

I was broke by then, having spent my last two dollars on the pretzels. But Darcy pulled a fifty dollar bill from her pocket, hidden somewhere in her dress, and so we sat on a bench and ate again, gathering our own flock of pigeons.

"I love how their feathers turn purple and green," she said, ketchup rouging her lips. "Iridescent."

"I love how they shit all over."

"Kind of Jackson Pollack," she observed.

"So how about you?" I asked. "What do you paint?

She had most of a hotdog stuffed in her mouth and could only shake her head. "Nothing," she finally managed to say. "I'm no artist. I'll probably be a housewife with kids that hate me, and a husband who's never at home."

Startled, I asked, "Why's that?"

"I don't know. I'm being dramatic. I think I need a napkin."

Darcy's hotdog was so smothered with relish it dribbled out from both ends. So I gave her my napkin and she daubed at her mouth, then spread it across her lap. "I have a big appetite," she explained.

"You've got the munchies. Are you still stoned?"

"I can't tell," she giggled. "It's just so different being here. With you."

"And why are you with me?" I had to ask.

She shrugged, smiled, licked mustard from her thumb. "Cause you're funny," she said, "and skinny, and tall. And your hair is never combed."

"I comb it!" I protested. "I just don't put that *stuff* in it!"

"And your jeans smell like turpentine, and there's paint on your fingers, and you're always reading a book. And I like the way you look at me when you think that I can't see."

Caught, busted, revealed as a spy, I flushed with embarrassment, recalling that moment in history class when she'd bent to retrieve her pencil. "Hey," I said, "I'm sorry—"

"*Noo*, it's okay. You made me laugh. It was really kind of nice. Like this …"

Leaning back against the bench she gazed up at the leaves, infused at that moment with a lemony glow, warm, sunny lozenges of fluttering happiness daubed amidst cool purple shadow. "It's like Monet here," she said of the trees. Then, without prelude, "Tell me something about your father. Do you miss him very much?"

Staring at the ground, studying my loafers, I searched for something to say. I was not in the habit of discussing my father, not even with my mom. But there was something about the events of that day that made me want to share, to frame some portion of my family's past to hang on the wall of the present. Handing Darcy what remained of my hot dog, she took a huge bite without looking away and I began telling my story.

"We'd always go down to Yankee Stadium when the Red Sox came to town, the oldest rivalry in the history of sports, going all the way back to the Babe."

I looked to see if the famous name registered with her, if Darcy knew anything about baseball. She didn't, apparently, and swallowed the last of my ungarnished hot dog in two enormous bites.

"First time we went I was eight years old. It wasn't my birthday or anything like that, but he'd bought me a brand-new mitt, an adult-size Rawlings that I spent the whole night greasing, kneading, pounding with my fist. We drove to the Bronx in his unmarked police car, a gray Ford Fairlane with spotlights mounted on the doors. I told you before, my dad was a cop, a detective with the Parkway Police. That car always smelled like Aqua Velva, Lucky Strikes, and spilled coffee. A twisty black cord draped down from the dashboard, hooked to a handheld receiver. "Go Yankees!" my father yelled into the mic, pretending to press the button.

"He knew all the players from over the years and had memorized their stats: Mantle and Maris, Bobby Richardson, Tony Kubek and Cletis Boyer. Elston Howard was the first negro Yankee—a catcher, like Yogi Berra.

"We talked about baseball all the way down, cruising through the parking lots, walking up the ramps that wound from level to level. I'll never forget the smell of the stadium—chewing gum, hotdogs, cigar smoke and sweat, the oil from greasing my mitt. Peanuts shells crunched like gravel under foot, glued to the concrete in pools of spilled Coke.

"Our seats were on the level in back of home plate where a net draped down from the upper deck so no one got hit by foul balls. I wore the mitt anyway, always glancing at my hand, at the red Rawlings label on my wrist. When the Yankees got a hit, the whole stands would jump up and I would jump up with them, though I couldn't see anything, just the back of a shirt, or the seat of a fat lady's dress. Mostly I stared at the green-painted columns that vanished away into shadows, studying the arches on the stadium's rim, ribbed like the pipes of an organ. One time a bat cracked, and we leaped up cheering, the crowd going wild with excitement. My dad turned to me with a grin on his face and a new Spaulding baseball in his hand— 'Wow!' he said, shaking his fingers, pretending he'd caught it barehanded. 'Did you see that, Bud?' he grinned, looking down, plopping the ball in my mitt. 'Regular Bobby Richardson, huh?'"

"Bobby Richardson was my father's favorite Yankee. He didn't hit a lot of homers, but he always got on base. 'One bag at a time,' my dad always said. 'That's how you win at baseball.'"

"That's … perfect," said Darcy, as though speaking to herself, lost in some personal thought. A pigeon hopped up on the bench beside her and she didn't even flinch. "Wait here," she said and bolted away as the pigeons scattered before her, their shiny wings flashing like transparent coins then folding again like umbrellas. I watched her lean by a vendor's cart and dash back as quickly as she'd left. Bent at her waist, heel touching heel, she stood like Alice before me. Pulling the purchase from behind her back, she offered it up with both hands. "Happy birthday!" she smiled, enjoying my surprise, waiting for me to smile back. It was a navy-blue Yankee's cap with the NY on its crest; the most famous, most recognizable symbol on the planet, except for maybe the peace sign.

"Jeez, Dar," I stammered, the first I ever uttered that name.

Setting the ball cap atop my head she tugged it this way and that, until finally she paused to examine her work, her attempts to get it just right. "Wait!" she said and tapped its brim. "Now you look just like Bobby Richardson!"

There was no way she knew what the short stop looked like, but I hardly cared at that moment, so recently returned—at least in my mind—from the hubbub of the House That Ruth Built. With the cap on my head, I felt strangely at peace as I sat on the leaf-mottled park bench, wondering what magic had led me to Darcy and her gift of recalling my father.

"C'mon!" she prompted, already turning, "we really *must* visit the Plaza!"

But we first had to pet the horses, a dozen of them snuffling and clomping their hooves by the fountain where the hansom cabs gathered, Darcy forgoing a carriage ride until we had more time, until after we'd gone fishing, and to Yankee Stadium.

"Shall we see if Eloise is home?" she called, dashing ahead across Fifty-Ninth Street. We sat in the lobby of the grand hotel amidst bouquets of fragrant flowers, surrounded by bell hops in silly round hats, their tunics cinched tight at their throat. Rich ladies tittered in falsetto voices while men tapped their pipes in glass ashtrays, black shoes buffed like mirrors, white sandals like lattice with nail-polished, rose petal toes. Darcy sprang lithely from sofa to chair, giving each cushion a wiggle. Pulled by my sleeve, I hopped around with her as she circled the elegant room, tethered to her wrist like the miniature poodles whose long leashes glittered with jewelry. Mirror by mirror I observed myself in my brand-new Yankee cap, each image connected like a paper doll cut-out unfolding across the grand lobby.

"It must have been fun growing up in the Plaza," Darcy said of Eloise, the mischievous storybook character. "I sure wish I had. It's gotta beat living at my house."

Ten minutes later we were standing in Saks where the salesgirls spritzed perfume on our wrists. Holding them up to each other's nose, Darcy's eyes framed by our forearms—"Lavender," she whispered, and licked my hand, her tongue like a Persian cat's. Abandoned in the crowded shoe department, I slouched in an armchair while she tried on heels, her calves even more elegant in four-inch spikes, hiking up her dress in the mirror. Darcy's good looks served to open doors, and the pretty young salesgirls flocked like pigeons, oohing and ahhing as they snatched gowns from hangers, pressing them each to her chest.

Bent over a counter, she was modeling hats, the old-fashioned kind with feathers and nets that bisected her cheekbones like shadows. "Try this," she giggled, swiping the Yankee cap from my head, replacing it with Audrey Hepburn's beret. Donning my ball cap, she pulled us to the mirror and leaned with her face next to mine. "You're beautiful," she said.

"You're handsome," I countered. "You could play ball, you look so convincing."

"That's half the game," she smiled a bit sadly.

She acquiesced to a stop at Saint Patrick's, though not without some pouting. Passing through the massive wooden doors of the church we were instantly plunged into darkness, much like the zoo, but with the smell of incense, and the penetrating stare not of a tiger but Jesus Christ on the cross. Dipping her fingers in holy water, she pressed them to my forehead, then turned to the altar and crossed herself, touching a knee to the carpet. I did the same, so as not to offend, lost in a world of ritual passions I knew absolutely nothing about.

There were few parishioners present, the pews mostly empty, and the distant alter abandoned. The vast chamber echoed not only with voices but a solemn, intimidating propriety. "Over here," Darcy whispered, leading me along a wall to where arched alcoves flickered with the light of votive candles.

"What are these?" I asked, staring up the statues, rosy in the glow of red glass.

"You can pray to the saints," she explained. "Here, do you want to?"

"Pray?"

"Whatever, light a candle." Plucking a taper from a wooden box, she lit it from another then passed it to me like a joint. "Go ahead, light one."

"What saint is this?" I asked.

"I don't know. Does it matter?"

I did as I was told and lit a candle, its wick taking slowly to the flame. "There," I said. "Am I Catholic now?"

"Minus the knee socks and pleated skirt."

Standing outside on the wide stone steps, I asked, "Think we should call our parents?"

Darcy shrugged, sulking for some reason. "Go ahead," she said, "I'm not calling mine. I don't want this to end that way."

"I don't have money for the train," I confessed.

"I do," she said, and sighed dramatically. "I've got all the money in the world."

"We have to go now," I was forced to concede. "Unless we can crash with Eloise."

Hanging a left on Forty-Second Street, within minutes we were in the maze of shops and newsstands beneath Grand Central Station. Darcy bought a copy of the Times and two coffees, *regular*, though I told her I didn't drink the stuff. It tasted great though, and it perked us right up, making me realize how tired I was, how far we'd walked that day. On our way to the lobby, we passed a candy shop, a chocolatier, and paused to look in the window. Dark chocolate, white chocolate, milk chocolate everything, cherries and caramels, nuts and crèmes, all wrapped in tutus of frilly white paper, sugared like Christmas Eve.

"Hungry?" she asked.

"No, but ..."

"You got a sweet tooth? C'mon, I can fix that."

We got two of everything and took our bounty to the grand concourse, where we sat on the marble stairway with paper cups balanced on our knees, craning our necks at the ceiling. Twice as tall as the vault of the Met, we studied the light-bulbed constellations described in green and gold paint, the arrival and departure board clacking away on a wall, informing us of a 4:20 Local/Express leaving on track 117.

Borrowing some quarters from Darcy, I screwed up the courage to call my mom from the bank of pay phones by the restrooms. A nurse at Phelps Memorial Hospital, my mother often worked the night shift, and I was relieved to have to leave a message with the ER operator, relating our arrival time, and conveying my sincerest apology. It was a cowardly way out, but I felt much better after making the call, having mentioned that Darcy was with me.

She was reading the paper when I returned, deeply engrossed in the sports section. "I'm looking for a baseball schedule," she said, "to see when the Red Sox come to town."

"You ate all the cherries," I observed, pawing through the white paper bag.

"Sorry. Did you really like the gooey ones?"

"I prefer caramel."

"Did you talk to your mom?"

"I left a message. You're not gonna call?"

Diving back into the newspaper, she said, "The Yankees are in Boston the first week of June. We could maybe ride up on the train."

"Nah. Wrong stadium."

Nodding her agreement, she returned her attention to the sports section, her silver hair bouncing with each toss of her head, with every turn of a page. All these plans, I thought, all these dreams… Was any of it real? Does this girl truly mean the things she says, or will I see her tomorrow in history class and she'll barely acknowledge my existence? I hardly cared at the moment, stargazing at the ceiling with the Yankee cap tipped off my forehead. Anything could happen, and actually *had*, I realized, a mini satori like I'd read about in books, about things that never happened to me. Then Darcy was smiling, reaching with her thumb to wipe dark chocolate from my lips, and I wanted to lick that perfect finger, sweet cherry sucker that it was.

"Oh my!" she cried, noticing the blue Met button still fastened to my sweater. "Where's my button?"

It was missing from the neckline of her cotton dress, and the look on her face, the flutter of her eyelashes, the oval pout of her lips was so pretty, so fetching, that I removed my button and clipped it to her collar, my knuckles barely grazing her skin. She smiled at me then with sparkling eyes, the same color robin's egg blue, and I wished I had a thousand more buttons to press to the warmth of her chest.

At four o'clock we descended to the lower level and boarded the train with the gray-suited hordes, dashing to the front of the farthest car, taking a seat on the left-hand side where you could look at the river riding north. The wicker seats were brittle and old, chilly to the touch, and Darcy hugged her arms to her chest, her bare legs goose-pimpled with cold. Chivalrous as hell, I stood in the aisle and tugged off my birthday sweater, tucking it gingerly around her shoulders, wrapping its arms like a scarf. She looked up at me with grateful eyes, the warmth of her smile all the comfort I needed.

Propping our feet on the back-facing bench, we hoped that no one would choose to sit there, increasing our chances by pretending to sleep, extending our private time together. She'd let me have the window seat, and in the darkness of the tunnel I studied my reflection in the glass, the bill of the ball cap shading my face, concealing my eyes as I stared. On my first day with Darcy I'd spoken more about my father than in the three years since his passing, and now this perfect stranger knew more about my life than anyone other than my mom, while I knew almost nothing about her.

Turned toward the window, I both saw and felt her head fall against my shoulder, her arm gently twine with mine. "I'm so tired," she mumbled, as the train lurched forward, the green lights of the tunnel flickering past. Watching her reflection as her eyelids drooped, I studied her in secret, as I had in history class. She was perhaps even prettier asleep, her eyelashes splayed, shading her cheeks, her full lips dimpled at the corners. The lights in the compartment flickered on and off, and in those brief intervals we vanished from the window and the darkness outside rushed in.

Suddenly, I too was tired and slouched down deeper in the seat. Darcy moaned and slid a bit closer, raised her chin and placed two tiny kisses on my neck, the barest breath of a kiss, a mere dampness of lips. "Happy, happy birthday," she whispered.

When we exited the tunnel on the elevated tracks, the echoes abated and sunset flooded in. Tenement windows leered empty as skulls in the canyon of derelict buildings, kids shooting hoops in graffiti-sprayed playgrounds ignoring the train as it passed. By the time the conductor called 125th Street, Darcy was asleep and my life had been changed, a feeling like spring taking root in my soul, creeping through the rubble of my ravaged heart, infusing the world with a young lover's joy and a tiger's wistful eye.

Chapter 4

JUST AS I FIGURED, rumors circulated at school that the NYPD had searched for us all over Manhattan, that Darcy's father had called the FBI. It was all bullshit, but it came with a kind of celebrity that was difficult not to enjoy. I'd gotten off the train at Tarrytown that evening, while Darcy went on to Philipse Manor, the stop at the affluent end of town just a few of miles north along the river. So I didn't know how her parents reacted, if they were waiting for her at the station.

Mom and I squirmed on uncomfortable chairs as we waited in the principal's office, watching Darcy and her mother through the glass slotted door, enduring the same plastic seats. Principal Hammer—the *Hamster*—sat straddling the corner of his desk, a balding man whose bulbous forehead reflected the ceiling light. Jabbing a finger to emphasize a point, he leaned menacingly toward his captive audience, and I saw Darcy's mom flinch and shrink lower in her chair, her attention directed to the floor. Stylishly dressed in a tailored spring jacket the color of daffodils, Mrs. Saint James appeared older than my mother by at least two decades, though it was hard to say if her hair had grayed or was naturally silver like Darcy's. Their startling eyes were the same color blue, their profiles as perfect as cameos. When Darcy's lips pursed and drew suddenly tight, I could tell she was getting upset, the blood running quickly to flush her cheeks, as crimson and bright as her bra strap. Turning toward her mother, their knees came together and she squeezed her mom's gloved hand, like circling the wagons in Indian Country, the Hamster's hair already scalped.

"She's very pretty," my mom confided. "I can certainly see the attraction. But that doesn't excuse what you did." Mom had been pissed when I first got home, waiting for me on the red checked sofa, her hands folded neatly in her lap. Oddly, though, she'd had nothing to say, and after some minutes of awkward silence she rose and went straight off to bed. But the next day at breakfast she gave me a lecture and cut my allowance for a month, leaving me just enough money for lunch, and to pay Darcy back for the train. But as stern as she'd acted, Mom seemed happy that I finally had a girlfriend, relieved that the world was returning to normal, or what little of normal remained, measuring our lives against the state of the world before the death of her husband.

"She asked about Dad," I mentioned as we waited.

"And what did you tell her?"

"Nothing really. She didn't say much about her father, except that he wasn't dead."

"Doctor Saint James? I should say not," said Mom. "He's a prominent member of our community, active in civic affairs."

"Then why isn't he here?"

Mrs. Saint James minced out of the office, tugging at the hem of her jacket. Darcy, behind her, was holding her hand, eyes front as they headed for the exit. Then leaning back quickly as they passed through the door, she blew me a kiss with her one free hand in the fashion of young Chinese girls.

"Well," said my mother, "she certainly is charming," and it was all I could do not to smile.

We spoke to the Hamster, or he spoke at us, counting my transgressions on his fingers. I studied the ribs of his transparent socks where his blue-veined ankles were exposed, the tiny perforations on his wing tip shoes a vortex of curlicqued spirals. Mom sat through it all with a stoic demeanor meant to conceal her impatience—convincing Principal Hammer perhaps, but hardly fooling me. I promised to never skip class again and he promised to be angry if I did. The faint smell of flowers still hung in the air; the sweet scent of Darcy's shampoo.

Walking my mom through the parking lot, a sleek yellow Cadillac was parked by the bleachers, its dark windows darker in the shade of a tree, exhaust drifting blue from its tailpipe. I could barely make out the bright yellow jacket posed rigid in the passenger seat. As the car pulled away, I saw Darcy's hand pressed to the glass in the rear, not waving, just held there, a delicate doily, her splayed fingers shaped like a star.

Later that day I went to library and looked up "charming" in Webster's: "to delight by compelling attraction," it read, "to affect as if by magic." Recalling the old saying, I laughed out loud, drawing the librarian's scowl, thinking, *Look up* charming *in the dictionary and there's a picture of Darcy Saint James.*"

Sentenced to detention, we spent the next three weeks in Mrs. Ibanez's after-school study hall, located across from the auditorium where she was the drama coach. The class hosted the usual compliment of fuck-ups, mostly greasers and negroes, one of whom was Antoine Jones, Bosco's older brother. Mean and lean in his black leather jacket, T'won claimed a section at the back of the room, slouched at his desk with his legs stretched out and his high tops blocking the aisle. Doodling in his binder, he'd glance up occasionally to glare at those who threatened his solitude, an island of calm amidst the braying of donkeys, primarily Steve Railsbeck, the biggest ass in school.

Mrs.I was gone most of the time, popping into the room between acts, her spiked heels announcing her approach. Darcy and I talked through the ninety-minute sessions, our desks shoved together by the windows. We horsed around, laughed a lot, Darcy sometimes squealing, which always drew a wisecrack from Railsbeck. But Steve never crossed the invisible line enforced by Antoine Jones, a frontier as palpable and fraught with danger as the DMZ in Vietnam.

After a week, when Mrs. Ibanez's habits became predictable, we began cutting class after the second of her two checkups, a brazen act I would never have contemplated prior to meeting Darcy. There were no other teachers around, just the phys-ed coaches, who cared only about jocks, so it was easy to sneak through the locker rooms and out the gymnasium doors to the parking lot. From there it was a short sprint to Bedford Road and the Aqueduct, the old, stacked-stone waterway that wound high and lonely through forest and fields all the way to Croton, snaking past the cemetery where we went to be alone.

I knew the old graveyard like the back of both hands and had named all my favorite haunts in it: The Jesus Place, The Van Gogh Place, Conover's, and Archuletta's Island. I explained it all to Darcy on the way there, walking along the Aqueduct trail, the crowns of trees and scattered rooftops sloping west toward the river, the wooded hills of Rockefeller's estate rising to the east. Darcy whooped as she galloped ahead of me, a sandal in each hand, her hair streaming back and shirttails flying so she could *feel the air all over!*

We dropped off the Aqueduct at desolate Douglas Park, cutting through the woods to the slow-moving Pocantico River. More stream than river, we slipped off our shoes and waded across at the dam, the crumbling waterfalls all that remained of a three-hundred-year-old grist mill. Entering the burying ground by the Old Dutch Church, the bucktoothed headstones rippled in rows beneath trees much younger than they were. Cracked and pitted and wafer thin, they sprouted with the abandon of wildflowers. Threading the graves on the dandelioned path, we leaned into a window of the stacked-stone church and pressed our foreheads to the glass.

"It's beautiful inside," said Darcy. "Is that a real wood stove?"

"They mull spiced cider at Christmas time. You can stay after service and drink some. My ancestors actually built this church back in the 1600's. And look," I said, barely touching her waist, "ours is the first family buried here."

Crowding the path near the front of the church, the first row of headstones leaned russet and crumbling, severe as ladder-back chairs. Jacob, Catalyna, and Winey Van Couenhoven were the names inscribed on their surface. Carved in an ornate, archaic hand, they were overseen by angels, moon-shaped faces with childish wings, their eyes closed fast in slumber. I explained how our name had been bastardized over the centuries, dropping *Van*, then shortening the spelling to *Conover*. "It's in the historical society. You can read it in the book."

We strolled up the path to a narrow road where a giant gray oak cast a parasol of shadow, shading the headstones blue at its base, bordered by wrought iron railings. One white headstone stood out from the rest, and Darcy pushed open the creaking gate to study the name on its face. "Washington Irving," she read aloud. "This could be Rip Van Winkle's tree! It's already making me sleepy!"

Tracing a maze of gravel paths no wider than a wagon's wheels, the grass grew tufted with forget-me-nots, drifted in dandelion fluff. I took her to the Conover Place, a tall, miter-topped pinnacle bearing our family's name, standing just beyond the boundary of the burying ground where no records survived to connect us. Beside it was the grave of an unnamed infant, its headstone crowned by a baby lamb, the dates on its face revealing that the child had died at birth. In some past century the pitted stone had been snapped from its base, and tipping it forward you could place a penny, or a roach, or a yellow dandelion head in the small depression beneath it. Fishing a buffalo head nickel from my pocket, I left it there in homage, promising Darcy we'd soon return.

A stone's throw from there was the Jesus Place, where His beatific, contemplative likeness stood barefoot atop a pedestal, surrounded by angels with their granite heads bowed and arms raised in eternal supplication. Darcy picked daffodils and slipped them through the loops of the angel's fingers, taking Jesus' hand in hers, staring up at the hollows of his pupils.

We paused at the Revolutionary War Memorial to recite the names of long-dead soldiers, noting how many streets in town had been named in their honor. Lying on the barrel of the cast iron cannon, Darcy imitated its roar, falling on her knees in the dewy grass to eyeball where the shot might have landed. Everywhere around us was the pink of rhododendrons, the blue of hydrangeas, and the ever-present perfume of lilac. Slate-roofed mausoleums lined the twisting avenues like so many rabbit warrens. Carved into the sides of the grassy hillocks, draped in wild morning glory, their cracked stone facades had grown purple with violets, orange with honeysuckle. Cupping our hands to bracket our faces, we leaned against the slotted doors, patiently waiting for the darkness to deepen and the stained-glass windows to resolve. They came alive in glowing colors of lavender, ruby, and lime, thin rays of sunlight fingering the chamber like peering through the eye holes of a mask.

Pure white dogwood and pink magnolias overhung the bumpy old roads, hedges of juniper and arborvitae shielding the more famous vaults from view: Andrew Carnegie, Samuel Gompers, R. H. Macy, and the Rockefellers. Slipping back into those dark recesses, we bent beneath curtains of cedar boughs and slow-blooming clumps of azalea, wending through a maze of bird baths and benches enveloped in carpets of ivy, red veined coleus climbing through trees amidst bright purple periwinkle jungles.

Standing by the *Bronze Lady*, an oversized statue of a robed woman enthroned before a mausoleum, I told Darcy the story of how the *Lady* was the lover of the man entombed, how the tears she cried—the green streaks of oxidation on her face—were tears of grief, jealousy, and guilt that she had murdered her philandering husband. "On Halloween," I explained, "we'd get some poor kid to sit in her lap while we told the story, whispering at the end that when the *Bronze Lady* cries, she will kill again. Then we'd all scream and run away laughing, stranding our victim in her cold, iron arms."

"Cool," said Darcy, "hoist me up."

"No way. Not till Halloween. Then I'll sit there with you."

She made me promise I would, hooking our pinkies together like grade school kids, and we strolled the paved loop of affluent mausoleums with Tiffany windows, where local scenes of the Hudson and the marshes at the Restoration shone gold as honey, purple as jelly in the musty dark. I showed her the Maurice Fromkes headstone with its engraved palette and paintbrushes, and the Bascomb family crypts bored directly into native rock. Then the Van Gogh Place, a narrow, hidden, shelf-like flat where juniper hedges stair-stepped down a hillside, and a grassy ledge lay mottled in sunlight, the river and the Palisades dramatically revealed through the tops of swaying maples.

"This place is magic!" Darcy cried, letting herself tumble to the grass.

"Wait a sec," I said, stepping toward the ivy-covered vault. Slipping an arm through the wrought iron gate, I groped near the top of the archway until I felt the blanket I'd stashed there and tugged it out with a theatrical flourish. "Ta-da!" Darcy laughed, as I shook the green plaid quilt, dislodging dirt and leaves and probably spiders before furling it out on the grass.

"Your mobile boudoir," she observed.

"My moth-eaten picnic blanket. Minus the picnic."

"I'll make sandwiches next time we come. What would you like?"

"Choke and lusterslime; hold the Wonderbread."

"What's that?"

"White bread that's 90 percent air."

"No, silly, choke and lusterslime."

"Peanut butter and jelly, man. Get hip."

We collapsed on the blanket, looking up at the trees, their leaves rustling crisply in the breeze. She tip-toed her fingers across the blanket until they found their way into mine, gazing at me with a smile on her face like a white feather balanced on end.

"You look like your mom," I finally said. "Your eyes the same color of ice."

"Cold," she said, "like the rest of my family, though Lena's were almost black."

"Who's Lena?" I asked.

"My oldest sister. Don't worry, you won't have to meet her. She's dead."

"I'm sorry," I said, somewhat shocked.

"Don't be, I hardly knew her. She was thirty something when she died, drowned in the ocean in Florida. It's okay," she said, sensing my discomfort, "I have another."

"Another sister?"

"Kara's twenty-five. She lives in Vermont. She's married and has a baby. I remember her vaguely from when I was young, and now I only see her at Christmas. Her room looks the same as the day she left, photos on the bureau, jewelry in the drawers. Her telephone's still hooked up! But Lena's room is completely empty. No phone, no pictures. Nothing."

"What about your dad?" I asked.

"What about him?" she yawned, and I laughed at her transparent deflection.

"He wasn't there in Hammer's office, but I saw him out in the car."

"No," she said, "he never comes. He's way too busy for that."

"For meetings with the principal? You do that often?"

When her eyelashes fluttered, I knew I'd upset her, and wished I could take it back.

"My dad's a surgeon, an ophthalmologist," she said. "He commutes every day on the train."

"And …" I coaxed.

Artfully cornered by my repartee—and confined to the musty blanket—she continued to speak as if to the trees, their branches bending to listen. "I remember sitting for my eye exam in his creepy old leather chair. The seat was cold when he pushed me against it and swung that big thing in my face. It looked like a giant insect head ready to suck out my brains, the lenses like eyes, the grips like antennas feeling their way through a tunnel. I was trapped in that chair as he twisted the dials and flipped through the charts on the wall. When I closed my eyes I saw zigzags and squiggles and patterns like Indian blankets, like the weird looking symbols you see on TV when stations are going off-air. He finally gave up when I wouldn't sit still, so he called my mom to come get me.

"My parents are ancient, in their sixties," she sighed. "I don't even know why they had me."

She could have stopped there, and I would have let her, but she went on anyway, unprompted.

"My father comes home every night at seven, as predictable and inevitable as the train. He eats his dinner alone in the kitchen, then sits in the living room reading the *Times*. All I ever see is the back of his head where his hair is beginning to thin, smell the stink of his awful pipe, hear its clink when he taps it in the ashtray. He never bothers to talk to my mom, like she's too dumb to converse with. He's always right and we're always wrong. He's *so* self-righteous, wrapped up in himself—he actually believes in the devil!"

"Really?" I said, absorbed in it all, imagining her every description.

"He *is* the devil, in my book!"

The angriest look distorted her face, and it scared me how quickly she'd changed, recalling the day at the Central Park Zoo when she'd stormed off after the tiger.

"So what *is* your favorite book?" I asked.

"Are you changing the subject?"

"Yeah, but really, everyone's got a favorite book."

She told me about *The Little Prince*, how her mother used to read it to her, the two of them stretched out on towels at the beach club, the stem of a wine glass buried in the sand. "I'll read it to you sometime," she promised, crossing her heart with her one free hand, leading my eyes to the swell of her chest that rose with the rhythm of her breathing.

We floated like leaves on the silence that followed, the mutual abandonment of all pretension creating a vacuum that drew us together, both of us leaning, lifting our chin, watching ourselves in each other's eyes until the second before our lips touched. We were spun into darkness and cool sensation, the taste of our tongues, the damp of our mouths, the warmth of her breath when our cheeks brushed together, filling my ear like a conch shell. Her skin smelled like summer in the cavern of her hair, the down on her neck turned a soft, fuzzy gold in the floating tattoo of the sun.

"Darcy …" I whispered.

"Yes?" she said, leaning to look in my eyes.

"Nothing, I just felt like saying your name."

"*Do* wear it out," she giggled, and kissed me again.

It wasn't the first time I'd kissed a girl, but the first time I wasn't half drunk at a party, then embarrassed the next day at school. Darcy was the first girl I ever *really* kissed, who could have kissed anyone but instead chose me.

We stayed at the Van Gogh Place until the sky turned purple, hugging, talking, studying our faces just inches apart, amazed at not feeling self-conscious. Darcy held a lightning bug cupped in her hands, her cheeks blinking yellow as she watched it. "I just can't believe you," I said out loud. "There's no part of your face that I don't want to kiss."

"There's no part of me that you can't."

Closing her eyes, she awaited my kiss, her lips like the petals of a rose. I, too, closed my eyes as our mouths came together, and the amber light blinked on inside me.

Chapter 5

ANTOINE JONES, THE KING OF DETENTION, got into a fight with Steve Railsbeck that sent Steve to the hospital, and in the process it was discovered that Darcy and I had skipped class. Railsbeck was an asshole, but I'd known him all my life and I felt kind of bad that his broken hand and dislocated shoulder had effectively ended his high school football career. Antoine, who'd stayed back a year and had already turned eighteen, was arrested. His high school career, for what it was worth, also ended, and because he was draft age, he enlisted in the army to spare himself possible jail time.

I'd also known Antoine all my life, mostly because he was Bosco's brother. He didn't play sports in high school, but had always been an incredible athlete, pitching for my father's team when Dad coached Little League baseball. T'won could play at any position and hit homers every time at bat. He had a fastball that no one could hit, but eventually he beaned a batter—some said intentionally—and he quit the league, pretty much giving up on school as well. It was a shame, Dad said, as Antoine showed real potential.

Darcy and I met with the principal again, accompanied by our mothers.

Mom was less forgiving this time, but when the Hamster tried to blame it all on Darcy, and I spoke up to defend her, she seemed pleased that I'd actually stood my ground and at least owned up to my part.

Darcy and I got detention again, though not together like last time. I was back in Ibanez's class, but Darcy had to sit in the principal's office on the uncomfortable plastic chairs. It was only a couple weeks till summer, so it didn't seem like a death sentence. We saw each other in history class, grabbing a minute together before and after the bell rang, but Darcy was grounded, and I couldn't visit her at her house, or even call there. She called *me*, though, sneaking into Kara's old room where the phone was still hooked up. She'd call every night between eleven and midnight, and if Mom was home, I'd keep the phone smothered beneath my pillow, the receiver in my hand and a finger on the button so I could pick up first ring.

We talked about everything: school, art, books, the Yankees, and when we ran out of interesting personal stuff she read me the newspaper, anything to fill the hours. I loved just listening to the sound of her voice, her laugh when she read me the comics. Mickey Mantle was shooting for his 500th homer, and *Rosemary's Baby* was due. *Portnoy* complained too much for Darcy, so she skipped to the movie reviews: *Blow-Up*, *The Sting*, *Bonnie and Clyde*—"Hey!" she said, "that sounds like us, but minus the bullet holes!" The headlines read, "US Warplanes Bomb Hanoi." "Israeli Rule in Jerusalem." "Ali Indicted for Draft Evasion."

"This sick guy in Africa got a new heart!" Darcy exclaimed. "Can you believe it? Sounds like Frankenstein, or grafting apples. What if I asked them to cut out my heart and put it in you?"

"I'll take it however I can."

"I'd give you my heart in a second!" she blurted.

"Or maybe we could swap."

Darcy fell silent. "Are you saying you love me?"

"Maybe," I answered. "Would that be okay?"

"Only if you meant it."

"Okay, then, I love you."

"I love you, too."

And there it was, laid out on the table, or more like the green plaid blanket.

"Have you ever been in love before?" she asked.

"Nope," I said, "Have you?"

"No. Never. Okay then, goodnight."

"Goodnight?"

"Yeah. I just want to lay here and think about it."

"Then go think about it in your own room, in case you fall asleep."

I'd never told anyone I loved them before, except for maybe my mom, and I lay awake in the dark for hours, amazed at how quickly we'd fallen in love, if love was what we were feeling. If it was, I thought, then you didn't actually *fall* in love as much as love somehow leaked out, was already in you, biding its time, crouching like Clyde in the getaway car, leaping at the chance to escape.

Chapter 6

Senior graduation was the sixth of June and that night there were parties all over town. Darcy was still grounded and couldn't go to any of them. The last time we'd spoken, the night before on the phone, she told me she was thinking of running away and asked if I would go with her.

"Sure," I said, "I'll be right over."

"Are you serious?"

"Are you?"

She was silent a moment, then laughed. "No. I just wanted to see what you'd say."

"Have you ever actually thought about it? Running away?"

"Why would I? A boy just told me he loves me."

"Who? Like, after I did?"

She laughed and told me how silly I was.

"Really, though, have you ever considered it?"

"No. I could never run away."

"Why not?"

"I just couldn't. Now go to your parties."

I told her I couldn't go without her, but she made me promise I would. "Please," she said, "don't let me ruin things for you. Have fun while you can."

"You mean, before they draft me?"

"Don't even say that!" she scolded, and smooched the receiver before hanging up.

So, I went to the parties with Todd, a couple of them down by the river, by the railroad tracks where we used to hang out as kids. Todd's father had been killed in Korea, so we'd pretty much grown up like brothers, doing sports with my dad in the dog days of summer, sleeping over at his house on weekends. We weren't much alike in size or demeanor, Todd big and strong, and me kind of gangly. He was fun, I was pensive. He laughed when I shrugged, like he got the joke before I did.

We hooked up on Beekman Avenue where Deloit Mason, a senior, bought us each a couple of quart bottles of Colt 45 at Rose's Corner Store, and two of the fattest cigars we'd ever seen. Deloit was a greaser, his hair slicked back in a cheesy pompadour, but he was cool, so we caught a ride with him in his brother's Mustang, Carter being in Vietnam and in no position to object. Todd pretended to know about cars, and he talked about dual carbs, fuel injection, and things I didn't give a shit about.

"Hey, Conover," said Deloit, "you going out with that Saint James chick?"

"Yeah," I said, "I guess so."

"You *guess* so? Guy oughta know something like that."

"I am, then. We are."

"You banging her?"

"She's my girlfriend," was all I could think to say.

"But does she fuck?"

"You writing a book, Del?" Todd intervened. "Jacqueline Susann or something? Oh shit," he lied, "I just spilled beer on your seat."

"Fuckin' dickwad!" Deloit exploded. "Are you queers wasted already?"

"You flyin' solo tonight?" Todd asked. "Big date with the hand? You *did* graduate, right?"

"Wise-ass prick!" Deloit growled, jamming on the brakes. "Get outta my car, you fuckin' juniors! Last time I front for you!"

Deloit peeled away, smoking his brother's whitewall tires, stranding us on the deserted streets of Philipse Manor where the houses were huge and the trees even bigger, smothering out the stars.

"Should I thank you?" I asked.

"Defending your honor, bro."

"And now we're walking."

"Now we're *bopping*!" Todd cackled, breaking into the street strut, his shoulders thrown back, his stride grown long, an exaggerated grin on his handsome face. We were both wearing jackets with inside pockets for the illicit transport of booze, and our shadows stretched long beneath the leaf-mottled streetlamps, cigar smoke trailing like flags.

Minutes later a red Saab pulled up beside us and Jonah Gold rolled down the passenger window. "You headed to the party?" he asked. "Hop in!"

There were three people in the car, Jonah, his brother Silas, and Mary Ann Hicks—Mouse, as we called her on the Ave. We climbed into the back with our lifelong friend, who was busy toking hash from an empty beer can.

"Put out those cigars, will you?" said Silas, jerking the car out of gear. Silas was an older, chunkier version of his brother, sporting the scraggly facial hair that Jonah had foretold.

"Thanks for the ride," I said. "We just got booted outta Deloit Mason's car."

"His brother's classic Mustang coupe," Todd corrected.

"That guy's a hood," said Jonah. "He probably carries a knife."

"Can you put out those stogies?" Silas repeated.

Mouse was choking, her cheeks bulging with smoke, and she passed the can to Todd.

"Is this really hash?" he asked.

"Hell yeah," said Jonah. "Silas got it at college!"

I took a tiny hit, struggling not to gag. Jonah said, "So you and Darcy are an item now, huh?"

"I guess."

"You *guess*?" Todd laughed. "A guy oughtta know something like that!"

"Will you please put out those cigars."

"I knew her in grade school," said Mary Ann, her voice turned husky from the hash. "All the Saint Jameses went to Saint Teresa's."

"What was she like back then?" I asked.

"Same as now. Quiet, pretty. I don't think she had any friends."

We were driving across the railroad bridge, the Hudson River stretched wide before us. Hanging a right down the narrow dirt road toward the Beach Club, cars were parked everywhere, some off in the weeds, half smothered in brush, or driven up on the rip-rapped banks where water slapped at the rocks. Silas cruised around the Eagle Statue, then nearly back to the bridge before we found a place to park, right behind Deloit's Mustang.

"That guy carries a knife," said Jonah.

"His brother carries a gun," said Todd, and Jonah's eyes widened. "He's in the army, man, relax. Let's party!"

The Beach Club gates were padlocked, but you could sneak around the fence on the river rocks and onto the shingle by the docks. Across the point was the swimming beach where a bonfire was burning, kids strewn around it in the sand, or on folding beach chairs stolen from the bins along the sea wall. Bosco Jones was there, and a bunch of other jocks from the football team, dripping with cheerleaders and drill squad wannabes. Tiny Dionne Hayes sat beside Bosco, his shadow in the firelight twice her size. I'd known everyone there since the dawn of time, from sports when I used to play, church when I used to attend. Todd wandered around slapping backs, doing the bro hug and the handshake with his teammates. A starting linebacker in his junior year, Todd wasn't huge or mean or overtly hairy, just a naturally gifted athlete who won hearts as well as games. Ol' Deloit Mason sat by himself in the shadows along the wall, giving us the evil eye.

Our fat cigars were half dead by then, or half alive, as Todd would say, and we puffed them while savoring what remained of our beer, also swigging from bottles of wine and liquor making the rounds. Silas and Jonah kept their hash under wraps, Mary Ann sitting alone and cross-legged in what looked like a drug induced trance. The jocks dragged driftwood logs from the jetty and tossed them onto the fire, plumes of smoke and orange sparks spiraling up toward the stars. I was sitting on a log, wishing Darcy was with me, imagining her hip pressed to mine, when a really drunk cheerleader plopped down beside me and squashed her boob on my arm.

"Hey, Teal," she winked, "how did you like the Met?"

"It was … great," I stammered. "You should try it."

"Where did you go, to a hotel or something?"

"Kind of. We hung out a while at the Plaza."

"You're kidding!" she gasped, her breath like a burp.

Her bleary eyes widened and her lips formed an O as she clumsily grabbed at my hand. I tried not to laugh at this really drunk senior who had never even noticed me before, who had always ignored the boys from the Ave, except for Todd, of course. I said, "We went to the zoo and shopped at Saks, lit a candle at Saint Pat's Cathedral. We just talked, you know. We talked, and ate, and Darcy read me the newspaper."

"Really? You did that?"

"Yep."

"Huh," she said, "that does sound fun. Maybe I *would* like to try it."

It was Darcy, I realized, who lent me this sudden cachet, a newfound coolness by association with the mysterious and beautiful new girl. "Excuse me," I said to my new, wasted friend, patting her head as I rose.

Mary Ann sat alone some ways from the fire, looking stoned, and sadly alone. Few of us called her Mouse anymore, though the nickname remained appropriate. A brown haired, willowy wisp of a girl, her face was cute as a button, her big brown eyes and pouty lips like an urchin from Oliver Twist. We had known each other since kindergarten, since the playground days of ring-a-levio, hopscotch, and kick-the-can. We'd fed stray kittens under her porch and flown kites into TV antennas, made crafts out of noodles and poster paint that we taped to our fridges at home. As the only person who'd professed to know Darcy, if only briefly, and many years before, I suddenly I needed to speak to her, and lurched off across the sand.

Hopping, leaping over groping couples, I headed in her general direction, my path like the trail of the Candyland game through a lemon drop forest of bodies. Some really drunk guys were trying—and failing—to sing "House of the Rising Sun," segueing directly into "Eve of Destruction." A hundred people had gathered by then, with more arriving all the time. I caught a quick glimpse of Deloit Mason conspiring with some other Avenue boys, most of them older than me, draft-age dropouts dressed in black leather rather than olive drab. When the chorus of jocks began singing "Ballad of the Green Berets"—really badly, mocking the song—Deloit staggered to his feet and got right in their faces. "My brother's a Green Beret," he shouted, "so fuck off, you hippie bitches!"

The singers, the offense, looked nothing like hippies in their red letterman jackets and class rings, and they laughed at Deloit, who stood his ground with his fists clenched tight at his sides. The Avenue boys hopped off the wall and squared off with the football team, dramatically so in their shit-kicker boots, backlit by the flames of the fire. Bosco Jones, silent until then, stood to his full and considerable height and pointed his finger at Deloit. "Cool out, Del," he issued a warning. "Ain't no one making fun a yo brotha." Bosco was also from our side of town, growing up in the projects on Cortland Street, just a few blocks down from the playground. "My brotha, he's in the service, too. Y'all don't see me gettin' pissy."

Suddenly, theatrically, Todd strutted from the wings in an exaggerated crouch, whistling the theme from *West Side Story* and snapping a beat with his fingers. His one hand was raised as though wielding a knife, carving a path through the tension, singing—"Here come da Jets, we are Jets all da way, from our first cigarette to our last dyin' day!"

That was all it took, and the drunken beach party exploded into a scene from *The Blob*, with chicks screaming, sand flying, somebody yodeling or badly hurt. Just like Jonah said, Deloit had a knife, its blade flashing orange in the firelight, sweeping it back and forth before him as partiers leaped from its arc. Bosco snagged Deloit's leather jacket, picked him up with one massive arm and threw him like a javelin into the river. Then everyone was laughing, hooting, singing, and somebody, little Dionne Hayes I think, dragged Del from the water and left him on the sand. The greasers went home, or to the next party, and when Todd stumbled up with a grin on his face and sat next to me on the wall, I saw that he was bleeding from a gash on his forearm, a pretty deep one, and then Jonah was saying, "See, I told you that creep had a knife."

Mouse—Mary Ann—gripped the neck of a square liquor bottle and poured its contents over Todd's wound, then gulped down a slug for herself.

"You wanna go home?" I asked Todd. "Or to the hospital?"

"Fuck no. It's only like, eleven o'clock."

"Let's split, though," said Jonah. "There's another party happening at the Yellow Rocks. All the heads are up there."

So that's where we went, up the dirt road another quarter mile to where an old train trestle had once crossed the tracks. There were fewer cars parked there, and a bunch of motorcycles, and when we scrambled down the steep embankment and burst laughing from the trees, we were greeted with a mighty chorus of cheers and a bristling of arms extended, offering us joints and apple core pipes, even a genuine hookah. There was no sandy beach at the Yellow Rocks, just humongous boulders—thus the name—and partiers lounged amongst them like seals, poured into the hard, mossy contours like melted candle wax. Wine bottles clinked, pot and wood smoke swirled, and the twinkling lights three miles across the river shone red, green, and blue.

A circle of people played guitars, trying to sound like Peter, Paul and Mary, but settling for the Smothers Brothers. Phillipe Holland III—PH3 we called him—mused aloud about quasars and quarks, while Erik Neumann, dressed all in black, in ironic imitation of his minister father, preached about turning on, tuning in, dropping out. Kids from my art class posed tragically by the fire, their faces made abstract by the flames, while the drama club gulped wine from a stage prop skull, addressing the purple-stained chalice as "poor Yorick" and beginning each sentence with, "Alas ..."

We smoked more hash and lots more pot, and Todd rekindled what was left of our cigars with an actual flaming brand. A really fat stogie could last all night if you knew what you were doing, tamping it carefully, stashing it in a pocket until the Cuban mood returned. Todd's cigar hadn't weathered the rumble very well, but was still sound enough to puff on, which he did as Mary Ann washed his wound, binding it with a relatively clean white sock wrestled from the foot of PH3, the only guy we knew who still wore socks.

After attending to Todd's bloody arm, Mouse wandered off down the shore, her skinniness mocked by the fire's glow as she crouched on her haunches by the water. I followed her down there, announcing my presence with a forced, if not satisfying burp. She looked up at me with a glassy stare, the light shining wetly in her eyes.

"Mind if I join you?" I asked, to which she shook her head, indicating either that she didn't mind or I shouldn't sit, but I hunkered beside her regardless.

"You want to talk about Darcy," she said.

"Yeah," I mumbled, embarrassed to be so easily read.

"You really like her, huh?"

"Yeah, I do."

"Well, that's too bad," she said.

"Why?" I asked, truly surprised. "Is there something I should know?"

Mouse shook her head, revealed a sad smile, her face mostly hidden by her hair. "I already told you what I know," she said. "We went to Saint Teresa's together, or at the same time, I mean. Lots of girls thought Darcy was a snob, too pretty, too good for the rest of us. The only time she spoke to me was on the bus going down to Saint Pat's. Sister Marqusa seated us together, so it's not like we had a choice. I was really surprised by how much she talked, since she'd never even once said hello."

"She talks a lot," I was quick to agree. "It kind of surprised me too."

Mouse said, "Darcy could have any boy she wants. All these jocks are in lust with her, but I really thought that you'd be different. I thought you'd be *you*, you know?"

I didn't know, and I found myself shaking my head.

Mary Ann sighed, sniffling back tears that had suddenly welled in her eyes. "Darcy just told me about her family, how rich and important they were. One of her sisters was a teacher in Florida. Another got killed while skiing."

"No, no, it's the other way around. One sister's married and lives in Vermont, the other was drowned at the beach."

"Could be, this was years ago."

"No, really, it's just like I said—"

"Look, I really don't know, or care, okay? She told me this stuff, and I didn't believe her—no one believed her, you see? Her father was crazy, her mother was a saint—none of it made any sense."

I was staring at the hollow of Mary Ann's throat, barely aware I was doing it.

"Is it just because she's pretty," she cried, "and I'm not? Just tell me, and I won't ask again."

It took me a moment to grasp what was happening, fucked up and stoned as I was. Mouse flipped her hair and looked right at me, waiting for me to respond. Then she leaned and kissed me square on the lips, then sat back, and averted her eyes. "That was a total surprise for you, huh? You really don't even know."

Too stunned to answer, I looked out at the river, at the glittering necklace of the Tappan Zee Bridge that wound its way over to Nyack.

"Medic!" Todd hollered at that imperfect moment. "Somebody find me my medic!"

Mouse glanced toward the fire, then back at me, swiped at her tears and bolted away. Crouched in the darkness I watched her go, wondering what the hell had just happened. First the drunk cheerleader, and now Mary Ann. The world that I knew had been turned upside down in the course of a single night, and all of a sudden I was Mister Cool, or Mister Totally Clueless, and it was all because of Darcy.

An anemic chuckle then rose from the rocks not twenty yards away, and I spied a dark figure rise from the shadows, drunkenly attempting to stand. He managed to close half the distance between us before stumbling and collapsing in a pile.

"I fucked her once," the shadow spoke.

"Deloit?" I asked of the darkness.

"Little fucker stole my car. I loved that car, man."

"Carson? I mean … Carter?"

"Close enough. It don't mean nothin'. I know you?"

"It's Teal. Conover. I know Deloit."

"Little fucker, been driving my car this whole damn time. He can have it, I don't care. I can't even drive no more. Hey, find my fuckin' crutch, willya, 'S here somewhere."

I searched around and found the crutch not far from where Deloit's brother lay half sitting, half sprawling in the cold, slimy rocks.

When I handed it to him, he said, "Yeah, I fucked that chick, the little bitch. She acted like she didn't want it, but … I'd fuck her again in a New York minute. I'd fuck anything now, you know?" Then he was crying, or maybe laughing, and when I tried to move toward him, he swung out with the crutch, and it ricocheted off the rocks. It clanked with a tinny, metallic sound, and then he was coughing, gasping for air, a ragged, breathless, soulful mantra much like Darcy's tiger.

I felt kind of sorry for him, and a little afraid. Did anyone know that Carter was here? Did Deloit even know that his older brother was back from Vietnam? Carter *could* have known Mouse, I supposed. They might have met in the neighborhood, or maybe at the playground. Or he could just be lying, trying to impress me, or anyone else within earshot. I couldn't imagine the two of them together, not sweet Mary Ann. She'd just never seemed that desperate to me, but then again, what did I know? Not much, apparently.

"Hey, you got a cigarette?" Carter asked.

"I don't smoke."

"Fuck you, then."

"Fuck you, too."

He laughed. "That's the spirit, kid."

"You need a hand?" I asked.

"Sure," he cackled. "Or maybe a leg. How 'bout a new fucking foot! No, just get the fuck outta here."

I was walking away, happy to leave him, when he said, "Her sister ain't really dead, you know. The bitch is a fucking liar."

"What did you say?"

"Don't mean nothin'. No fuckin' thing," said Carter

"What did you just say?" I repeated.

When I made to move toward him, he swung out again with the crutch. "Fuck off, man! Don't come near me! Don't *anyone* fuckin' touch me. Back the fuck off, or I swear to God I'll kill you! Swear to God I will!

"Don't mean nothin'!" he mumbled again, laughing as I stumbled away.

Back at the fire, Mary Ann had wrapped a second sock around Todd's forearm, the first one sodden with blood. Mouse wouldn't look at me, and Todd said, "Conover, you look terrible, like you just seen a ghost."

"Yeah, Casper's hiding over there in the rocks. You look a bit pale yourself."

"He needs to go to the emergency room," Mary Ann insisted, grabbing Todd by his one good arm. "Jonah," she commanded, "find Silas! We need a ride."

Scrambling up the trail to the car, I wondered how Carter had managed the hill, and how he would climb back up; Silas was having a difficult time and he had two feet, though both, apparently, left. Silas was way too drunk to drive, so Todd slid behind the wheel, not that he was in much better shape, having quaffed more brews than me. "Put out those fucking cigars!" Silas snarled as we peeled away down the road.

Halfway there I threw up in my mouth and Todd had to stop the car. Tumbling out of the passenger seat, I fell to my knees on someone's lawn, the huge house dark, as were all the others on the quiet street at two o'clock in the morning.

"Go!" I said. "Split! I'll be alright."

"Don't leave him," I heard Mouse say.

"Yes," I insisted. "I'm cool, I'll walk home."

"Oh yeah," Jonah chuckled, "you're *cool*, alright."

I waved them off, and finally they left, leaving me sprawled on the lawn.

Laying on the grass looking up at the trees and the few stars shining through branches, I tried to piece together what had happened that night, reducing it all to what I wanted to believe, and what I totally didn't. I *didn't* believe what Carter had said, whether he was talking about Darcy *or* Mouse. But was that really Carter Mason in the rocks, and not some derelict bum? And how could he come all the way from the Nam without his family knowing?

It didn't make sense, but then what did—the war, the riots, my father dying, Darcy so strange and painfully beautiful that it hurt just thinking about her. I don't know how long I lay there like that, but when a glaring white light shone right in my face, I thought at first it was morning. It wasn't the sun but the beam from a cop car idling by the curb beside me, pinning me to the lawn with its spotlight.

"On your feet," said a disembodied voice, emanating from the glaring light.

When finally I managed to stagger erect, shielding my eyes with one hand, the cop said, "Hands down, kid. What's your name?"

"Teal. Conover," I added.

A silence ensued as the gears slowly turned, as the cop made the connection to my dad.

"We got a report of a possible stabbing," said the voice. "You okay? You know anything about that?"

"No, I'm just … taking a rest."

"Well, go home and rest, and don't pass out on a stranger's lawn."

I never got to see the cop, though I probably knew him, and he almost certainly knew me, a friend of my dad's from work, or sports, or summertime PBA picnics. Cops are quite different when they're not on the job, not dressed up in leather and blue. In tee shirts and shorts, with a beer in their hand, they're pretty much like normal people.

I got home at four and tiptoed to my room, even though Mom was at work, probably sewing stitches in Todd's wounded arm, scolding him as she did it. I slept—if you could call it that—with the phone by my pillow in hopes that Darcy would call, knowing she probably wouldn't. I dreamed that it rang, and I heard her voice, purring and slinky as a cat. *Don't mean nothin'*, she kept repeating … *Love you* … then smooching the phone.

Chapter 7

THE NEXT DAY I STARTED a summer job with Parks and Recreation, finagled, of course, by my mom. I didn't make a great first impression on Mister Napolitano, the foreman, but there wasn't much competition from the rest of the crew. Mr. Nap, as we called him, seemed to realize we were victims of poor timing, and he took pity on us, and that first day we raked leaves in Douglas Park, propped on the handles of our rakes, chugging bottles of Fanta and Orange Crush that our boss supplied at break. Damian White was on the crew, a totally weird Avenue guy who thought it was funny to piss on other people's shoes or fart in their face when they were kneeling in the grass. Nobody liked him or sat with him at lunch. Mr. Nap explained the job to Damian, who only grinned and did whatever he wanted to do, which was mostly nothing. But we weren't exactly building the pyramids, just spiffing up the park, and Damian's help wasn't missed.

When I spoke to Darcy on the phone that night, I never mentioned Carter Mason or Mouse. I lied and told her that the parties were fun, that there had been a fight and Todd got slashed but was mostly doing okay. Darcy didn't know Todd, or any of those people, so it was all a documentary to her.

"I wish I could have gone, though," she said. "Do you still love me?"

"Probably," I said. "What's your name again?"

"Stop it, Teal. That's not funny."

"Sure it is. I can feel you smiling through the phone."

We made a date for the following Sunday when her sentence was to be lifted. We were going fishing in the river, down at the Yellow Rocks. Bring a bag lunch.

That Sunday morning broke sunny and clear. I got up early to collect my father's fishing gear, stashed in a closet where it had languished for years. I planned to walk down there, so I did what rigging I could at home—oiling the catch, tying the bobber, crimping the sinkers—so I wouldn't have to carry the heavy tackle box.

Sitting at the table by the kitchen window, the pole stretched out on the linoleum floor, I cut the line with a pair of pinking shears from Mom's sewing drawer. There was a drawer for everything at our house: pads and pencils, rubber bands, hammers, screw drivers, and nails. Mom was heavy into bright, cheerful colors, the kitchen painted sunflower yellow with red, plastic place mats on the faux marble table. A rainbow of Fiestaware lined the glass-paned wall cabinets, teacups and coffee mugs hanging from hooks on the wall above the stove. Our apartment was a palette of patterned hues: braided rugs, frilly lampshades, red and white checked armchairs in the wallpapered living room. Even the toaster cozy was red, as were the oven mitts, tea kettle, and salt and pepper shakers.

Through the window and across the street I could see my old grammar school and the sunny, second-story art room where little kids' finger paintings were taped to the glass. Old Mrs. Hoppstaeder had been my teacher back then, scribbling away at her wobbly easel, her charm bracelet jangling like a tambourine. I'd told her once that I couldn't draw waves, and she told me that drawing anything was like drawing a breath—you did it without thinking, without wondering how. It was the first real thing a teacher had ever taught me. That, and in fifth grade when we learned to crawl beneath our desks and cover our head with our arms, practicing for the day when the A-bombs would drop, the warheads flying from Cuba.

Farther down Pocantico Street I could see the old playground where we used to play games—basketball, stickball, up-against, anything that bounced. In block-wide games of ring-a-lario, Todd, Mouse and I always tried to hide together, crouching behind dumpsters or the fenders of cars, dashing like mad toward the monkey-bar prison, shouting "Olly, olly, in come free!" at the top of our lungs. One year, on Labor Day, Mary Ann and Dionne won the talent contest, dancing atop a picnic table, grinding their skinny hips, singing "Jimmy Mack" into opposite ends of a jump rope.

The tetherball pole was gone now, but the slide and monkey bars survived, pelted with eggs and festooned with toilet paper every Halloween. The crabgrass field had since been paved and new basketball hoops installed. In the evening you can still hear kids playing H-O-R-S-E, bouncing the ball until dark, the rhythmic thud like the ticking of a clock, as faithful as the bells at Saint Teresa's.

With the pole on my shoulder and the Yankee cap on my head, I Tom Sawyered my way down Pocantico Street, bluebirds and robins singing in the trees, lemon drop bursts of bright morning sunlight winking through the leaves. Hopping the fence at the Restoration, I loafed across the narrow footbridge, the flat of the millpond reflecting the sky, transected by the V-shaped wakes of swans, white as the clouds overhead. Red and yellow tulips bordered the gravel paths, planted there by women in rough wooden clogs and traditional hoop-shaped skirts. The historic old homestead was shuttered at that hour, the gates not officially opened to tourists until midmorning. Just across Route 9A, kitty-corner from the Restoration, The Old Dutch Church marked the entrance to the cemetery, high on its headstone-prickled hill. Closer still, the three-story Tudor structure that was George's Tavern leaned from the weight of the centuries, its yellowed façade a busy geometry of diagonal beams and cracked stucco.

Just past the barns and the frog-croaking tide pools, the marshes shone lime through weeping willows draped like maiden's hair, the Pocantico River biding its time before emptying into the Hudson. Red-winged blackbirds flitted through reeds alive with electric-blue dragonflies, their transparent wings sparkling like prisms in the slanted morning light. We used to build rafts out of old bald tires that sank in the pollywog mud flats, the smell of the muck like a salve on our skin, caked in the soles of our sneakers. In winter we'd play hockey with branches and rocks, striped scarves wound around our faces, whooping and hooting through the hoar-frosted wool until somebody fell through the ice. All the way home we'd press cattails to our lips, pretending they were fat cigars, exhaling white plumes of our breath toward the sky, a star-speckled bruise overhead.

Passing through woods I hopped another fence, then the gate at the Town's new ball fields, then crossed the bridge to the Eagle Statue where it lofted its wings by the river. Hopping off the southbound platform at the Philipse Manor Station, I followed the railroad tracks north for a bit before climbing back up to the road, feeling suddenly anxious, plagued by the lies that Carter Mason had told, and to a lesser degree by what Mouse had revealed, how everyone in parochial school thought Darcy was a snob, not believing a word she said. But when I got to the bluff above the Yellow Rocks and squinted down through the trees, all my fears evaporated, dissolving like fog in the heat of the day, in the crystalline clarity of morning.

Perched on a rock in her ragged cutoffs, her silver hair ruffled by the breeze, Darcy glanced up and looked right at me, spotting me easily through the leaves. On my way down the hill my pole snagged a branch, and she laughed as I struggled to free it. Arriving at her aerie, she wrapped me in her arms and smacked a loud kiss on my cheek, a green leaf glowing at the periphery of my vision, stuck to the bill of the ball cap.

"You wore the Yankee hat," she said, rewarding me with another kiss.

She was holding a paper bag in her hand, half hidden behind her back. "Worms?" I asked.

"Worm *sandwich*," she smiled, holding the bag before me. "And look what else I got!" she added, pinching a charred, damp roach in her fingers. "I found it here by the fire."

We searched through the dregs of last week's party looking for more castaways, but found nothing but a burnt, bloody sock.

"How's your friend doing?" she asked.

"He'll live, but they couldn't save the arm."

Waiting for my smile, which wasn't forthcoming, Darcy broke into a grin of her own. "You're such a comedian," she said.

"*Asshole*, I'm told."

"I've yet to see that side of you," she said, at which point I spun around and showed her the seat of my shorts.

We dug through the woods looking for worms, rewarded with only one in ten minutes of searching. "Kind of pointless, anyway," Darcy observed, pointing to the fishing pole, "since you forgot the hook."

She was right. I'd tied on the bobber, then the sinkers, then nothing, the hook part of the ritual escaping my attention. "It's an existential exercise," I explained. "The fish are merely a symbol."

We wandered down the strand to a place where the shore merged with the railroad embankment, where the steel tracks gleamed in the morning sun and the smell of creosote rivaled the musk of the river. The jumble of rocks morphed into smooth gray slabs, flat planes of granite where small pools of tidewater pocking their undulant surface, flocks of brown sparrows dipping their beaks and fluffing their downy wings. We sat cross-legged on the flattest, widest rock, face to face and knee to knee, and resumed where we'd left off at the Van Gogh Place, doing what I'd been dreaming of doing every day since Darcy got grounded.

We hugged and kissed for an hour or two, not looking up when a train roared past or seagulls dropped from the sky, airplanes droning far out on the river, a distant, melancholic sound. My arms were tanned from working in the sun and our skin was a perfect match, our fingers laced together like braids. "Teal," Darcy whispered, as though testing my name, "is that for the color of your eyes?"

"Nope. It's got nothing to do with color, or ducks. It's my full name, Thomas Lee."

"Thomas Lee," she repeated, trying it out.

"My dad's name was Thomas, so I was *Tommy* for a while, just to tell us apart. Then it was TL, which soon became Teal because that's how my cousins pronounced it."

"You have a big family?"

"Yeah, I guess, we've all stuck close to home. For like, four hundred years."

I saw an opening then, and took it, curious to learn more about Darcy's dead sister who drowned in a skiing accident. "So," I said, "you don't see much of your sister Kara?"

"Not really. She used to visit when she was in college, but not since having a baby."

"She went to school where? In Miami?"

"No, in Boston. I went up to see her a couple of times, but … hey," she said, avoiding my question, "let's try smoking that roach."

I'd left it out in the sun to dry, and we each got a couple of tiny tokes before it was played. It was good shit, as they say, and we were instantly hungry. "What's really in that bag?" I asked.

"Worms, I told you."

"I love a good worm," I said. "Bust them out."

She'd made CLPs: choke, lusterslime, and potato chip sandwiches, two apiece. Darcy ate both of hers and half of my second. "Did you bring anything to drink?" I asked.

"Did you bring any hooks?" she replied. "Can't we just drink from the river?"

"Are you crazy?"

"Apparently," she said, "I just made out with you. Let's go fishing."

So, I showed her how to cast, which she did a dozen times until she got it just right. I loved just watching her, standing aside while she whipped the pole around, her tanned legs slender, her bare feet in the water, her back a perfect trapezoid beneath the sheer fabric of her blouse.

"You're a pro," I said.

"But we don't have beer cans, like you and your dad at the lake."

"That's okay. The fish won't be biting anyway."

Propping the pole in a cleft of a rock, we watched the red bobber drift on the waves, bouncing hypnotically, bright sparkles in its wake, a dozen yards out from shore. Our shadows were reduced to a gray cape around us as the sun blazed hot overhead, Darcy leaning against my chest with her brown arms draped over mine, across the twin bumps of our knees.

"Your neck's getting burned," I cautioned, and taking off the Yankee cap, I cocked in on her head.

"Do I look like Bobby Richardson?" she asked.

"Elston Howard, if we don't get out of this sun."

She dipped her hand in a bird bath pool and sprinkled cool water on my arm.

"That feels great," I said, and did the same for her.

The water lay beaded like diamonds on our skin, glittering in the demon sun. I poured a cupped handful down her back and she giggled, poured another down her front and she shivered. "It feels like mint," she said, looking up from beneath my chin, "air-conditioned."

Wetting both hands, I slipped them in her blouse where her nipples were hard as candy. "More," she said, and I repeated the process, my penis pressed hard against her spine where no doubt she could feel it.

"Wait," she said, and crossing her arms pulled the blouse over her head. I ladled more water on her smooth brown shoulders, watching it dribble down her back. Turning, she fiddled with the buttons on my shirt, peeling its sleeves from my arms. Face to face and breathing hard, we kneaded our sweaty skin, a salty taste like potato chip crumbs stuck in the corners of our mouths. "C'mon," she said and grabbed my hand, pulling me toward the river. Kicking off my sneakers, I waded in beside her, our feet turning white beneath the surface, wiggling ovals of reflected sunlight lapping against our shins.

We waded up to our bellybuttons, where the sand was soft underfoot, and stood there kissing as a train rushed by, the wind of its passage rattling the leaves in the copse of surrounding trees. And I wondered how we looked to the passengers inside, if they even glanced up from their newspapers, a couple of kids half naked in the river, floating like bobbers on the bouncing waves, tethered to nothing but themselves.

Darcy plunged in and pulled me with her, and the water rushed over our bodies, cooling those parts that a second before had been burning, scorching hot, merging our flesh in a shivering mass of caramel-colored goose bumps. She shrieked, and I hooted, and we dragged ourselves ashore where we lay half out of the water, Darcy's back glistening like a sunbaked gemstone of burnt sienna and chrome.

"My popsicle," she said, tickling my ear with her tongue.

We couldn't stop squeezing, squirming together, the lapping water a precious oil everywhere we touched, allowing skin to slide on bone and hair to adhere to muscle, the river and the sun both icicle and spark that arced all over our bodies. I tugged at her cutoffs, and she did mine, shimmying to slide them off, moaning in frustration when they clung to our hips, our pockets filled with sand. We froze in an instant when we heard distant voices coming from somewhere above, our heads, our noses just inches apart as we looked in each other's eyes.

Three young boys came prancing up the tracks, laughing, leaping, flailing their arms with joyous, childlike abandon, performing grand acts of selfless bravado, if only in their minds. Bereft of ego at eleven years old, they parried and stabbed at the air, grabbing their hearts in sustaining grave wounds, vying for the hand of a fairy tale princess who looked, I was sure, just like Darcy.

The boys never saw us, engaged as they were in young male companionship, and once they were gone and the silence returned, Darcy and I just lay there, the water lapping against our legs, the sun sliding sideways across the blue sky. With her head on my shoulder, I felt her teeth bite down on my sunburned flesh, but softly, slowly, the faintest impression revealing the trail of her lips. "Hey," I said, "who's got the sweet tooth now?"

"This smell," she said, sounding distant, distracted, "the river, the trees, the railroad tracks, it reminds me of when I was a kid, hot summer days at the beach club."

"Diving off the raft," I added, "for the lurid benefit of Jonah Gold. I bet you're a good swimmer."

"My father taught me," she said, and fell silent.

A single white cloud appeared in the sky, and we chose to watch it awhile, Darcy patting the sand with her hand, impressing the shape of a star fish. Eventually she said, "My mom had bought me this cute little swimsuit, black and white checks with a frill at the bottom. I was probably five, maybe six years old. Kara was a teenager, still living at home but mostly off with her friends. She had tried and failed to teach me to swim, giving up after several attempts.

"I was playing in the shallows in my brand-new swimsuit, floating face down on a plastic raft with a transparent window in the bottom. I was lying there, dreaming, absorbed in that world of tiny little seashells and sand, when suddenly my father scooped me up and carried me out to deep water. I was crying, panicking, but he held me on the surface with his arms stretched out beneath me. He said, 'Row like a boat, paddle your feet. I promise I won't let go.' And he didn't let go, and pretty soon I was floating on the surface, still in his arms, but dog paddling out toward the raft.

"I'd forgotten to be scared, and was giggling, in fact, when suddenly he let go. I sank like a stone, thrashing my arms and gulping down water as I screamed. I splashed my way over to the red and white cork line where finally my toes touched the sand, where I choked and shivered as he walked down the beach, never once turning around, water still dripping from his baggy gray trunks, his skinny legs shining like fish scales.

Pausing a moment, looking up the cloud, her voice found a sudden resolve. "I went right back out there and paddled and kicked until I could stay above water, and by the time my father paid attention again I could swim even better than Kara."

Absorbed by her story and her face as she'd told it, I tried to say something to lighten her mood, to bring her mind back to the present. "There's better ways to learn to swim, but maybe he did you a favor."

Too late by one second, I saw my mistake, and Darcy's face darkened in the shadow of the cloud, but then as quickly brightened again when the cloud, or the moment, passed over. Her moods were as fleeting and quixotic as the weather, once threatening, then stormy, then calm as pond. "That's my dad," she exhaled with a sigh, "always doing nice things for people."

We continued to ladle cool water on our skin, parched in the stifling heat, Darcy scooping a hatful with the Yankee cap, pouring it over my head. Her skin had turned pink on the bridge of her nose and the hollow beneath her eyes, and I found myself kissing her cheeks, her forehead, and the elegant curve of her chin. The water kept rising as the sun moved west, eclipsing the Palisades, the trees on the cliff tops writhing like flames, bright orange in the afternoon light. As the slack tide rose, our island got smaller, and the lapping of waves grew louder, our footprints erased from the flat of the sand, seaweed now dancing in the rocks.

Darcy's yellow flipflop floating in a pool, bobbing like a small rubber boat, the perfect impression of her heel and toes in the slanted, golden light—that is the picture I keep of that day, my haiku of summer, my first taste of love.

In the absence of sunshine, we grew suddenly cold and gathered our few things together, cutting the fish line, freeing the bobber to drift away north along the shore. Hand in hand we crossed the tracks and scrambled up the bank by the absent trestle, kissing in the street at the edge of the Manor, not caring if anyone saw. Darcy kept the Yankee cap cocked on her head, saying it was her turn to wear it, her ponytail bouncing like a long silver tassel as she flip-flopped her way toward home.

She called that night and talked for hours, reading me the comics while I sprawled atop my sheets, slathered in sunburn ointment. Imagining Darcy on her sister's bed, as fiery and naked as I was, there was plenty of time to do what I needed while listening to the sound of her voice, imaging her face, her tongue, her lips, the ski slope rise of her breasts. She would pause only briefly to ask silly questions I was never expected to answer, saying, "Poor Charlie Brown, will Lucy ever love him? Will Linus give up his old blanket?"

Chapter 8

AFTER THE FISHING TRIP we saw each other as often as we could, which wasn't easy because of my job. We didn't spend a whole day together until the Fourth of July, a hot, muggy, east coast day when the town hosted a grand parade with high school bands, volunteer fire departments, and Little League ballplayers marching to the cemetery where the VFW fired rifles at the clouds.

Perched on the roof of a mausoleum, peeking through dogwoods on Archuletta's Island, Darcy and I watched the old hunchbacked veterans line up at the Civil War monument, a bird-stained statue of a Union soldier with a garrison cap and musket. Standing at attention in their ill-fitting uniforms, their wrinkled hands held to their hearts, there was sorrow revealed in their weepy old eyes while behind them the color guard cocked their rifles and fired three rounds in succession. Darcy flinched at the sound of each shot, leaning back against my chest with her head tucked under my chin. Little boys scrambled on hands and knees to pluck the brass cartridges from the grass, the old men oblivious to the innocence of youth, immersed in the trauma of their past.

"Were you one of those kids," Darcy asked, "racing after the bullets?"

"Casings," I corrected, "and yeah, I was one of them. Still got some in my sock drawer."

I told her about riding in the parade with my father, he on his black-and-white police Harley, me on my Huffy with baseball cards affixed to the forks with clothes-pins. I'd been so proud to ride along with him, everyone watching from the curbside, babies in strollers, grandmas in lawn chairs cheering us on as we passed. He'd goose the throttle to make it growl when the neighbor kids twisted their wrists.

"You really miss him, huh?"

"Sure," I answered.

"You say that like its natural, like anyone would."

"Would what?"

"Miss their father."

It was hot and muggy, and even in our cut offs we were sweating, my bare feet sticky in my Weejun loafers, Darcy kicking her flipflops down the road as we headed for the green plaid blanket. The Stars and Stripes fluttered everywhere we looked, fastened to sticks poked into the earth, perfectly blending with the blue lobelia, red geraniums, and white mums that blanketed the graves of the veteran's.

"Those soldiers," said Darcy, "those sad old men … What will you do about the draft?"

"Nothing. I'll be in art school."

"That's why you're going?"

"No. It's just where I'll be."

"Would you go, though, to war?"

"Maybe," I said, "if you'd fit in my pack. You and the little Chinese girl. Did I tell you I once tried out for football?" I added, looking for a way to explain. "Only because I thought I had to, because boys *need* a letter for their sweater. I was skinny, though, and pretty slow, and the coach just used me for a tackling dummy. Football, it's so macho, you know? Guys snapping towels in the locker room, laughing real loud like hyenas. The ego stunk worse than the sweaty jock straps, and I quit after only a week. That's what I figure the army is like—same crap, different uniform."

"You're funny," said Darcy.

"Why? You think I should join the army?"

"No! I don't want anyone to go. Especially you! Why didn't you go out for baseball instead?"

"Huh? I don't play baseball anymore."

A crow swooshed low and croaked overhead, straight out of Van Gogh's wheat field.

"Was your dad in the war?" she asked. "World War Two?"

"Yeah. Was yours?"

"No." she said, "he had a deferment, something to do with his heart. Tell me more about your dad. Tell me how he died."

I shrugged, sighed, shook my head, but told her anyway. "He'd been in a car wreck, a high-speed chase that left him paralyzed on the whole left side of his body. My dad was a southpaw, just like The Babe, meaning he threw left-handed. That was the end of his Little League coaching, as well as being a cop. Even the end of his nighttime job down at the corner drugstore. But he'd still go down to the pharmacy at night to hang out with Larry and Paul. What used to be a five-minute walk took him half an hour with the crutch. His arm was like a noodle, his leg like rubber, casting it out as he walked. He wore a brace on a special shoe that I had to help him strap on, lifting his foot, tying the laces, cinching the buckle to his calf. It weighed nothing, his leg, the muscle like dough. There was just nothing left anymore."

We'd paused on the path by the Archuletta vault, dandelions dotting the grass. "I'm sorry," said Darcy, grabbing my arm, offering me the opportunity to stop. But I went on anyway, wanting to tell it, needing her to hear.

"On the nights he went down there, my mom fixed him supper, meat and potatoes on a red dinner plate with aluminum foil tucked around it. It was my always my job to take it to him, and … I don't know why, but I dreaded that trip, like I dreaded touching his leg. On the way to the drugstore, I'd walk really slow with the plate held out in both hands, islands of vapor forming on the foil, twinkling under the streetlamps, swirling around as the steam leaked out, like the sky from *Starry Night*. I'd study the bottles in the drugstore window, check for nickels in the gumball machine, putting off that moment when I'd walk behind the counters and see him slouched on his stool, his hair turned white, his face stubbled gray, but smiling, always smiling. 'Hey, Bud,' he'd say, 'thanks for the chow. What did your mom make tonight?' He always called me Buddy, or Bud, like guys always say in the army.

"He died a year later. A vein in his head; they said it was over in seconds. I'd *run* to the drugstore now if I could. If he was still down there, waiting."

Darcy was silent, inspecting her toes, her nail polish seashell pink. "How come you never visit his grave? I don't even know where it is."

"I don't come here to be with the dead. It's more like escaping the living."

"C'mere," she said, and cradled my head, and I cried like I hadn't for years. After drying my tears with the tail of her blouse, she led me down the steps to the Van Gogh Place and spread the green blanket on the grass. We lay without speaking, just holding each other, till I noticed the sound of her measured breathing and realized she was asleep. Moments later I too was dozing, the heat of our bodies like a warm glass of milk easing me into unconsciousness.

I awoke to find Darcy yawning beside me, one knuckle rubbing her eye, her lips describing a capital O as she stretched her arms toward the treetops. The polka dot pattern of sunlight and leaves speckled the grass around us, and Darcy said, "It feels like photosynthesis. Like my blood's all green inside me."

"My flower," I said, and kissed the crook of her arm.

"That felt great, our little nap. We must have been really sleepy."

"It's probably the heat. Or I'm so boring."

"So easy," she said, falling back in my arms. "I'm just so comfortable being with you, it's hard to stay awake. What if we woke up in the mountains somewhere, in Albert Bierstadt's cabin. You think we'll ever live together? You think we'll leave this town?"

"Maybe," I stammered, at a loss for words. "Someday."

"Sorry," she said, seeing my confusion. "I just never know what I'm going to say."

"That's alright. I can't think of anyone I'd rather shack up with."

"Mia Farrow? Michelle Phillips?"

"Who?"

"Michelle Phillips, from the Mamas and the Papas."

"Well, maybe her."

She laughed and buried her head on my shoulder, and a few seconds later she was biting my neck, her teeth faintly grazing the skin. "Hey!" I laughed, "I was only kidding. I'm hot for Mama Cass!"

We wrestled a bit, pinching, tugging, squeezing our bodies together. Darcy was strong and gripped me with her legs, pressing her weight on my hips, her long hair dangling down in my face where it tickled the tip of my nose. Suddenly she froze with her head bent low, her breathless giggling abated.

"Feel that?" she asked.

"What, your heart?"

"Guess again," she smiled, rising on an arm, directing our eyes to the lump in my pants. "Feeling the sweet tooth, are we?"

Straddling my stomach, she crossed her arms and pulled her top over her head, the gleaming aurora of silvery hair ignited like rays of the sun. She slid back slowly with her rear in the air and wiggled her shorts down her hips and, rolling away, she kicked them off and stretched out flat on her back, naked, dimpled, tanned all over, my blonde palomino in the grass. Smiling at me with parted lips she waited for me to act, to do whatever I wanted to do, not quite certain what that was. She helped me do it, we helped each other, melting together like cherry filled chocolates, caramels, and soft centered creams, our clothes strewn around us like crenelated wrappers, the blanket balled up at our feet.

The smell of the grass was intoxicating, prickly soft on our skin. As the sun slipped down behind the trees we huddled beneath the blanket, like Indian lovers in the days of yore, or little kids playing with flashlights. It was warm in there, full of our scent, Darcy purring, then growling like a tiger, her fine hair pasted to my skin. Suddenly she hiccupped and sat up straight, tossing off the blanket, exposing us both to the goose-pimply air.

"Darn!" she said.

"You always get the hiccups?"

"No! So why now?"

"You're allergic," I said. "To me. Try holding your breath."

She tried, but with no success. "Ohhh!" she groaned. "Is there something I can take?"

"I've given you all I got. But wait," I said, rising, striding to the stone wall of the mausoleum where I reached my hand through its ivy facade. "There might be water in this tap."

Hidden in the foliage was a rusty old pipe turned green and moldy with age, but when I opened the spigot water streamed out, running cold and clear at my feet. Splashing a handful on my red, flushed face, shivering with the rush, I ran back to the blanket and wrapped it tight around me. "Go ahead," I said, "drink a bunch. It'll cure those hiccups."

Darcy did, and it worked first try, and she stood there naked, water dripping from her chin, dribbling down her tummy to her sun-tanned toes.

"Darce," I said, from my place on the blanket, "forgive me for saying this, but you are so fucking beautiful …"

She did forgive me, but I never said that again, having learned my lesson from the tiger. I told her I loved her a million times, but beauty is a truly mysterious thing, existing solely in the eye of the beholder, not in the object beheld.

Wild strawberries grew at the edge of the grass and Darcy knelt there to pick some, crouched with her bottom exposed to the breeze, the tips of her breasts like red berries. Returning to the blanket we wrapped it around us and ate from the palm of her hand, Darcy's lips scarlet, tart when I kissed them, sugary deep in my throat. She smeared the red juice on both our cheeks then bent to write something on my belly, shielding my eyes so I couldn't watch as her wet finger tickled my skin. "Peace," she had written, when she allowed me to look, upside down so I could read it. And peace it was, that day, and for many days thereafter, the kind of peace you can't win at a conference table, arguing about money, politics, and war, about the shape of the table itself.

"Hey," I said, "what is the sound of one hand clapping?"

Darcy's brow furrowed, then relaxed in a smile as she tapped her stained fingers on my belly, where the flat of her hand made a slapping sound before coming to rest on my heart. Stunned at how easily she'd answered the riddle, an ancient kōan resolved, I pressed my ear to the fragrant grass and heard Buddha roll over in his grave.

Chapter 9

I DIDN'T REALIZE HOW MUCH TIME I spent with Darcy until Todd called, inviting me to Laughing Hill to watch the solar eclipse.

"It's a total eclipse, man. Bring Darcy if you want. I still haven't met her, you know."

"Get out."

"Seriously. I haven't seen you since the rumble, the Jets and the Sharks."

It had been six weeks since the graduation party, my longest Todd-less period since kindergarten.

"Should be quite a gang," he said. "I got a nickel bag from Neumann, so he'll probably be there to mooch it. He follows the market, religiously, you might say."

Todd was always joking. He cracked me up.

"So, bring your squeeze. She can hang with Mary Ann, catch up on old times."

"Mouse is coming?"

"I'm kind of seeing her."

"You're dating?"

"I guess."

"Hey, that's my line."

"Eclipse begins at four fifteen," said Todd. "You gotta bring something to look through, though, like a dark negative, so you don't burn your eyes. And hey, her name isn't Mouse, its Mary Ann."

"I know. Force of habit."

"They're habit forming, chicks."

"Tell me about it."

I wanted to call Darcy but realized then that I didn't know her phone number, she being the one who always called me. I wasn't supposed to call her anyway, since we'd gotten in so much trouble. I'd never even been to her house. So, I looked up her number in the telephone book, figuring the statute of limitations must be up. It rang a bunch of times, and I almost hung up until on maybe the hundredth ring her mom answered.

"Hello, Mrs. Saint James," I cooed, totally Eddie Haskell. "This is Teal Conover. May I speak to Darcy, please?"

"No," she said, quite matter-of-factly, "I'm afraid not. This is not a good time."

"Is everything okay?"

"Of course she's okay, if you must ask. Darcy is not accepting calls at the moment."

"Will you tell her I called?"

"Perhaps," said Mrs. Saint James, and she abruptly hung up.

I'd been tempted to leave a message about the solar eclipse, about meeting me at Laughing Hill, but thought better of it. It seemed wiser, sneakier, to keep our time together a secret.

So, I made a CLP sandwich and stuffed it in my pocket, wrote Mom a note and headed out the door. Banging down the cellar stairs, I remembered about the negative and ran back and pawed through the closet, through a box full of family photos dating back to the Revolution, until I found a piece of celluloid obscure enough to do the job.

It was a long walk to Laughing Hill, a private section of Rockefeller's property along the river, in back of the hospital where Mom worked. I cut through the cemetery just for fun and crossed 9A at the Little League fields where I used to play ball with my dad.

It was there that Antoine Jones beaned Moses Frye with a fastball, same pitch he always threw, right down the pipe. Watching from second base, I didn't think T'won had done it on purpose. Moses went straight down, KOed, even wearing the clunky old batter's helmet. He flopped around on the ground for a minute, getting lime all over his uniform. There were two ballfields, and both games were suspended while Dad and the other coaches knelt beside Moses. He seemed alright, but they called the fire department anyway, and the aid car came and took him to the ER, where Mom treated him for a mild concussion. Neither he nor Antoine played ball after that, which was a shame because while Moses sucked—I always thought he leaned into that fastball— Antoine Jones was great, feared even, as the best pitcher in town. After that he was just plain feared, a really tough kid that nobody fucked with.

I cut through Kirk Mabry's backyard and into the Manor and walked the quiet streets to the cul-de-sac with the hole in the fence, where I crawled through onto Rocky's property. Coming out of the woods onto sloping fields, I gazed up at the stone breastworks of Rockwood Hall, the crumbling parapet all that remained of what once had been the most opulent mansion on the Hudson. It sat at the top of Laughing Hill, where kids went tobogganing in winter, laughing and screaming all the way to the bottom, where a cliff dropped off to the railroad tracks. A dozen people in colorful jackets stood silhouetted against the blue sky, and when Todd called my name, everyone joined him, shouting, "Teeeal! Teeeal!"

"It's really you!" he said and slapped my shoulder. Shoving a warm can of Piels in my hand, he clunked it against his own. "No Darcy, huh?"

"Her mom answered when I called, so I didn't get to talk to her. Hey, Mary Ann," I said.

Sitting alone on the foundation wall, Mouse tossed her hair as it snapped in the wind and tucked it behind one ear. She nodded briefly, faked a smile, and quickly looked away.

"Toke?" asked Todd, holding out a joint. I pinched it, puffed it, and held my breath, then tried to pass it to Mary Ann, who folded her arms across her chest as though hugging herself for warmth.

Erik Neumann grabbed the joint from my hand. "Don't mind if I do," he said, taking a single, massive hit that burned halfway down to the roach. "Good shit," he choked, glancing at me. "Looking to score any weed? "

"No thanks," I said.

"You're working, aren't you? You got some cash."

I shook my head again, and he said, "That Darcy chick must be draining your funds. The girl is high fucking maintenance."

I had to laugh. Everyone thought they knew so much about Darcy, how she was rich, and wild, and stuck-up. What if I told them that we just walked around, or talked on the telephone, went fishing in the river without hooks. "I'm saving my money," I said.

"Teal's headed out west!" said Todd. "Aren't ya, bro?"

"Yeah?" said Neumann. "Like what, Haight-Ashbury? You gotta be kidding."

"I'm not going anywhere. Just saving my money."

"What the fuck time is it?" asked Steve Railsbeck, who'd wandered over to snag the doob from Erik. "Yo, Teal," he said, "gracing us with your presence?"

"If that's how it feels, roll with it."

Railsbeck still sported a cast on his arm from when Antoine had broken it in detention. It was covered with names in black and red marker, a half-ass peace symbol with a grinning skull. "How's the hand?" I asked.

He held it up, the plaster filthy underneath. "Kinda hard to jerk off with," he snickered, grinning directly at Mouse.

Todd said, "Maybe your mom could help." Leaning between us he took Mary Ann's hand and led her toward the massive chestnut tree that crowned the top of the hill.

Mouse lit a cigarette and slid down against the trunk, while Todd and I stood gazing at the sky, sipping our lukewarm beers.

"Sorry about that," he said, apparently referring to the convo with Erik Neumann. "I didn't know you were keeping it a secret."

"Keeping what a secret? Who says I'm going out west?"

"I just thought … someone said … you know how you've always said you loved mountains, the lure of wild, wild west."

"I always said *what?*"

"It's Darcy, huh? You're sticking around for her?"

"It's not that. I'm just not going anywhere. And where would I go with only six weeks left of summer?"

"Okay, cool out. I'm on your side. I'm glad to keep you around. Hey," he said, "there's that fucker Dwayne. I gotta go talk to him."

Todd hustled off, leaving me alone with Mary Ann. She wouldn't look up at me, so I slid down beside her against the bark of the tree. "Can I bum a cig?" I asked.

Staring at me for an overlong moment, she said, "You don't smoke."

"How do you know?"

Looking away, she took a drag of her Salem, stabbing the butt to her lips. "I know lots about you," she said, exhaling white smoke. "I'm sorry, Teal, about the party. I shouldn't have done that. I was really drunk." She added, "I don't love you, anyway. Now I'm in love with Todd."

I'd never even known that Mary Ann loved me, but hearing her say that she no longer did hurt somehow, in ways I couldn't account for. Mouse had just always been Mouse to me, a girl from the neighborhood, my kindergarten friend. But now her affections felt more like love lost, one I never realized I had, much less reciprocated. For weeks I'd been so full of passion and lust that the loss of even this secret morsel was like a devastating punch in the gut.

Watching her shred the cigarette filter, I sought to do something with my hands, stuffing them in the pockets of my corduroy jacket where I felt the CLP sandwich. "Here," I said, holding it out like some kind of goofy offering.

She looked at the napkin, squashed from its journey, and wrinkled her nose in confusion.

"Sandwich," I said. "Peanut butter and jelly. With potato chips."

"Choke and lusterslime with chips?" Mouse knew the lingo, an old playground adept.

"It's good," I said. "Try it."

When Todd came back, we were eating the sandwich, passing it back and forth between us.

"Hey," he said, "don't bogart that sammich, my friends."

"Want a bite?" Mary Ann asked, talking with her mouth full.

"Hell yeah," said Todd, and leaned and kissed her square on the lips.

"Gross," she said.

"That *is* good, darlin'. How 'bout another bite?" He kissed her again, and this time she giggled. It was good to see, and it made me happy, and just like that I was over being jilted for my best and oldest friend.

We shared a cigarette after we ate, the sky beginning to darken, erasing the afternoon shadows from the grass. "Hey," said Todd, "you don't smoke."

"So they say. How's your arm?" I asked.

He held up his forearm where the remnants of over a dozen stitches were still visible. "It's hard to jerk off with," he said, mimicking Railsbeck. Throwing his arm around Mary Ann's neck, he hugged her to his side. "But I don't much need to these days. Hey, it's happening," he said, athletically jumping to his feet. "Did you bring something to look through?"

Searching through my pockets, I drew out the old negative and handed it to Todd. We were all standing then, Todd holding the celluloid to one eye.

"Not so close," said Mary Ann, squinting at Todd and away from the sun. I turned away, too, but was peeking at her, wondering how I'd ever missed her feelings for me.

"Yeah!" said Todd, "it's happening all right!"

The mob of people lining the wall were looking through negatives of their own, or waiting their turn, Railsbeck wearing an actual welder's hood, apparently unwilling to share it.

"You didn't bring a negative?" I asked Todd, who shook his head sheepishly, and handed me the film. "Nah, I fucking forgot."

"Who's the asshole now," I said, and passed the film to Mary Ann.

"It's incredible," she offered, "the moon and the sun. Makes me feel kind of ancient, eternal."

Laughing Hill had turned ghostly gray, the Hudson dull as lead. "Here," said Mary Ann, and passed the negative to me. The first thing I saw was not the sun but the image of my father, his empty grin and silver eyes gazing directly at the camera, my mother's young face revealed in profile, her curly head pressed to his shoulder. She held one hand to the front of his shirt with two fingers slipped between buttons, as though feeling his chest for the thump of his heart, assuring herself of its presence. The circle of moon now passed through them both in a virtual wedding band of light, their existence eclipsed by celestial time, exposed overlong to its passage.

"Hey," said, Todd, "don't overdo it. You can really fuck up your eyes."

When I looked away I was all but blinded, my hands, my sneakers, the grass around me gone blurry and out of focus. Mary Ann blotted the tears from my cheeks, daubing my face with the jelly-stained napkin.

"Medic!" Todd joked. "Keep your eyes closed, man. Relax them for a sec. Jeez Louise, Conover, this is the last cosmic event I'll ever take *you* to."

Mom had made meatloaf when I got home, and we ate it in the living room on TV trays while watching the evening news. A Black Power conference was convening in Newark; Che Guevara was dead in Bolivia; and a really skinny British chick named Twiggy was the most photographed subject since the Grand Canyon.

I told Mom about meeting Todd for the solar eclipse, not mentioning the old negative. She asked me how his arm was doing, if he was keeping it clean. I was right about that night—she'd been the nurse who sewed him up, eighteen stitches in all.

"He's fine," I said. "He's dating Mary Ann Hicks."

"Angie's daughter? We went to high school together. Her mom, I mean. I remember Mary Ann from the playground gang, from the summer crafts program. She was a cute little thing."

"Still is."

"Do you remember Carter Mason?" Mom asked. "He hung out at the playground, too."

"I know him alright. Deloit's older brother."

"Well, Carter lost his leg, poor thing. I mean, he literally lost his prosthetic limb, somewhere out in the woods. He was badly wounded in Vietnam, stepped on a mine, I believe. He's been back for a month, but no one knew. He just got off a Greyhound bus and headed straight for the woods at Rockefellers. The police have been up there looking for it, the leg. They said his camp is just a few sheets of plastic and a filthy sleeping bag. It's sad, pathetic, and he's drunk all the time. Been to the ER twice."

"What will they do?" I asked. "They can't just leave him up there."

"I don't know. Call the VA, I guess."

Thinking back to the graduation party, I felt kind of bad for Carter. Maybe I should have been nicer to him, tried to help him out. But the guy was being such an asshole, like he was *trying* to piss me off.

"Darcy called," said Mom, "said she'd try again later. How is she doing? You two sure see a lot of each other."

"She's fine."

"You really like her, huh? How much do you like her?"

"Like what, from one to ten?"

"I'm not trying to embarrass you, Teal, but you know about condoms, right? You know how to protect yourself?"

"C'mon, Mom."

"Sorry, hon, but it *is* my business, whether you like it or not. Are you two taking care of yourselves?"

"Of course."

But we weren't, really. I didn't have any condoms, and frankly hadn't thought about them. I started to count how many times we'd done it, which wasn't hard, not getting past the fingers of one hand.

A commercial on the tube showed little blue arrows attacking lightning bolts of headache pain. *Laugh In* started right after that, this really cute blonde chick dancing in a bikini, a lady in a hairnet swatting a homeless person with her purse.

"Mom," I said, "when you and Dad met, how did you know you loved him?"

"I'd known your father forever, from way back in grammar school. I guess I always loved him."

"Really, though. I mean, you didn't actually *love* him in third grade."

"In high school, then," she said. "We dated, he took me to the prom, all the stuff you kids think is corny."

"I don't think it's corny that you and dad went. It wasn't lame back then."

She laughed. "No, it wasn't lame. Not at all."

"Even then you knew you loved him? You knew you wanted to marry him?"

Mom grew thoughtful, showing me the face I'd grown to anticipate, to even dread in the months after Dad died. I'd hated to see her cry, and she knew it, always trying to hide her tears, adopting instead a stoic facade I hated even more.

"You don't have to—"

"It's fine," she said. "I don't mind telling. I guess it was when he went overseas—that's what we used to call it back then, going off to war. It just sounded safer, though it wasn't, of course. There was no television, so you only saw the war at the movies, on the newsreels, big gray battle ships shooting guns, airplanes dropping bombs. You didn't see soldiers getting killed, not like you do now. You couldn't watch your husband, your brother, your son die on the evening news. But yet, you knew how terrible it was by just the sheer numbers of dead, the boys coming home in wooden boxes, or horribly wounded, like Carter Mason.

"He wrote me letters as often as he could. He was at Okinawa, did you know that? They landed on the beach in those open boats exposed to all those guns. Your father would never tell me about it, except to say that many of his friends had died. In his letters he only talked about home, always asking about our friends, if I saw his dad, or Uncle Walter, especially his mom.

"When I got a letter, I was overjoyed, my heart was so starved for him, and because it meant he was still alive. But not really, you see? Because I always thought, after the happiness—What if I'm reading his *final* letter, and now perhaps he's dead? It took several weeks to get mail from the Pacific, weeks in which he might have died, been killed without my knowing. With each letter I got it was always the same—the joy, the pain, then the waiting.

"That's when I knew I truly loved him, how empty the world would feel without him, the absence of love in my life."

Had we been sitting closer, my mom would have reached out to finger my hair, push a lock behind my ear, like Darcy often did. "Oh," I said.

"Oh?" she laughed. "Just *oh*?"

"Thanks, I mean. For telling me that."

"You think you really love this girl? Do you think that she loves you?"

"I guess, but how do I—how do we know what real love is? How can you actually tell?"

Mom sighed and smiled with her hands in her lap, her fingers constantly moving. "It's not like the answer to a math problem, dear. There's no official way that love feels. After the war, I suppose I loved your father even more, and I knew that he loved me. But he was different then. They were all different, coming back. We were older, too, and I won't say wiser, but we'd seen and felt a lot more things, not all of them wonderful, like life had been in high school."

"You think that high school is too young to know?"

"I'm not saying that, but you might see things differently in a few years. You will. Maybe your idea of love will change. Maybe who you love will change too."

"Did the war change your love?"

"Yes, but I can't say how, or how much. I wish there was something I could tell you, Teal. I know you really like this girl, and it appears she really likes you. I truly hope you don't get hurt, but chances are you will. Maybe not by Darcy—I hope not by her—but eventually … you'd be the first person to escape life's pain, and likely the last to know it."

She smiled at me then, the look I dreaded vanished from her face.

"You think I should go in the army?" I asked.

"No," she said, without hesitation. "I wasn't suggesting that war helps you love. You can know love right here. I just can't help you know if love's real. Only you can do that."

"Us, you mean, me and Darcy."

"No, I mean you. People can be in love all by themselves. That's what I mean by life's pain."

My hand was on the phone when finally it rang, startling me from a dream about Darcy, where she stood at the top of Laughing Hill staring directly at the sun.

"I wanted to talk to you so bad!" she cried. "It's horrible here! They've been fighting all day!"

"Calm down," I said, surprised by her intensity. "I called you this morning, did your mom tell you?"

"No, but I knew. I could hear her talking."

"What's going on?"

"Ohhh, the same old thing. It's always the same. She drinks, he gets angry. He's angry, so she drinks. I guess she loves him, like she just can't help it! She never does anything but cry and drink, and he just loves that, you know? You know why? Because … because then he gets to be *him* again! He gets to do what he loves best, and she won't stop him, she never has, and it just goes on and on!"

She was crying like I'd never heard anyone cry, even when my father died, and I wanted to squeeze her, to stroke her hair and erase her tears with my lips. "You want me to come over?" I said. "I could be there in twenty minutes."

"No! I don't want you to see this!"

I looked at the glowing clock on my bureau, its hands converging at midnight. "Are they still fighting?" I asked.

"She's in the bedroom. I can hear her from here. He's downstairs with his stinky pipe, reading The New York Times. He's reading the fucking newspaper, Teal, as if he didn't just crush her completely! I'd fucking kill him if I could. I swear to God I would!"

Those words, how she said them, reminded me of Carter, the venom in his voice when he'd swung with his cane, warning me to keep away.

"I think I need to come down there," I said.

"No!" she screamed, her voice shrill through the phone. "Aren't you listening? Do you not fucking hear me?"

I was shocked, stunned, unable to respond. Darcy had never sworn at me before, her voice like that of a stranger. Looking for something to cut through the tension, I blurted the first thought that came to mind.

"My mom and I talked about my father tonight, about being in the army, going to war, the stuff he wrote in his letters. She was trying to explain about falling in love, the ways you could tell you were in it. She spoke about pain—*life's pain*, she called it—how you could end up in love with somebody who doesn't love you back."

"You think I don't love you?" Darcy cried.

"I'm talking about your father, Dar. Like maybe if you actually tried to love him—"

"Did it kill your mom when your father died?" Darcy interrupted. "Do you think she'll ever get over it?"

"People get over everything."

"You haven't."

"C'mon, Darce. What if your father died?"

"I should be so lucky," she said.

Something switched off when I heard those words, and I just couldn't listen anymore.

"You really don't know what you're talking about," I said. "What do you know about death?"

Soon as I said it I wished *I* was dead, forgetting about her sister. "Wait," I stammered, "I didn't mean—"

"Please!" she insisted. "I want to know. I want to hear all about dying."

Staring up at the plane of my ceiling, at the checkerboard pattern of ambient light that fell through the panes of my window—the fridge switched on, water pipes clunked, a car passed down on the street. It took me a second to gather my thoughts, searching for where to begin. I said, "It's the little things that get you the most, nothing you'd have noticed before. His coat, his cap, the shoe with the brace, the smell of Vitalis on his comb. His name on a cup, a tie on the doorknob, a bookmark holding a page, everything waiting like he's still coming back, like he'll walk through the door any minute.

"The first few days you can't even think, like everything's turned upside down. The apartment is packed with relatives and friends and people you don't even know, cold cuts laid out on the dining room table, cigarette smoke in the bathroom. The scent of carnations is sickeningly sweet from the wreaths stacked up in the hall, delivered by men from the funeral home where there's no room left by the casket. Your aunts and cousins are hugging, or laughing, crying when they think they're alone. One uncle promises he'll take you fishing, another to a Yankee game. It's like … everyone's trying to make you feel normal, like life will go on as before. But it won't. It can't, cause there's no going back, no escaping the fact that he's dead."

I thought that I'd maybe said something important when Darcy fell silent on the phone. A minute went by and her sniffling subsided; then I heard a long intake of breath.

She said, "Its worse missing someone who's still alive, watching her die every day. Do you think I *want* my father's love? You think I would care if he died?"

And the click of the phone filled the shell of my ear like a mine going off underfoot.

Chapter 10

Two days passed without word from Darcy, so finally I called her house. The first few times the phone rang and rang, and I freaked out thinking they'd changed their number, or maybe even moved. On the seventh try her mom finally answered and asked that I please stop calling. I asked her why, but she hung up abruptly, much like her daughter had. A week went by and I was feeling depressed, just going through the motions at work. It was mindless labor, digging and raking, with plenty of spare time to think, always thinking of Darcy and how much I missed her, how my life had turned quickly to shit.

Crazy fucking Damian White didn't help. He brought a gun to the job one day, a CO2 pistol you primed like a pump, and he went around shooting at birds. Bradford Raines, this fat kid from school, pleaded with him to stop; Damian shot him right in the belly, a small red hole in his t-shirt. The hollow lead pellet was stuck in his skin and Mr. Nap plucked it out with his fingers. He sent Bradford home for the rest of the day but didn't fire Damian. I figured Mr. Nap must have known the White family and felt sorry for their nutty son. Damian was all smiles after that, like he was special, that he could do any dumb thing he wanted and get away with it.

Mom was just leaving when I got home from work. "Lasagna's in the oven," she said. "Just turn it to 350 and wait for it to smell good." So I ate alone in front of the television, watching American Bandstand, Soul Train, and the Monkees, which I always pretended to hate. I turned it off when *Bonanza* came on, cringing at Little Joe's grin, hoping that maybe the phone would ring and Darcy would tell me she loved me. When that didn't happen, I did the next best thing and called Todd instead, who had just returned from the tennis courts.

"You play tennis?" I said.

"I'm just learning. Mary Ann is teaching me."

"Mary Ann plays tennis?"

He enthused about how good she was, then asked if I wanted to play sometime.

"Yeah, I guess."

Todd laughed. "You gotta quit *guessing*, man. This ain't no game show. This stuff's all real."

"Right, tennis is so vital, the white shorts and V-neck sweaters."

"So what's up?" he asked.

"Nothing. I'm just waiting for Darcy to call."

"Explain yourself, Riddler."

I told him how she'd gotten kind of mad at me—"Not *at* me, but with me, you know?"

"I can dig it."

"You can dig it, you big jock?"

"So, like, what's up with Darcy anyway? People keep seeing her walking alone, late at night in the Manor. You really love her, huh? Well, good luck."

"Why do you say that?"

"No reason. She's just … a beautiful girl."

"She doesn't think so."

"Get the fuck out."

"Really, she hates when people say that."

"I'm kinda that way myself," he said, and I had to laugh. That's what I loved about Todd—I always felt better after talking to him.

"So you wanna play tennis?" he asked.

"Sure. I'll call you."

"No you won't."

"I just called you, remember?"

"That's cause something's wrong."

"What's wrong?"

"I don't know. You're not saying."

I watched my reflection on the TV screen, forgetting for an instant that I'd turned it off. "I'll let you know," I said.

"About tennis?"

"About everything."

By Saturday morning Darcy still hadn't called and I felt anxious, antsy, stalking around the apartment, changing my tee shirt once, twice, then stripping completely and hopping in the shower. I used Mom's shampoo, which smelled nothing like Darcy's, and combed my wet hair with my fingers, pulling it back in a ponytail about as long as Silas Gold's beard. Wiping steam from the bathroom mirror, I noticed I was getting muscles from chopping and shoveling and all the hard work I was doing at my job. It felt cool to be strong, like I was growing up, finally becoming a man.

I decided right then to go down to Darcy's and get to the bottom of things. I was out the door by 7:30, cutting through the Restoration to the Manor, following a kids' trail through a dozen backyards until I stood by the stop sign on her corner. I'd never seen her house in the daytime before, having only snuck around it at night, walking Darcy home from the river or the cemetery where we went to make out. It was truly imposing in the morning light, a square white monolith with columns and porches, surrounded by trees and well-trimmed lawns. The Coupe Deville was parked in the driveway, a black BMW beside it, and a much smaller car of unknown make gathering dust in the garage.

Walking down the center of the leafy street, I crossed the sidewalk, then the lawn, and was approaching the front door when I spotted Mrs. Saint James around the corner of the house. She was down on her knees in a flower bed with a wide-brimmed hat on her head. I was just about to speak when she glanced my way, gripping her spade like a knife.

"Hi," I said, "remember me? From Principal Hammer's office?"

Raising a dirt-smudged glove to her forehead, blocking the morning sun, she said, "Yes. You're Darcy's partner in crime."

Not responding to her provocation, I asked, "Is Darcy here? Is she okay?"

"Okay? Is my daughter okay? What exactly do you think is going on here?"

A man's voice called from inside the house, drifting like pipe smoke from an opened window. "Connie? Constance! Where are my leather gloves?"

"Go!" Mrs. Saint James pleaded. "Please go!"

"But, Darcy—"

"Back porch," she whispered, waving me off. "Now leave!"

I hustled away, ducking beneath windows like a cat burglar as I scuttled along the prolific flower beds. Rounding the corner of the house, a creeping wisteria smothered the porch in blue tassels, creeping up and over the white-painted lattice and onto the roof itself. Plumbing its depths, I found an opening and stepped up onto the porch, my eyes adjusting to the cave-like shade, finally discerning a white wicker glider where Darcy lay sprawled on its royal blue cushions. Tanned in cut-offs and a halter top that revealed her belly button, she stared at me with saucer eyes, a look of real shock on her face.

"Dar," was all I managed to say before she leaped up and grabbed my hand, pulling me quickly across the lawn to a hedgerow of fragrant roses. We didn't stop there but followed a path behind the garage to an overgrown, paved-stone patio where an ivy covered birdbath spewed no water, and a carpet of periwinkle devoured the cast-iron lawn furniture. Arrived at last, she hopped up like a bunny and wrapped her legs around my waist, twining her fingers at the back of my neck.

"My God, Teal, what are you doing here? I have such a sweet tooth!" She kissed me then, her tongue in my mouth like a snake as it coiled around mine.

"Cool it," I said. "Are you okay?"

"I'm fine. Now that you're here!"

"Why haven't you called?"

"Please don't ask. Can't you just kiss me? Let's go somewhere!"

Ignoring her charms, I maneuvered to a bench and sat down on the purple flowers, Darcy clinging, cuddled in my lap with her hands up the front of my shirt.

"I missed you so much!" she giggled.

"Then what's with the silence? You sounded so panicked on the phone."

"I told you," she cooed, "I'm a total flake! Forget all the stuff I said."

"How can I forget it? Are you in trouble, or not?"

"No!" she assured me. "I overreacted. Just like Daddy said."

"But you were crying on the phone. I was ready to call the cops."

"Please Teal, stay out of this," she said, quite seriously. "I'm handling this my own way."

"You're way? What's that supposed to mean?"

"It means I'm done talking about it. I'm just gonna have to grow out of this thing, grow up, and put it behind me. Wait here a sec," she winked, "I got us a little present!"

Just like that she was up and away, dashing through the arbor and gone. A minute later she galloped back with a white paper bag in hand and a wicked grin on her face. Reestablishing herself on my lap, she slid the contents from the sack. "Viola!" she laughed, revealing a slim box of condoms. "I actually bought two, but … they found one."

"Fuck!"

"Let's!" she squealed.

"Who found them?"

"My father, who do you think? We have to use them, Teal. It's stupid not to."

"And that's what the fight was about? That's why you were so upset?"

She hung her head, released a sigh and allowed her shoulders to slump. "They're making me go to a doctor, Teal. Sending me to a specialist."

"Are you sick? Or hurt?"

"You know the kind of doctor I mean. It's not the emergency room."

"A psychiatrist?"

"A shrink," she said. "A witch doctor. A guy in a long white coat."

"That's bullshit."

"I know," she said. "It's just for show, to make my parents look better. Like somehow it's all my fault!"

"But you just said that everything was fine, that you'd overreacted."

Sitting up suddenly, she crossed her legs, a bare foot bobbing in the grass. Her skin was the color of coffee—regular—striped in blades of blue shadow. "I better go," she said. "They'll be looking for me."

"Your mom already knows I'm here. She told me where to find you."

"She did?" Darcy gasped, genuinely stunned but recovering quickly with a practiced aplomb. Smiling, fawning, she went on speaking as though I hadn't mentioned her mother. "Doctor Fiona Deveroux is my shrink. Don't you just love that name?"

"When do you start?"

"I already did. I went yesterday, and the year before that."

"What?"

"Not to Dr. Deveroux, but up in New Hampshire where I went to school. I can't remember the first one's name, and the second one had two. You know how some women keep their maiden name, like Darcy Saint James Conover? But that would be almost four names, wouldn't it?"

"So you've been to a psychiatrist before?"

"Psychologist. There's a difference."

"Like what?"

"Well … I don't know!" she giggled. "Maybe they were psychiatrists. I don't recall. It's all just a silly game."

"What happened at your school?"

"Nothing really. I had no fucking interest in Bible study. There were tons of books I wanted to read, but they wouldn't let me, so I just stopped going."

"And they kicked you out?"

"The first school, yeah. The second one I left."

"You split? Where did you go?"

"Nowhere. I walked to the highway and stuck out my thumb, ended up someplace in Maine."

"Fuck, they must have freaked. I bet they were really pissed."

"They were. My father, he—"

"What? What did he do?"

"He's such a jerk. I truly hate him."

"Jeez, Dar, is that all you can say? You can't blame your parents for everything."

Just at that moment her father called, and both of us flinched at the sound. "Darcy!" he shouted, "Where have you gone? You were told to remain on the porch!"

"I better go," she whispered. "And please don't worry. Everything's under control."

Whose control, I wanted to ask, but didn't get the chance. Kissing my cheek, she sprang from my lap, spilling the condoms on the grass. I remained in the garden for several more minutes, expecting to hear angry voices. When silence ensued, I rose from the bench and peered through the bordering hedge row. Posed in the center of the sunlit lawn, a tall man stood with his hunched back turned, his hands clenched in fists where they hung at his sides, his face revealed briefly in profile. He looked nothing like Darcy from what I could see, which wasn't a lot from my vantage point. Looking this way and that way he scanned the yard and its oblong islands of landscaping, sweeping the corner of the three-car garage where I watched from the safety of roses. When his eyes met mine he paused for a moment as if he knew I was there. So intense was his gaze I could see nothing else, just the round, black holes of pupils. Tiny brown wrens peeped and flitted through the arbor, bumble bees buzzed in the grass, and time felt suspended in the few, fleeting seconds before Darcy's dad turned away. Once he was gone and the screen door slammed, I stared at the jungle around me, tangled clematis and roses with thorns abandoned to survive on their own. It was pretty in its way, and it smelled like my girlfriend: sweet, luxuriant, and wild.

Later that evening I spoke to Mom, having practiced what I'd say all day.

"If I think Mr. Saint James is hurting Darcy, do I have the right to do something?"

Curled in her chair with a crossword puzzle, bent toward the light of the lamp, she turned to me with her pencil poised and her glasses slid down on her nose. "What makes you think he's hurting her? Did Darcy say he was?"

"Not in so many words."

"That's quite an accusation, Teal, for her to make, and you to repeat. Have you seen some wounds, or bruising?"

I hadn't, and I'd kissed every inch of her body, finding nothing but unblemished skin.

"Is he verbally abusive, physically intimidating? That's as harmful as actual assault."

"She just says he hurts them, is all."

"Well, that's terrible. Tragic, if it's true."

"Of course it's true!" I said. "Why would she lie to me?"

Mom set the puzzle on the table beside her, unfolded her legs to face me. "I'm not saying she's lying, hon. But Darcy is a young, emotional girl, and quite rebellious from what I've seen. It's very serious, what she's saying. I hope it's not true, that she's just exaggerating a little, if only in her mind, which I'm sure is no less painful. But you can't repeat what you're telling me, Teal. Not without significant proof.

"I know Phil, a little," she continued, "or Philip, as he prefers to be called. He is somewhat arrogant, pompous even, but he's never struck me as a violent man. He's just not the picture of an abusive father, or husband."

"What about her," I asked, "Mrs. Saint James?"

"Constance? She's a very nice woman, your aunt Katherine's age, so we were never friends. But I do remember Lena, the oldest daughter. She was an odd one, or so they said, stunningly beautiful, like Darcy."

"Darcy said she drinks a lot."

"Lena?"

"No, her mom."

"Please don't repeat that either, Teal. It's different when you're an adult. Rumors like that can damage people."

"And they don't hurt kids?"

"I'm not saying that. You know I'm not. It's just that when you're older—part of a class-conscious society—labels like that stick."

"But I believe her, Mom. I don't think she's crazy."

"I never said Darcy was crazy. When did I say that? Honey, I know you like her, that maybe you love her, but please don't do anything rash. Doctor Saint James is a powerful man."

"Like what, he'd hurt me too?"

"Please don't put words in my mouth, Teal, and don't let a very young girl put words in yours. It's difficult enough growing up, and when parents are so much older than a child—they're forty years older, at least—it makes it even harder. I'm trying to protect you, dear."

"But I want to protect *her*."

"I know, and that's admirable. I just think it's premature to say anything, and especially to do anything. I don't want you to get hurt, emotionally, or otherwise. Do you understand?"

"Of course I understand, Mom. I'm not an idiot."

Mom rose, crossed the room, waited until I stood as well, and gave me her customary hug. "I know you're not an idiot, Teal. And Darcy isn't crazy. But maybe she's confused, and that's no crime, but neither is parenting a child. Can't you just wait and see what happens? Perhaps all it needs is time."

"That's what she said, that she'd have to grow out of it."

"Then why not allow her to do so?"

Mom stepped away, looking suddenly weary. "I think you really do love her," she said. "This must be so hard for you."

"She's dead, you know, her sister Lena. Do you happen to know how she died?"

"No! My God, that's awful news. Did Darcy say when it happened?"

Turning away, I faked a yawn. "I'm going to bed," I said.

"Teal, hon, before you go … will you let me know what happens? Believe me when I say I'm on your side, even if it feels like I'm not."

Chapter 11

WHEN SCHOOL STARTED IN SEPTEMBER I had over five hundred dollars in my savings account. Mom wouldn't let me touch it, giving me money from her dresser drawer whenever I needed something, including the five bucks I used to buy a nickel bag from Neumann, telling her the cash was for the movies. I felt bad lying, but like Erik said, that's the way it goes with your parents; you can't actually tell them the truth about your life.

Darcy and I didn't have any classes together. It's like they knew better and were trying to keep us apart. Hammer even called me to his office for a pep talk, saying it was a new year, a new day, and that he hoped to be seeing a good deal less of me as I accrued the requisite credits for art school. He didn't mention Darcy, but she told me he'd spoken to her too, with no mention of preparing for college.

Darcy and I saw each other every day at lunch, walking out beyond the wall where the smokers went, climbing the boot scuffed path to a place where we could see the river, the bridge, and the Palisades north to the nuclear power plant. There was a bare log to sit on, carved with initials and burned by cigarette butts, and Darcy would drink her bottle of Yoohoo and eat most of the bag of M&Ms I bought every morning on my way to school. We didn't talk about her father or her visits to the Doctor, and life was fun and sweetly goofy as we sat there kissing and holding hands. Everyone knew to leave us alone, even Todd, who finally quit bugging me about heading down to Malandrino's for a wedge.

I made the mistake of telling Darcy about baseball cards, how we used to collect them as kids, playing games where you flip them heads or tails, or touching corners, or toss them to lean against a wall. After that she made me buy M&Ms *and* a pack of Topps on my way to school, Ollie at the counter thinking I was crazy buying baseball cards at my age.

We played every day at the log, chewing the pink gum that came in the pack, and pretty soon Darcy had won nearly all my cards, loaning them back to me on credit, payment to be "meated" out, as she put it, on her terms. She was always bugging me about the Yankee cap, saying it was her turn to wear it. Why was I bogarting it like that? I didn't tell her the real reason I kept it—because it smelled like her hair, that at night I would lay with it pulled down on my face like some kind of New York cowboy, dreaming about singing around a moonlit campfire, just like the James Taylor song. My second mistake was saying that I'd buy her a brand-new cap so she could have one of her own. She turned away quickly at hearing my offer, and it wasn't until I literally heard a teardrop plop on her fat deck of cards that I realized she crying. "I'm sorry, Dar, that was stupid of me," I said. "It's *our* hat. I'll bring it to school tomorrow."

"

Football season had started, and the leaves were turning red, and sitting in class, watching them twirl past the window, I devised a plan of how Darcy and I could get together without her parents knowing. The biggest game of the year was always against the Ossining Indians, the Headless Horsemen's foremost rival. In the buildup to the game, kids volunteered to paint posters in the hallways, and in the gymnasium where they held the pep rally, even painting the bus that the booster club rode to the big event, taking place that year in Ossining. Darcy volunteered to help, staying after school an extra hour in the week leading up to Saturday's game. Mrs. Saint James chauffeured her home at 4:30 instead of 3:30, passing by the playground on Beekman Avenue where she observed me shooting hoops with the little kids, proof that Darcy wasn't spending that time with her partner in crime.

When the big day came, Mrs. Saint James dropped Darcy off in the school parking lot and watched her daughter cue up in the bus line before driving away. Darcy never got on the bus, hooking up with me instead by the big culvert where the brook flowed through, just beyond the cyclone fence. From there we crossed the deserted playing fields, sprinting around the oval track to Old Sleepy Hollow Road where we walked its crumbling shoulder to the tree-lined corridor of Rocky's property. Cutting off on a black cinder horse trail, we wove uphill through bright autumn leaves the color of Darcy's plaid skirt, tapping the surface of icy puddles with the toes of our sneakers, the tiny sound of their tinkling demise like xylophones in the crisp morning air.

She gave me the Yankee cap to wear as we entered the bright sunshine of the first yellow field, a red barn leaning atop the rise, its doors wide open and a sheer mist swirling in the knife-edge shadows. Three horses, tawny as dry leaves, hung their heads over the fence rail as we approached, the image of Darcy and I curved across their glossy eyeballs. Rubbing their noses, petting their groomed forelocks, their jaw muscles rippled spectacularly as they chewed the crab apples Darcy had gathered from a nearby tree.

"They like you," I said.

"I like them. I've loved horses all my life."

She leaned and kissed a horse square on the nose, on a pink spot soft as satin.

"Do you ride?" I asked.

Huffing a laugh she tossed her hair, much like a horse's mane.

"I used to," she said, "a long time ago. Another swell gift from my dad."

I wanted to ask her what that meant, but she turned her face to avoid the question, dancing away through diaphanous mist, shredding its cloak with her fingers.

We came out of the woods in Pocantico Hills, not a town but a cluster of cute white houses with wrap-around porches, geranium filled window boxes, and fluttering American flags. The homes were immaculate and nearly identical, the tidy lawns mowed, the leaves raked, the ubiquitous trees well-trimmed. The gated entrance to Rockefeller's mansion stood less than a quarter mile away, and I remembered my dad telling me how these homes once housed the staff, the maids, butlers, and gardeners who maintained the estate when John D was still alive.

"I love these little houses," said Darcy, sneaking up to peek in a window. "There's even a white picket fence."

"We'll be looking through black bars if you don't get away from there," I said, thinking of my dad again, how I used to hang out in the empty jail cells at police headquarters.

By the time we got to the gray stone church with the Marc Chagall windows, the noon sun oozed through the leaded glass in tubes of vibrant color—wine, gold, sapphire blue—dripping like syrup on the wooden pews. Darcy stood in the opened doorway and let the warmth play on her body, her arms and legs splayed in the shape of a leaf, the living embodiment of autumn.

The church was deserted on a Saturday morning, everyone gone to football games or golfing at the country club. Just as I'd hoped, we had the place all to ourselves, and we strolled up the wine-colored carpet and sat in the front pew, looking up at the pulpit, the cross, and the tasseled wall hangings lit by the magnificent windows.

"Chagall lived in a monastery," I explained, "and when he

got too old to paint, the monks tied scissors in his crippled hands so he could cut the shapes from colored paper and paste them to the wall."

"Wow," said Darcy, "what passion. And really sweet of those monks!"

"Or maybe it was Mattisse with the scissors. I really can't remember."

Darcy kicked her sneakers off and lay out on the pew. I did likewise in the opposite direction, our heads side by side as we stared up at the vaulted ceiling. The stained-glass reflections pooled like water in the corners where arches merged, the color of grapes and lemonade in the upside-down chalice of dormers.

"This feels so different than Catholic church," she said, "more relaxed, less fakey."

Pulling a crabapple from the pouch of my hoodie, I took one bite and blanched. "How do horses eat these things?" I gagged. "It's worse than licking Sweet Tarts."

Out of the blue, she said, "I went to Saint Teresa's with Mary Ann Hicks, did she tell you? I thought she didn't like me then, but now I think we're friends."

"Mouse and I grew up together," I mumbled. "I've known her all my life."

"Todd really likes her, I can tell. Do you think that Todd likes me?"

I sat up straight. "What do you mean?"

"Not like *that*, you goof! Just … do you think he likes me? Does anyone like me, besides you?"

It took me a second to absorb the question, unconsciously shaking my head. "Of course they do," I said. "Why would you ask that?"

"I'm just saying. No one talks to me unless you're there, and really, they just talk to you."

I sighed and flopped back down again, my skull clunking hard on the pew. "It's all in your head," I said.

"Look who's talking."

I sat back up again. "You said that before. What's it mean?"

"Nothing, forget it. You're angry now."

"No, tell me."

She'd worried a dime-sized hole in her leggings with the tip of a nail-bitten finger, the windows igniting the curve of her iris like a shard of colored glass. I realized suddenly that I was kind of angry, that maybe I knew what she meant.

"Fine," I said, adopting her own diversionary tactics, "you don't have to tell me if you don't want. I'm used to it by now."

It was sneaky of me to turn it around so that Darcy appeared at fault, and she sulked a moment, ruining her stocking, the navy blue stitches unraveled.

"I was ten," she said, when finally she spoke. "It was almost Christmas, and my sisters were home, and all I wanted were these ruby red shoes."

It took me a second to realize what she was doing, recounting the story of her dad's swell gift that she'd avoided telling me before. Its own kind of gift, she offered it as penance for having made me mad, but it only made me feel worse.

"I'd seen them at Macy's in the shoe department, sparkly and red like Dorothy's slippers in the *Wizard of Oz*. I tried them on in a full-length mirror with a pair of frilly white socks, turning my ankle like Mom always did, pivoting on each toe. Clicking my heels like Judy Garland, I whispered, 'There's no place like home, there's no place like home.' But home was the last place I wanted to be, a dark old castle full of goblins and ghouls, alive with flying monkeys.

"I told my mom they were all I wanted, and she said she'd mention it to Dad, but on Christmas morning when I came downstairs there were clothes, and a bicycle, and an easel with paints, but no red shoes to be found. I began to cry and ran back to my room, my father shouting how ungrateful I was, not respecting of the spirit of Christmas. Red shoes were garish, cheap, he said, not befitting a young lady like me. Lena and Daddy had a fight that night; you could hear them all over the house. Kara holed up in her room with the phone. Mom went to bed with her wine glass.

"The next day he came home with an oversized box and set it on the dining room table, then sat in his chair with his stinky old pipe and rattled the pages of the Times. My sisters coaxed me down from my room and watched as I opened the present—a pair of black leather riding boots and a lifetime membership to the Briarcliff Equestrian Academy. Lena went home without speaking to my father and that was the last time I saw her. The night before she had sat by my bed until she figured I'd fallen asleep. The light was turned off, but I saw her face reflected in a pane of the window. The rain fell on the glass like tears on her cheeks; there was no way to tell them apart."

"Wait," I said, confused toward the end. "You were ten years old, and Lena was there? You told me you hardly knew her."

Lost in her thoughts, ignoring my question, she went on as if I hadn't spoken. "Mom drove Kara back to college, leaving me alone in the house. I took a tube of vermillion paint from my brand-new set of oils and painted the riding boots red, set them on the cushion of my father's chair where he couldn't help but see them.

"When Daddy came home exactly at seven, I waited for his reaction, crouching at the top of the third floor landing where I always sat to listen. But I heard no response, just the crinkling of the paper and the clunk of his pipe in the ash tray. Hours later he went up to bed and I waited for his footsteps on the stairs. But I knew he wouldn't come up to my room, not when he'd have to address me, when he couldn't just sit on the edge of my bed and pretend I wasn't his daughter."

"What?" I said. "Pretend what?"

A voice then boomed from the rear of the church, back by the doors where we'd entered. "Hello up there! It's time to close!"

Darcy stood, smoothed her sweater and tugged the Yankee cap level on my head. Heading toward the sunlight she took my hand, her face flushed with the colors of the glass. I can picture us still as we walked down the aisle, imagining ourselves getting married. So sure was I that we shared the same thought, it filled me with tempered excitement, conjuring a lifetime spent strolling the hills through a forest of ruby red slippers, in love with a girl as fragmented and fragile as the luminous Darcy Saint James.

The sun arced west toward afternoon as we headed toward home on the horse path, Darcy shedding her bulky sweater, cinching its arms around her waist. Dawdling on the hillside above Swan Lake, shading our eyes to look out, white clouds floated on its mirrored surface, erased here and there by the thumb print of the wind, cast like a net on the rippling water amidst arrowhead patterns of geese. A handful of deer cropped grass in the meadow, their antlers gnarly as treetops. They flinched when juncos swarmed overhead, the shape of them furling like flags. Down by the lake we saw horses approaching, the clop of their hooves echoing off the fiery hillside. "This way," I said. "There's an old BB gun trail through these woods."

"BB gun trail?" said Darcy, following me into the brush.

"We had wars up here when we were kids, sneaking up on the greasers' beer parties, shooting their cars while they were making out."

"That wasn't very nice," she said. "How would you like it?"

"That's why we called them wars. No one got hurt except Eamon Doherty, who got a pellet stuck in his forehead—way worse than Bradford Raines. Todd dug it out with a pocket knife; that's where the medic joke comes from."

"The what?"

"You had to be there," I explained.

Halfway up the hill we stopped to watch the riders go by. There were three of them, two women and a man, the ladies dressed in red jackets and white pants, the man in khaki and black.

"Maybe that's Happy Rockefeller," said Darcy. "Or Princess Grace. Are we hiding from them?"

"Sort of," I said, "force of habit from the old days. Did you wear the tight pants and pith helmet?"

"You had to at the academy. I looked like a snob."

"At least the jackets are red," I said. "You didn't have to paint them."

That finally got a smile from her, the first since the church, and we climbed up the hill to its crest. From there you could see the river, Eagle Mountain, and Rockefeller's mansion through the trees.

"Wow," enthused Darcy, "that place is a palace! I hear there's an actual golf course."

"What's this?" I said, my attention drawn elsewhere.

Darcy took my arm and pressed close to my side, both of us staring at a mound of dry leaves and a shred of black plastic suspended between trees. The green wink of wine bottles sparkled across the forest floor, and the duck patterned corner of a sleeping bag protruded from an edge of the tarp.

"Is someone camped here?" Darcy asked.

"Looks like it. I think it's Carter. Carter Mason."

I looked for some reaction to his name, but there was none.

"Who's he?" she asked. "How do you know him?"

"He's an Avenue guy. You might know his brother, Deloit."

She shook her head. "C'mon," she said, squeezing my hand, "let's get out of here."

But just then the leaves rustled and the mound of plastic came to life, a shredded wing of it flying away to reveal Carter

Mason himself, all one hundred pounds of him, a scraggly beard obscuring his face, his long hair tangled and unwashed. His one foot was shoeless, its sock full of holes, the other—from the calf down—was missing.

"You find my fucking leg?" he growled, his voice raspy, ragged with sleep. He glared at us, and Darcy and I stared anxiously back. "Who the fuck are you? You got a cigarette?"

"Please," said Darcy, pulling at my arm, "let's go."

"I know you," said Carter, smiling, his teeth crusted yellow, a humid stink rising off him as the afternoon breeze stirred his plastic cocoon. I held my breath, though not just from the smell. "You're that kid," he said, "your dad used to coach Little League. I played on that team, man. The Vikings, or some such crap."

Darcy inhaled, her fingers kneading my forearm.

"That's right," I said. "Me and Deloit were on that team."

"You know my brother? The little cunt. Stole my goddam car. You seen my leg? I can't find the fucker. Fucking VA. It don't fit anyway."

"We gotta go," I said. "We'll look for your leg."

"You," said Carter, pointing a bony finger at Darcy. "How'd you get so pretty? Do I know you?"

Darcy pulled hard at my arm, yanking me off balance. "We'll look for your leg," I repeated, allowing myself to be led away.

"What about that cigarette? You got one on ya? Hey!" he shouted, so forcefully we had to turn and look. "Go Yanks," he grinned, observing my cap, raising his fist in salute.

We were well down the hill before we stopped to catch our breath, Darcy leaning against a tree, her forehead pressed to the bark. "You okay?" I asked.

"That was horrible," she said. "Why doesn't somebody do something? How can they just leave him here?"

"The cops took him to the hospital, my mother said, just to get fed and clean up. But they can't hold him for anything."

"*He has no leg!*" Darcy cried.

She turned to me then and we held each other. "I'm such a coward," she said. "I couldn't even speak to him."

"I was hard for me, too, and I know the guy."

If Darcy actually knew Carter Mason then that was the time to say so. But she didn't, and I decided right then to chuck my suspicions and live life only for the moment—as surreal as it was—and not linger in the past, Darcy's, or my own.

Darcy didn't dance on the way back to school. She was glued to my side, her arm twined in mine, her head always finding my shoulder. Our progress would slow till we'd stop all together and kiss in the center of a field, in the middle of the trail, then the road, then the playing fields above the gym where we waited in the bleachers for the buses to return.

"Find out who won," I said, instructing her on how to successfully complete our charade. I felt guilty doing it, lying, but there was no other way we could be together. "And make sure to tell your mother."

"When will I see you again?"

"Monday, lunch," I said.

"I mean *really* see you!"

"Next Ossining game?"

"Be serious!" she scolded, squeezing my hand. "We can't wait that long."

"We'll see. We'll figure something out."

Because we always did.

Chapter 12

WE DIDN'T HAVE TO FIGURE TOO HARD, because after that, with the trust that Darcy had falsely garnered, her parents allowed her out on weekends under the guise of hanging with Mary Ann Hicks, who Mrs. Saint James remembered from Saint Teresa's. We had picnics alone on Laughing Hill, drinking Yoohoos and eating CLP sandwiches, smoking miserly pin joints while Darcy read fortunes from a bag of Chinese fortune cookies, the pink and blue slips blowing everywhere across the grass. I read to her from *Franny and Zooey* in the boiler room of the Manor train station, sitting together in a funky old overstuffed chair, its back and arms covered with melted candle wax, trains rattling past the paint-blackened, arch-topped window.

A few times, when her parents weren't home, when it was too cold to hide on the porch, we'd sneak into her kitchen and make hot chocolate, listening for the tell-tale clunk of the brass door knocker. *Let's go upstairs*, I'd say on those occasions. Darcy had described how she'd decorated her room in the likeness of Van Gogh's room at Arles, with blue walls, an orange bed frame and bright red blanket—even a yellow chair. "No way," she'd say when I prodded her to let me see it. "It's a mess up there, a huge pile of clothes on the floor."

Things were fine at school, neither of us visiting the Hamster's office, my grades no worse than usual. I'd actually improved in

English class, where I did extensive book reports, reading *Dharma Bums*, *Naked Lunch*, *Soul on Ice*, and *Walden*.

Mary Ann was in my Driver's Ed class, she and Steve Railsbeck, and Dionne Hayes. Mr. Hash was the teacher, the source of many dumb jokes, mostly from the wise mouth of Railsbeck. It was a cool class because we drove around on lonely back roads, usually starting out on Old Sleepy Hollow Road, driving up through Pleasantville, and Briarcliff, coming back through Pocantico Hills and around the Tarrytown Lakes, the fall colors fading, but still bright enough to rouge the water's surface.

I was driving the new Impala one afternoon when Steve reached from the back seat and tugged my hair, long enough then to tie in a ponytail. "Really going hippie on us, huh Conover?"

"Don't do that," Mr. Hash scolded, "it's distracting."

"Yes sir, Mr. Heesh. I mean, Hash."

"That's enough banter, Mr. Railsbeck. You can fail this class if you choose."

We were driving past Brandywine, the ornate stone tower rising above the treetops, solitary and solemn as a monk's chant. Elegant homes lined the leaf-strewn road, mansions with stables and white-painted fences that wound through the forest until vanishing from sight. Rolling through Westchester, the wealthiest county in the nation, I thought of Carter Mason, wondering how he fared in the chilly weather, winter yet to come.

"Pull over here," said Hash, pointing to a narrow turnout. "Dionne, if you would."

Dionne and I switched places, she seeming lost behind the wheel, Mr. Hash working with her to scoot the seat forward as far as it would go. I jumped in back, wedging Mary Ann between Steve and myself.

"How lovely you look today," he told her, actually sniffing her hair.

"Fuck off, Steve," she said, not looking at him.

"Blinker," said Mr. Hash, instructing Dionne. "Anyone coming?" Turning in his seat, he glanced between us in the rear, checking for traffic. "Clear," he confirmed, and Dionne pulled the car onto the road.

"No need to be rude," Railsbeck whispered, dipping his shoulder against Mary Ann. "That was a compliment."

"Not coming from you."

"That's cold," he smiled. "Are you always this frigid?"

"Shut up, Railsbeck," I said. "You're such an asshole."

"Defending Todd's honor, are we?"

"Enough chatter," said Mr. Hash, without turning. "Not another word."

A few minutes later, on the outskirts of Pleasantville, Mr. Hash shouted, "Light, light, light!" as Dionne drove straight through an intersection, the oncoming traffic blaring their horns.

"Brilliant move, Einstein," Railsbeck jeered, "almost got us killed!"

Without instruction from Mr. Hash, Dionne swerved the car across the yellow line, parked it halfway on the shoulder, and jumped out crying, covering her face with both hands. Mr. Hash got out and hustled after her, timidly patting her shoulder.

Slouched in the back seat, Railsbeck said, "One of us should probably move the car, before we get killed again."

"You're such a dick, Steve," said Mary Ann. "Where's Antoine Jones when we need him?"

Steve laughed. "Teste, are we?" he said, making sure we caught the pun.

"Seriously," I said, "shut the fuck up."

"You gonna make me?"

"Oh please!" said Mary Ann. "Let me out! Teal, let me out!"

I climbed out of the car, holding the door open for Mary Ann, who walked around back and went straight to Dionne. Wrapping an arm around her waist, she led her a few steps away, Mr. Hash getting the message, motioning to me. "Mister Conover," he ordered, "move the car off the road. And turn the damn thing off!"

I did as instructed, remaining in the front seat while Steve hummed an annoyingly mindless tune behind me, but at least not speaking. Not until Mary Ann glanced toward the car, forcing a wan smile. "So," said Railsbeck, "you ever done it with Mary Ann? You guys act like you have."

I was never much of a fighter, but I felt like hitting Steve right then, smashing his repugnant, freckled face. But Hash opened the driver's door and ordered me out. "Mister Railsbeck," he said, "drive! And not a word, or I swear you will never drive with me again!"

Mary Ann helped Dionne into the seat Steve had vacated, walked around the car and slid into the middle beside her. I cracked open the window, the cold air feeling good on my face, and we drove back to school in silence. Coming around the Lakes, watching geese paddle along the shore, I became aware of Mary Ann leaning against me, her head just brushing my shoulder. Curled up small, she looked like a waif, her brown eyes closed and her nostrils barely moving as she breathed. Glancing at Dionne I saw she was watching, but just for a second before turning away, her forehead pressed to the flat of the window where clouds of white vapor appeared on the glass.

Chapter 13

ON THE SATURDAY JUST BEFORE Halloween, I walked out of Rose's Corner Store with my morning M&Ms and Topps baseball cards, intending to meet Todd for tennis, when a beige Karmann Ghia pulled up to the curb and beeped its tinny horn. It was a cold morning, and I couldn't see through the car's frosted windows, so I just kept walking, figuring they couldn't be beeping at me. But the headlights blinked, and the passenger window cranked down, and Darcy leaned across the seat, flashing a smile as she waved.

"Hey," I said, bending to speak, tapping a finger on the door panel. "Where'd you get this?"

"Get in!" she commanded. "C'mon! C'mon!"

Soon as I hit the passenger seat she took off, my door still open, and we sped up Beekman Avenue as fast as the little car would go.

"So, what's with the car?" I asked.

"We're going to the March!"

"What march?"

"The anti-war March on Washington!"

"Darce, are you crazy?"

"This time, yes!"

It was Kara's car, Darcy explained, or had been, purchased for her years ago in college. Kara hated to drive the thing, hated driving, period, and it had sat abandoned in her parents' garage ever since.

"It smells pretty bad, and the heater doesn't work."

"I noticed," I said, wiping the foggy windows with my sleeve. "V-Dubs are like that. Do they know you took it, your parents?"

"Not yet!" she giggled.

"How do you know there's a march?"

"Jonah told me."

"So people do talk to you."

"You want out?" she said. "I'll pull over right here, Teal. If you don't want to come with me, just say so."

"Take it easy! I'm the boyfriend, remember?"

"You sure are!" she said, smiling again. "And don't you forget it!"

We took the Henrick Hudson south to West Side Drive and crossed the George Washington Bridge into New Jersey, Darcy driving with both mittened hands on the wheel, her red winter coat buttoned to the top toggle. I was freezing in my navy-blue sweater, cursing myself for ignoring Mom's plea to wear my corduroy jacket. Every few minutes I wiped moisture from the windshield, leaning across Darcy to reach her side.

Somewhere in Newark I said, "Let's stop for coffee. Warm us up."

"I thought you didn't like coffee."

"Once in a blue moon."

"What's a blue moon?"

"I don't really know. Just something people say."

Darcy pulled into a gas station off the Interstate. "Check the oil or something," she called from the door of the store. "I'll get the coffee."

The oil was fine, but the gas gauge was on zero. "I hope you got money," I said when she returned, holding two paper cups and a box of chocolate donuts. "We're driving on fumes."

"It was hard to start," she said. "I wonder if that's why."

"I'm surprised it started at all. How'd you learn to drive a stick?"

"Kara taught me when she came home from college. It's kind of like swimming—you never forget."

Darcy had plenty of cash, and I stood there topping off the tank, looking at the brick tenements around us, wondering if anyone had been killed in them during last spring's riots. Watching it happen on television, it had looked like something from Europe or Japan, like pictures in a schoolbook where whole cities were destroyed, entire neighborhoods engulfed in flames. Twenty eight people had died.

I thought about the day ahead of us, what might happen in the capital city where cops and soldiers were bound to greet us with night sticks and tear gas, like they did at all the big protests. I was suddenly nervous to be going there, heading into history, stepping into those grainy old photographs of marching soldiers, flaming beach heads, mushroom clouds.

I washed the windows vigorously with a squeegee, pushing so hard the rubber squeaked and Darcy tapped on the windshield for me to stop. The clarity lasted just a few miles before steam from our coffee cups fogged the glass again, mine so sweet I could barely drink it. Darcy ate the miniature donuts by the handful, her upper lip mustachioed with dark brown frosting. Leaning to wipe the windows again, I tried to daub the chocolate from her mouth, and the next thing I knew she was kissing me, the Karmann Ghia slowing dramatically, car horns blaring in streamers of sound as the Interstate traffic whipped past.

"Whoa!" I said. "Save the love for the rally!"

I ate two donuts, and Darcy ate the rest. Discovering a full pack of Newports in the glove box, she insisted we smoke one. "They're probably ten years old," I said.

"But it's never been opened," she pleaded. "Please! We'll just smoke one."

So we did, and I honestly couldn't tell how stale it was, because all cigarettes tasted like shit to me. We shared one, and it felt like smoking a candy cane.

"It's not too bad with coffee," Darcy opined.

"All smokers drink coffee. It's like peanut butter and jelly. And potato chips."

"I love you, Teal," she said suddenly, turning to look directly at me.

"Good," I said, placing an extra hand on the steering wheel, "just don't prove it till we get there."

An hour later we pulled off 187 into DC. There was a ton of traffic, the sky full of helicopters, we figured because of the March. All the way down we'd been passing buses painted with flowers, peace symbols and anti-war slogans, Darcy beeping the horn as we sped by, people waving to us from the windows, flashing the two-fingered peace sign.

"Where's a bus now," she said, easing off an exit ramp, "we could follow it to the rally."

The pinnacle of the Washington Monument rose above the buildings like a giant Conover headstone, and we headed in that direction, knowing it was close to the Lincoln Memorial, where Martin Luther King had given the Dream speech. "Park anywhere," I said. "We can walk wherever we're going."

After cruising the block a couple of times, we pulled into a parking garage and took a ticket from a bored, negro woman in a security uniform. It was cavernous dark in the garage, and Darcy ran whooping down the echoing ramps, attempting to yodel like Gene Autry. "I'm hungry," she said when we hit the street. We'd eaten all the donuts, and my bag of M&Ms, split the pink bubblegum from the pack of baseball cards. "Do they even have pretzels in Washington, DC?" she asked. "I don't see any umbrellas."

We headed toward the Monument and soon merged with throngs of people holding up placards and waving banners, wearing peace symbol armbands. They all seemed confident of where they were going, so Darcy grabbed my sleeve and we dashed ahead as the crowds swelled and the destination became apparent. Tens of thousands of demonstrators were gathered at the reflection pool by the Lincoln Memorial, both sides of the plaza as crowded as Sixth Avenue at Thanksgiving. A greater crush of people I'd never seen, whole Yankee Stadiums' worth, people of all ages, all classes and races. Some had ponytails, beards, and bandanas, others wore sports coats, silk stockings, and ties. Children sat perched on their parents' shoulders with names tags pinned to their sleeves, and dogs ran wild through the forest of legs, high on the palpable energy. Above our heads and all around us, banners snapped in the wind, cardboard printouts and hand-painted signs declaring, "Peace Now!", "No More War!", and "War Is Not Healthy for Children and Other Living Things!"

"My heart is pounding!" said Darcy, squeezing my arm. "It's like we're on the ocean! All these people are the sea!"

Taking her hand, I shouldered through the crowd to the concrete pool where we stood atop a stubby wall and looked out over the thousands of marchers that lined both sides. The ebb and flow of constant chanting was like the tide of the ocean, the hum of conversation the surf. People swayed and jostled everywhere, their mouths opened wide, shouting, laughing, some even crying, unable to contain their emotions. Whether joy or grief, I couldn't tell, and I figured it must have been both.

"What are they saying?" Darcy asked. "I can't hear a thing."

Someone was speaking through a bullhorn at the top of the concourse, their message echoing, drifting, indecipherable. But the chanted reaction ran through the crowd like a tremor in the earth, a whitecap on the water, the wave of rising voices breaking, rushing back through the masses until the words became a single roar at the distant tail of the dragon. *Peace! Now! Peace! Now! Peace! Now!*

Darcy turned and crushed me in her arms. "Thanks so much for coming with me!" she squealed and then finished the kiss she'd begun in the car.

Peering past the shoulder of her brilliant red coat, it seemed that everyone was hugging, touching, kissing, the love I felt for Darcy spreading everywhere, my personal feelings coursing through the crowd like blood through veins, the sense of it intoxicating, like the minty rush of a million menthol cigarettes.

"Let's go!" I said, grabbing her green-mittened hand, diving back into the mob. "I have to hear what they're saying."

Wiggling, ducking, bobbing through bodies, we made our way toward the front, bumping into people, stepping on toes, saying *peace* by way of apology. College kids gathered in bright sweatered clusters with banners declaring their school, striped scarves wound around their necks like fabulous woolen stoles. Negros in overcoats, suit jackets and ties held hands while bowing their heads, singing, praying, swaying together as though standing on the deck of a ship. Scruffy looking men in green fatigue jackets held a eulogy at the top of the key, the more able members protecting the others from the crush of the growing mob.

The crowd surged forward and we with it, the tide of marchers sweeping us along in a river of people now headed across the Potomac River, to where those around us said we would attempt to levitate the Pentagon.

"What?" Darcy laughed. "We're gonna what? That's so cool!"

"Don't get too excited," I said, instantly regretting the remark, it sounding so cynical, so adult.

"Why? You think it's impossible? Is peace impossible?"

I didn't think so, but my range of possibilities wasn't as expansive as Darcy's, as limitless in scale. My idea of moving a building, of changing people's mind, was slower, more incremental. Winning peace was like winning at baseball—you did it one base at a time.

We crossed over a bridge, the flow of people slowing at the bottleneck. The Police cordon began on the other side, cops on horses and motorcycles, a phalanx of them on foot wearing visored helmets, carrying truncheons and clear plastic shields. But the march was peaceful, people singing, the bright sun high and warm on our faces. Some started stripping off their coats and hats, Darcy and I among them, and she took the opportunity to swipe the Yankee cap from my head. She'd previously clipped the blue Met button to its brim, and now she pinned a small black and white peace symbol to its crown, the crest stiffened by a Yogi Berra baseball card slotted in the sweat band.

"Where'd you get the pin?" I asked.

"Stole it from an Orioles fan. Is that the Pentagon?" she asked, as off in the distance a long, low building came into view, surrounded by hundreds of national guardsmen in khaki uniforms, their green helmets shining in the sun.

We walked in silence for some time, glancing behind us as the column grew narrower, longer along the road to our uncertain fate. We spoke to people as we walked, exchanging names, explaining where we were from, talking about the war and how we got into it, and why we must get out. It was stuff I hadn't heard before, the phony body counts, the attack on US warships that never happened.

Word passed through the crowd that people had been arrested at the head of the column, Abbie Hoffman, Benjamin Spock, and Norman Mailer among them, one woman handcuffed for placing a flower in the barrel of a soldier's rifle. When we finally arrived at our destination, the plaza-like steps of the Pentagon, the War Department itself, those of us that remained sat cross-legged on the concrete apron, listening to arm-banded march leaders speak into bullhorns, while a flat-bed trailer full of TV cameras set up fifty feet behind us. An equal distance away, stretched across the towering façade of the building, the line of silent soldiers stood three deep. With heels locked together and rifles at their chest, they blocked the massive doors of the building, above which tall windows ran narrow and deep, slotted like the portals of an ancient castle where archers readied their bows.

As the day wore on, it grew bitter cold and people began to leave. Those who stayed were advised by the *armbands* to remain seated, though it was okay to stand and stretch, which Darcy and I did, kind of slow-dancing in place, hugging each other for warmth. A few protesters tried to speak to the soldiers, who didn't respond or even move. The Guardsmen were young, not much older than we were, and you could see that they were nervous, apprehensive as the daylight waned. I'm sure that some were angry, too; such was the feeling all around, those who were *for*, and those who were *against*, and not just confined to the war. Earlier that day there'd been people waving a red, yellow, and black banner, the flag of the Viet Cong. "What are those people doing?" Darcy had asked. "Don't they get it at all?"

The TV cameras filmed everything, and I wondered if my mother was watching, who I knew would be on our side, the side of peace. I also knew she'd be pissed as well as worried. As the sunset paled to a greenish gray, then purple in the west, the camera crews turned on their floodlights, bathing the plaza—the huddled protesters and the phalanx of soldiers—in a harsh white glare. Deep, black shadows were also cast, and from their depths US Marshals in white cowboy hats leaned through the wall of soldiers and swung at the squatting protesters with long truncheons. The protesters cringed and turned from the blows as the crowd shouted and booed, calling for the TV cameras to film the attacks. But the Marshals drew back behind the troops, popping out farther down the line to swing again. The bullhorns blared that we should all remain seated, lock arms, and weather the attacks.

"Don't break ranks, people! Do not strike back! Don't give them an excuse!"

But still some people struggled to their feet and left, afraid or hurt, telling those around them they were sorry, apologizing for their fear.

"Do you want to go?" I asked Darcy. She didn't answer, just shook her head. "It's okay, you know. There's no shame in leaving."

"I know," she said. "I'm fine. Just a little nervous."

"Everyone is," confided our neighbor, a middle-aged man with his wife, eavesdropping as we all were on the conversations around us. "Stay or go," he said, "we've made our point. When the cameras leave, you don't want to be here."

An hour later the media started packing, rolling up their cords and cables, some of them pointedly looking away from us, others obviously distressed, gazing anxiously down at the crowd as the bullhorns beseeched them to stay. Our neighbors, Lydia and Ben, stood to leave. "Good luck," said Ben, holding out his hand, "and thank you." Lydia bent and kissed Darcy's head, and then they left, wading back through the thinning crowd. They were older, maybe wiser than us. They could have been our parents.

"What do you want to do, Dar? I believe things are gonna get military."

"Close ranks everyone!" the bullhorn blared. "Take up the slack as people depart!"

The remainder of us scuttled around like crabs, scooting together on our butts, on our haunches, an undulating mass of shoulders and heads in the black-and-white monochrome of the floodlights.

As if on cue, as if we were part of Mrs. Ibanez's school play, the guy with the bullhorn stood. "Lock arms, people," he said. "Remain seated. Don't resist. Keep your heads down—but never bowed!"

He was looking directly at Darcy and me, or so it seemed, and then the lights went out behind us and the Pentagon plunged into darkness. In the silence that followed you could hear people breathing, sense the drumming of a thousand hearts as we all crouched cross-legged in the sudden night. With our heads pressed together, our knees touching, arms looped around the shoulders of strangers, Darcy and I waited with the others, and as our eyes learned to see in the shadow of our truly huddled masses, the ranks of soldiers began to march in place, their boots striking in cadence against the concrete, the pounding of their many soles louder than the pounding in our chests.

I had to look up, and when I did, I saw the first soldier inch forward, moving in abbreviated, incremental steps until he'd progressed a full body's width, when two others closed behind him, creating a wedge, the tip of an arrow penetrating the heart of the crowd. There was a murmur of voices along the front line, and a girl cried out as the wedge grew wider and the arrow burrowed deeper. Still, we continued to grip hands and arms, and some began to sing, but only briefly until someone stood and fell awkwardly forward, soliciting another round of shrill cries and stumbling attempts to stand. "Keep cool, people!" the guy with the bullhorn shouted, a disembodied voice floating above us all. "Don't resist!"

Somebody issued a full-blown scream, a deep-throated, soul-rattling wail of pain, and a rifle rose in silhouette against the Pentagon wall and plunged down swiftly, the rifle butt eliciting a solid crack on bone as another scream sailed and a growl vibrated through the knot of tensed muscles. The white cowboy hats were suddenly everywhere, and as the crowd erupted into tumbling, tripping, half-erect shadows, the soldiers' rifles rose and fell like pistons, the steps of the War Department writhing with bodies and unabated screaming, faces suddenly covered with blood, the manic atmosphere of violence and panic enshrouding the scene like smoke.

Darcy was too afraid to scream, I could see it in her eyes, her lips drawn tight, restricting the impulse as her fingernails clawed at my arm. She was trembling visibly, and so was I, having fallen to our knees, then lying on our backs as people stepped over and around us in their rush to escape. Out of the tangle of vertical shadows something tumbled and landed heavily on my chest, knocking the wind out of me. As I lay curled up there, trying to draw breath, a girl with long, dark, beautiful hair turned her head to look at me, her blanched face a shaman's mask of fear and confusion, her entire jaw cocked drastically to one side, her almost-smiling mouth a crossword puzzle of crimson, shattered teeth. She either sprang up or was wrenched away, but suddenly she was gone, and there was blood on my hands, and anger in my heart.

The pounding of the soldiers' boots went on forever as the endless supply of them broke the demonstrators apart, more and more of us breaking arms and ranks and running away into the dark. The forest of bodies and legs around us suddenly went from denim and corduroy to olive drab, and I rolled on top of Darcy, thinking this was it, we were about to be smashed, when a hand reached down and ripped me to my feet.

"Get her the fuck outta here!" shouted one of the bearded war Vets. "Now!" he ordered, and for that brief second I knew what it felt like to be in the army.

We ran then, both of us gripping some part of the other, into the hysterical mass of people doing the same, everyone helping or inadvertently hindering the flight of others as we stumbled and fell and got up to run again, the stamping boots never missing a beat, a ticking clock of methodical brutality echoing off the façade of the Pentagon. The guy with the bullhorn was shouting the whole time, but no one could understand or care what he said. Then his tinny, measured voice whelped out and there was only crying, and groaning, and panicked pleas for help.

Clots of people were sprinting down the street toward the bridge, Darcy and I among them, when red and blue lights began to spin and high-pitched sirens squawked, splitting us apart like pool balls in a rack, sending us off in different directions along even darker side streets. Some stopped to huddle in the alcoves of buildings, futilely prying at locked glass doors. A taxicab fishtailed to a stop in the center of the street, and a Black man got out and motioned us to him. "C'mon! C'mon! Git in here!" he called. "Move it now!"

Six or seven of us piled in and the cab peeled out, its wheels squealing, the hyperventilating driver mindlessly switching off the taxi light. None of us cared where we were going, as long as it was away, and we were silent for the duration of a two-minute drive, watching out the windows as cop cars sped by with lights flashing and sirens screaming, frightened people limping, staggering down the deserted sidewalks. One of the guys in the cab was bleeding, and Darcy pulled a wad of Kleenex from her pocket and pressed it to his forehead.

"I'm sorry, I'm sorry," he kept repeating, as dark blood dripped on her sleeve.

"It's okay," she stammered, her anxiety peaking. "My coat is red. It's red already."

"Where y'all going?" the cabbie asked.

"Anywhere," said the woman with the bleeding man. "Anywhere is fine."

"I'll take you where you want. Just say it."

She gave him the name of a local hotel, the other folks asking for the bus station, and Darcy handed him the ticket stub from the parking garage. "That's just a couple blocks," he said. "I getcha there first." When he let us out at the parkade entrance, Darcy tried to give him a twenty. "No mam," he said, "this one on me. This one on Willy B."

"Thank you, Willy B," she said, and the yellow taxi sped off in a cloud of exhaust, pearly pink in the glow of the streetlamps.

"You drive," said Darcy, when we got to the car.

I'd never actually driven a stick, but didn't choose to remind her, and snagged the keys when she tossed them to me.

It wasn't the same lady at the ticket booth, but another woman who looked just as bothered to be distracted from her magazine. I jerked and stalled the Karmann Ghia through downtown, looking for a sign for I87. Neither of us had a watch, so we didn't know what time it was. Darcy twiddled with the radio dial, searching for news of the riot, but there was nothing on that time of morning but religious talk shows and phony sounding DJs.

"Turn here," Darcy directed, pointing to the red and blue Interstate crest. She snuggled against me as close as she could get, curled around the knob of the gear shift. "I'm so exhausted I can't even cry," she said. "Do you believe that actually happened!"

"No," was all I could offer, remembering the girl with the broken jaw, how pretty her hair was, how awful her crooked smile.

"Those guys in the cowboy hats," she said, "they were just trying to start something. And the soldiers! What were they thinking all that time, just standing there, waiting, watching us come, crowding right up to their feet. Do you think they were afraid?"

It surprised me how Darcy saw the world, feeling sorry for soldiers who bludgeoned pretty girls. Driving to Washington, DC, that morning had felt like going to a ballgame, heading for the bleachers at Yankee Stadium, expecting, at best, to eat hotdogs. But now it seemed more like a full contact sport, a brand-new national pastime.

Miles clicked by and Darcy fell asleep, stretched across the console with her head on my thigh. In the dark, in the cold, it was even harder to see through the windshield, the fog of our breathing coating it with frost, then ice. I rubbed with my sleeve, scraped with my fingernails, but managed to create only a small window within a window, the probing headlights of oncoming traffic descending like pop flares in the night. Looking for something to scrape with, I found the hard-edged pack of ancient Newports. It did a better job than my fingernails, and repeated applications broadened my view and allowed me to relax a little. A familiar song came on the radio, and I turned the volume up a notch, mindful of waking Darcy, my thoughts drifting with the music as it filled the darkened cab. *Toss me a cigarette I think there's one in my raincoat. We smoked the last one an hour ago ....*

Knocking a candy cigarette from the pack, I lit it, coughed, and took another drag. Darcy shifted, mumbling in her sleep, and the warmth of her against me, the buzz from the menthol, and the perfectly woven voices of Simon and Garfunkel made my eyes water, then tear. Everything that had happened that day, everything that was happening and would happen caught up to me suddenly and I was overwhelmed with a strange apprehension, squeezing the wheel as the feelings leaked out, struggling to erase them like ice from a windshield, to create even the smallest opening through which I could see an end, a goal, a destination.

Reaching for Darcy in the dash-lit dark, I touched her shoulder, then her hand, reassuring myself of her presence, that there really was a girl who loved me, and who I loved back, who was willing to force me to change my life, and perhaps even change the world.

The Newport burned down to its cottony filter, and the stink filled the confines of the tiny car. Cracking the window, cold air blew in, snapping me from my reverie as we crossed the George Washington Bridge, the lights of Manhattan thrilling in scale, so many strangers pressed together, the sense of it rising like clouds from the smokestacks, like steam from manhole covers.

Arriving at the Van Tassel apartments, I squeezed Darcy's shoulder until she sat up. "Where are we?" she mumbled.

"My house. Can you drive yourself home? I'm too tired to walk back."

Blinking, yawning, she gave me a kiss. "We never levitated the Pentagon," she said.

"But we elevated the dialogue."

"Think so?"

"Yeah. Maybe. It sure did for me. We've all come to look for America."

Tiptoeing quietly into our apartment, I made it as far as my bedroom door when Mom appeared in her robe and slippers and just stood there, waiting for me to speak.

"I'm sorry, Mom, I should have called, but … I couldn't. You won't believe what happened—"

"Dr. Saint James had a heart attack," she said. "They've been looking for Darcy all day. Where is she, Teal?"

"She's home," I said. "She's on her way."

"You look terrible. Are you okay?"

"Yes. No. This is really fucked up."

"Yes," said my mother, "totally fucked up indeed."

Chapter 14

Darcy didn't come to school the next day, or the day after that. I called a couple of times, but no one answered. Mom said Dr. Saint James had been sent to Monte Fiore in the Bronx, where he'd had by-pass surgery. My mother was pretty pissed off at me, and Darcy, but I was right about her supporting the peace effort. She said she couldn't blame us for that, but she gave me a scolding for doing stupid stuff like sitting on the steps of the Pentagon, where the chances of getting hurt were almost guaranteed.

"You're only seventeen," she said, "let older people do that. And don't put young girls like Darcy at risk."

I didn't tell her it was Darcy's idea in the first place. I figured she was in enough trouble. No one even mentioned the March at school, not in class or even just bullshitting in the halls. It was like it never happened, and it kind of bummed me out. I told Todd, and he was shocked.

"You went to that? What the hell for? I saw people on the news waving Viet Cong flags!"

"I saw that, too. In person, I mean. But only a few did that. Most folks were just normal, like you and me—"

"Not like me," Todd shook his head. "You'd never see me do that!"

I was truly surprised to hear him say it, Todd who was so

accepting, and easy going. "Why not?" I asked. "You think the war's a good thing?"

"I think it's what it is. Our guys are dying in Vietnam, and you shouldn't criticize them."

"They're not criticizing the soldiers," said Mary Ann, who stood beside us hugging her books.

"They're waving the fucking Viet Cong flag!"

"Teal just said that most people don't support that. You think that means a hundred thousand protesters support the Viet Cong because someone holds up a flag?"

Todd smiled at Mary Ann, but it wasn't a good smile, a happy one. "Whose side are you on here?" he said. "You're supporting these wackos—"

"Teal's a wacko? Is that what you're saying?"

"No! No way! Teal," he said, turning to me, "I'm not calling you anything, but c'mon, this isn't you. This is Darcy's thing. She's dragging you into it."

I didn't know what to say, because it was partly true. It was Darcy's idea to go to the March; I hadn't even known it was happening. But still, it was something I truly believed in, something I would do again in a second. I was proud of what we'd done, and maybe that was part of what bothered me: I wanted some credit for myself.

"It's true, isn't it?" said Todd. "It was her idea to go down there, am I right?"

"Leave him alone," said Mary Ann. "You're bullying him."

She leaned against him then, put an arm around his waist and gave him a little tickle.

"Don't!" he said. "Don't try to make up for this."

"This what?" said Mary Ann, looking hurt.

He stalked away angry, showing us his muscular linebacker's shoulders as he hustled off down the hall.

"I gotta catch up," said Mary Ann. "I shouldn't have butted in like that."

"Mouse!" I called as she strode away, wincing as I said it.

She stopped and turned. "It's alright," she said, referring to her nickname. "I don't mind if it's you."

"Thanks, is what I meant to say. For butting in. Sometimes that's just what you have to do."

Todd called that night and apologized. "Sorry, man. I didn't mean anything by that. I just lose it sometimes with all the protesters. I guess I just never knew one."

"Knew two," I corrected him. "And you were right. It was Darcy's idea, but I'm glad we went."

Todd was silent a minute. "Okay. I'm not gonna start another argument. But hey, tomorrow's Halloween, man, you up for the séance?"

"We gonna do that again?"

"Sure. It was fun."

Last year we'd held a séance at the Old Dutch Church. It was kind of a tradition, a very loose one, generations of teenagers with Ouija boards, or chalk and a water glass, trying to raise the dead at the cemetery. Everyone there got really drunk, and Ph3 set some chick on fire. Not really on fire, but her filmy costume got too close to a candle, and Bosco Jones poured beer all over her.

"Okay, I'm in," I said.

An hour later the phone rang again, and it was Darcy, the first time I'd heard from her since her dad's heart attack.

"Everything's totally crazy here!" she said. "My sister Kara came down from Vermont—she's about to have another baby! Her oldest daughter is three, and into everything, and I have to watch her all day, make sure she doesn't hurt herself, or break my mother's collection of knick-knacks. Mom finally told them they had to leave, that it was all too much for Daddy."

"How is he?" I asked. "I heard he had a by-pass."

"He got home yesterday and went straight to his room. They let us go in there one at a time to see him, like at Kennedy's funeral, like he's lying in state or something. He's not really talking, at least not to me."

"I'm sorry I didn't drive you home that night," I said. "That must have been terrible walking in on that."

"It was easy, actually. There was no one home, just the hall light on and a note from my mother saying they'd gone to the hospital. So I parked the car in the garage again and they never found out I took it, just that I stayed out all night. Mom was afraid to tell my dad because of the heart attack, so I pretty much got away with it. Cool, huh?"

"Cool?"

"I don't mean the heart attack, but … you know what I mean."

I didn't really—know what she meant—but that was becoming the norm. She wanted to see me on Halloween, so I told her about the party.

"A séance! Far out! I'm excited!" she enthused. "What are you gonna be?"

I was dumbfounded by it all, her dad's near death, her excitement about the séance.

"What time?" she asked when I didn't respond. "I'll meet you there."

"Ten, I guess. Or thereabouts."

"Ten thirty! Listen, Teal, I gotta go, they don't want to tie up the phone. I love you!"

Bosco Jones was Blackman, dressed in a pair of tight pajamas and a cape with a big *B* on it, *Black* becoming the new word for

Negro in the newspapers and on TV. Todd got hold of an Ossining Indians football jersey and wore a headband of feathers with a rubber tomahawk sticking out of it. Mary Ann dressed as Peter Pan in bright green tights and jacket, a felt hat with one of Todd's feathers protruding from its band, and a pencil-thin mustache as fine and curved as—I hate to say it— a mouse's whiskers.

"I'm King Tut!" said Jonah Gold, "like from the museum, remember?" He wore a striped bath towel wrapped around his head, tucked and folded and draping to his shoulders. His baby face was painted gold, his eyes made up like Elizabeth Taylor. "My dad fucking freaked," Jonah laughed. "Our people just kicked Arab ass in six days, he'd ranted, and my son pretends he's Egyptian!"

I didn't dress as anything, just borrowed my mom's eyebrow pencil and drew a pair of glasses around my eyes, outlined my nose, including my nostrils, and scribbled a fat mustache above my lip: the poor man's equivalent of the cheap, plastic version of same.

There were quite a few people there, most of them heads, and the scene reeked of pot smoke. It was a perfect Halloween night, the moon almost full, silver clouds sailing, a sparkling of stars in their wake. Snaky black tree branches loomed above the church, its weather-vaned steeple spooky in silhouette, shredding the chilly mist. We gathered in back on the grassy bench that dropped steeply toward the bumpy old cemetery road. Narrow and flat and hedged in by bushes, a wrought-iron fence further defined it, tasseled with chains and drooping medallions, the ornate pickets pointy as spears. In its center, not a dozen feet from the church wall, a rectangular sarcophagus about four feet tall, four feet wide and eight feet long rose as though sprouting from the grass. The séance was held on its rough, stone surface, and Neumann, dressed as always in black, and wearing a preacher's collar stolen from his father, was busy drawing numbers and letters on its surface with a nub of white chalk.

"Wait a fucking minute," said Steve Railsbeck, slapping at Neumann's hand, "it's way too early for that shit." He handed Erik a bottle of hard liquor, its amber color beautifully illuminated by a row of candles burning along the crypt's edge. Railsbeck was appropriately dressed as the devil, wearing clothes hanger horns, a red hooded Sleepy Hollow High School sweatshirt, and red face paint. He didn't really need to highlight his features, as they already conjured the overlarge, exaggerated likeness of evil.

"Let's levitate somebody!" he said. "C'mon! Who's up for it?"

I was standing in the shadows with my hoodie pulled over my Yankee cap, so I don't know how Darcy recognized me, but she did, creeping out of the bushes to slip her arm around my waist. I jumped, and she said, "Boo!" though she looked anything but scary. Lots of chicks dress up all sexy on Halloween, showing off their cleavage, wearing tons of makeup, ruby red lipstick accenting their come-hither smiles. Just looking around, I could see half a dozen of them in slinky black witch outfits, with pointy hats and even pointier breasts. But Darcy was dressed as a pirate, with a kerchief tied around her head, a gold hoop earring, a black eye patch, and a charcoal, five-o'clock shadow. The only lipstick involved was a big red scar drawn ragged across her cheek. She wore a pin striped vest, baggy pants bunched at the knee, and black Converse All-Stars. "Argh!" she growled, "Have ya seen me parrot, matey?"

She was a beautiful pirate. There was nothing she could do to not be beautiful, and I wanted to tell her that but couldn't. "Hey," I said, giving her a hug. "You're looking … salty. How are you doing? How's your dad?"

"He's fine. Look at you," she said, pulling my hood back. "Oh, I get it. Teal, you're such a minimalist."

"That's me. The bare essentials."

"Accent on *bare*," she giggled.

"C'mon people!" Railsbeck shouted. "Let's get somebody up on the table. Mouse, how 'bout you? No? You're too skinny anyway, could lift you with *one* finger. Where's Bosco? Mister Jones? Oh, didn't see you there, Blackman, it being so dark an' all."

Bosco glared at Steve, his look more threatening than the devil's.

"Woulda been a real challenge," said Railsbeck, "but hey, shiver me timbers, here's the Pentagon girl! Couldn't levitate *it*, but I bet we could levitate you!"

"Huh?" said Darcy.

"C'mon over here. Jump up!" he said, slapping the lid of the crypt.

I shook my head. "Don't do it," I told her, but she smiled, patted my stomach, and sauntered over. "What do I do?" she asked.

"Just hop on up here," said Steve, who without warning grabbed her waist and lifted her onto the lid. "Now just lay back! And mind those candles! Where's Three? You stay the fuck away, man! No playing with matches! There you go, darlin', kick back and relax. All right everybody, gather round! You know the program."

The program was that everyone places a single finger beneath the victim, in this case Darcy, and upon a signal, and after great cosmic concentration, lift her in the air. We'd done it before, and it actually worked, though I can't pretend to know why. I didn't want her to do it, especially because of Railsbeck, but Darcy was up for anything, and there was no stopping her. The candles burning at each end of the platform cast a warm glow on her forehead and cheekbones, the gold hoop earring poking through her hair winking in the sputtering light.

"Alright team," said Steve, "fingers now, fingers!"

A bunch of people then crowded around the crypt. There wasn't room for everyone, so I gladly stood back. It truly did look like a ghostly cabal, characters with horns and filmy wings all huddled around the pitted slab, the candle's flames dancing eerily, reflected in the arched windows of the church. I moved to where I could see better, peeking around winged shoulders and furry arms. I didn't trust Railsbeck; he was such a dick.

"Mumbo jumbo, crawfish gumbo," he said. "We offer this maiden as a sacrifice to the gods. Do with her what you will! I would! Now *lift!*"

I watched as Darcy's dark form stiffened on the slab, flashing back to the Pentagon and my rational dismissal of the notion of levitating. Yet here we were, against all logic, lifting a human being with the strength of a single finger, albeit a dozen of them. Because Darcy did rise up from the crypt, her body relaxed, but rigid, two inches, six inches, one foot above its surface. Suddenly she shouted, "You fucker! Get your hands off me!" Swinging out with one free arm, she fell back to the lid, some quick-thinking hands cushioning her fall, but still bonking her skull on the stone.

I shouldered over there and helped her to her feet, rubbing the back of her head. "Railsbeck, you prick," I said.

"Don't look at me, I didn't do anything."

"Yeah, right!" said Darcy, "guess that was the devil feeling my ass!"

"Not this devil! 'Twasn't I."

Blackman appeared in an effort to save the day. "You might consider gettin' the fuck outta here," he told Railsbeck.

"No need for violence," Steve replied, "this is a peaceful gathering. Make love, not war!"

"Cool out, man," said Erik Neumann. "I got something right here to put our minds at ease." He held out a small white cube of sugar and rotated it in his fingers, its planed geometry brilliant in the candlelight. "Who'd like to start the bidding for this truly sweet peace of mind? Don't panic, I have plenty for all. I'll add it to your accounts."

Darcy was the first to eat one, plucking the cube from Erik's fingers, popping it in her mouth. She got one for me and held it to my lips until I swallowed. A bunch of people ate some. Neumann, it appeared, was already tripping, bent over the crypt with chalk in hand, scribing the letters for the séance with a mad scientist's absorption.

Todd handed me a beer. "I hope you know what you're doing, man," he said. "You get that from Neumann, you don't know what the fuck it is."

"I guess I'll let you know."

"Just don't do anything crazy," he whispered. "And don't let her talk you into anything, either."

I didn't respond to his warning, too aware of our last conversation about Darcy's influence.

"Hey," said Todd, turning to Mary Ann, "what are you doing? You're not gonna eat that, are you?"

Mouse was about to pop a sugar cube in her mouth. "I thought I'd try it," she said. "I've always wanted to."

"Please," said Todd, "don't eat that, okay? Can't you just do it some other time? I mean, I don't want to tell you what to—"

"Okay," she said, "I'm saving it, see?" and she slipped it in the pocket of her short green jacket, patting it for good measure.

Todd gave her a hug, glancing over her shoulder at me, his look both accusatory and apologetic.

"Alright you freaks!" Neumann shouted, "all aboard for the soul train!"

We gathered around the crypt, Erik looking manic, authentic in the preacher's collar, the old-fashioned Puritan kind with lapels that hung down like a neckerchief. He held what looked like a kitchen stanchion for a pointer, one of those metal things you set hot pots on. "Whom shall we call forth?" he said, "Washington Irving, perhaps?"

"Done that," said Jonah. "Nobody home."

I was worried they'd pull a name off a headstone, the first ones being my ancestors, who I wasn't anxious to disturb.

"Let's go for the gold," said Railsbeck, unfortunately still among us. "Let's call the real deal. Let's call the Headless Horseman."

"Yeah, man!" the cry went up.

"Outta sight!" said Erik. "Let's fuckin' do it! Get your hands on the pointer, people, one fingertip a piece. Don't press hard, and no pushing!

"Oh, Horseman," he began, "headless though thou be, we call upon you to appear before us. Do you, can you, heed our call?"

The pointer began to move across the rough surface, screeching as it traveled. It stopped on the letter *Y*, then glided to *E*, then *S*.

"Yeah, man, or…. Yea, he approaches!" said Erik. "Praise be! Can I get a hallelujah?"

"Hallelujah!" everyone shouted.

"Are you near to us?" Erik asked, and the pointer spelled Y-E-S again.

I wasn't quite sure if I was feeling a buzz, what with the weed and the beer, but I felt tingly, my fingertips vibrating, ears echoing, my jaw kind of numb. Darcy squeezed my hand a bit harder, her eyes focused on the Ouija board, her other hand touching the pointer.

"Can you *feel* his presence?" said Neumann, posing the question to us all.

"Yea," we answered.

"Do you will his presence?"

"Yea!"

"Can you abide his countenance?"

"Hell, yea!"

"Do you hear his approach?" he said, cupping a hand to his ear.

In stony silence we listened intently for the thunder of hooves, the jangle of spurs.

"Horseman!" Neumann shouted, "we beseech you! Ride! Gallop! Enter this circle of black-hearted souls!"

I was totally unsurprised when a wild shape then burst from the surrounding hedges and fell flailing in our midst, a manic flurry of grasping arms and one bare foot, the other as absent as the fabled Horseman's head.

It was Carter Mason, looking ragged as a scarecrow, and as frightening, no more demented and possessed of demons for its being Halloween. Rolling and cackling, he grabbed at our legs in the ever-widening circle he created as classmates danced away. Pulling himself erect, he leaned against the séance crypt, knocking candles to the grass where they sputtered out in the dampness. He was skeletal, filthy, his wild eyes gleaming in their sockets, his beard long and matted, confettied with dry leaves.

"Tricker treat!" he shouted, and laughed, the sound of it as crazy and theatrically arcane as any Boris Karloff/Bella Lugosi movie, but real, genuine, and therefore chilling. "It's me!" he cackled, "The Legless Horseman, searching for my fucking foot!"

No one responded, most not knowing who Carter was, or how such a madman had come to be in our midst. "Fuck," Todd whispered, "is that who I think it is?"

I nodded, and when I did, Carter looked right at me. "Well, if it ain't Mickey Mantle again. What's happening, *Slugger?*" Looking closer at my cap, he noticed the peace button pinned to its crown, and chuckled. "Peace, brother!" he said, and flashed us all the two-fingered sign. "And hey, I bet Captain Ahab there is that cute little blonde." He was grinning, leering at Darcy.

He said, "You don't remember me, but I remember you. It took me a while, but I damn sure recall. You got me fired from mowing your lawn, always stretched out half naked on your lounge chair, covering up with a towel. But I saw you alright! Didn't I, Miss Saint James?"

Darcy squeezed even closer to me, standing almost on my toes, her arms wrapped tight around my waist. "Not true," she whispered.

"What's that?" said Carter, leaning forward, then falling back against the crypt, needing its support to stand upright. "You saying I'm a liar, like you don't know me, you completely forgot what you did?"

"Where's your crutch?" I asked, stepping in front of Darcy.

"Why?" said Carter, "you gonna help me? Give the poor cripple a hand? Ain't that something. Ain't that grand! Well it ain't! It ain't no fuckin' thing!" He lunged at me then and our arms locked together, pushing me back into Darcy, knocking her to the ground. I was the only thing holding him up, and Carter laughed in my face, his breath foul, his body as light as papier-mâché, yet maniacally strong.

Railsbeck stepped out of the shadowy circle and sucker-punched Carter in the side of his head, sending both of us down and on top of Darcy where she lay crying on the grass. A trickle of blood wormed out of Carter's ear, and there rose from within him a werewolf's howl of pent-up torment and despair. I felt Darcy scramble out from beneath us and heard her crash off through the bushes. Carter was sobbing, helpless now, mumbling incoherently in my arms, crushing me in a desperate embrace.

Then Todd and Mary Ann were peeling him off, and Erik helped me to my feet, saying, "Better go find her, man. You got about five minutes till that shit kicks in."

I ran off blindly into the dark, cracking my knees into headstones, tripping over tree roots and wrought iron chains. Finally stopping to collect myself, my brain cascaded with fluid imagery, tingling sensations traveling through my extremities. I tried to develop a plan, mapping in my mind the places I would look for her, the places we both knew. But would Darcy know them now? Would I, the back of my hand turned transparent as glass, filigreed with veins like a leaf?

The terrain was rolling, constantly morphing, and I more or less watched myself find the footpath and follow it up to Washington Irving's plot, the naked oak writhing in a hurricane wind, Van Gogh stars swirling in its branches. I wandered through the headstones, the maze of old rails and fences sending me in circles, into square geometries of abstract thought, of observing my sneakers cut through the grass. Drifting through angels at the Jesus Place, I touched their cold hands, looping my trembling fingers in theirs. Jesus appeared to see right through me, the hollows of his irises filled with love and compassion.

At the Van Gogh place I lay down on the grass, the frozen, black tips of it stabbing my hands, prickling the back of my neck. Then I was standing by the ivy-covered door, sticking my arm into its dark recess, expecting a tiger's claw, or an owl's talon to reach back, but finding only the blanket. Holding it to my face, taking in the scent of Darcy's hair and the damp, moldy essence of the cemetery itself, I suddenly knew where I'd find her. She was at the Bronze Lady, where I'd promised to meet her months before, and as I walked up the stone steps, past the solitary angel with wilted flowers in her hand, I pictured Darcy huddled in the Lady's lap, the solemn face above her streaked with green tears, always crying, eternally sad, the throne upon which the girl I loved held court.

"Hey," I said, reaching out to her, Darcy reaching back, our fingers knitting in a tactile sensation like raindrops striking a pond. Standing on the granite pedestal, I waited as she leaned to kiss me, another explosion of feeling and taste I would never have dreamed was possible.

"I knew you'd come," she said. "I knew you'd find me, save me."

"I'm here now."

"You're beautiful," she said, stealing the thought from my head.

"You're … unbelievable."

"You don't believe me? About what he said?" she asked, speaking of Carter Mason.

She was shivering, the cold of the metal penetrating her body, absorbing all its heat.

Nudging her gently, I squeezed into the Lady's lap beside her. It was cozier under the blanket, both of us radiating warmth, love to the other.

"Don't think about anything," I said, "just sit here with me. Just breathe. Just hold me."

We did, for how long I don't know, because although I promised not to think, not all thought is containable, controllable. Some thoughts flow like invisible water, moving, sliding, contouring around all things in their path. Thought becomes color, imagery, blooming in your mind like snowflakes rushing at a windshield, kaleidoscopic symmetries of unrecognizable organization crowning one upon the other, sound, taste, scent, shape, together and the same, undifferentiated, inseparable, yet each fantastically distinct, rising like fish to the surface of a pond, silent, otherworldly, *underworldly*, touching some membrane with the tip of its nose, breaking all understanding into endless ripples that expand and grow outward to the edge of nothing, to no definable end, toward the idea of infinity.

Knowledge, intuition rose pale on the horizon, bleeding into waking life like a sunrise, pink amidst gray, then scarlet, then silver, streaked with daybreak like honey poured over the Palisades, sparkling the Hudson with flakes of precious gold.

"Teal?" I heard her say. "Are you awake?"

"I think so. Did you sleep?"

Neither of us could say if we had. There was no way of telling, nothing to compare. "Are you still tripping?" I asked. "Are you cold?"

"I'm numb, if that's what you mean. I was really scared. How did you find me?"

"I just knew."

"You're in my head, always inside me," she said, and tried to cuddle deeper. "That weird guy at the séance, the thing he said about—"

"You don't have to explain."

"But I want to! I want you to know." She sat up to look at me, her damp eyes pink, a single tear pooled in a corner. "I really didn't recognize him until last night. How could I? He's like a whole different person.

"Carter used to work for us," she continued. "He mowed lawns—everybody's lawns, not just ours. He seemed like a nice guy, was always polite. He smoked cigarettes, though, and he tossed their butts on the grass. One afternoon I was laying out back, reading my stupid magazines on a lounge chair. I could hear the mower running, like it always was in summer, everybody tending their oh-so-perfect lawns. Suddenly the noise stopped and I looked up, lying on my tummy with my top untied. Carter was just standing there, smoking his cigarette, staring at me in my Bermuda shorts. I was only fourteen, fifteen at most, so who knows what he thought he was seeing. I'd folded a towel across the chair and I tugged it quickly around me.

"Suddenly my father raced across the lawn, yelling, screaming at Carter. I really don't know how he got there so fast—he must have been watching from a window. 'What do you think you're doing!' he shouted. 'Put out that cigarette! And Darcy, put some damn clothes on!'

"I did as I was told, clutching the towel as I ran toward the house. I saw Carter smirk, then smile at my father and flick the cigarette on the lawn. I remember it smoking in the fresh-cut grass, my bare feet stained the same color green. He fired him, my father did, for tossing the butt, the grounds truly littered with his filters. But I didn't get him fired! It's not like I squealed! Nothing really happened in the first place!"

"Maybe that's why Carter's pissed," I said.

Darcy shook her head. "He's angry at lots more than that."

"I just mean … you know … at you."

"He's mad at *me?*"

Darcy didn't know what Carter had told me that night at the Yellow Rocks, the nastiness, the meanness of it. "He's harmless," I assured her. "He doesn't know what he's saying."

"He remembers me, though," she said.

"He's crazy. Who knows what crazy people think."

"Crazy people like me?"

"Give me a break, Dar. I'm not talking about you."

The sound of tires crunched loudly up the gravel road, headlights sweeping the foliage. We ducked out of reflex as the cop car slowed and pointed its spotlight at the rhododendrons. "C'mon out of there," said the voice on the bullhorn.

"Stay here," Darcy whispered, "they're looking for *me.*" She kissed me then, and ran toward the headlights. Through the tangle of branches, I heard her laugh, heard the car door open and close. I waited in the bushes until the taillights faded before bounding away down the hill, leaping over headstones, skirting the vaults so I could reach the gate before they did. Sprinting across the blacktop of Route 9A, I was into the Manor and racing over lawns, in and out through the trees, the sky vaguely brightening, the partial moon waning, slowly erasing the stars.

They beat me to the corner of Darcy's street, where I saw the cop car pull into her driveway, its headlights sweeping the side of the house before coming to rest on the rose hedge. Running through backyards as fast as I could, I stumbled upon the derelict bird bath in the overgrown garden behind the garage, where ivy devoured the lawn chairs. From the cover of azaleas, I peered through the branches, squinting at the halo of headlights.

A screen door screeched open and shut with a bang as the Doctor rushed out of the house. Dressed in pajamas and an Indian print robe, he clutched an aluminum pole like a lance, an IV bottle attached to its top, swinging like an old-fashioned lantern. "Turn off those damn lights!" he shouted toward the cruiser, shaking his fist, the long tube of the drip line attached to his forearm. Posed in the high beams, his robe billowed out, his torso truncated by shadows, severing his head like the legendary Horseman, his vile presence conjured at last. Limping around the front of the squad car, furry white slippers slapped on the asphalt with a comical, repetitive sound; his wife's slippers, no doubt, jammed on in his frenzy to confront his delinquent daughter. Reaching for the door on the passenger side, he gave it a mighty yank. "Do not provoke me!" he screamed at the window where Darcy held her finger on the lock button.

I heard her laugh when the colored lights swirled on the rack atop the cruiser. In the pinkish glow of their metered rotation, I saw through the window of the darkened garage another car parked beside Kara's Karmann Ghia, a battered old Dodge with Florida plates that I had not noticed before. It appeared for a second, then was quickly gone when the twirling lights blinked off. In the vacuum of silence, I heard the cop say, "You're abusing Village property, miss. Please step out of the vehicle."

As soon as Darcy opened the door her father grabbed her arm, wrenching her up on the toes of her sneakers, their faces just inches apart. "How dare you upset your mother like this!" he shouted. "Hasn't she enough on her plate?"

The backdoor squeaked open and a voice called out, "Philip! Please! Remember your heart!"

"Stay out of this, Constance!" the Doctor barked, yanking his daughter toward the wisteria-cloaked porch. I was just about to leap from my hiding place when Darcy pulled free from his grip, spinning toward the cop car where the officer sat with his blue sleeve hanging out the window. "Why don't you do something now!" she cried. "Why don't you come when *I* call?"

Snorting with derision, she looked toward the house where her mother leaned out from the porch. "Are you alright, Mom?" I heard her say.

"Of course she's alright," the Doctor insisted, his voice turned syrupy sweet. "Come now, my beauty," he cooed like a dove, and my mind flashed back to that day at the zoo and the strange encounter with the tiger. Darcy went rigid and growled in his face, and he bristled at the depth of her insolence. But only for a second before spinning toward the squad car, his grand smile instantly returned. "So there you have it, officer," he said, his tone implying dismissal. "Please know how much we appreciate your efforts. And if you catch the other scamp, I'll be happy to press charges."

I continued watching as the car backed out and Darcy ran into the house, the Doctor alone now, leaning on his pole, its utility reduced to a crutch. He glanced both ways down the length of the street while discreetly knotting his robe. No longer as headless as I wished him to be, I still couldn't make out his face, his posture suggesting a sick old man beset with concern for his daughter. His borrowed slippers slapped ever so softly in making his way to the porch, the screen door barely clicking as it closed.

I crouched in the rose bushes, listening for voices, watching for shadows to move past the windows. Ten minutes later the lights winked out until only the one remained lit, and I pictured him sitting in his wing-backed chair with a copy of the New York Times, a pipe in his mouth, the IV in his arm as he basked in the ruin of the world.

Chapter 15

I**N *FRANNY AND ZOOEY* THERE'S THIS** there's this "pea green" book about a pilgrim with a withered arm. He's lost his family in a plague or a war and wanders around searching for truth. Everyone's nice to him, but that doesn't help, so he keeps on repeating a prayer to himself, invoking God's name with every breath while waiting for a miracle to happen. That's how I felt after Halloween when Darcy got exiled to her sister's. "Just for a while," she'd written in her note, scribbled on the back of a postcard.

I went through school by rote every day, attending classes in body alone, mindlessly checking boxes on multiple choice tests, ignoring questions that required real thought. I got a warning in math, and biology too. The only class that interested me was art, and I spent as much time there as possible. I was getting into Japanese art—Hokusai and Hiroshige— the perfection of their composition so obviously derived from nature, so reflective of it, like the cemetery wrought on linen. I could see how much it had influenced Van Gogh, his perspective, his colors, the flowery geometry of cherry blossoms.

At lunch on the log, I began reading the haiku of Basho and Issa: "Oh snail, climb Mount Fujiyama…." In D.T. Suzuki's books on Zen Buddhism, I discovered things I'd never thought of before, the riddle of kōans and the promise of satori, exciting a hope that transcended my loneliness, that utilized it, in fact, suggesting a moment when all things could be known, or intuited, a great revelation exposed in plain sight, a thunder-clapped hand striking air.

One day in art class I found Mr. Arstahl staring at me, peering up from his desk where he was always scribbling in a notebook. Next thing I knew he was standing beside me, looking over my shoulder as I slashed away at a fresh sheet of vellum, holding the paintbrush upright in my fingers, Japanese style. "Mister Conover," he said, "I wonder if I might have a word with you."

"Did I do something wrong?"

"Why would you say that?" Dewey sighed. "How I wish the student/teacher relationship could be more about reward, and less about punishment."

I didn't know what to say and said nothing.

"Do you happen to know when Miss Saint James will return?" he asked.

"No sir, I don't."

He sighed again, his posture slumped, resolving himself to whatever he was about to say.

"You two know each other well. Quite well, in fact," he added. "Miss Saint James left rather abruptly, leaving her work, her portfolio, lying about, subject to public perusal. I thought it best to protect her privacy, and I believe that's what I've done. So, I'm going to ask you to look at Darcy's portfolio, as I suspect she wouldn't, couldn't really mind, considering. I just want to say, by way of my status as a teacher, as well as an adult, that sometimes a young person's intellect— their sophistication—exceeds their ability to suppress their emotions. Oh God!" he gasped, slapping a palm to his forehead, "listen to what I just said!"

Dewey leaned and planted his big hand on the table, looking down at me with his droopy gray eyes. "Sometimes," he began anew, "one's intent does not anticipate all outcomes. That is the gist of this commentary, poorly presented as it is. But please, do not ever suppress your emotions. I never meant to suggest that, as it would constitute the end of all art.

"If you would," he said, prompting me to rise and follow him to the rear of the classroom where oversized lockers stored our assignments. He bade me sit at a table away from the other students, laid Darcy's thick, black portfolio in front of me, and walked away.

I flipped it open to charcoal sketches of horses running, jumping, grazing. Then a pencil drawing of a pigeon, then a tiger, then a naked man sprawled on his back in the grass, his penis lying flaccid on his thigh. It took me some seconds to realize it was me, as was the next nude figure, and the next, all posed at rest, sprawled out on a blanket, one even wearing a Yankee cap.

What really struck me, shocked me, was not that I was looking at my naked self, but that the quality of the drawings was incredible, like Di Vinci renderings, or Michelangelo, so well-proportioned and composed were they, done from memory alone, I was sure, by the most talented hand I'd seen outside of a museum. I'm ashamed to say that my first reaction was jealousy, then embarrassment, as I thought of all our conversations about my going to art school, pursuing a career in the art world. Darcy smoked my ass with her talent, and as I flipped through more pages I began to feel deceived, tricked into believing that, in at least this one way, I was her superior, or even just her equal in terms of how I saw her, how she'd become everything to me, embodying all the beauty, all the tragedy and unbounded passion that I attributed to the human spirit.

When I looked up again Mr. Arstahl was standing beneath the clock by the exit sign, watching me. Closing the portfolio, I folded my arms atop it and sat observing the clock, and Dewey, until the bell rang and everyone but me raced for the door.

"I suppose you've divined my thoughts," he said, when finally I stood before him. "You could say it was none of my business, and you'd be correct, so I won't give you the lecture about birth control. I'm talking about something else here, something as pregnant, if you'll pardon the term, with danger and consequence as the act of love, with which, and please forgive me again, I believe you are both familiar.

"You are two of my best, my favorite students," he said. "Darcy is a very… impulsive, sensitive girl. You are also sensitive, thoughtful, and by that, I mean inquisitive as well as considerate. You two have crossed an emotional boundary and you should understand the responsibilities that entails. It's not often that teenagers are accused of wisdom, but I think you may actually possess some, and so I implore you, Mister Conover, employ it, use what fledgling wisdom you've accrued and protect your heart, protect her heart, and for God's sake, use a condom."

Darcy's drawings, her artistry, haunted me for days. What surprised me more than her skill was the form her work took. I would have expected her art to be bright with color—sunflower yellow, rose red—as vibrant and splashy as she was. Instead, her drawings were black and white, linear and exacting, executed with an architect's finesse. It made me wonder who she really was, who else she was, besides the girl I thought I loved. And it made me love her even more, made the mystery of her that much deeper, the sadness of her secret self more alluring, and her love for me an even greater kōan.

By Thanksgiving weekend she'd been gone a month and I hadn't heard anything from her. I tried to find Kara's phone number in Vermont but had no luck. I figured I'd give it another week, when the holiday was over, then call her house and hopefully speak to her mom. But that same day, moping around the apartment by myself, I checked the mail and there were at least two dozen postcards in the slot, all from Darcy, from Miami, where her other, *dead* sister once lived.

I was reading them at the kitchen table, each colorful sunset and swaying palm tree describing her love for me, when there was a knock at the door. Annoyed by the interruption, I tore myself away from my first taste of Darcy in weeks, and when I opened the door, prepared to be rude, I was amazed to find her standing there, brown as a berry and beaming at my shocked expression.

We stood in the hallway for who knows how long, hanging on each other, not even speaking until my neighbor, Mrs. Angevine, came up the stairs with groceries in her arms and I helped her into her musty apartment, littered with doilies and cat hair. Coming back out, I grabbed Darcy's hand and pulled her up the stairwell to the roof.

The metal door squeaked when I kicked it open, and we stepped outside into brilliant sunshine, in a treetop world of fluttering clotheslines and aluminum TV antennas. The rooftops were staggered, connected by ladders that rose from one level to the next, and with Darcy behind me on the cold, steel rungs we climbed to the tallest section.

"It's beautiful," said Darcy, squeezing my hand, "it feels like the top of a mountain." Huddled like pigeons on the cap-stoned wall, we dangled our legs in the air, six stories above the tree lined sidewalk on Elm Street. "Look!" she said, pointing a finger. "There's the Old Dutch Church, and the Beach Club, and the Yellow Rocks where we went fishing!"

"Almost fishing," I corrected.

"I caught you!" she giggled and kissed me on the lips.

The pointed steeple of Saint Teresa's rose above the rim of the building, and just then the bells began to toll and birds swirled chirping from the branches below our feet.

"So what the hell?" I plunged right in, "you were in Miami all this time? With your dead sister?"

"Did you miss me terribly? Do you still love me?"

"Stop it, Dar, listen to me. I saw what happened on Halloween night, your dad in his bathrobe, the car in the garage. Tell me what's going on."

"What does it look like? They sent me away to my sister's."

"But you told me your sister was dead!"

"She used to be! She was dead to my father, or that's what he told me when I was a kid! I *believed* him, Teal! I guess I was stupid. I'll always be stupid to him!"

I was hugging her then, maintaining our balance, our legs swinging out from the cornice.

"Daddy would never even talk about Lena. He sent all her clothes to the Salvation Army, tore all her photos off the wall. Mom put them back up when Lena came home—"

"Came home?"

"—Which only happened twice, once when Kara had just started high school, and the Christmas when they fought over shoes."

"The red shoes?"

"Dad had said Lena was better off dead. We would never see her again."

"And you believed him."

"I was ten years old, Teal! What should I think—that he *wished* his daughter was dead?"

"I get it," I said. "It kind of makes sense. And I'm glad your sister's not dead."

But I didn't really get it, how Lena was dead, then suddenly alive, then just as quickly dead again when Darcy told me she'd drowned.

"Let's celebrate!" Darcy squealed, instantly animated, rocking us both on our precarious perch. "Long live Lena! Lena forever! And she gave me this incredible pot!"

So, we smoked a roach in the afternoon sunlight and she told me about Miami, how the weather was hot and the ocean warm, a tropical paradise in the absence of her father. Lena was single and lived on the beach, in a bungalow with a dozen cats. "She's a loner," said Darcy, "a widow with a shawl, pining for a sailor at sea."

The Hudson Valley stretched long and lush before us, remnants of autumn collected like chaff amidst pockets of hunter green, the forest as dark and mysterious as the days before the Dutchmen arrived. I told her the story of the Leather Man, who had lived in the woods with the Indians somewhere between Ossining and Sleepy Hollow. His heart had been broken by a beautiful maiden, and he traveled the hills alone, roaming the forest as though searching his soul, communing with the spirits of the trees.

"Is that how you felt while I was gone?" Darcy asked. "Then let me console you in your room!"

"The Leather Man slept in the leaves," I said. "His clothes were tanned from hides."

"You can skin me, nature boy. I might even strop your knife!"

The weed made it crazy descending the ladders, peeking at Darcy's cute butt. We stopped at each clothesline and dumbwaiter shaft and fell kissing and panting against the door, stray hairs caught in the corners of our mouths, hands tangled up in our shirts. When we got to my room Darcy flopped on the bed and sprawled there with limbs akimbo, looking around at the stuff on my walls, the top of my dresser cluttered with keepsakes.

"This place is like a museum!" she said. "Everything has a meaning!"

She asked what each ribbon and trophy was for, the story behind every pennant. Sniffing the leather of my old Rawlings mitt, she said she could still smell the oil. I showed her the shell casings stashed in my sock drawer, the badges from my Cub Scout troop. She said, "I feel like I'm lying in the center of your life, a snow globe swirling with memories. I gotta pee!" she squealed. "Don't even breathe till I get back."

A door in my room led directly to the bath, and I watched Darcy close it behind her. Waiting impatiently, I stared at the art prints and magazine clippings I'd tacked to the walls over the years, pictures of the Mick and Roger Maris, M. C. Escher postcards, Warhol's silk screens of Marilyn Monroe, and a woodcut by Edvard Munch. *The Scream* showed a woman posed on a bridge with both hands clapped to her ears, as though stifling the voices that wailed in her head, escaping through the oval of her mouth. The silence of her scream was more deafening than sound, visually piercing the inner ear, the inner being of the viewer.

I'd been staring at the print for quite some time before I realized the shower was running and had been for a while. Tapping on the door, Darcy didn't answer, so I waited until the noise and the splashing stopped and tapped again. "Darce?" I said, leaning closer, my forehead pressed to the jamb.

I could hear her in there, the shower curtain rattling, the tap now running in the sink. "What are you doing?" I asked a bit louder.

"Just playing!" she sang. "Checking out your razor. Feeling what's it's like to be you!"

I flinched at the sound of the apartment door slamming, and then Mom called out, "I'm home!"

"Shit!" I whispered to Marilyn Monroe, the other nude blonde in my room. Pacing the floor while my girlfriend got dressed and Mom banged around in the kitchen, I decided it was best to defuse the situation before Darcy stepped dripping from the shower.

Mom had groceries spread out on the counter, the refrigerator door opened wide. "I see you got some mail," she said, smiling, eying the stack of postcards.

"Yeah, finally."

"How's Darcy?"

"She's, uh, fine. In fact—"

"Are these from Florida?" Mom asked, squinting at the palm trees in the photos.

"Turns out she wasn't in Vermont," I said. "She's actually here. Right now."

"You spoke to her?"

"I mean she's here. Now. In the shower."

Darcy breezed into the bright yellow kitchen before my mom could respond. "Hi!" she smiled, extending her hand. "Happy to finally meet you!" Even soaking wet her hair was still blonde, her brown skin tanned through her hairline.

Always gracious, Mom shook her hand. "Welcome back, dear. You were sorely missed."

Darcy blushed and hopped to my side, slipping her arm in mine. "I missed him, too," she said. "More than you'll ever know."

Mom seemed surprised, or simply touched. "Are you kids hungry?" she asked. "I was thinking of making breakfast for dinner, since Teal never eats in the morning."

"You don't eat breakfast?" Darcy was amazed. "You never told me that!"

"Darcy eats like a horse," I explained.

"That's not true," she countered. "Horses have a very limited diet. I eat everything. Can we make pancakes?"

The girls broke out the whisks and flour while I stuffed groceries in the fridge, falling into an easy banter as Darcy cracked eggs in a bowl. She talked about surfing, palm trees, coconuts, and snorkeling in coral reefs. I pictured her slithering through turquoise water in a swimsuit the color of sunset, her silver hair riding the current like seaweed, yellow fish darting around her.

"Do you have a turkey baster?" she asked.

Mom fished one from a drawer, and Darcy drew the batter into its long, narrow neck. Squeezing the bulb, she squirted a variety of shapes on the hot skillet, easy ones at first, Mickey and Minnie Mouse with round heads and ears, segueing into more complex designs, showing off with butterflies and long necked giraffes, dinosaurs with spiny, archipelago tails. The last one was mine, a Thanksgiving turkey with a dollop on its chin and a fantail of lumpy feathers. Mom was impressed and squeezed Darcy's shoulders as she watched. "Where did you learn that?" she asked.

"Mom taught me when I was little. We used blueberries for eyes, canned peaches for lips and ears."

"Your mom's a good cook, huh?"

"Not anymore."

"So, your dad cooks?"

Darcy laughed, a smirking huff.

Seeking to fill the stilted silence, Mom said, "Teal's dad didn't cook either, and I'm afraid his son is just like him. He'd exist solely on peanut butter if I let him."

"Choke," Darcy corrected. "And lusterslime. With potato chips."

"Potato chips?"

"Yeah, Mom," I said, "you gotta try it."

"Does Teal look like his dad?" Darcy asked. "Do you have any pictures?"

Dragging a chair down the hall to the closet, I stood on its wicker bottom, rearranging old Macy's bags and round hat boxes where our past was stored safely on shelves. I could hear them talking as I pawed through collections of Christmas ornaments, Halloween decorations, and rolls of musty wallpaper. Buried at the bottom of all that stuff was a half dozen leather-bound photo albums, the older ones worn and beaten around the edges, smelling like ancient parchment. It took some effort to pull them free, and in the process I knocked a Bloomingdales shoe box off the shelf, spilling it onto the floor. Stepping down from the chair, sitting on its edge, I sorted through its contents, mostly old letters with faded post marks, their crinkled edges candy-caned with red and blue stripes. From out in the kitchen, I heard Mom ask, "So, how is your father, dear? Is he recovering well?" Mom called everyone *dear*, or *hon*. It's just what old people did.

"Sure," said Darcy. "He's fine."

"And your mom's holding up? It must be extra tough for her right now."

"I guess. It's always tough for my mother."

I was afraid my mom would ask Darcy why and ruin this special moment, but she didn't and instead asked, "Do your parents even know you're here? Why don't you give them a call right now, tell them you're having dinner—*breakfast*—with us."

I could picture Darcy's face as she shrugged, and then I heard her say, "No, that's okay. They don't care where I am."|

All the old letters were from overseas, postmarked in the forties and addressed to Mom, written by my father. They were already opened, so I didn't think I'd be intruding by taking a look, to hear what Dad had been thinking all those years before. His handwriting was tiny, cramped at times, then large and erratic as if scribbled in a hurry, anxious to scratch down his thoughts.

> Hi, Honey, sorry I haven't written for a while. We're on the troop ship and mail is difficult. We're all writing letters tonight, as tomorrow— this morning—we'll be landing on the beach. It's difficult to find a place to write as we're packed in here so tight. Some of the men around me were crying, and I just can't talk to you unless I'm alone,

so it feels like you're almost here. So I'm up on deck with my Zippo lighter trying to write by its light, the ship blacked-out as we approach the coast, as are all the others around us. It's hard because the wind keeps blowing out the flame, and besides, I really don't know what to write except to say that I love you, that I think of you always, and hope you are thinking of me....

"Don't you think they'll be worried?" Mom asked.

"My father probably isn't home. He only stayed in bed a few weeks and then went right back to work. My mom is in bed as soon as it's dark. She really likes her wine."

My father's handwriting changed dramatically, the letters exploding on the page, wild and edgy and smudged with decades-old dirt.

Almost a week has passed since I last wrote. I couldn't bear to mail what I'd written on the ship. I somehow felt that if I did, I would surely be sealing my fate, that I wouldn't survive to speak to you again. But I have survived, though there were many times I felt I wouldn't, or wished I wouldn't, so terrible are the things we've seen, too terrible to describe. All I want is to be free of these thoughts, to be with you in our home, in our town, walking at Rockies, sitting at the Yellow Rocks, just being with you and putting all this behind me....

Reading those words, I was truly shocked, realizing that my parents had lived their lives in all the same places I did, with the same thoughts and feelings that I now felt for Darcy.

"Certainly, your parents care, dear," Mom was saying. "I know it seems we don't sometimes, but we always care. It's human nature. Someday you'll know what I mean."

> A dozen of my friends are gone. I'm so sorry to burden you with this, but I must tell somebody, and there is no one left here who cares, who is even capable of it. We've all lost friends, and feel terrible, even guilty for it. All I can think of is holding you tight and feeling safe in your arms, keeping you safe from all this. But I fear that when I do return, I'll be changed, and you won't be able to love me anymore, not like you did before, before all this. No one can understand what it's like who hasn't been here, and none of the men who sent us here can know unless they come themselves. And then they could never do it, could never ask men to do this to each other....

"You think I'll have kids someday?" Darcy asked.

No doubt Mom was surprised, not used to Darcy's curve ball questions, but I imagined her smiling, nodding her head, being her comforting self. "Of course you will," she said.

"With Teal?" said Darcy. "Do you think he would marry me? Do you think we could have a family?"

Looking up from the page, I listened to the silence, ticking like the clock on the mantle, pancakes sputtering in the greasy pan, Dad's letter crinkling in my fingers.

"I don't know, hon. That would be up to Teal, and you. But there's plenty of time to think about that. You two are so young and—"

"But I love him," said Darcy, "and I know he loves me."

"Time will tell, hon. But right now, your parents are wondering where you are. Why don't we give them a call."

"No," said Darcy, "it's really not necessary. We have an understanding."

"What kind of understanding?"

"I'll tell," said Darcy, as simply as that, and more batter spattered in the pan.

On the floor by my sneaker was a creamy brown photograph, wrinkled and curling with age. Three men in uniform posed by a Jeep, smoking cigarettes while grinning at the camera. One of them was me, a bit older, maybe taller, but equally skinny with long ropey arms. His eyes followed mine as I turned the photo, leaving me no place to hide, and I felt myself wobbling on the deck of a ship that pitched and rolled beneath me.

"Sometimes," Mom said, "parents do things their children consider intrusive. But that doesn't mean they don't love them, and kids need to figure that out. You can't take something you don't understand and wield it like a weapon."

"I love my mother," Darcy assured her.

"Of course you do, dear. Loving your parents is only—"

"I love my *mother*," Darcy repeated.

Slipping the letter back in the box, I returned it to the shelf, then moved the chair, closed the door, and waited in the darkened hallway. The aroma of butter and warm maple syrup infused our small apartment, yet now I wasn't hungry. I'd almost forgotten why I'd gone to the closet, and tucking the picture in the pocket of my shirt, I could feel my heart pound through the fabric, through the years since my dad was a teenager.

"When Teal's father returned from the war, he was different," Mom said, "and I missed the Tommy I knew. He hated the war, he hated the Japs and the fear that never subsided. And he hated hating everything, was afraid it would never release him. How could I love him, in the midst of all that? How could he really love *me?*

"Honey," Mom soothed, and I pictured her face, the tilt of her head as she smiled, "sometimes hate is just fear in disguise. It's hard to tell one from the other."

Darcy was silent for quite some time, considering how to respond. She said, "Teal is a lot like his father, I think. Afraid of being afraid."

"My son is afraid?"

"My mom cried for a year after Lena left, or that's what Kara told me. My sister was only eighteen when she ran. She calls it *escaping the past.*"

I waited for Mom to ask more about Lena Saint James, who I'd told her had drowned in the ocean, resurrected now at the very worst moment. Resolving to end the bizarre conversation, I made to stride boldly into the kitchen when Darcy said, "I was always afraid my mom didn't love me, that she needed *him* more than me. Teal feels the same way about his dad, that he died wanting death more than staying alive, or what his life had become. He can't really tell if he's angry or sad—he's even afraid to find out. I hate my father while he's still alive. I'm just not ashamed to admit it."

Chapter 16

WHATEVER UNDERSTANDING DARCY had with her parents appeared to be real, because we saw each other often after Thanksgiving, anytime we wanted, in fact, as long as it wasn't a school night. Mom was both taken and taken aback by her first meeting with Darcy. Despite the strangeness of their conversation, they still spoke often when Darcy called, sometimes talking until I grew impatient and picked up the extension in my room.

That night after breakfast I drove Darcy home, even though I didn't have my license yet. Breaking the law was a big deal for Mom, but she'd wanted to impress us with her trust, how she knew we'd act responsibly. When we got to Darcy's house, she made me wait in the car while she ran inside. A minute later she returned with a photograph of herself taken at Miami Beach, standing in the surf in a lemon-yellow bikini, trying to look like a starfish.

"Lena took it," she told me. "It's for you, for your museum, so you'll always think of me."

"I'm always thinking of you anyway," I said.

"Now you'll think of me in a bikini."

Before we knew it, Christmas arrived and I broke into my savings account and bought Darcy Berne Hogarth's *Dynamic Anatomy*, a big hardcover book about figure drawing with pencil and charcoal. Not that she needed it, so good was she at drawing the human body.

I didn't mention that Dewey had shown me her portfolio. I wanted to, but something made me hesitate, not a little of which was my ego, recognizing how much better an artist she was than I.

I invited Darcy to Christmas dinner at Grandma Conover's, but she declined, saying she'd feel too Catholic. What she did was invite *me* to Christmas Eve service at The Old Dutch Church, which was actually my church, First Reformed, services held there only twice a year at Christmas and Easter. I hadn't attended church—the big church near the high school—since my father died, when I'd volunteered to read a passage from the Bible, standing at the pulpit in front of a bunch of strangers. I thought it would be fitting, or somehow life-changing in the midst of all that grief. But it wasn't, not for me, and I never went back again.

It snowed a few days before Christmas, a couple inches that stayed frozen in the shadows and around the trunks of trees, but by Christmas Eve it hadn't snowed again and the roads and paths in the cemetery were patches of ice. We agreed to meet at the Jesus Place, and I waited under a giant tree now foliated only with stars, wearing my corduroy coat and the tie I'd last worn at Dad's funeral, the Hogarth book in its candy cane gift wrap tucked beneath my arm.

I saw her coming a long way off, the tiniest wink of a candle's flame at the end of the winding path. The closer she got the brighter the flame grew, its halo splashed over the brilliant red background of her toggled coat. She held the candle in both green-mittened hands, and as she drew nearer, her smile gleaming with the light, she was to me the perfect Christmas gift, wrapped in the scarlet package of herself, the entirety of her being the brightest star, the truest beacon for questing Magi wandering the surface of the Earth, eventuating here on the icy old path, in the circle of angels at the Jesus Place.

"Come on," she said, stepping onto the frozen grass, the figure of Jesus waiting patiently atop the pedestal, His eyes cast down in transcendence. Standing on tip toe, she dribbled a pool of creamy wax in the palm of the Holy hand, holding the candle there until it stood alone, the light of it painting the face of Jesus much as it had her own. "Happy Birthday," she said to the statue, returning to take my arm. "Merry Christmas, Teal," she smiled, fingering a lock of my longish hair, "my other favorite Jesus."

"Merry Christmas, Dar," I said, and handed her the book.

"You got me a present?"

"Don't open it now."

"But I don't have yours."

"*You* are mine," I said. "I can't begin to tell you."

She kissed me then, a long slow kiss that glowed inside me like a candle. I couldn't believe how much I loved her, the cold of her hair as it brushed my cheek, the wintry smell of her coat. Frozen stars winked brightly overhead, millions of galaxies and far-off worlds, while I only cared about this one, this tiny, mysterious, personal universe described by the halo of a candle.

Skating down the icy path toward the church, Darcy whooped when she almost fell, tripping me when I caught her. She tried to scrape a snowball from the frosted ground, to hit me when I was down. "I wish it would snow," she said, expressing every child's sentiment at Christmas.

The stone steps of the Old Dutch Church were crusted with ice, sprinkled with salt that crunched under foot. The old Deacon winked and handed us programs with the Christmas Star on the cover. I pointed Darcy to the narrow stairway that led up to the gallery where the choir sat. Paper-collared candles lined the wooden pews, and we sat in the front row along the balcony where we could lean over the railing and point down at the parishioners, giggling into our hands at the silly hats, assorted sneakers, and pretentious fur stoles.

There was no electricity in the centuries-old church, and candles flickered on the whitewashed walls, the air perfumed with fragrant greens festooned with scarlet ribbons. The apse smelled like a Christmas tree, and looked much like one too, winking, glowing, garlanded with light, replicated faithfully in the tall, arched windows in a triptych of shadow and light. Candlelight painted the Protestant faces, pearling the steam that rose from the kettle set on the old wood-stove.

"What's that smell?" Darcy asked.

"Apples. They serve mulled cider at the end of the service, if you feel like sticking around."

"Oh, yes!" she said. "I'm sticking!"

Everyone rose when Reverend Neumann ascended the pulpit, its prow protruding like a masted ship above the waves of wooden pews. "It's just like Catholic church," Darcy whispered.

And I said, "But no kneeling."

The choir stood and began to sing, their voices booming beside us. I scanned the text of the program to see if we were supposed to join in; we weren't, but a minute later we were, and Darcy pressed her cheek to my shoulder as we sang from the pamphlet in my hand. "O come, all ye faithful, joyful and triumphant, O come ye, O come ye to Bethlehem!"

"I love this singing," she said between hymns. "You have a wonderful voice!"

I didn't have a wonderful voice, but I let her say it anyhow, content to listen to hers, which was of course beautiful, as was everything about her. "That's Erik's dad?" she asked, pointing her mitten at the reverend.

"Recognize the collar?"

Darcy stared, stifled a laugh, and clapped a hand to her mouth. "From the séance!"

"Erik wears it all the time," I said. "He leases it, on credit."

The Reverend would speak, we'd sing, he'd speak, and then we'd sing again. It was all very cool because I really loved Christmas, everything about it, the joyous and the solemn, the religious and the not. Leaning from the balcony, gazing down at it all, I imagined my ancestors building the church three hundred years before, digging at the earth as I had at my job, their faces and voices as familiar to others as mine was to Darcy and Todd. I felt a great sense of history in the old church at Christmas. Or not-history, perhaps, feeling the centuries fall away, replaced by the nowness of things, the idea that the only real time is the present, and the only real moment this instant.

Darcy gasped and squeezed my hand. "Look," she said, nodding toward a window where near its bottom, in a triangle of candlelight that painted the world outside, snow was falling, big white feathers of it shaken from the ermine robe of Christmas, from the downy wings of the peaceful dove itself.

"Let's go!" she whispered, nudging me along the pew.

"And miss the mulled cider?"

"It's snowing!" she said.

A few robed choir members glanced our way and winked as we departed. The deacon stood at the foot of the stairs, his hands clasped firmly behind his back, an old Christian soldier at parade rest. "It's snowing," I told him, by way of explanation, and to my great surprise he broke into a grin and leaned to open the door.

"I know!" he laughed as we stepped outside, where the landing was tattooed with his footprints.

Darcy let go a muffled shriek and packed the fresh snow in a snowball. I figured I was in for a fight, but she held it to her lips, licked it twice, and took a timid bite.

"Vanilla?" I said, and she threw it at me. We stood gazing up as the flakes zigzagged down, melting on our foreheads, our cheeks and chins.

"If this was a movie," she said, "I wouldn't believe it."

"If this was a movie, you'd fall asleep."

That warranted another snowball, which I dodged as easily as the first. We were standing, playing, on the path where my ancestors' headstones had stood for centuries. "This feels so historic," I said. "Almost psychedelic. Think of the Christmases they spent here. And now you. Now us."

She drifted to the trunk of a candlelit tree, where she leaned to peer through the church's window. I slipped up beside her, knowing we could not be seen from inside, and watched in secret as one after another the parishioners lit the candle of their neighbor, until every face wore a warm yellow glow as they opened their mouths to sing, the sound of their voices like steam on the glass, muffled but not silenced by the thick stone walls. "Hark! The Herald Angels sing, Glory to the newborn king! Peace on earth and mercy mild, God and sinners reconciled!'"

Through the grid of the window the church became a lantern, its warmth defined by the warps in the panes, the dark night absolute in contrast. "It's like one of those old-fashioned advent calendars," said Darcy, "you open the little door and find a mouse or a candlestick inside."

"More like spying on Tiny Tim, Scrooge freezing his ass in a nightgown."

After the service we went back inside to grab Darcy's gift from the balcony where she'd left it. Only the smiling deacon remained, and he poured us hot cider from the kettle on the stove.

"Hey," said Erik Neumann, appearing suddenly beside us. "Merry fucking Christmas, comrades."

"Hey," I said back. "I didn't think you attended service."

"I don't. I came for my father. He likes a little spice with his cider, if you dig my meaning. Speaking of which, you guys wanna get high?"

Why not, we figured, and headed back out into the cold. The snowflakes grew thicker as we walked through the Manor, everything mantled in white. Darcy pulled up her scarlet hood, her face a pale crescent in its oval shadow, smiling when I fished the Yankee cap from my coat pocket. We passed a joint between us as we walked, our voices rising, keening higher as the doob burned down to the roach. Muffled by the storm, our laughter hovered like the cones of snow swirling beneath the streetlamps, elegant garlands of descending joy that followed us from corner to corner.

Peaceful and silent, nearly midnight, we strolled down the middle of the road, the colored lights of surrounding houses draped like winter's robe. "This is so cool," said Erik. "I can't remember the last time it snowed on Christmas Eve."

"What about your dad?" Darcy asked. "The spiced cider?"

"That was just my lame excuse. I actually like Christmas service."

"I wanna go every year," she said, adding, "but only if Teal will take me!" And she slipped her hand in the pocket of my coat where I held it all toasty in mine.

"Hey," said Neumann, squinting at his watch. "It's midnight, straight up. Merry Christmas, amigos."

"Merry Christmas!" said Darcy, and gave us each a hug. After which Erik hugged me, and I, caught up in the spirit, hugged him back.

"I won't forget this," Erik said, walking away backwards, the snow piled high on his shoulders. "It's so far out, you know? It's snowing! It's Christmas! I love you guys! I love this fucking night!"

"Where are you going?" I shouted, the figure of Erik growing smaller in the distance, his gray shape fading in the see-sawing flakes. Seconds later he was totally gone, only his footprints remaining in the snow, running backwards down the center of the road.

"What the hell?" I said.

"You think he'll be all right?"

I shrugged. "You know Neumann. He's probably on acid."

Arm in arm, we arrived at Darcy's corner, where we paused to try sliding on the snow. It didn't work, its being so cold, the temperature dropping toward the teens. "Wait," she said, fumbling through her pockets, retrieving the little candles from the church pew.

Slender and white in their round paper collars, she handed one to me, lit it with the lighter she'd kleptoed from Erik, and held its wick to her own. Standing button to toggle on the corner of her block, she leaned from the shadow of her hood. Her face, in the guttering crescent of flame, was the luminous face of an angel, and her voice when she sang was an angel's voice, rising on wintry wings. "Silent night, holy night, All is calm, all is bright …"

Darcy was my Miracle on 34th Street, my Clarence from Bedford Falls, the answer to my long-ago letters to Santa delivered at last to my stocking. So happy was I at that perfect moment, that tears froze brittle on my face, overjoyed at the center of so selfless a love as I struggled to sing along with her—"Round yon Virgin Mother and Child, Holy infant so tender and mild, Sleep in heavenly peace, Sleep in heavenly peace."

"Peace, Teal," she said, blowing out the candles, then pressed her cold lips to my cheek.

"What's the matter?" she asked. "You're not sad, are you?"

"Maybe. A little."

"Because of your dad?"

She hugged me so hard I heard myself wheeze, like a gasp from the old church organ.

"C'mon," she said, pulling me toward her house. "I want to give you your present."

No lights burned in the dim foyer as the door knocker clunked behind us. Waiting in the dark for my eyes to adjust, there were no decorations in sight, no Christmas tree or evergreen boughs or mistletoe hanging in a doorway. All I saw was a crèche on a table by a window where the curtain was drawn. Ceramic sheep and hand-painted shepherds gathered around the crude manger, the Virgin Mother and Holy Child tucked away inside it, Joseph and the Three Kings looking regal in their robes, staffs held rigid in their hands.

Observing me study the age-old scene, Darcy said, "My parents haven't gone to church in years. I don't even know why they bother. Wait here," she winked as she kicked off her shoes and ran up the stairs in her stockings.

I'd only ever been in the Saint James's kitchen, and never when they were home. The house was quiet except for the clock, and the sound of its ticking and the embers in the fireplace drew me toward the darkened living room. The place smelled strongly of pipe tobacco and the vaguest hint of wood smoke. The wingback chair that I took to be the Doctor's was tall, wide, and heavily upholstered, so much like a throne that I was tempted to kneel like a peasant before it. Ornately framed paintings hung on walls patterned with velveteen wallpaper, still lifes of flowers and stately white horses, hunting dogs flushing quail. Marble-topped end tables held porcelain vases and an assortment of cut-glass ash trays, figurines filigreed with hairline cracks curtseyed on knickknack shelves. Startled by the tumble of a log in the fire, I realized how anxious I was, the Master reclining in his dread antechamber somewhere above my head.

A photograph leaned by itself on a table, red embers reflected on its glass. Leaning to take a closer look, I picked it up in my hand: A black and white portrait of the happy couple taken on their wedding day, Mrs. Saint James as beautiful as her daughter, with a bouquet of dahlias in her arms, the Doctor severe in a tailored black suit and charcoal boutonniere. He was grinning more than smiling, as though amused to be married, enjoying some personal joke.

From somewhere in the darkness came an intake of breath, and I gulped down a breath of my own. Gripped by the notion that I wasn't alone, I inched nearer to the Doctor's chair, easing abreast of its tack-studded arm where I leaned to make sure it was empty. Relieved that it was, I released a sigh, and a hoarse voice then spoke from the shadows, from the smaller, less pretentious chair beside it. "Merry Christmas, love" whispered Mrs. Saint James, and the room returned to silence.

Darcy's cool hand encircled my wrist as she raised a finger to her lips. "Shh," she instructed, drawing us back where I caught a quick glimpse of her mother, curled like a cat in her wing-backed chair, her slippers aligned on the carpet.

"She's drunk," Darcy whispered, once safe in the shadows. "She probably thought you were me. Tomorrow she won't remember a thing—it's like you were never here."

We hugged for some minutes in the dark foyer, orange coals popping in the hearth. "Merry Christmas," she smiled, and presented the gift she'd been hiding behind her back, a gold-wrapped cylinder tied with the bow so recently removed from her hair. "Don't open it till morning," she made me promise, "and thank you so much for this wonderful Christmas, my very own advent calendar. Whenever I open its tiny door, I will always find you inside."

All the way home I relived the night, retracing our tracks in the snow, mouthing the words of Christmas hymns that drifted in clouds of my breath. I kept an eye peeled for Erik Neumann, hoping he was okay, and wondered what manger Carter Mason had found on Christmas Eve, 1967. Nearing the fence at the Restoration, a cop car tracked slowly up the road; at the crest of the hill its light bar flashed—a cheery red glow through the snowflakes.

I waited until morning to open Darcy's present, when Mom and I opened ours. Drinking hot cocoa, watching the *Yule Log* on TV, we nibbled at the jelly rolls she made every year. Mom gave me a sketch pad and a box of pastels, some charcoals with cardboard nubs. I'd bought her a package of cookie cutters—reindeers, wreaths, and stars.

My present from Darcy was *The Rocky Mountains*, a print of the painting we'd seen at the Met. A card in the shape of a candy cane was scribbled in loopy green ink. "To my adventurous boyfriend with the wild, pure heart," it read. "May you follow your dreams, may I always be in them."

In that last respect, Darcy's wishes came true, every day, every moment, for the rest of my life.

Chapter 17

ERIK NEUMANN WAS ARRESTED ON Christmas Eve and taken immediately to the hospital. I had unknowingly witnessed the initial stages of his arrest, the flashing red police lights sending him running stark naked through the snowy backyards of Manor residents in a half-hour chase that ended only when he slammed into the grill of another squad car. Erik said later that he'd thought it was Santa's sleigh, Rudolph the reindeer with a strobing red nose. They found his pants stuffed in somebody's mailbox, his pockets full of LSD, and he was charged with possession of an illegal substance with the obvious intent to sell. He'd shivered so badly in the back of the car that the cops took him straight to the ER, where he was determined to be hypothermic, and hospitalized for what eventually became pneumonia.

We visited him there, Todd, Mary Ann, and I, on New Year's Eve, and popped a bottle of sparkling cider just before visiting hours were over. Erik expressed confidence that his charges would be dropped, or at least reduced, due to his family's good standing in the community. And also because the reverend had retained an expensive lawyer. He tried to sell us acid as we left, saying he didn't have any on him, but could describe exactly where to find his stash. We declined, saying we were keeping it light that evening, which we did, splitting a couple of six packs that Todd bought legally—he'd turned eighteen in December—and drinking it in the boiler room of the Manor train station where the heat had been turned on for the season.

It was sweltering hot in the musty basement, a deceptively small room, nowhere near the dimensions of the lobby above it. The rear wall was an outcrop of natural bedrock blasted from the bluff behind it, where an ancient boiler with Isinglass windows grew from its face like a crystal, syrupy flames licking its innards in mesmerizing, airtight, slow motion. A wobbly, wooden table and equally wobbly stool took up half the space, the overstuffed chair now crusty with candle's wax from when Darcy and I sat reading books together. The arched expanse of a floor-to-ceiling window was painted with multiple layers of black paint, the enamel so thick you had to scrape it with a quarter to create the tiniest peep hole.

We lit the candles, stripped down to our t-shirts, and settled into our respective posts: Todd and Mouse cuddled in the big green chair, me sprawled out on the table. I moved only rarely to swig from my bottle, drops of sweat beading my forehead. A late train delivered its cargo of commuters, their wing tips clunking loudly across the floorboards overhead, dust drifting down to powder my face when I was too lethargic to stir.

"Yo, Frankenstein," said Todd.

"Yes, master."

"Where's your date this evening?"

"Darcy?"

"No, Twiggy."

I explained how she wasn't feeling well, or that maybe her mom had the flu.

"A confusing chick," Todd opined.

"Don't say that," Mary Ann scolded. "How rude."

Todd guffawed. "C'mon, don't go getting all sensitive, now. Teal, you're not sensitive, are ya?"

"Moi? Hell no. Bullets bounce off me."

"See," said Mary Ann, "that's humor. You've made him defensive."

Todd tickled her midriff and she acted annoyed but laughed when he tickled some more.

When she finally stopped squealing—when Todd quit tickling—she said, "Speaking of bullets, Teal, did your best friend tell you the big news?"

"News?" I said. "What news? Friend? What friend?"

"Go ahead, tell him," she said, slapping Todd's muscular arm.

"Ah, shit," he groaned, "I enlisted in the army. I don't even go till I graduate."

"What?" I shouted, lurching erect. "You fucking *what?*"

"Calm down there, Frank. Get back on the gurney. It ain't that big a deal."

"No big deal? They'll send you to Vietnam!"

"I know that," he said. "I'm doing what's right—"

"*Right?* Are you totally crazy? Are you that fucking *stupid?*"

"Watch it now!" he warned, zero levity in his voice. "It's what I believe. It's what *I* think is right! And what's so smart about what you're doing? You go to some hippie demonstration, and now you're straight with the world? Grow up, Teal. Grow a fucking pair—"

"Don't talk that macho crap to me! That's what starts wars in the first place!"

Todd leaped from the chair like a bull from a chute, Mary Ann tumbling from his lap. "I don't have to listen to this shit! If you weren't my friend—"

"What, you'd hit me? Is that how it works for you?"

"Stop it!" yelled Mary Ann, grabbing Todd's arm as he jabbed his thick finger in my chest. "Don't do this, Todd. Teal is your friend. You know how much he loves you."

"Funny fucking way of showing it!"

"He's just … upset."

"He's *pissed*, is what. I've transgressed somehow, not living my life the Teal way. People can't even die without offending him!"

"Shut *up!*" she shouted, and silence descended like dust from the ceiling. "What is wrong with you two? Just think for a fucking minute."

It was Mary Ann's swearing that made us stop, Mouse who never swore, never raised her voice above a whisper.

Both of us were sweating like pigs by then, Todd's broad chest revealed through his tee-shirt, muscular, and kind of scary. Todd was half a year older than me, and he used to joke about how he was wiser, more mature. He was only kidding, but physically he really was older, hairier, more developed. Todd was a man, about to join the army. I was a boy, not yet willing to join anything.

Todd sat down, and Mary Ann with him, her skinny butt perched on his knee. He kissed her bare shoulder where she'd rolled up her sleeve, then glanced up and showed me his grin. "I'm sorry, man" he said sincerely, his chiseled features softening.

That was so Todd, and it killed me to hear it, always the first to say he was sorry, to do whatever it took to right our shared wrongs.

"How sorry are you?" I asked.

He smiled at the game, his dark eyes twinkling, knowingly nodding his head. "Real sorry."

"*How* sorry?" I repeated, and Todd broke out in his patented version of Brenda Lee's torturous torch song, whining, "I'm sorry, sooo sorry! Won't you accept myyy a-pol-o-gy!"

"Apology accepted!" I shouted, feeling great to laugh again.

Mary Ann kissed him, and they engaged in an extended little make-out session I was forced to endure from the table, my eyes averted and mind adrift as I stared at the cob-webby ceiling. A moth's shadow danced in the light of a candle. I tipped my warm bottle of beer. A train rumbled past just beyond the blackened window, a deep well of silence in its wake. In the vacuum of sound, I closed my eyes and thought about what Todd had said, how I looked at life my way—the "Teal way," he'd called it— unyielding as Biblical law.

Todd was my mirror, my opposite image, the negative through which I viewed the world. He saved me from looking too hard at myself, from burning my eyes on the sun. Both of us had suffered the death of a father, and at first it had bonded us more, but no one can miss what they've never known, possessing no means to compare. How would Todd feel if he'd known his dad, and could measure the depth of his loss? He'd be angry, and empty, and crazy as me, forcing it all to make sense, turning death into life like lead into gold, an alchemist's version of hope. I thought of what Darcy had said to my mom, how I hated my father because he died, as if he had chosen to leave us. But if hate was only fear in disguise, then what was I so afraid of?

"Hey," said Todd, his voice a near whisper. "Listen! It's him. It's the piper!"

I heard it too, the floorboards creaking, footsteps pacing a circle. The drone of the bagpipes filled the whole station, filtered by bedrock and layers of wood, yet clear, clean, and perfectly resonant in the high, vaulted ceiling of the lobby.

We sat without moving, just listening to the dirge, a melancholy sound like wind in the trees, breath blown over a bottle. It was truly a rare and mystical event to be present when the bagpiper played, a mysterious entity we'd never really seen, always seeming to arrive when we were up on the roof, or down in the bowels of the station. He was after the acoustics, or the privacy perhaps, and an open space large enough to march in. The last was imperative when playing the pipes: one had to maneuver in that slow, shuffling way, so martial was the music's tradition. And so appropriate, I thought, for Todd's big news, but hopefully not portentous.

The piper played for almost an hour before he abruptly stopped. In the ensuing silence we dared to crack open fresh bottles of skunky beer, holding our hands over the caps lest the tiny *psst!* give us away. Just when we figured he must have gone, the wailing began anew. It took me a moment to recognize the tune, but when I did a genuine shiver coursed down the length of my body. "Auld Lang Syne" was one of those songs that the passage of time could not diminish nor new-found cool negate. I think we all felt it, Todd, Mary Ann and I, the mournful reminder of years gone by and loved ones lost in passing. Even seventeen summers lent perspective to the world, and seventeen winters a story.

Struggling to stand, we faced each other, feeling kind of dopey, and a little bit drunk. "Well," said Todd, "happy New Year, you losers," and raising his arms, he embraced us. It smelled a bit skunky in there as well, in the huddle of tee shirts and armpits. But it felt good, it felt *right*, and Todd quickly wrestled me into a head lock and danced us around the table. "Don't be mad about the army," he said. "I'll be fine, you'll see. You know I'm cool, you know I'm bad. Who's the baddest cat in Sleepy Hollow?"

"You are," I mumbled into his chest.

"Who's gonna kick butt on the bad guys?"

"You are."

"Fuckin' A, brother. Fuckin' A!"

Todd staggered behind the boiler to take a leak, leaving Mouse and me standing there, face to face. Leaning in slowly, she looped her arms around my neck, and I pressed the damp back of her tee shirt. "Happy New Year, Teal," she whispered in my ear.

"Happy New Year," I repeated.

"Who's the baddest girl on Beekman Avenue?"

"You are."

"Who had the best arm in third grade?"

"You did."

"Who's always gonna love you, no matter what?"

I could smell the perfume in the hollow of her neck, feel her eyelashes batting my ear. I didn't know what to say, what to do, and ended up hugging her even harder, the sound of the bagpipes making me woozy, weepy as it floated above us. Released from the moment, she was quick to step back and wipe a tear from her eye, squeezing my wrist before letting me go.

We waited until after the piper had gone before gathering up our empty bottles, slamming the door shut in the same violent fashion by which we'd entered, the cold air instantly invading our coats. Todd was driving his mom's old Cutlass, armed with his legal driver's license, and he dropped me off in front of the VT. "Hey," he said as I climbed from the car, "no hard feelings, huh?" He was grinning, leaning across Mary Ann's lap to look me in the eye. "And try not to worry so goddam much. I got a good feeling about 1968."

Chapter 18

THE CHRISTMAS SNOW DIDN'T LAST very long. Within weeks it had been plowed, shoveled, and blackened with grime until its beauty had vanished, mounds of gray slush heaped up in parking lots, clogging the ice-dammed gutters. Mrs. Saint James was apparently well again. I saw her driving the Coup de Ville one day, wearing a pair of gaudy sunglasses that Darcy brought back from Miami. I didn't tell Darcy about Todd's enlistment right away. I don't know why, but I just couldn't bear to see her reaction. Neumann was still in the hospital, his trial slated for sometime in August. We visited him there, Darcy and I, where we were happy to learn that Carter Mason had also been arrested at Christmas. Not usually good news, but considering that he'd been placed in rehab, it was as close to providential as things get.

Darcy's birthday was coming up, and I planned on painting a portrait of her as a present, something very colorful—not quite Van Gogh, but maybe a little Renoir. I spent every art class and study hall working on it, struggling with it, and the work progressed slowly. I had my own personal corner of the room, a spot staked out by the window. None of my classmates dared use the easel where I hung my filthy smock—"the coat of many colors" they called it, all tacky with varnish and layers of paint. Dewey complained that I grunted while I painted, or hummed with my tongue sticking out. "An artist in love with his work," he joked. "Get yourself a room."

Darcy and I still climbed the smoker's path every day at lunch, perched on the log when weather permitted. I read her whatever book I was reading: John Knowles, Richard Farina, or a skinny little volume by John Muir, a crazy old guy with a really cool beard who had climbed a huge volcano.

Together we went over my applications to art schools: Parsons, Cooper Union, the School of Visual Arts, and Darcy read me articles from her dad's *New York Times*, swiped from the lawn every morning. Mohammed Ali had refused the draft and was likely headed to prison, dozens of US soldiers sought political asylum in Sweden, the government "cracked down" on LSD, and Zonker was headed to college. Charlie Brown sought counseling from Lucy.

I didn't see much of Todd after New Year's. I saw Mary Ann in Hash's driving class, and Railsbeck too, unfortunately. He told us Antoine Jones was in Vietnam, seeming to gloat about it, as if he'd gotten one over on the guy who'd broken his wrist. "Maybe you'll end up over there," I told him. "You could hump Antoine's gear for him." Mary Ann was sitting beside me, and she actually gave me the elbow. "That's not even funny," she said, and she was right.

At the end of January—the Vietnamese New Year—NVA troops attacked Da Nang, Hue, Saigon, everywhere. Dead and dying US soldiers were all over TV news. Five thousand marines were surrounded by twenty-thousand VC in Khe Sanh, where fifty-six Americans were lost in a single day. Bobby Kennedy declared the war unwinnable, saying that half a million US troops, plus over a million South Vietnamese, were unable to stop an enemy less than seventy-thousand strong.

The Tet Offensive went on for weeks, and there were anti-war demonstrations all over the world, in Paris, Buenos Aires, West Berlin, as well as universities across the US. College kids burned draft cards and went on hunger strikes when graduate student deferments were abolished and the draft accelerated. Just before

Valentine's Day there was a photo in the *Times* of a Vietnamese general executing a VC suspect, firing a pistol point blank in his temple. I cut the picture from the paper and tacked it on the wall of my room, next to the photo of my dad and his buddies, but opposite Darcy in her lemon-yellow bikini.

The first day of spring was Darcy's birthday, and my portrait of her wasn't finished. Or maybe it was and I just wasn't ready to give it to her yet, never quite satisfied, always finding a reason to change things. "Leave it alone," said Dewey, "the school can't afford you," referring to the many tubes of oil paint I'd gone through. So, when the day arrived, I got her a book, *The Little Prince*, figuring I'd save the painting for a rainy day, making a date to meet up at the train station, in the boiler room where I would read it to her. Turned out it was a rainy day, and when she got there, she was dripping wet, her hair plastered flat to her head, her blue raincoat soaked nearly black.

"What I really want for my birthday is the Yankee cap," she sniffled, shaking her coat, water droplets fizzling on the boiler. "It's my turn, anyway. Has been for a while."

"You okay?"

"Oh, sure," she said, squeezing into the green chair beside me. "I'm just cranky. I have a cowd, is all."

Reaching behind us, I grabbed her present, giftwrapped in a section of the *Times*. I'd already lit the candles on the table, arranged in the shape of a cake. "Happy Birthday, Dar," I said, handing her the book.

Ripping at the newsprint, she squealed to see *The Little Prince*. "You remembered!" she said.

"You bet. An elephant never forgets."

The book, which I'd flipped through, begins with a little boy's drawing of an elephant, an elephant *inside* a snake. When she held the book open to that page, I said, "Funny looking hat," and smiled. In the story, all grownups see the drawing as a hat. They never see the snake, or the elephant inside it.

"You read it?" she asked.

"A little. I was saving it for you."

She snuggled in against me as I read, the light of the candles wavering on the page, on her cheek and my arm as we studied the childish drawings of sheep, planets, and baobab trees. The story goes that a little boy, an apparently frustrated artist, older than six but of indeterminate age, crashes his airplane in the desert, whereupon a little prince appears out of nowhere and requests that he draw a picture of a sheep. It gets crazier from there, the Little Prince describing his home planet which is quote, "scarcely any larger than a house." He's kind of the caretaker of the planet, which has three knee-high volcanoes—one dormant, two active, upon which he cooks breakfast—a few sheep, a penchant for sprouting baobab trees, and one very beautiful, very thorny red rose with whom the prince is in love.

It was pretty funny, but deep, as they say, and I kept stopping to laugh and re-read certain parts, like when the Little Prince visits another tiny planet where he becomes the only subject of a lonely king, who forbids the young boy to yawn. The Prince says, about his yawning, "But I can't help it. I've come on a long journey and I'm tired." Whereupon the king says, "Ah, then, I order you to yawn!"

Whereupon Darcy yawned, my mellifluous voice narcotic in effect.

That's when I told her about Todd, figuring she'd be too sleepy, or too sick to respond. But I was wrong, and she got upset, wanting me to call Todd immediately and talk him out of it. "You can't let him do it!" she insisted. "He's your best friend!"

"What do you want me to do?" I complained. "I already had a fight with him!"

"Don't get angry at me," she sniffled. "Everyone's mad. Everyone's punching."

"Who's punching? We didn't hit each other."

I tried to kiss her, but she wouldn't let me. "Who's punching?" I repeated.

"Why didn't you tell me?" she asked.

"Because I knew you'd do *this!*"

The sound of her breathing was ragged and slow in the confines of the musty room. We opted for silence, as we often did lately, her forehead sticky against my cheek. The candles sputtered and the rain poured down, pelting the black-painted window.

"I saw your work," I finally said. "Dewey showed me your portfolio, and it was great. Your work is fucking *fantastic!* Why did you tell me you weren't any good?"

"I told you that? When?"

"On the bus. On the way to the Met."

"Maybe I wasn't good then. Not that I am now!"

"But you are," I insisted. "In fact, you're better than me."

"Don't say that! Was Van Gogh better than Gauguin? Picasso better than Braque?"

"I've wanted to tell you for a really long time. That's why I gave you the book."

"*The Little Prince?*"

"No, *Dynamic Anatomy*. It's written by the president of SVA, and you're even better than him. You lied to me, and I don't know why. You won't even tell me who's punching."

"No one is punching. And I didn't lie. Art is in the eye of the beholder."

"I believe the term is *beauty*, Dar, and you won't even admit to that."

"If everyone's an artist, like Dewey says, then I'm one too. There, are you happy now?"

I wasn't happy and told her so. "When am I gonna meet your dad? It's crazy I've never met him."

"Please don't start with the crazy again. And no one is punching, I told you that. Why can't you just believe me?"

Because the whole story was driving *me* crazy, the questions, the kōans and little white lies piling up to the height of a mountain, unscalable, undefinable, lost in the mist of the mysteries swirling around it.

Sighing, exasperated, I leaned back in the chair and stared up at the cobwebby ceiling. "It's your birthday, Dar. I'm just trying to give you a gift you already have. It's not mine to offer, only yours to accept. Just take it, and then I'll be happy."

Releasing a sob, she closed her eyes as tears rolled down her cheeks. Leaning to kiss me, her skin was red hot, a damp sheen waxing her lip. She said, "Thank you so much for the wonderful gift, and for loving a nut case like me."

In less than a minute she'd fallen asleep, her hand at the neck of my shirt. I sat there absorbing the heat of her body, listening to the rain drumming down, gurgling through the gutters as the boiler kicked on, its orange glow painting the rocks.

At the end of *The Little Prince*, on the last page, there's a childlike drawing of a single star shining above the desert. Readers are instructed to study the picture, to commit it to memory in case they stumble on that place in their travels, in their dreams, whereupon they'd be advised, in the words of the diminutive artist himself, to "wait for a time exactly under that star. If a little man appears who laughs, who has golden hair, and who refuses to answer questions, you will know who he is."

I already knew who he was, or who *she* was, as I waited impatiently, for what seemed like forever, beneath that lonely star.

Chapter 19

M y interview at SVA was on the last day of March. Darcy had promised to go with me, but the day before she was still sick, and begged off, apologizing profusely, though not convincingly. Jonah Gold volunteered to go instead, and I was glad for the company, feeling a little nervous, happy to have someone to talk to on the train.

Jonah's oldest brother, Seth, was traveling through Europe, smoking hashish, touring museums, and getting the clap. The anti-war sentiment was strong over there, and being an American was both a curse and a form of celebrity. It really helped him get chicks, he'd confided to Jonah, and apparently VD as well.

We talked about music: Dylan, Buffy Saint Marie, and Lou Reed and the Velvet Underground and Nico—the album with the big yellow banana on the cover. Jonah thought Nico was hot, and he figured Andy Warhol was actually a woman—"Kinda like George Elliot, you know?" He told me how he and Silas had gone to see the Mothers of Invention at the Bleeker Street Theater. They'd tried to smoke bananas before the show and had actually baked one in a pie tin, but it turned all black and mushy and they left it under a seat on the subway. "We even stuck a fork in it, man. Whoever found it must have puked!"

SVA was on East 23rd Street between avenues A and B. We took the IRT downtown, Jonah searching the train for the aforementioned pie tin. We switched off carrying my portfolio, which was a big help because it was so heavy. Jonah pawed through it as the stops rattled by, craning his neck this way and that, struggling to see in the flickering light. "Far out. Outta sight. Cool," he said, fingering each sheaf of paper, each cardboard-backed canvas. Jonah had applied to NYU, Lehmann College in the Bronx. He liked art, he told me, but figured he sucked at it, and decided to major in economics. "Jews are doomed to make money," he said. "It's kind of in our genes."

The school looked like a big warehouse, flat-faced, anonymous, sandwiched between other anonymous buildings just like it. Admissions was on the second floor, and Jonah waited in the student lounge, an industrial-looking cafeteria painted in midnight blue with silver stars taped to the ceiling. In the office, a woman whose name I immediately forgot sat me down in a chair facing hers and ignored me for several minutes while she perused my portfolio. She didn't say "Cool" or "Far out," but neither did she cringe, so I wasn't too uncomfortable waiting. She smiled when she was done and crossed her shapely legs, leaving my folder propped against her chair. There was no desk between us, and her bobbing ankle drew my eye until finally she spoke, saying, "So tell me, Thomas, why do you want to go to SVA?"

I almost said "I don't know," a response akin to "I guess," but instead I blurted—"I'm a fiend for art. I just ... love it."

She smiled again, her foot still bobbing, waiting for me to elaborate. When I didn't, she said, "Well, you're in luck, Tom. We have a preference for fiends."

"Teal," I said. "My friends call me Teal."

Suddenly friends, I was more at ease to explain that I'd heard the instructors at SVA were not teachers, but professional artists, and how I wanted to learn from those who *did*, as opposed to those who merely taught, or some variation on that cliché.

"What is it about art that you love?" she asked.

"I don't know," I said, no longer conflicted about saying so, because as I explained, "Who knows what art is? My teacher, Mr. Arstahl, said Tolstoy described it as the intent to exalt in humanity. That sounds cool to me, I can *feel* that. But art's always changing, right? People, artists, are always defining what art is. That's modern art, isn't it, always pushing the boundary, the definition, expanding it to include more things, more life, until maybe we're all artists, and everything we do is art, like Dewey says."

"Dewey Tolstoy?" said Ms. Weld, whose name I just then remembered.

"Yeah, the chubby gay Bolshevik," I laughed, shocking myself.

"Was Tolstoy gay, do you think?"

"No." I said, backpedaling. "My girlfriend thinks he is. Dewey, not Leo."

Ms. Weld smiled, seeming to enjoy my discomfort. "Would it make a difference if he was?"

"Of course not. He was a pacifist before Martin Luther King. Before Gandhi, and Thoreau. He wrote a book, *the* book on non-violent civil disobedience. You probably knew that, but I just found out."

Ms. Weld re-crossed her legs, her right foot bobbing now, her high heel falling to the carpet. I watched it drop, reminded of Darcy, and said, "She just *thinks* he's gay. Mr. Arstahl, I mean. She said girls can just tell. But as long as people love each other, who cares, right? Cause it's all about love, Jesus says. And the Beatles," I added, grinning absurdly. "And art, the thing about humanity, that's love too. The intent to love. And you know, really, that's what I love about Darcy."

Walking out of her office, thinking about what I'd just said, I figured that even if Ms. Weld thought I was crazy, I didn't care. Because something about it made sense to me, maybe for the first time, and I began to feel a little like a real artist, and not just because of my filthy smock.

A minute later I was back in the lounge, collapsing on a plastic chair, letting my heavy portfolio slam to the floor. Jonah didn't even look up, so engrossed was he in the copy of the *Village Voice* spread out before him. "So," I said, "I think that went well."

Jonah raised a hand, impatiently waving me off. "What's up with you?" I asked. "Are there naked pictures in there?"

"Check it out," he said, and shoved the paper toward me across the table. The photo on the front page was of a young Vietnamese girl running naked toward the camera, her burned arms lofted like wings in the air, her mouth opened wide in a scream. She was Edvard Munch wrought in the flesh, scorched as it was, the road behind her strewn with bodies; her village, her home, an aurora of flame.

Jonah related the text of the story, how Madame Binh, a representative of the National Liberation Front at the Paris Peace Talks, had accused the American Division of the 23rd Infantry, fighting in the vicinity of Son My, in the hamlet of My Lai, of slaughtering five-hundred unarmed civilians—men, women and children—shooting them, burning them, blowing them up. Some soldiers, though not enough, had refused to participate, and women had been raped and sodomized, food and water poisoned, and the entire hamlet raised. At divisional headquarters, deputy operations officer Major Colin Powell dismissed the accusations as unfounded.

"How could anyone do that?" Jonah asked. "I just can't imagine."

But you had to try, I thought. You had to try to imagine what happened to those soldiers—kids not much older than Jonah and me—that allowed them to do such terrible things, made them susceptible, rendered them capable, depleted their souls enough to commit those acts. *Could that happen to Todd?* I wondered. *Would that happen to me if I found myself in that situation, if I had seen what they'd seen, and felt what they'd felt?* I didn't think so. Not every soldier had joined in. But how could anyone know for sure unless they had actually been there?

The ride home on the train wasn't as sunny as the trip down. Jonah told me that Silas had another year of college before graduate school, and if the war was still happening, he intended to escape to Canada, where an elaborate network existed to help draft resisters. "I guess you heard Bosco's brother is in Nam," he said. "One out of four guys over there is Black. No wonder Ali chose jail. I wouldn't go to Canada, though, I'd go to San Francisco, to Haight-Ashbury. I heard you were going this summer."

"I'm not going anywhere."

"Why not? You got all that money."

"All that money? I have five hundred bucks."

"So, what are you saving it for?"

"I don't know. What do *you* save money for?"

"I don't. We're rich—to the manor born, literally. You should go, man," he said. "Face it, Conover, you're a hippie."

"I'm an artist."

"Same fuckin' thing. Hippies, beatniks, revolutionaries …. The pump don't work cause the vandals took the handle!"

Chapter 20

"TODD," I SAID, "I KNOW YOU DON'T like to talk about this, but please, just listen a minute." We were in gym class, up at the football field, jogging on the track that ran around it.

"Talk," he said, not even breathing hard. "I'll listen, long as you can keep up."

"No," I said, grabbing his wrist. "Just stop a minute, let's walk."

So we did, our skanky sweatshirts soaked with sweat, haloed darker around our necks and under our armpits. It was a blustery afternoon, the clouds as gray and stained as our clothes, trees near the bleachers bending in the wind, their branches divested of leaves. In seconds I was shivering.

"Did you see the news last night?" I asked. "Cronkite says we're not winning the war."

"We ain't losing it either."

"We can't win, is the point."

"Says who?"

"Says Cronkite, and Kennedy. Says everybody who's not in the army, or the Johnson Administration. And even some of them."

"So, what's your point? I shouldn't go, right?"

"Yes! What's the point of going now?"

Todd sighed, his cropped hair wet, his handsome face splotched red. "My dad was in the army," he reminded me.

"I know. So was mine."

"My dad *died* in the army, in Korea."

"What does that mean? That you have to die too?"

"Who says I'm dying, Walter Cronkite? Look, it's just something I feel, like you feel you're against it. I'm not *for* it, you know. I'm not for war. But there is a war, *our* war, and I feel I should serve my country—"

"It's not *our* war! I don't want it. You're serving a bunch of politicians! They don't give a fuck if you die over there."

"But I do! I give a fuck that my father died. Did he die for nothing? Is that what you're saying?"

"No, I—"

"Then don't say that. Don't tell me I shouldn't go, that I'm ignorant, that I don't understand. Because I do, okay? I just don't analyze every fucking thing like you do."

My teeth were chattering, sweat chilling my body, the wind whipping cold at my legs. "Did you hear the stuff about My Lai?"

"Oh Jesus," he said, "don't start that shit. It's just a rumor, propaganda. And even if it's true, it's only a few guys. That's war, that's what happens sometimes."

"How do you know what happens?"

"How do *you* know?"

"I don't, but at least I don't pretend to. You think any of those guys knew they'd be bashing babies' heads in, burning people alive—"

"C'mon, man—"

"What, am I making this up? That stuff doesn't happen? What if it's not what you think? What if it's like nothing you ever dreamed, could never imagine, and you come back changed?"

"*That's* gonna happen anyway. And that's what you can't deal with."

"Don't turn this back on me. When we went to the Pentagon— and don't fucking run away, just stand there and listen—When we went to the Pentagon, there were soldiers there, veterans, guys who went to Vietnam and made it back, some of them in pieces. Those are the guys you should talk to, Todd. Those are the guys who *really* know. Don't listen to me if you think I'm so wrong—"

"I don't think that."

"Listen to *them*, Todd. Listen to Carter Mason, not fucking LBJ."

"I can't get out of this, okay?" he said. "I'm going, and that's that."

"What about Mary Ann? You're just gonna leave her?"

"I can't take her with me." Todd grinned.

"That's not funny," I said, remembering her saying the same thing in Hash's car. "What if you never see her again?"

"Then you can see her for me. That shouldn't be too hard for you."

"What's that supposed to mean?"

"Fuck you, Teal," he said, and sprinted away.

Chapter 21

THE NEXT DAY THEY KILLED Martin Luther King, shot him on a hotel balcony somewhere down south. They said it was a white guy acting alone—they saw him with the murder weapon. But lots of people didn't believe it any more than they'd believed a weeping Walter Cronkite when he'd announced that President Kennedy was dead, that police had surrounded a single gunman in a Dallas movie theater. Bobby Kennedy preempted a campaign speech to announce to a crowd of black supporters that their greatest hope had been shattered, expressing his heart-felt commiseration for their loss, asking that they assuage their pain with prayer, instead of violence.

But there were riots all over the country, in one hundred and twenty cities, according to the Times. They showed it all on television: New York, Detroit, Chicago in flames, Mayor Daley ordering his police to shoot to kill. "Now that they've offed Dr. King," said an angry Stokely Carmichael, "it's time to end this non-violence bullshit!"

Darcy missed a week of school with her sinus infection. She called me every night and we talked for an hour, her voice croaky, her vowels rounded. Her mom was taking good care of her, she said, and it was kind of fun, both of them enjoying the fuss, like in the old days. "I miss my mom," she told me.

"How?" I asked. "You live in the same house."

That week in history class we were studying about Marco Polo and the opening of the trade routes to China, when Dionne Hayes raised her hand and asked old Humpty why we weren't discussing our own country, why we didn't talk about the riots in DC and Los Angeles, or in Harlem, less than twenty miles away. Humpty said that history, by definition, concerned itself with the past, not the present, which prompted big ol' Bosco Jones to stand and say that history wasn't squat without the present. "Before don't matter except for now," he said. "Otherwise, who gives a shit about yesterday?"

I saw Todd later that day in the hall and we spoke for a minute, but I didn't tell him about what Bosco and Dionne had said. We were still kind of touchy after our talk on the football field, and I didn't want to get into politics. But to me it was all the same—the riots, the assassinations, the counterculture, the war. I didn't know if Todd looked at it that way, all lumped together, or whether he thought about it at all, analyzing things, like he said I always did. All I knew was that it felt like I was losing my oldest friend, and there was nothing I could do about it.

Later that night, I was almost asleep when the phone rang. I figured it was Darcy, but it was Todd, inviting me to drink some beers on the occasion of his father's birthday, the following weekend at George's Tavern.

"Cool," I said, "but *my* birthday's not for another month," meaning that I was still underage.

"No prob," he said, "not at Georges."

I was staring at a print of Picasso's *Guernica* on my wall, a tiny copy of the huge monochrome canvas that hung at the Museum of Modern Art, depicting the carnage of the Spanish Civil War. I'd promised Darcy I'd take her to see it that same Saturday, but I didn't think she'd mind if I canceled for something as important as this, and that's what I told her when Todd hung up and the telephone rang again.

"I'm glad for you guys," she said.

"You wanna come?"

"No, this sounds like a guy thing."

"A manly thing."

"A macho thing."

"Nah, it's not like that," I told her. "Me and Todd grew up together. It's more about people than men."

I arrived at George's early that night and sat outside on the stacked stone wall. Across 9A, at the Restoration, the mercury vapor lamps lit the weeping willows a garish pink, their yellow branches orange, nearly florescent in their brightness. It was barely seven, and George and a couple of old guys were the only people inside, flanking both sides of the bar, the juke box playing an old Frankie Vallee song about carrying your girlfriend's books from school, which I suppose I'd actually done for Darcy.

It got cold on the wall, so I went inside and sat at a table by the window, next to the juke box, which went blissfully silent after one last song about peanut butter. George glanced over and held up a finger, which prompted me to nod, which prompted him to tilt a schooner beneath the tap and expertly pour a nearly headless beer, which he delivered to my table. He waddled more than walked, his belt buckle lost beneath his huge belly, his round face like custard, stubbled gray, a cigar poking out where his mouth might have been.

I threw a dollar on the table and George made a face, which I interpreted as a smile, and he said, "I'll run ya a tab," then waddled back to his place behind the bar. I sipped at the beer, wanting to conserve my coherence for Todd, but fifteen minutes later he had yet to arrive and my sips got bigger, and then the glass was empty and George appeared with another, so quiet in his slippers he was hustling away again before I even noticed. More patrons arrived, singles sitting at the bar, groups settling at tables, their winter coats draped on the backs of their chairs. I was beginning to feel guilty sitting alone at my large table while couples looked for a place to sit, when a half dozen jocks in Ossining letter jackets strutted in and brazenly eyeballed the scene. The hunky one, the obvious leader, the quarterback or something, looked right at me and smiled. The rest of them just glared, foregoing all pretense, and then I was standing, sliding my chair back and gesturing. "Have a seat," I said, "I was just leaving."

"Nah, nah," said the QB, pulling up a chair across from me. "Finish your beer, we'll join ya. You mind?"

"Knock yourself out," I said, still standing, until the tight end squeezed my shoulder and we all sat down. "Where's the chicks?" the QB asked.

"Yeah, where's all the chicks?" echoed the stubby one with Elvis sideburns.

"Who do I answer?" I asked.

"Anyone you want," said the leader. "It's a free country."

"Yeah, free fucking country," the parrot repeated.

It was clear what I was in for. There was no sense trying to talk my way out of it. "If you're looking for chicks," I confided, leaning across the table, "I hear they fuck like rabbits up in Ossining."

"Right on!" said the QB, staying the arm of a less suave compatriot. "I hear that, bro! You're kinda cute yourself with that long hair an' all. I bet you swing both ways."

I glanced at the clock, Todd half an hour late. Then I remembered that the bar clock was ten minutes fast, that the cavalry might still arrive, about to ride in like John fucking Wayne at the Alamo.

"No swinging involved," I explained, "fucker sticks out like a javelin. Last quarterback poked his damn eye out."

Even the QB flinched, and all the cynical grins disappeared.

"Listen," I said, "I gotta go. Big date with your coach. But here," I added, and pushed my full schooner across the table, "have a beer on me."

"Fuck you, hippie!" the quarterback snarled, a thread of white spittle on his lip.

"Okay then, on you," I said, and toppled the glass with the tip of my finger, spilling its contents across the table to cascade into his lap.

It was all pretty crazy after that, and later I couldn't say who hit me first, but I do remember who kicked me last, because all of sudden Elvis had blood all over him, and it wasn't mine. At first I figured it was Todd, quo vadis himself, come to save my bacon, but it was some bald guy—buzz-cut anyway—who went through those Ossining Indians like butter, like margarine, smashing them with every chair and coat tree in the bar until they all ran away but the King and the quarterback, prostrate on the beer-soaked floor.

I hadn't even landed a punch, and then Deloit Mason was propping me on a stool, smearing even more blood on my face in an effort to clean me up. George washed a dish towel under the tap and tossed it across the bar toward what remained of my table. It reeked of stale beer and a hint of bleach, but eventually I began to recognize myself in the mirror behind the bar. "Hey," said George, speaking to Deloit. "you want I should call the police?"

"Fuck no. No cops."

"Deloit, man," I gurgled, my mouth full of blood, "where the hell did you come from?"

"I seen what was happening," he said. "It don't take no genius to figure out."

"But why? Why'd you help me? After that shit at the beach."

"Fuck all that," he said, "don't mean nothin'. Sure, you're an asshole, but you're my asshole, from the Avenue, man. Them dicks don't fuck with us."

"Thanks," was all I could say.

"Don't mention it. In fact, don't say fuckin' nothin'."

But I did, of course, still feeling a bit cocky. "You're in the army, huh? That where you got the haircut?"

He was still scrubbing my face, blood oozing from my nose, my eyes beginning to swell. "Yo, Einstein," he said, "just shut the fuck up."

"Why?" I asked, "after your brother, an' all? Why would you sign up for that?"

He tossed the bar rag on the floor where it landed with a splat. "I shoulda just left your ass to die, you dumb bastard," he said. "Maybe I should kill you myself."

"It didn't even hurt," I said. "Even when they kicked me in the face."

"That don't last," Deloit assured me. "Another hour, you'll be in agony."

Then George was looming over me, a clean rag in his hand. "You're Teal, right? Teal Conover?" He tossed the rag in my lap. "Telephone," he said.

"Hello?" I was leaning against the wall by the Men's room, supported by the ice machine.

"Teal," said Todd, "look, buddy—"

"Whatever it is, don't worry about it. Me and Deloit got it handled."

"It's Darcy," he said. "We got a problem. You gotta get over here."

"Where? What are you talking about?"

"We're at Mary Ann's. Darcy took something, man. She keeps asking for you."

Deloit was gone when I looked around. I stumbled outside, then into the road where I jumped in front of the first orange Mustang I saw. "Are you fuckin' crazy?" he shouted. "You actually *trying* to die?"

"Hey, Deloit," I said, "do me a favor?"

He dropped me off in front of Mary Ann's house, lights burning in the basement, in the whoopee room where we used to play Wiffle basketball, throw darts when we were kids.

"Holy shit!" Todd said when he saw me. "What the fuck happened to you? Did Deloit do this?"

"Hell no," I said. "Deloit was my savior. He went bananas on those guys."

"What guys?"

"Ossining guys. A bunch of fucking jocks. Where is she? Where's Darcy?"

She was curled on the sofa in a crocheted afghan, a lifeless lump beneath zig-zagged designs. Mary Ann was sitting with her, perched on the edge of a cushion. "She's better now," she said, "calmed down a bit."

"From what? What's going on?"

"I don't know, man." said Todd. "I was driving to George's when I saw her staggering down the street, I mean literally staggering. I whipped over and grabbed her, and she freaked fucking out, yelling and screaming, beating on me like crazy. Do I have a shiner?"

"Couldn't tell you, dude," I sneered. "I can't see through my black fucking eyes."

Mary Ann rose when I knelt by the couch, Darcy balled up like a fetus. I touched her, and she yelped. "Dar," I whispered, "are you alright? Did Neumann give you some acid?"

She was moaning, trembling, breathing in spurts, her puffy eyes squeezed into slits. Pulling me to her, she hugged me tight and buried us both in the afghan. My nose was so swollen I couldn't breathe and had to come up for air. When she opened her eyes, she let out a scream, "Look at your beautiful face!"

Cooing, caressing, she kissed my cheeks as if I was a child with a boo-boo, a kid with a bruise or a skinned-up knee soothed by her healing lips. "Shh," she kept saying, as if I was crying, and I realized then that I was.

"Darcy, tell me what happened."

"Mom," she cried, and said it again, repeating it over and over.

"Did he hurt her?" I asked. "Did he hurt you? Are you tripping on something, or not?"

She wouldn't say more, so I just let her cry as I breathed through a crust of dried blood. Minutes went by as her panting subsided and the tension drained from her limbs. When I heard a soft sigh and her arms slipped from mine, I knew she had fallen asleep.

Easing up slowly, I crossed the room to where Mouse sat cross-legged in an armchair, the Wiffleball hoop mounted on the wall above her head. I stood there a minute, incapable of speech, until she tossed me the old foam basketball and I chucked it at the rim. "Swish," I said as the orb passed through, dropping soundlessly into her lap.

Mary Ann rose and touched my face. "You look horrible," she said. "Does it hurt?"

"Only when I breathe. Where's Todd?"

"Out there," she said, pointing at the back door.

Todd stood leaning against a post with his head craned up at the stars. Puffing away at a fat cigar, he pulled another from his pocket and poked it in my swollen lips, hoisted his warm can of Schlitz toward heaven and said ,"Happy Birthday, Pop."

"Happy Birthday," I echoed and then tore off the stogie's cellophane wrapper, careful to not rip the paper cigar band. Slipping it onto my finger like a ring, I glanced at Todd's hand and saw that he'd done the same, sliding it on his pinkie instead, his hands way bigger than mine.

"What do you figure she took?" he asked.

"I don't know if she took anything."

He regarded me coolly, a smirk on his face. "Look, man, I told you how I found her. She was totally freaked out, barely walking."

"That doesn't mean she's on something. She might just be … fucked up, you know?"

"No, I don't know. Nobody's that fucked up over nothing."

"It isn't *nothing*, Todd! She doesn't have to be *bleeding* to hurt!"

"Okay, okay. But she needs help, a doctor, the ER, or more drugs! Even if it's only in her head, get off your ass and *do* something!"

I told him I would, because Todd was right, like he almost always was. But it didn't happen that night, because in less than an hour I could barely move, my ribs aching, my eyes swollen shut, my cheeks and lips merging in a brittle, fleshy mound.

Back in the house, Mary Ann said, "You and Darcy can stay here tonight. My dad almost never comes down here. I'll get you some pillows."

"I'm leaving," said Todd, when she went upstairs.

"Sorry about tonight."

"That's cool. I shouldn't have said that shit."

"I mean about your dad, drinking some beers and stuff."

"Another night."

"Cool, though I doubt George will have me back."

"Sure he will. It's great for business."

Todd smiled, clapped my shoulder, which hurt like hell. "Sorry," he said, wincing along with me. "Take good care of our girlfriends."

Chapter 22

Mom freaked out when she saw me, but she didn't cry. I didn't really think she would, having seen much worse in the ER. The swelling went down in a couple of days, but my face was badly bruised, the whites of both eyes turned completely red with tiny, broken blood vessels. It was weird to look at myself in the mirror, like seeing a whole other person, and for once I was glad I didn't shave. I saw Deloit at the Corner Store one morning and he barely nodded, though I'm sure he recognized me, the only blue-faced, red-eyed kid on Beekman Avenue. He'd told Ollie he was home from Parris Island for a couple of weeks and then was headed for Viet Nam, places like the A Shau, and Khe Sanh. He was a marine, like my dad.

Darcy explained what had happened that night, though it sounded kind of fishy, blurting out first thing that morning that she'd taken a handful of her father's meds and chased it with some wine. I figured it had something to do with him, but it was pointless to ask her more. One day in the library I asked Mrs. Brooks for the old high school yearbooks from the forties, after the war, when Lena Saint James had attended. The books were all cardboard and flimsy back then, the photos in black and white, the nicknames beneath the pictures—*Skitch, Pickles, Rollo*—sounding corny and old fashioned. The football team wore weird leather helmets, the cheerleaders in skirts to their ankles. But the banner they waved looked much the same—an Ossining Indian being scalped by the Headless Horseman.

I picked out Lena without reading her name, staring out from the center of a page where all the guys had crew cuts. Raven haired and ivory pale, she looked nothing at all like Darcy, but was just as beautiful in her way, a mysterious smile, perfect teeth, her dark eyes emboldened by jet black eyebrows slanting across her forehead. Someone had drawn a halo above her head, explained in part by her nickname beneath: *The Saint.* But nothing could account for the impression she gave of a child staring out through a mask, standing on tip toe to peek through its eye holes behind which another girl lurked. Her *likes* were "cute boys", her *dislikes* "old men", her *ambition* one word: "escape".

Never married and living alone, she'd be easy to find, I guessed. Calling Information from the phone in my room, I listened to a long list of Saint Jameses in the Miami area. There were no Lenas, but I narrowed it down to a dozen L's and jotted their numbers in my binder. If anyone could explain what was going on I felt it would be her, the mysterious Saint, the abductor of young girls. But as one by one my calls came to nothing, my resolve and enthusiasm faded and I wondered if maybe it was wrong to pry into Darcy's life, as well as her oldest sister's. On the next to last call, on the fifth or sixth ring, a woman picked up and spoke breathlessly into the phone, as if she had run a long distance. "Hello?" she panted. "Hello?"

Suddenly *live*, I was slow to respond, and a pensive silence ensued, the rhythm of her breathing subsiding at length in the long-distance tunnel of the phone line. I was about to answer when she spoke again, a little girl's lilt to her voice. "Darcy?" she whispered, then said it again, the word filled with tender compassion, "I'm so, so sorry, honey, but you just had to know. It cannot go on like this!

I wanted to tell you in person, in Miami, but I waited too long, and you ran. She loves you so much, and God knows you love her …. We can't let him take that away. Darcy?" she repeated, when I still hadn't spoken, and I let the phone drop from my hand, the sound of her voice far away on my pillow where it lay until the dial tone buzzed.

Whatever I thought I would learn from Lena only deepened the mystery, and I felt like a burglar breaking into their lives, replete in dark clothes and black mask. The next time I saw Darcy I didn't mention the call, pretending to accept that she'd just taken drugs that night in Mary Ann's basement.

Neumann was finally released from the hospital, freed on bond until August. He looked terrible, worse than me, the pneumonia having taken its toll. But he still had plenty of drugs for sale and I warned him to be careful, that the cops were probably watching, but he just laughed. Steve Railsbeck turned eighteen and received his draft notice. He wasn't headed for college, and he sure wasn't gonna enlist, so he bragged how he'd do something crazy down at Whitehall Street, something really wild so they'd classify him 4F. Mary Ann just shook her head, saying, "The draft board will see right through you, Steve. You're just the kind of crazy they want."

My birthday, May thirteenth, fell on a Saturday that year. It was also our anniversary, Darcy's and mine, and so we decided to go to the city and relive our past, brief as it was. Waiting for the train at the Manor station, the weather was sunny and warm, much like the previous year, with trees budding everywhere and commuters wearing sports jackets, their winter coats mothballed for the season. A month had passed since I'd gotten my ass kicked, but I still drew quite a few stares. The bruising on my face had receded to just the rims of my eyes and I looked like a Pharaoh, except that the whites were blood red. I could have been cast in a

Fellini flick, some kind of Egyptian transvestite.

Darcy was carrying my birthday present when she arrived. It was wrapped in real wrapping paper, sky blue with red balloons, and she insisted I open it right away. It was a shirt, a really nice dress shirt with a button-down collar and slots instead of buttons on the cuffs. "I'll buy you cufflinks later," she smiled, "or maybe I'll steal some from Dewey."

White with a piping of fine blue pinstripes, the shirt was reminiscent of a Yankees jersey, and she made me put it on right away. Pretending to read their *Wall Street Journals*, a dozen weekend commuters watched as Darcy peeled my blue sweater over my head, pulled the tissue and cardboard from the shirt and snapped it open on the breeze.

I stood like a scarecrow with my arms held out, Darcy jabbering through a mouthful of pins, tugging and tucking, fumbling with eyelets until she'd buttoned the shirt to my chin. It was way too big for me, and not just because of the cuffs. The tails draped down to the tops of my knees, the shoulders drooping to my biceps. But it felt so new with its crisp, starched collar, I decided I loved it, and gave her a big hug.

All the way down on the Local train, seated on the river side, Darcy rested her head on my shoulder as the conductor called out the stops—"Irv-ington! Dobbs Fer-ray! Yonkahs! Spy-ten-dyval!" When we reached the East River the conductor called "University Heights!" and Darcy jumped up from her seat.

"C'mon," she said, grabbing my hand, "we're getting off here!"

It finally made sense, the shirt, the date—we'd arrived at Yankee Stadium.

"Are they even playing today?" I asked, as we ascended the stairs to street level. It was the beginning of the season and with all that was happening in my life I hadn't been following the Yankees, not like I had as a kid.

"I don't know. I don't *care!*" she sang, pulling me up the sidewalk.

The blocks around the stadium were packed with people, like a game had just ended, which it actually had, a guy in a silky Yankees jacket informing us that we'd just whipped the Tigers 10–2. Plowing through the crowd to the front of the stadium, we craned our necks at the huge blue "YANKEE STADIUM" sign. Fans still poured from the exits, the clean-up crew already pushing brooms, wheeling garbage bins amongst them. Catering trucks were backed to the service bays, loading or unloading food stuffs, and Darcy yanked my arm in that direction. "What are you doing?" I asked, "they're trying to close."

"Not yet they aren't, and the door's wide open."

Just like that we slipped inside, ignored by the workers loading hot dog buns, bags of peanuts, crates of Coca Cola. We ran up a stairwell and found ourselves in the wide, concrete corridors that led from ramp to ramp and floor to floor, die-hard fans still descending from the upper levels, whooping their joy at having witnessed a Yankee rout.

"Where are we going?" I asked.

"You tell me," said Darcy. "I've never been here before."

I followed wherever she wanted to go, always up, then around, then up again until we couldn't go any higher and walked out of a tunnel onto the top level above the first base line. Workers were scattered across the infield, raking the batter's box, the mound, even the on-deck circles. A noisy gang-mower trimmed the grass in center field where the old timer's monuments were enshrined like headstones. I pointed them out, and Darcy clapped her hands, her grin like the arches on the stadium rim.

"This is so cool!" she said, "I can't believe we're finally here! Happy Birthday, Teal!" she squealed, and gave me a juicy kiss.

We sat holding hands on the green-painted seats, Darcy's eyes darting at the flutter of pennants, at the squawking of seagulls where they perched in the lights. It was warm, muggy, and bittersweet as my thoughts drifted off through the stands, sweeping the aisles for those scenes from my past when I'd sat eating hot dogs with my dad—there by the dugout; way up in left field; directly behind home plate. I'd be pounding my mitt while he scratched out a score card, his profile embossed by the sun; he'd give me a wink and ruffle my hair when I pressed my cheek to his arm, the size of his knuckles, the bump of his nose as grand as the tumult around us.

Tethered to the present by Darcy's hand, I sensed her emotions like the nibble of a fish, in the tentative touch of her fingers.

"You're thinking about your father," she said.

"Sorry. I should be thinking of us."

"No," she soothed, "that's just what I wanted. It's like I can be there with you."

Slipping the Yankee cap off my head, I tucked it gently on hers. "Now you are," I said.

Darcy looked radiant, glowing with happiness, the girl from the Marc Chagall church. "If only we had hot dogs," she laughed. "Then it would be perfect!"

"Know what would make it really perfect?" I said, summoning the courage to finally do something, like I'd promised Todd in Mary Ann's basement. "If you told me about your father."

Down on the field a guy stepped on his rake, bonking himself on the forehead. It was classic Three Stooges, or Laurel and Hardy, but we both let it pass without comment.

"Please," I said when she closed her eyes and withdrew her hand from mine, her toes tapping madly on peanut shells, the wind making tinsel of her hair. Like waiting for the scratch on your favorite record, or counting the seconds after lightning, we sat in the stands without touching each other, our hands like small birds in our laps.

"When I turned six," she finally said, "they threw me a party at the Beach Club. I remember it clearly because Mom made cupcakes, pink, with a candle, and a frosted number 6."

Turning her eyes away as she spoke, addressing the empty stands, she adopted the tone of a Shakespearean actor standing alone on a stage, engaged in internal soliloquy.

"When the sun went down and my friends had left, it was time to change out of my swimsuit. Mom was asleep on the seashell blanket, so Daddy made me hold up a towel, a green and white striped one that smelled like coconuts from the bottle of suntan lotion. "Up high," he instructed, turning me around, hiding us from bathers down the beach. Kneeling before me, he peeled off my wet suit, letting it drop to my ankles.

"Brushing sand from my shoulders, from my elbows and arms, Daddy was humming to himself, rubbing my knees, then the cleft of my bottom, then the place between my legs. The lapping of waves made a hiss on the beach and air bubbles popped on the sand, and far away across the water a big boat moved without sound, white curls at its bow, green lines in its wake that faded away in the distance. "That's my little beauty," Daddy kept saying, over and over as I cried.

"When he was done, he pushed me aside and snatched up my black checkered swimsuit. Shaking it out, sand blew in my face and stuck to the tears on my cheeks. Wrapped in the towel I ran to my mom, who had passed out there on the blanket, and I stepped on her wineglass balanced in the sand, jamming the stem in my foot. I bled all over my parents' blanket, all over the pure white beach. I was crying, *crying*, and Mama wouldn't help me, her wine the red color of blood. Daddy looked on with a look of impatience, disgust on his sunburned face. He dumped melted ice from the Styrofoam cooler and tossed in the ball of my swim suit. Pinching a corner of the bloody striped towel, he carried it dripping to the car."

Darcy's lips continued to move even after she'd finished her story, recounting in silence whatever came next, if the tale ever truly ended. Looking for something to do with my hands, I was tempted to reach for hers, but she was so elsewhere, so far away, my arms couldn't equal the distance.

In the most painful way, Darcy answered my question with a much greater truth than I'd asked for. Riding home on the train, she drifted off with her silvery head on my shoulder, and I wondered at such moments if she was truly asleep or perhaps was just hiding somewhere, tending to the baobabs on her own tiny planet, watering her version of a flower. "I am not at all afraid of tigers!" the thorny rose said to the Prince. And the Prince had said of his own red beauty, "But I was too young to know how to love her."

And I was too young to know how to care.

Chapter 23

ON THE LAST DAY OF SCHOOL there was an assembly in the gym for seniors. They marched us through the movements of our graduation ceremony, practicing how we'd walk on stage to receive our diplomas, shake Hammer's hand, etc. After gym they took us to the cafeteria and served us Cokes while we waited to be fitted for caps and gowns. Senora Ibanez and Mr. King, the only black teacher at school (no relation), worked with the ladies from the rental store. It was just a half day, with no real work, hardly like a school day at all.

Darcy wasn't there, having gone home early, offering no excuse for her absence. It had been three weeks since Yankee Stadium and we'd settled into awkward acquiescence, never speaking of that day, especially her disturbing confession. Part of me wanted to ask her more, yet another part felt guilty, having trapped her in a moment when she couldn't say no, a victim of her own grand design. I carried her photo in the pocket of my shirt, posed on the beach in the yellow bikini. She was smiling in the picture, and I needed to see it, to remind me of what I was missing.

Gathered in the cafeteria with all my friends, everyone was in a pretty good mood, smiling, joking, laughing out loud; everyone except Steve Railsbeck.

He shuffled over and flopped down at our table, totally

uninvited. "I'm going to Whitehall for my physical today. When are you going?" he asked Todd.

"Been there, done that."

"Yeah, what's it like?"

"Same old. They squeeze your balls, you turn your head and cough. They ask you if you're crazy and you say no, or *yes*, in your case. Either way you sign the papers and then your ass is theirs."

"My dad's taking me down this afternoon, soon as we're out of here."

"Are you scared?" asked Dionne.

Railsbeck snarled, "What's it to you? You ain't going. You ain't even American."

Dionne blanched and turned away. Her oldest brother, Carlos, had been killed in Vietnam, one of the first advisers. Steve was such a jerk.

"So, what's your plan?" said Mary Ann. "You said you were going to do something crazy so the army wouldn't take you."

"My dad's gonna be there, aren't you fuckin' listening?"

Steve took such a huge swig of Coke that bubbles fizzed out of his nose. Slamming the bottle hard on the table, it foamed out over his hand. "Fuck!" he swore.

"You remember my brother," Bosco smiled. "Ol' Antoine, he was in Saigon when the gooks hit the embassy. You know, at Tet? He said all them sappers just blowed themselves up—*ka-boom!*—right in front of him. Them little fuckers ain't afraid to die, are you?"

Steve didn't answer, and so I asked, "How is Antoine?"

Bosco chuckled. "I ain't supposed to say nothin', but he's in jail, what they call the brig. He be comin' home soon."

"Don't they go for a year?" Todd asked.

"Usually," said Bosco.

No one wanted to ask why Antoine was in jail, and in the silence that followed Steve slammed his bottle again, and Mary

Ann snatched it away from him. "You're getting us wet," she said, pulling napkins from the dispenser, spreading them over the table.

She wiped the bottle too, and held it for a minute while Steve said, "Guess if I was some rich asshole, I'd be going to college, getting deferred from this shit!"

Everyone watched as Steve's face turned red, everyone except Mary Ann, and me because I was watching her as she slipped a hand in the pocket of her jacket—the green one she'd worn on Halloween—and pulled out a crumbling sugar cube and dropped it down the neck of the bottle.

"Toast!" I said, holding up my Coke. "Here's to us, the class of '68! Forever young! Forever Horsemen! Even you, Railsbeck!"

We all drank, gulping down our sodas to the last fizz.

Railsbeck was bound to do something crazy now, if he even made it to Whitehall Street before his dad found out, if Steve didn't freak out first. I had to hand it to Mary Ann; few people had more reason to hate Steve, but in the end, she put differences aside and tried, in her way, to help him, to assist him in avoiding what she figured was in store for Todd, which she felt powerless to change.

That night on the phone I told Darcy what Mary Ann had done. "Wow!" she said, "that's insane! You think Steve's all right?"

"I don't know. Why don't you call him?"

"No thanks," she laughed. "But if Steve ends up in Vietnam, I guess I'd kind of miss him."

"Railsbeck?"

She was silent a minute. "Do you think about it?" she asked. "About Todd?"

"What about him?"

"When he leaves, you may never see him again."

I had thought about it, but despite all I'd said to the contrary, I felt sure he'd be back and life would go on as before. It was Darcy's presence I wasn't convinced of, her question seeming more about us, how our time together might end. "What about you?" I asked. "Have you applied to any colleges?"

"You're avoiding my question."

"And you're not?"

I could picture her shaking her beautiful head, sense her resignation.

She said, "It's just not something you'd understand. Why don't you ask your mother?"

On June sixth, at graduation, we performed as instructed, shaking Hammer's fish-like hand, tossing our cardboard hats in the air, and shouting like we gave a shit. I noticed Mr. *No Relation King* standing by the bleachers where the parents sat, holding a transistor radio to his ear, a look on his face unbefitting the occasion. Parents mobbed the hardwood floor, everyone pumping hands, hugging each other, girlfriends searching for boyfriends separated by the alphabetical seating. I found Darcy and we hugged and kissed, same with Mary Ann, though we were self-conscious about it. I hugged Todd too, a manly abrazo; he smelled like the crappy cologne he wore after gym, and I remembered what Darcy had said about never seeing him again, and it floored me. But then Steve Railsbeck slapped my back so hard I hyperventilated. "Conover," he said, "what the fuck did you do to me? You put something in my drink!"

I didn't know what to say. I couldn't deny it, couldn't snitch on Mary Ann, but it all proved moot when Steve said, "I don't know what that shit was, but I was so fucked up by the time I got to Whitehall, they sent me straight to the shrink! He knew what was happening, and said I had to come back. But fuck, man, I'll just take more of that stuff. Where can I get some?"

"What about your dad?" I asked.

"Pop? He don't take drugs!"

"Noo, dumbass," I said.

"Oh, fuck him, man. *He* ain't going to Vietnam!"

"There's your man," I said, pointing to Erik Neumann, who was busy giving my girlfriend a squeeze.

"Of course," said Steve, "I shoulda fuckin' known."

The crowd flowed out of the gym and into the parking lot, where the sky was just turning pink. Kids milled about, talking, making plans to meet later for the parties. The greasers revved their engines, beeped their horns, music blaring from their radios, and that's how we found out. It was on all the stations, and after a few minutes everyone grew silent, leaning by opened car doors as news of Bobby Kennedy passed through the crowd, until only the white noise of radios buzzed, a dog barking far in the distance.

I was standing with Mom when we heard the news, how he was shot by a *lone gunman* in a hotel in California. Mom hugged me and I hugged her back, her fingers like claws on my shoulders. I knew she was crying—lots of people were, white people this time, those who hadn't found their tears when Doctor King had died, just two months before. Looking around, I saw so many faces, so many kinds of emotion, some people still laughing, some sobbing, or stunned, twisting their diplomas in their hands. I remembered when President Kennedy got shot, right after my father died, how Todd and I posed like marines in my living room, saluting the funeral on TV. A black horse pranced sideways down the middle of a street, black boots turned backwards in the stirrups, thousands of people lining the curbs with tears frozen solid on their face.

All of my life I had watched people die, on the news, in the movies, at a distance. But only my father's death had seemed real, and his loss lent its truth to the others.

I saw Darcy and her parents over by the gym where news of the killing had yet to arrive. She was smiling at her mother, her father's back turned, his black hair shiny as a crow's wing. *That's my little beauty*, I imagined him saying, picturing Darcy in the green striped towel, and I wanted to rush there and pummel his face, to erase his dark presence from the world. Mrs. Saint James appeared to be crying, the pink wash of sunset in her eyes. Whether tears of joy at this rite of passage or sorrow for innocence lost, her grief was embedded in the lines on her face as though carved by the stem of a wine glass, deep as the hole in a Kennedy's head, grave wounds in the soul of a nation.

Darcy and I had intended to hook up at the Yellow Rocks, skipping the party at the Beach Club. But the assassination changed all that, and instead I went home with Mom, where we sat on the couch, watching footage of the shooting playing over and over on TV. I figured Darcy would eventually call, but by nine o'clock she hadn't, so I dialed her house and listened to the phone ring until finally I gave up. I hated to leave Mom, but I had to see Darcy, knowing she'd be just as upset, and with no one to talk to about it.

A half hour later I was standing on the lawn in front of her house. The lights were out, and I briefly considered throwing rocks at her window, like people do in the movies. With my luck, though, I'd probably break it, her room so high in the eaves. *But maybe I should*, I thought. *Maybe I should shatter the Doctor's window and have it out with him right now, right here on the lawn where he'd fired Carter Muson.*

Engrossed in the thought, I jumped when a car horn beeped, and turned to find Todd in his mom's gold Cutlass idling by the curb. The car was packed with tipsy people—Todd, Mary Ann, and Erik in front; Jonah, PH3, and Belinda Cake (gooey on the inside, the tale was told) in back.

"I was looking for you," said Todd. "The party's a bust, literally. Someone set fire to a boat at the Beach Club. The cops roused everyone at the river."

"You seen Darcy?" I asked.

"I saw her down at the Yellow Rocks," said Mary Ann, "walking around in the water."

"Shit, she's probably freaked."

"You heard then?" said Todd.

"Of course I heard. It's all over TV. The end of the Kennedy Legacy."

"No," said Erik, "our own local legacy. Carter Mason jumped— or hopped—off the Tappan Zee Bridge. Who knows what went on in his mind."

"It's all gooey!" shrieked PH3, high on Neumann's acid.

I took off running, headed for the Yellow Rocks, Todd still calling my name. When I reached the buttress of the old railroad bridge I descended to the tracks, blindly slid down the river embankment and tramped along the shore, wading through the water as the tide came in. Stumbling onto our fishing rock, I found the wet stars of Darcy's footprints and followed them back to the tracks where they disappeared in the gravel. The moonlit rails led me straight to the Beach Club where headlights shone in an exodus of cars, partiers escorted by flashing police lights from the scene of the burning boat. On the roof of the station, a match head flared and the wick of a candle flickered. It had to be Darcy, the only person besides Todd and me who even knew how to get up there.

She surely was watching as I jogged up the tracks, lit by the halo of moth-fluttered lamps, then up the long stairs of the pedestrian walkway to the grated scaffold where red lights blinked in the darkness. It was easy to hop the metal railing and scale the ladder to the overpass roof. Crunching across its graveled surface, in three quick moves I surmounted the wall, and the summit of the train station was mine.

Darcy sat bundled in a pale blue blanket, one of many we'd stashed around town. She was silent for a moment, then opened the blanket and allowed me to wiggle in beside her. Her cut-offs were soaked, and I struggled with her blouse, pulling it over her head, a comic if wordless interaction that left me half naked and Darcy wearing my pin striped birthday shirt.

"Darce," I said, "I'm sorry about Carter. There was nothing that you—that we could do."

There were tiny holes in the fabric of the blanket, and through its weave we could see stars winking, bridge lights blinking, the black silhouette of the Eagle statue that had once crowned the roof of Grand Central Station. "You're shivering, Dar. Want me to make you warm?"

She nodded forlornly as I wrapped her in my arms, squeezing her tight against me. "Aren't you gonna talk to me? Tiger got your tongue?"

"He's out there now," she finally said, "floating around with the fish. I never wanted that to happen. I would have talked to him, told him I remembered."

"Remembered what?"

"*Him*, Teal! The way he was before!"

"Are we talking about Carter?"

"About everyone!" she cried, suddenly angry. "Him, me, you, my mom … whoever we used to be! I can't take being your *normal* anymore, your empty old beer can that drags on the rocks whenever the boogieman comes."

"What? My father, you mean?"

"You can't accept anything that threatens your dream, your 'perfect world where things never change.'"

She was quoting me from the first day we met, the story about fishing with my dad.

"Like what?" I asked.

"Like poor Carter Mason, who *you* think I fucked! As if no one could love me but you!"

Throwing off the blanket she leaped to the parapet, her long hair electric with static. A train roared past on the tracks below, illumined in silver-blue flashes, snapping her shirttails in the gale of its passage, the smoke from the boat fire swirling. Raising her arms as though intending to fly, she mimicked the pose of the Eagle. "Get down from there!" I shouted. "You're acting crazy!"

"Acting?" she laughed, her tongue sticking out as she tight-roped the length of the wall. "That's yet to be determined, though everyone has their suspicions."

Darcy was too athletic to fall, and I knew she wouldn't jump. That much was an act, and it pissed me off to think she'd try to play me. Then she curtseyed and swung her leg high in the air, balanced on one bare foot. "How *beautiful* am I now, Teal?" she asked, the train like a sparkler in the distance.

"So you did fuck Carter, is that what you're saying?"

"You mean did I fuck him *back?*"

Had she actually admitted it, or was she trying to hurt me? Were we even still talking about Carter?

"Speaking of boogiemen," I heard myself say, "next Halloween we'll conjure your dad, the original Heartless Horseman."

Without really thinking I grabbed for her foot, snagging her ankle as she tried to hop away. "You said you bled all over the beach the day you stepped on the wineglass. I guess that would leave a pretty big scar, so why don't we take us a peek?"

A real look of panic came over her face as she teetered atop the wall. I could barely see in the half-lit dark, not enough to inspect her heel. "Which foot was it anyway? I bet there were plenty of stitches."

All of the arrogance washed from her face as her legs began to tremble, and suddenly I truly was afraid, divested of my own arrogance, my mistaken belief that I knew this girl dispersing as fast as the smoke. "Darcy," I said, releasing her foot. "Will you please just sit—"

"Go away, Teal," she cut me off. "Leave me the fuck alone."

I didn't understand how she meant it exactly. For tonight, for a while, or forever?

"What?" I said. "You want me to go? Do you want me say I'm sorry?"

Reaching for the collar of my birthday shirt, she held my eyes with a stare, as one by one she unbuttoned its length until the sleeves slipped away down her arms. Sailing aloft like the ghost of our love, her gift billowed out on the wind, assuming the shape of a Renaissance torso before coming to rest on the tracks.

Posed on the wall, she was naked as David, the moon making marble of her skin. She said, "I'm just some old painting you hang on your wall, a book you make up as you read. You pretend that you love me, like Gatsby loves Daisy, like Franny loves Bloomberg the cat. You think I'm a liar, but that's a lie, too. It's *you* who's afraid of the truth."

Barefoot, shirtless, she climbed off the wall and tip-toed across the sharp gravel. If the thousand cuts hurt her, she didn't reveal it, absorbing the pain as she had all her life, disappearing down the ladder like a half-naked Brahmin, like Venus de Milo into shadow.

PART
TWO

Whlle Truth in most cases is impossible to deny, much is offered like candy, an assortment of answers in the palm of one's hand, from which only the sweetest is chosen. Not so very different from the age-old techniques employed in the sculpting of history, verities plucked from the meadows of time to brighten the room of the present.

For many weeks after that long ago night, I relived the scene in my mind, slicing and splicing the things Darcy said until painless enough to swallow. She couldn't have meant that she'd let Carter touch her, and that day at the beach was long past. Who was to say what had actually happened and what a little girl saw in her mind.

These were the lies I told myself as I tried to make sense of the world, a senseless endeavor, I realize now, from the lofty perspective of age. Darcy was right when she called me a liar, a dreamer afraid of the truth. But those who cannot forgive their youth will never forgive themselves, and by extension, all of humanity. Just writing these words, I have to smile at their tone of noble intent, the pathos and passion of that troubled time long since gone out of fashion. Two men had died on that memorable day, one famous, and one unknown. Unfamous was Carter in history's eyes, unforgettable in my own.

The past stretches back like the tail of a comet, the present the thinnest veneer, the flare of a match head revealing our hands poised in the process of being, that brief, flaming instant we think of as life before it devolves into smoke. Learning to live there, to exist in that moment and not the dark well of the past; that is the canvas, the raw block of granite that all artists strive to give shape to, to reflect the beauty they see in their minds, proof that our lives are worth living.

When I was a child, I hoped nothing would change, that life could go on as I'd known it, dappled with sunlight and puffy white clouds, the sultry nights studded with stars. But at eighteen years old, a crack breached the firmament and grew with the vengeance of lightning, splitting the canvas like an El Greco painting, revealing the summits of mountains. Why mountains? Who knows … their symbol I guess, gleaned from great paintings and books, the lofty objective of snails on a quest, where life is returned with the seasons.

But as Bosco had said in Humpty's class, "Yesterday ain't nothin' without today." While each of us strives to live in the moment, the whole of us lives for tomorrow, to make sure there is one for our children, our kind, in the far away land of the future. Nothing is lost that can still be remembered. All life resides in the mind. Who can't recall their first kiss, their last heartbreak? Which would you chose to forget?

Chapter 24

Standing on the platform at the Tarrytown station, waiting for the train with my mom, our eyes were puffy from holding back tears, keeping anxiety at bay. Leaving home was a rite of passage my mother had never experienced, my father departing only for war and in some ways never returning. I alone, of generations of Conovers, was attempting to make my escape, transgressing perhaps against centuries of tradition that had seen us all buried in one place.

After that night on the roof of the station I had called Darcy repeatedly, but none of my calls were returned. Standing on her corner, walking past her house, skulking around on her lawn … if she saw me at all she never came out, cloistered away in her room. Not since the year my father died had I cried so much, hiding it, as always, inside. When a week went by with no word from Darcy, I told my mom I was leaving, buying a ticket to San Francisco, where cast-offs like me belonged. *Why not,* I thought; it's what everyone expected, what my friends had been saying for a year. It sounded much better than the actual truth—that I was simply running away, escaping the pain of my broken heart like a drunk driver leaving a car wreck. I'd write Darcy a letter from far away and tell her how much I missed her. She'd write back and say that she loved me, and we'd meet somewhere in the mountains, floating like ducks in an alpine lake with the sun burning hot on our skin.

That was the part I mentioned to no one, my second real reason for leaving—I was heading out west to the solace of mountains, to "seek their good tidings," as John Muir had written in his book about climbing volcanoes. Darcy had told me I wanted wild places before I knew it myself. The pure kind of landscape my ancestors found when they first stepped off their ship, a harsh world, ageless and grand beyond measure, the place where all beauty derives.

That's what I dreamed of as I waited for the Greyhound in the lobby of the Port Authority, junkies and winos drooling on my sleeve, bums checking phone booths for change. When the bus gained the farmlands of Pennsylvania, I finally began to relax, the country beyond the green-tinted glass looking fresh, vital, and clean. I found myself humming the words of a song that ran in a loop through my head, reminding me of Darcy with her hair soaking wet, the ten-year-old Newports found in the glove box of Kara's abandoned car. *Toss me a cigarette I think there's one in my raincoat. We smoked the last one an hour ago ....*

Stopping in Chicago, I wandered the terminal looking for a Mrs. Wagner pie, but all there was were pop machines and broken candy dispensers, so I bought a slice of pizza and a bottle of cherry Coke. It turned out to be the last good pizza after leaving New York—west of there it was all pretty crappy, covered with pineapples and dumb shit like that. I called Mom collect, but she wasn't home, still working her crazy hours. Todd said I could call him collect any time, that he'd call me right back at my phone booth. But I figured I'd wait until I had something important to say, not just my second day out.

We ended up crossing the Continental Divide at night, and all I got to see of the mountains was the inside of a long tunnel, a florescent-lit cave that made the tires hum like turbines. At dawn we were creeping down an endless grade toward Salt Lake City and another stop where I bought a postcard of a cactus and scribbled a self-portrait on the back, a sad looking elephant inside a snake, perched on my head like a hat. I had planned to mail it to Darcy that day but never came up with a stamp. Calling my mom, she got all excited, asking if I was eating well. I lied, of course, and said that I was, though all I'd eaten in the past three days was pizza and M&Ms. "Call me when you get to California," she said, making me promise I would.

I didn't though, because we got into the bus terminal in downtown San Francisco late at night. It wasn't as creepy as Port Authority, but it had its share of weirdos, mostly Blacks and longhairs nodding off on the benches, a cop and a janitor keeping a watchful eye on things. The guy at the ticket window guessed where I was headed before I even asked, saying I could catch a transit bus on Market Street, take me straight up Haight Street all the way to Golden Gate Park.

So that's what I did, getting off at Ashbury because … why not? I shouldered my pack, a crappy canvas bag left over from Boy Scouts, and walked up the sidewalk, crossed the street, then back to the brightly lit donut shop where I'd started. Standing out front was a wild looking dude with huge, frizzy hair and an even bigger, frizzier beard, his completely round profile electric with neon, a pink and blue dandelion in silhouette. "Hey, brother," he said, "buy me a donut."

It wasn't a question, but neither was it a demand, so I couldn't think of a good reason not to.

"Sure," I agreed, whereupon he laid his arm around my shoulder and said, "Outta sight, man," and escorted me inside. We ordered a couple of chocolate donuts with multi-colored sprinkles on top, and two large cups of coffee—*regular*— I told the waitress, who frowned like I was crazy. My new friend told me his name was Beau, that he was from New Orleans, but now lived nowhere in particular, though presently he was crashing in the Park. "I don't own nothin', man, and nothin' owns me," he said. "I used to be married, owned a house and a car, or thought I did."

I figured he was going to tell me how he got divorced, how his wife took him for everything, but he didn't.

"She died, man, my wife. I loved her so much. She was so far out, a beautiful soul. But now, you know, I'm free of all that. I love everything now, you dig?"

Thinking of Darcy, I wanted to say yes, but I honestly didn't know. I told him instead what the Buddha had said, that life was sorrow, but also change.

"Far out," said Beau, rainbow sprinkles in his beard. "That's very cool. You're very cool."

He asked me my name, and I told him.

"Like a duck," he smiled, reminding me of Darcy again.

"Right on," I said, caught up in the moment.

Beau said he was thirty, but it was hard to tell, his face all hidden in hair. He'd tuck a lock behind one ear while trying to sip his coffee, but it popped right out again, tensile as bed springs. He could have been older, his voice kind of gravelly, but he smiled so often it made him seem young, his pink eyes twinkling with mirth.

"Where you crashing, man?" he asked.

"I don't know. I just got here."

"You crash out with *Beau*, I got me a place. It's just a bush, by a tree in the park, but the cops don't hassle ya. You're welcome to it. You got a blanket?"

I had a sleeping bag, also left over from Boy Scouts, with a fucked-up zipper and ducks printed on the inside—maybe teals, maybe mallards, I didn't know. It was just like Carter Mason's.

We drifted up Haight in a chilly fog, tendrils of it wreathing the lamp posts. Bus cables bellied down the middle of the street, sparking with arcs of electricity. Neon signs sputtered and candlelight flickered in bay windows over the storefronts, God's eyes and peace symbols taped to their panes, tapestries lit with globs of color from slow-pulsing lava lights. It was three in the morning and only one other person passed us, a black dude swaddled in the American flag, a red, green, and yellow tam perched impossibly atop his monstrous Afro.

"That's Freedom," Beau told me. "And don't say hello. He gets nasty if you wake him up."

"He's sleeping?" I asked.

"Sleep *walking*, bro. There's a difference."

When we got to the crosswalk at Stanyan and Haight, where it tee-boned into the park, a lone Harley passed with its twin pipes blatting, punctuating the silence of morning. Beau held my arm as we showed our respect, nodding at the rider in polite recognition. Dressed all in leather and stagged-off denim, the Hell's Angel flashed us the peace sign, white fangs glowing in the cavern of his beard, long hair floating behind him.

"Keep 'em smiling," said Beau. "We all stay healthy that way."

Two square columns flanked the park's entrance, perched upon by squatting figures wrapped in blankets, silent sentinels of the foggy night. "Blanket people," Beau called them. "Hell," he said, "I'm one, too, but I just like my privacy."

We walked through a tunnel, crossed a wide lawn then ducked into a dark copse of trees. "Watch it," said Beau, "take care where you step. There's other folks in here, too."

I couldn't see anything, so I held Beau's hand until he stopped at the base of a tree. "Honey, I'm home!" he whispered, patting the bark like a lover's cheek. Fishing around on his hands and knees, he came up with a blanket and furled it on the ground. "Go ahead," he said, "spread out anywhere." The nub of a candle appeared in his hand and he planted it cockeyed in the tree's gnarly roots. "I got a little wine, a little weed," he said. "What's mine is yours, brother Teal."

We smoked a roach, but I skipped the wine. A few stars twinkled through branches. "This reminds me of home," I said, "spending the night in the cemetery." Beau was all ears to hear about that, and I talked until I'm sure he was asleep, rambling on about Darcy and how beautiful she was, how I doubted my heart would ever mend. I nodded off writing her a letter in my head, convinced I'd remember it in the morning. But that never happened—the letter, not morning—because beginning the next day I was stoned all the time, forgetting about mountains, at least for the moment, and sometimes, admittedly, about Darcy.

Chapter 25

Beau was gone in the morning, the sun shining bright through the treetops. The rhythmic thumping of a half dozen bongos woke me, the sound of voices singing, dogs barking. I rolled up my sleeping bag and stuffed it—leaves and all—into my pack. Stumbling out of the woods, the expansive meadow of Hippie Hill was dotted with people throwing Frisbees and blowing bubbles, musicians playing flutes and guitars on benches lining the path. The grass was wet and the air smelled of ocean, and at the top of a distant tree-covered hill the fog hung like pink cotton candy. A fluorescent orange Frisbee careened through the air and landed in the grass at my feet, chased by a wiry black-and-white dog that tumbled on its belly to avoid me. He sat up quickly, comically in fact, one haunch planted atop my sneaker, as if expecting some form of praise. "You gotta pet him," said a girl in a long flowing dress, braids in her hair, but no shoes. "He's a real panhandler," she explained.

Her name was Honey, and she was big and blonde and constantly smiling. Her old man's name was Jude and he was tall and skinny, her exact opposite, except for the duplicate smiles that never left their faces. The dog's name was *Panhandle* and he didn't belong to them, or to anybody. He belonged to *everybody* it seemed, as passersby stopped to give him a pet or a piece of whatever they were eating, an apple, a carrot, half a donut, or a hunk of fish and chips.

We tossed the Frisbee around for a while, me, Honey, Jude, and a crazy Black kid called BeBop, who would break out dancing without provocation, the Frisbee sometimes bouncing off his head. We talked, shouting as we played, Jude saying he was from LA, Honey from eastern Oregon where she'd grown up on a ranch. BeBop was from the Fillmore, just below the Haight, and that's all he seemed willing or capable of explaining, belting out a Chamber's Brothers tune whenever the spirit moved him—"Time! Tick, tick, tick, time! Tick, tick …"

The bongo playing would continue all day, I learned, and after some hours of tossing Frisbees and smoking joints, I got hungry and headed up the path Beau and I had taken the night before, Panhandle choosing to go with me, soliciting pets from whoever we passed. Everyone seemed to know the dog, and I felt kind of famous by association. Arriving at the park entrance on Stanyan, the blanket people still squatted Buddha-like atop the columns, others playing guitars on the low stone walls. One chick was throwing the I Ching with a handful of pennies, the book open in her lap where she sat on the sidewalk, the soles of her bare feet black and calloused. "Panhandle!" she called to the dog, who wiggled over and collapsed against her flat, boobless chest.

Her name was Sunshine, and she wore jodhpur pants and a purple blouse so sheer you could see through it. The beads she wore around her neck were wound as thick as Christmas wreathes, her leather headband so soaked with patchouli oil she squinted at me through the fumes. A single hoop earring hung from one ear, matching the stud in her nostril, anklets stacked up on both bony legs where tattoos of butterflies swarmed. She shared a red vine licorice with me, even giving a piece to the dog, who dropped it, sniffed it, and left it on the sidewalk. "He likes the black ones," Sunshine explained, retrieving the licorice and eating it herself. She threw the I Ching for me, each penny—heads or tails—representing a line, solid or broken, which together formed a symbol appearing in the book. Reading the name and text of each diagram she interpreted their meaning, the whole process pretty intriguing, an elaborate version of fortune cookies, or flipping baseball cards.

Sunshine took me to the fish-and chips-joint just up Haight Street where I bought us lunch wrapped in a folded newspaper, the newsprint turning soggy with grease and the vinegar she splashed liberally on everything. Loitering on the sidewalk, passersby stopped and shared our food, offering bananas, ice cream cones, or joints—whatever they had—in return. One of the grubby hands dipping into our newspaper was Beau's. He knew Sunshine and gave her a hug, stooping also to pet Panhandle, the dog licking his greasy fingers. We walked up Haight together, the fish and chips gone before we hit Belvedere.

It was a beautiful day, breezy and warm, throngs of people consorting on the street dressed in gauzy, flowing clothes, the air redolent of incense, pot smoke, and patchouli oil. The scent of fresh bread drifted from the Russian bakery, whiffs of charred meat gushed from the Love Burgers joint across the street, and exhaust smells spewed from a line of Harleys leaning by the curb. Parked outside the I/Thou Café, an Angel's van sat with its doors opened wide and a tarp jerry-rigged overhead. Caked head to foot in blackened grime, a somber biker dismantled a chopper, its parts spread out on the bubblegummed sidewalk where a huge Saint Bernard lay panting in the shade, its wide collar bristling with metal spikes, belying a placid, lackadaisical nature when Panhandle sniffed at his butt.

Music blared from a loudspeaker at the Psychedelic Shop, Grace Slick promising yet more volunteers, Jimi Hendrix's psychotic guitar riff just now *comin' ta getcha!* A short, fat, bald guy wrapped in a bed sheet pontificated to all who would listen, platform huaraches on his bare, taloned feet, his toenails grown overlong. Every other tie-dyed, long-haired freak was dealing, calling out their wares in the tradition of peasant markets everywhere—"Orange Sunshine! Blue Cheer! Humboldt bud!" There was a festive, carnival atmosphere along the street, wherein perfect strangers treated each other like dear old friends, and in other circumstances I could easily picture Todd amongst them, slapping backs and shaking hands, exhorting the team to the proverbial goal line, whatever the goal here was.

A poster in front of the Straight Theater declared Santana to be the house band, and Sunshine stopped beneath its marquee to rap with a chick in a rainbow-painted wheelchair. The girl's name was Crystal, and she smiled with crooked teeth, her eyes almost purple and her hair so long it lay coiled in her lap with a tambourine and a basket of fuzzy kittens. A little kid, maybe four years old, was climbing all over the wheelchair, so long-haired and cute I at first couldn't tell if he was a boy or a girl. Rolling Panhandle onto his back, young Twig rubbed his pink belly, the dog eating it up with his tongue hanging out, prompting the kid to do the same. Everyone laughed, Beau braying like a donkey, Sunshine's titter as tinkling as wind chimes. Not much bigger than the little boy, she'd recently turned fourteen.

At the corner of Ashbury, a red, white, and blue striped panel truck sat with its doors and windows open and beautiful, young, hippie chicks—mostly runaways, Beau explained—hanging from every portal. Their flowing hair was braided with flowers, just like in the song, their smiles transcendent and sloe eyes dreamy, their hands and feet painted in spider webs of traditional Afghani design. Captain America, overseeing the blonde harem, was dressed in a tailed waistcoat the colors of the flag, the top hat on his head starred and striped like the logo of the New York Yankees. Tipping my cap, I was quick to exclaim, "Go Yanks!" but he seemed not to understand.

Beau knew him too, and after hugs and kisses the Captain leaned into the rear of the truck and returned with his hand cupped before him. Like birds in a nest or Catholics at communion, Beau, Sunshine, and I opened our mouths and the mad top-hatter placed tiny squares of Window Pane on our tongues, ritually performing the sign of the cross before flashing us the peace sign.

Minutes later the street sounds blended into something like music, a weaving of voices and blaring horns with a base line of grumbling Harleys, Ecloff the Angel dog barking in counterpoint to the jangle of Crystal's tambourine. A fairy in braids and tiara of flowers leaned from the truck and exhaled a cloud of pot smoke directly into my nostril, as saffron-robed Krishna girls with heads shaved like peaches danced barefoot out into traffic, the ting of their finger cymbals filling the air with an essence akin to incense. *Hare Krishna! Hare Krishna! Krishna Krishna! Hare Hare!*

At some point we drank wine, smoked more pot, and then ate something like raisins. I strummed a guitar I couldn't play, and sang a song I did not know the words to. We sat in a pink-painted room with big windows and glass beaded curtains for doors, where dangling crystals suspended from the ceiling shot miniature rainbows on the walls. A girl all in feathers washed my feet with a sponge, and then I was holding a baby, watching her watch me, her eyes blue as sky as palm trees swayed in the window. By evening I was barefoot and up on a roof with people I didn't recognize. We silently watched a smoldering sunset descend over Golden Gate Park, turning sapphire, salmon, then liquid gold, a single star piercing the heavens. Panhandle lay coiled like a rope in my lap, his short legs trembling in a dream, and I thought of Darcy and almost cried, seeing her face, smelling her hair, craving her touch like milk chocolate.

I awoke on the roof in the middle of the night, wet and cold in the enveloping fog, feeling around for Panhandle, who had apparently deserted me at that late hour. I found a door that led below and entered the portal of a dark apartment. I couldn't see anything but heard the sound of a dog's tail thumping in the dark, Panhandle recognizing his friend of an entire day. Curling up against him I must have dozed off, and when I awoke there were other freaks scattered around me, some on mattresses, some on sofas, just me and the dog on the hardwood floor. A girl was wrapped in my sleeping bag, the one who had washed my feet. Glancing around for the blue-eyed baby, I wondered if maybe I'd imagined it all, hallucinated the whole adventure.

There were whispers from the kitchen, and the smell of cooking, and my stomach growled so loud that Panhandle growled back, a confused expression on his furry face. Tiptoeing through a maze of sleeping bodies, puzzled by the absence of my sneakers, I found two people drinking tea in the kitchen, an older guy with a balding pate, and a skinny woman in a halter top, a bandana knotted on her graying head.

"Helloo traveler," they said, nearly in unison, smiling at me, then at each other. "Tea?"

"Please," I said, and the lady sprang to her flip-flopped feet and lit a burner with a stick match. "Water'll be a minute," she said. "I'm Hannah. This is my husband, Jake. Welcome to our home." She motioned for me to sit in her chair, then leaned back against the sink, surrounded by plants that hung in the window, silhouetted by morning light.

"Come far?" Jake asked, posing the same question I'm sure he'd asked everyone there. His long gray hair hung stringy to his shoulders, his wire-rimmed glasses reflecting the light, as gleaming and bright as his forehead. He resembled Ben Franklin with a Fu Manchu and a sprinkling of Santa Claus's elf.

"New York," I said.

"Oh, my," said Hannah, "that *is* far."

"Far out," smiled Jake. "Been here long?"

I shook my head. "Two days, I think. How'd I get here?"

Jake made a *let's see* face, fingering his scraggly goatee. "Found you down at the Panhandle, I believe, chatting away with a seagull. I invited you up for tea."

"Do you have a little baby?" I asked.

Hannah smiled. "Amber's daughter, Little Angel. Or that's what we call her thus far."

"I thought so, but I wasn't sure."

"Amber must trust you," said Hannah. "And Little Angel, too, if she didn't cry."

"I held her," I said.

"She likes you, then," Jake nodded.

"Tea's ready."

Hannah poured hot water into a beautiful old weeping willow cup and dipped in a tea ball of rose hips and mint. "There's honey in the honey bear. Oatmeal in a minute. Sorry, that's all we've got."

"Sounds great," I said. "Seems like I'm living on M&Ms and acid."

"M&Ms are bad for you," Jake laughed. "Some water, Panhandle?" he asked the dog, whose claws clicked excitedly on the linoleum floor. Everyone, apparently, was Panhandle's friend.

After we ate there were sounds of movement from the rest of the house, and people with puffy eyes and pillow hair stuck their heads in the tiny kitchen and smiled, yawned, gave Jake and Hannah and even me a hug, before accepting tea and oatmeal. They patted Panhandle's head, and we rotated chairs until it was my turn to return to the living room and the battered old furniture and mattresses that formed an obstacle course through the apartment. One bedroom belonged to Jake and Hannah, but everywhere else belonged to the crashers, the trippers, the travelers, and runaways who oozed through the Haight like syrup through the honey bear, slow and sticky and golden with light.

My sleeping bag was rolled up and leaning in a corner with my pack, and Amber, minus the feathered hat, her fine red hair a mass of springy curls, was sitting cross-legged on an ottoman with the infant baby in her lap. There was something odd about Amber's round face and slanted eyes, her lips turned down in a permanent pout, though not at all unhappy. "Tank you," she said, and I realized she had Down syndrome. "Tank you for my baby, Little Angel. You made her not want to cry."

"That's right." I said, "the blue-eyed Angel."

Amber smiled, and she was pretty. As pretty as her baby. A child with a child.

Later I helped Hannah with her garden in the backyard, the vast, communal open space of trees and small garden plots that formed the center of the block of old Victorian apartment houses. She grew carrots, onions, and a variety of lettuce, even tomatoes in a ramshackle greenhouse made of old French-paned windows. "I can help," I said, chopping at the weeds with a spade.

"And so you are," she smiled.

"I mean I have money. I can buy food. I saved quite a bit from my job."

"Oh, no," said Hannah, "you keep your money. You can't be on the road without it."

She asked me how things were going at home, what led me to come to the Haight.

"I'm actually headed for the mountains," I explained, "seeking their good tidings."

"A quest!" she enthused. "That's exciting!"

"It is," I grinned, surprising myself. "But so far it's not what I thought."

"What did you expect?"

"That's just it, I don't really know. I've never known, but I figured I'd start in the wild."

"Nature, yes, Mother Earth," Hannah smiled, sifting damp soil through her fingers. "I thought perhaps you were headed for Canada. Lots of young boys are."

"Nah," I sighed, thinking of Todd, wishing that he would head north. "But the world's pretty wild right here," I added, not one week into my journey.

"*Human* nature. Yes, it's just as wild. And just as beautiful, too."

I told her all about Darcy then, or as much as I could as we kneeled in the dirt, right up to the night we broke up.

"And you don't believe her," Hannah asked, "what she said about her father?"

"She didn't really *say* it, is what I mean. I don't know what's real anymore."

Hannah smiled and brushed dirt from her forehead, her green glove sweeping the sky. "But that's what life is all about, deciding what's real, and what could be. You kids have a chance to do something special, something your parents could never conceive of—*totally* free, *totally* different, like nothing we've known before. I know it's hard, confusing at times, but some day you'll look back and the world will have changed. Only then will you realize the dream."

She looked so happy I almost believed her, polka dot thumbprints smudging her cheeks, teeth leaning crooked in her smile. "Sometimes," I said, "I'll see something so beautiful and … it's like I can almost forget."

"That's a gift," Hannah smiled, "to immerse oneself, to lose yourself in the moment."

"But I don't want to be lost," I said.

"Then how will you ever be found?"

I did help out as the weeks went by, going with Jake down to Cala Foods on Stanyan, slipping the cashier some money before Jake could object. Wheeling the cart up Haight Street, handing out food as we went, half the groceries were gone before we got home. We saw Beau and invited him up for tabouli and veggies. He had a salami in his pocket—no joke—and Jake said we'd have both meat *and* vegan dishes. I finally found a Mrs. Wagner's pie at the grocery store, hiding it in my pocket so no one would see. But up on the roof, alone at last, I fed most of it to Panhandle, shamed by the dog's soulful eyes.

That night in the narrow tent I'd made from an Indian-print bedspread, I wrote a long letter to Todd, explaining how it was so different here, how everyone shared what little they had, how little almost always sufficed. I told him about going to the Free Store with Sunshine and Amber, the girls trying on all kinds of crazy clothes, like Darcy had at Saks, or sitting on the roof with the latest crop of strangers, sewing patches and stars on our jeans. It was warm and beautiful in California, I wrote, where you could always smell the ocean, especially at night when I wandered the streets, much like the Leather Man.

I spent lots of time at the de Young Museum in the middle of Golden Gate Park. There was also an arboretum there, and an outdoor bandstand with rows of benches under gnarly, Mediterranean trees. I sat with my sketch pad in the echoing halls, sometimes drawing from the excellent Asian collection, sometimes just drawing from life, the people who passed, the school children and old timers who sat on the benches as I did, basking in the absolute radiance of art. I met a mysterious guy there named Art, and I couldn't say if that was his actual name or his handle, like Sunshine's name was really Luanne, which I'd learned from her address on an envelope. Art gave me a tab of purple Owsley and we ended up squatting in the Japanese Tea Garden, drinking tea that I couldn't taste, my tongue fuzzy, my jaw aching from yawning. After staring forever at the face of the Buddha, we materialized in the arboretum, which was naturally full of flowers, but the most beautiful flowers I had ever seen. The glass enclosure was infused with sunshine, light you could touch and breath and feel in every pore of your body, my skin like rose petals absorbing its warmth, its cosmic nutrients, traveling as it had from deep in space across stars and void, clouds and air to paint out the muscle in my arm, the fingers of my hand, the tiny veins of a tropical lily posed like the torso of a supplicant, a saffron, lemon, lavender pilgrim anchored in the flesh of the Earth.

One day I hitchhiked across the Golden Gate Bridge and was picked up by two Hare Krishna chicks in a yellow Toyota Corolla. Dressed in saris the color of sunflowers, their eyes were bright and their heads shaved bald, a white smudge like porridge striping their noses. Still, they were cute, and we smoked a doob, bouncing in our seats to a tape of Krishna music, the sweet scent of pine through opened windows overwhelming the reek of incense. Crossing the summit of Mount Tamalpais, we slowly descended to Stinson Beach where we played in the pounding surf, the girls' bodies lithe in their soaking wet saris, me in my jockey shorts, splashing in the waves with our arms flung toward heaven, praying, begging, daring a bolt of Buddha lightning to wriggle from the sky and strike us silly, glorious, alive!

Another time, another week, I thumbed up to Olema, where Jessie Colin Young lived, the old railroad car from the album cover rotting away by the roadside. I didn't see Jessie, but I met Cliff, who let me crash in the back of his old panel truck for the night, and in the morning introduced me to Haley and Trent who drove us all out to Point Reyes, where we ate magic mushrooms and watched cranes and seabirds soar against the wind, angling along the empty beaches. The clouds were gray and the sunlight silver, the ocean and the mainland merging in a dramatic slope that crested into the coastal range so that the planet appeared tilted, which it was, Trent explained, at eleven degrees, and though that was not what we were looking at, it was still really cool to ponder.

Sitting on a cliff's edge, staring at the sea, I realized how different life could be from the one I'd known back home. Just the trees, the ocean, its smell in the air were nothing like what I'd grown up with, the world itself a fresh sheet of vellum on which I could paint what I wanted, see what I wanted, feel truths beyond those I'd been led to believe. A reality all my own.

From the bank of phone booths at Cala Foods one morning I called Todd, collect, and he actually answered. I was pretty excited just hearing his voice, as if we hadn't spoken in years, and he told me to calm down, hang up, and he'd call me right back. It's what we'd discussed before I left, so I gave him the number of the booth and waited, waving to Sunshine across the street, who sat in her spot tossing pennies, Panhandle snuggled against her hip, begging for black whip licorice. Freaks kept asking to use the phone, and after I explained that I was waiting for a call—which they fully understood—they loitered around chewing sunflower seeds until somebody else was done talking. Finally, after ten minutes, the telephone rang and I grabbed it at the first ring. "Todd!" I shouted, "I thought maybe you forgot!"

"Never," said Darcy. "I could never forget."

"Darce? Is that you?"

"Are you disappointed?"

"No! Hell no! How—How are you?"

An echoing silence ensued on the line, and I thought I'd lost the connection.

"Do you miss me?" she asked, and I felt my heart leap, lodging itself in my throat. "No?" she cried when I still hadn't answered. "Do you just not love me anymore? Have you fallen in love with those girls?"

"Girls?" I said. "What girls?"

"The girls in your letter to Todd."

It took me a second to figure it out, my best friend minding my business.

"Amber is *mongoloid*," I tried to explain. "Sunshine is only fourteen."

"Have you slept with anyone?" she asked in a whisper, like someone holding their breath.

"No. Have you?"

"No! How could you ask that?"

"You just asked *me!*"

"Oh, Teal," she sighed, "I miss you so much. Is there any chance you still love me?"

"You know I do. I always will—"

"Please don't say that! That you'll *always* love me, like suddenly I'm in the past!"

In my other ear I could hear bongos thumping, Harleys revving, a street person hawking the Berkeley Barb on the corner of Haight and Stanyan. I studied pink bubblegum stuck to my sneaker, both toes inscribed with a face, one happy, one sad, scribbled in ballpoint the day I took acid with Art.

"If you read Todd's letter then you know how I feel. I've never stopped loving you for a second."

"He's leaving," Darcy blurted, as if she'd forgotten. "Todd's leaving today for the army."

"*Today?*"

"He told me just now, before he hung up. Do you want to call him right back?"

"No!" I said. "I'll call him soon, but right now I'm talking to you. Listen, Dar, you gotta come out here. You won't believe what's happening! It's like we're in some kind of mass satori where everyone's just waking up, thousands of pilgrims with withered arms trying to change the world! I'll pay for your ticket … there's places to crash … we could stay here and—"

"You're *staying*?" she cried. "You're not coming back?"

"If you came here, I wouldn't have to. We could go to the mountains together!"

"Come back *now*, Teal! Please say you will! My life means nothing without you."

What I told her was that somebody needed the phone, that I'd call back soon as I could. There *was* an emergency, but it was mostly mine, confronted with a life-changing choice: to stay out west where the world was fresh and continue my quest for beauty, or return to the graveyard of my family's past where everything was always the same.

I handed the phone to a hysterical chick whose bare feet bled on the sidewalk, her eyeliner streaked in black webs down her cheeks as she hugged her bare chest with both arms. I never called Todd, not knowing what to say, feeling only the distance between us, a difference that yawned like the miles between coasts, like the heights between summit and sea.

That night I couldn't eat because I had a toothache, or at least that's what I told Hannah. My tooth did hurt, but I just wasn't hungry, couldn't eat after talking to Darcy. In the morning, after a night of weird dreams about Carter Mason, my tooth was truly hurting, and Little Angel was crying, wailing even louder when I tried to pick her up. "You look like shit," Jake told me, when I declined his offer of tea.

"I feel like *your* shit," I said, making a joke, Jake being famous for his grumbling bowels. "My jaw's on fire. I hardly slept."

"We can fix that," he said. "C'mon, Pilgrim, we're off to the clinic."

The clinic was on the corner of Haight and Clayton, on

the second floor of an old Victorian building with bay windows overlooking the street. Jake sat with me in the packed waiting room, a cluster of miss-matched chairs and benches filled with sullen longhairs and little kids playing with trucks and dolls, scribbling in coloring books or directly on the walls. The staff looked identical to the clientele, wearing nose rings, beads, and peasant blouses with tiny mirrors embroidered on the sleeves.

We could hear someone screaming in another room, the male staff members rushing in on occasion, when the wailing reached a crescendo. "They bring the bummers in here, too," Jake explained. "It beats calling the cops."

A white-smocked doctor called my name, his long hair tied in a pony tail, a stethoscope and peace pendant dangling from his neck. His name tag declared him to be Dave, and Jake rose with me and the two shook hands like they knew each other, which I suppose they did, considering Jake's role in the crash-pad community.

"How are you feeling, Jake?" the doctor asked.

"Fit as a fiddle, flabby in the middle," he joked.

The doctor laughed, and showed us to a room down the hall. On the way there the screaming began anew, and when another door opened, I saw BeBop inside, wearing dingy gray underwear and one white sock, his hands wrapped in bandages, a strip of white adhesive taped across his nose. "Time!" he called out when he saw me, when he saw anyone. "Time!"

The doctor introduced me to yet another guy in a white coat, explaining that Mel was a dental student who worked for free, as did all the staff at the clinic. If my tooth could be fixed, Mel would fix it, free of charge. Jake and the doc left, and Mel checked out my mouth. He gave me my options and I said, "Pull it," which he did, painlessly, determining that I was not a hard-core drug addict come only to get high on Novocain.

Jake wasn't sitting in the waiting room when I got out, but

I found him down on Haight Street talking to Beau, Panhandle leaning against his ankle, trading affections when he saw me. Nero was doing his orator thing, spewing his radical rants, which sometimes involved some pretty lewd shit about farm animals. Jessie Colin Young was singing from the Head Shop speakers, bidding us to smile on our brother, everybody get together, and love … one … another … right … now. "Uh-oh," said Beau, and he nodded across the street where Freedom, wrapped in the American flag, struggled toward the window of the Bank of America with a cinder block raised above his head.

The implosion of the window eclipsed the manic hubbub of the sidewalks, the clatter of breaking glass having assumed special meaning in the American mind, in American society, where riots and street violence had become commonplace. In the brief silence that followed, everyone stopped and stared at the bank, its window gone, the alarm bells wailing, Freedom posed with his hands raised in fists, an activist athlete at the Haight Street Olympics. Then everyone cheered, the echo of it running up the canyon of store fronts like waves against a cliff face, resonating from wall to wall, Victorian to Victorian, where BeBop leaned naked from his safe house window screaming, "Time! Time! Time!"

"Fuck," groaned Beau, "we're in for it now. Our asses better get gone."

Moments later the sirens howled and people ran shouting in all directions, a kaleidoscopic vortex of swirling hair converging in the middle of the street. Ecloff rose to his massive paws, growling as the Angels tossed hog parts in the back of their van, Captain American battening his ship, the nymphets tucked safely in their clam shell.

"Let's go," said Jake, grabbing my hand, leading me to the safety of nowhere in particular. Beau went the other way, down toward the Panhandle, Panhandle the dog going with him. Crystal and Twig sat stranded under the marquee of the Straight Theater, and we literally skidded to a Road Runner stop and Jake said, "Go home, Teal, I'll meet you there."

"No way, Jose!" I replied and dashed across the street toward the theater, screaming "Medic!" at the top of my lungs.

Crystal was freaking as I bounced her wheelchair off the curb, Twig holding on as we plunged through the panicked crowd. All traffic stalled when a bus lost its electrical cables at the corner of Haight and Ashbury, where the Krishna dancers tossed rose petals in the air, chanting like the band on the Titanic. The police were as stymied by traffic as the rest of us, but not the motorcycle cops, who rolled down the sidewalks with sirens wailing, swerving to knock people down.

"Twig!" I called to the four-year-old, who appeared more excited than scared. "Hold on to your mom!" Spinning around the way we'd come, I tipped the wheelchair and regained the curb, pointing it in the direction of the I/Thou Café where faces were pressed to the steamy window and a black chick beckoned from the doorway. "Get in here!" she shouted, "getcha butt in here, Crystal!"

Shoving the chair at the waitress, I turned to look for Twig, snagging him just as a Harley ripped past, its siren intense for a second, then shrinking, fading, receding away to where others ran leaping from its path. Crystal and the waitress began to cry, then just as quickly were laughing again when Twig swiped a kitten from his mama's lap and pressed its wet nose to his own. Pussy, pussy, pussy, he said, and the café patrons cheered.

Later, in Hannah's kitchen, we drank chamomile tea we'd picked from the Kezar stadium parking lot, smoked a couple of doobs with Beau, Sunshine, her girlfriend Renee, and a guy named Tex from Minnesota. "How's your tooth?" Hannah asked me.

"Tooth?" I said, having forgotten about it in the excitement.

"You think Freedom's fucked?" Sunshine asked. "Think he'll go to jail?"

"Probably," said Beau. "No biggie for Freedom. He's spent most of his life behind bars."

"For real?" said Tex. "And his name is Freedom?"

"Like you're a cowboy from Minneapolis."

Everyone left when Little Angel began to cry, except for Rene, who stayed to take a shower.

When Jake went to bed and it was just me and Hannah in the kitchen, I asked her, "What's up with Jake? Is he okay? The doc at the clinic was asking about him."

Hannah smiled. "Jake is dying, love. He has colon cancer."

I was shocked, stunned, unable to speak, like Ecloff had ripped out my larynx.

"It's okay," she said. "It's tough to hear. Even tougher to know what to say."

"Does everyone know?" I asked.

"Most," she said. "Maybe not the new kids, but they'll learn, like you."

"I'm so sorry, Hannah, I just—"

She reached for my hand, touched my face, her green thumb buttoning my lip. "You don't need to speak," she said. "We're at peace with it now. We accept it."

"There's nothing they can do?"

Hannah shook her head. "Jake is full of love," she said, "as well as gas." She smiled then, joking at such an awful time, and I just started crying.

"Shh," she said. "Jake will never go away. His love won't die, and we know that. He knows it. Our boy, Chris … we lost him to the war, but he won't go away either. It's hard when people pass from your life, but love is forever, you see?"

I shook my head, because I didn't see, and I didn't want to accept it. Darcy, my father, Jake and his son … even the girl with the bare, bleeding feet—none of it made sense, and none of it seemed peaceful, no matter what flowers you wore in your hair. "I gotta go to bed," I said, and abruptly stood to leave.

"Wait," said Hannah, "don't go. Not yet."

But I did, and headed straight to my tent and curled up on my sleeping bag. Wind chimes tinkled in an open window, Joni Mitchell whispered through a wall. When the shower stopped running, I could hear Renee singing, reciting the words of a song, how life's illusions were all she recalled. She didn't know clouds at all.

Moments later Renee crawled into my tent, naked and smelling of talcum powder. "Hi," she smiled, "Teal, right?"

"Yeah," I mumbled.

"You okay? You seem kind of blue."

She flopped down facing me, her pale body curled like an *S*. Renee was cute, French-looking, like her name, with short brown hair and a turned-up nose.

"Cheer up," she said. "You wanna ball?"

"What?"

"You know, you wanna make love? I'm naked," she explained with an elfin grin.

"I thought you were—"

"What, gay?" She smiled again. "Whatever, you dig?"

"I got a girlfriend," I said without even thinking, realizing in that moment that I *did*.

"Far out, so do I. So how 'bout it, you wanna?"

I did want to, so badly it hurt. But something about it felt like lying, and not just to Darcy. Some things really do go away, vanish forever, never to return.

"Not tonight," I said. "But thanks anyway."

"Sure," said Renee, flipping on her side, snuggling her cute butt against me. "I'm so tired, ya know? It's been a long day."

I stayed awake for hours, thinking about Hannah and what she'd said, imagining a future alone. Not that Hannah would be alone, not someone who knew how to love like she did. But being *in* love was different somehow, a pie that you couldn't share, a personal trust like keeping a secret, or reading somebody your poem. I/Thou, yin/yang, little dots and dashes on a page … Could life truly be as simple as that, absolute opposites rolled into one, summoned with a handful of pennies? "Peace and Love," the posters declared, the Krishnas chanted on the corner. The two went together like Jake and Hannah, like choke and lusterslime. I wanted peace, I wanted love, but how could I have them both? Not with Darcy, Sunshine had said, reciting the *I Ching*'s decree, unknowingly reading the thoughts in my mind, as plain as the toes of my sneakers.

Renee was gone in the morning, and after showering I ran down to Cala Foods and stood in line at the phone booths. The whole time I waited, I practiced what I'd say to Darcy, how I knew I'd let her down and would continue to do so for at least another month while I went out in search of my personal dreams, what Hannah had called my "quest."

As the line got shorter, I began to panic, until finally, when a Hell's Angel handed me the phone, I could only dial Mom's number—collect— and wait for her to answer. She was elated to hear from me but also angry, saying she'd been worried sick for weeks. I couldn't believe it had been that long, trying to remember the last time I'd called or written her a letter. She said Darcy had phoned just the night before wondering when I'd return. Her mother had been admitted to the emergency room, injured in a fall down some stairs.

"Is Darcy okay?" I asked immediately.

"Of course, why wouldn't she be?"

"Her mom *fell* down the stairs?"

"Yes. Her wrist was broken, and—"

"How did it happen?"

"Well, I don't know, hon. Why don't you ask Darcy?"

Because she won't tell me, I wanted to say, at least not the actual truth.

I told Mom I'd call her right back, the same lie I'd told Darcy. Fumbling through my pockets for a fistful of change, I set a stack of quarters by the phone. It seemed like ages since I'd dialed Darcy's number, and I felt my heart pound with each ring, my fingers worrying the metallic cord like a loop of rosary beads. A dozen rings later the receiver picked up, and after some fumbling a weary voice rasped, "Hello?"

"Missus Saint James, this is Teal Conover."

Silence ensued, followed by a throaty cough.

"Hello, Teal. To what do we owe the pleasure?"

"Is Darcy there?" I quickly asked, already put off by her tone.

"Not at the moment," she said. "I haven't seen her all day, in fact. I was told you were in California."

"I was. Or *am*," I stammered, already confused about my plans. "I'm in San Francisco."

"Will you be returning?"

I pictured her sitting in her narrow-backed chair, a glass of wine in her damaged hand, the decanter on the table where a vase full of dahlias shed their white petals on the floor. "Ma'am," I said, "is everything all right? Are you and Darcy okay?"

I really expected she'd play the game, express surprise or offense that I'd ask such a personal question. But I heard a sigh, then the clinking of glass as she topped off her goblet of courage. Did I imagine the ticking of the grandfather clock, the tumble of logs in the fire?

She said, "I am not an eloquent person. I speak in clichés, I behave in clichés. My life is a cliché. You seem to think you know my daughter, listening to her tales, believing you have it all figured out—but you don't. Is it possible to know a person for … what, a few months, a year, and actually love them, enough to be responsible for their feelings? No, young man, it is not, so please don't give her hope just to dash it, not after all she's been through."

"What *has* she been through?" I asked. "And how is your arm, Mrs. Saint James? I know you hurt it. I heard it was broken."

"My wrist, yes."

"You fell, is that it?"

"Yes, in the garden. Stupid of me. I'm an old woman—"

"Don't," I said. "I *do* love Darcy, and if you loved her too, you'd stop this."

"What are you saying?"

"What are *you* saying? What happened when Darcy was a little girl? Why does she hate her own father?"

In the apparent tradition of Saint James women, she abruptly slammed down the phone, and I stood with the receiver clenched in my hand, knowing I'd totally blown it, wondering if Darcy would even speak to me again, much less love me when I got home.

Stuffing my clothes in my Boy Scout pack, I told Hannah and Jake I was leaving, returning to Darcy and my previous life. "What about your mountains?" Hannah asked.

"Hush, now, Mother," Jake chuckled. "The mountains are spirits, they'll always be there."

Hannah sighed and squeezed me tight. "Take care of yourself, and mind your heart. Don't live too much in your head."

"Do you really believe what you said in the garden?" I asked. "That someday we'll look back and the world will have changed?"

"I do," said Hannah, "though most won't notice. Children have no means to measure."

They tried to give me money, just a couple of bucks, but I told them I didn't need it, that I had plenty enough for M&Ms and bus fare back to New York. They gave me a God's eye that Amber had woven with a picture of Little Angel in its center, and I slipped a twenty beneath the honey bear, knowing someone would find it come morning. I lamented not saying goodbye to Beau and Sunshine and Panhandle, but Jake and Hannah just shook their heads and gave me a crushing hug, saying there was no need, that there were other souls in other places who would welcome me as they had, that hello and goodbye just came and went, spinning like leaves, like planets, like prayer wheels in the wind.

Chapter 26

I HAD PLENTY OF TIME TO THINK ON THE BUS, more than was probably wise. We passed through the mountains in daylight this time, and I saw all the things I'd be missing—great mountains in cloud, green forests in fog, a world of detachment and silence. *Don't live too much in your head,* Hannah had said. *The mountains are spirits, they'll always be there.*

As if to convey the gravity of my decision, the impact of my leaving, the headlines I read at midnight bus stops were illustrated with pictures of violence—army tanks rolling through the streets of Chicago amidst swirling clouds of tear gas, the same acrid scent that clung to my hair from the panic at the Bank of America; shirtless soldiers in dog tags and beads stacking bodies on a runway in Da Nang, the sun blazing down through great billows of smoke that could just as well have drifted from the homeland. I scanned their faces for a glimpse of Todd, the reality of his choice striking home, realizing in that moment, on the plains of Nebraska, that I'd finally made one of my own.

I caught the last train, the 11:20 out of Grand Central, and got home around one a.m. Dressed in her robe and floppy slippers, Mom hugged me as I walked through the door, pressing her hand to my clammy forehead, telling me I had a temperature. I'd caught a cold on the drafty bus, on my fevered trip across the country, and she ordered me to bed like she had in the old days, the smell of Vicks VapoRub smeared on my lip and the moisturizer rattling on a plate.

I slept twelve hours and awoke feeling great. Mom had gone to work, leaving me a note to thaw a steak for dinner. I jumped in the shower, my first since Hannah's, and standing before the mirror I noticed that I'd inadvertently grown a beard. It was hardly a big one, maybe an eighth of an inch long, not just a patch of wispy hairs but a uniform growth that darkened my jaw with stubble. "Wow," I whispered, thinking of John Muir's foot-long beard, wondering if Darcy would kiss me.

It was almost three when I headed down to Darcy's, taking all the short cuts to get there quicker, to be kissing her that much sooner. When I got to her house, I scanned the driveway and was relieved to find it empty. Still, I was apprehensive tapping on the door, the big brass knocker always intimidating.

No one answered, and I was tempted to just open it and call her name. I actually placed my hand on the knob, depressed the latch, but never pushed to see if it was locked. So, I walked around the lawn that Carter Mason once mowed, and stood by the flower garden where Darcy's mom had magically broken her wrist on the stairs. A variety of flowers were still in bloom, but no dahlias, and no bees buzzed around those that remained. I stepped quietly to the corner of the house where the back porch was enveloped in wisteria, hoping to surprise Darcy if she was there.

When I leaned enough to peek around it, I was shocked to see Antoine Jones, his head tilted back on the white wicker glider, his face even blacker in contrast, both eyes closed with his arms hanging limp, his chest barely moving as he breathed. Darcy was the mirror image of Antoine, his negative image, considering her startling pallor. Her head was thrown back on the wicker headrest in a perfect mask of repose, a look on her face not of no mind, but mindlessness, of complete withdrawal from the world.

Walking around the wisteria draped porch, I stood before her with one foot on the stoop, staring at the petals of her red-painted toenails, her bare legs stretched out on the floorboards. Antoine was the first to open his eyes, so white and commanding in his placid gaze, the shadow of flowers awash on his face turning his skin a dark blue. No other part of him appeared to move, just his heavy eyelids as he blinked, revealing no sign of recognition much less a gesture of welcome.

When I looked back at Darcy her eyes were just opening, narrow and blue as a Siamese cat's. She too stared with blank comprehension, unresponsive at finding me there, skinnier now in my rough patched jeans and tie-dyed shirt from the Free Store. After a long and agonizing moment, she raised her arms and whispered my name, and I dropped to my knees before her. Squeezing me tight, she began to cry, hitching violently, silently, the sobs shaking her body as she tried to contain them, as if to afford us a modicum of privacy on the now crowded seat of the porch swing.

She was trying to speak but failed to find words, her lips pressed wet against my T-shirt. Feeling a strong hand grip my shoulder, I turned to find Antoine leaning toward me with watery, unfocused eyes. "Yo, Teal," he said, his cropped head nodding, "welcome back, bro. She missed you, man. Big time."

I could only nod back, Darcy squeezing me so tight, rocking us all on the glider. Antoine rose, wobbling a little before assuming his predatory stance. He seemed taller now, bulked out from the army, from being in the brig. "I gotta split," he said, and Darcy reached out with feather-like fingers, her face still buried in my neck. When their hands came together, I noticed her skin—pale and translucent as candle's wax, spidered with delicate veins.

Antoine strode off and was nearly around the corner when I called, "Hey, Twon. Welcome back yourself!" Giving me the power sign, he showed us his smile, the same ivory gleam I remembered from Little League. It lingered in the air like the Cheshire cat's as he floated away across the trimmed lawn.

"Stop it, Darce," I said, when she went on crying. "I'm home. I came back for you." She kissed me then, and it was everything I remembered, wet and warm and filled with her scent, and I wondered how I'd ever even thought of not returning.

"You grew a beard," she said, smiling now, her glacial eyes sparkling wet.

"Not really. I just couldn't shave." Which was almost true. "You don't like it?"

"You're beautiful!" she said. "Your hair is so long, and it's blonde!"

I started to tell her about swimming in the ocean, running half naked on the beach with—

But she pressed a painted finger to my lips, followed by the taste of her own, and kissed me so long I couldn't breathe and had to come up for air. "Let's go upstairs," she said.

Standing abruptly, she grabbed my hand and led me into the kitchen, the only place in the Saint James's house I'd ever seen in broad daylight. Passing through the dining room, a crystal chandelier winked in the light from French-paned windows, rainbows of color splashed across wallpaper patterned like oriental rugs.

Rounding the foyer, we climbed a stairway with elegant, sculpted handrails, the wide treads silenced by brocaded carpet, studded with little brass tacks. Ascending the stairs, the walls were hung with photos ranging back over several decades, black and white portraits of men in suits, women in floor-length gowns. One showed the Doctor with a huge pair of scissors cutting a ceremonial ribbon, another of him holding a banner-sized check while aping for the camera. Further along there were children on horseback or playing croquet on a leaf-shadowed lawn, posing with ribbons in their platinum hair, dressed in their Sunday best.

"Is this you?" I asked, pointing to a picture of a tow-headed girl in a stroller.

"That's Kara," said Darcy. "This one is me. My first picture ever, I guess."

Darcy lay cradled in her father's arms, her eyes squeezed shut against the flashbulb, her tiny fists clenched as though defending herself against the world into which she'd been born. You couldn't see the Doctor's eyes, but I could tell that he was smiling, his widow's peak drawn like the point of an arrow, his nose like the blade of a knife.

More photos showed Darcy propped in her high chair, or holding an Easter bunny, dressed as an angel in a Catholic school play with filmy wings pinned to her gown.

"Who took all these pictures?"

"My father," she said. "He once had a passion for cameras."

"No Lena?" I asked, and she squeezed my hand and led me to the second floor.

A corridor availed us of several rooms, and I tried to guess which was the Doctor's, crawling with spiders and vipers no doubt, guarded by the aforementioned flying monkeys. Marching me toward one corner of the house, Darcy kicked at a door with her toe, the paint there visibly worn. A minty coolness drifted from the room as sunlight streamed through its windows, a fluttering mosaic of teal green stars from maple leaves pressed to the glass.

We entered the bedroom of a teenage girl, its bureaus lined with porcelain jars and fancy perfume bottles, its single bed teeming with teddy bears, dolls, and a skinny green frog in top hat and tails. Satin ribbons polka-dotted the pink-painted walls, red, gold, and blue badges of accomplishment in equestrian events, tennis matches, even a beauty pageant. There was a graduation picture of a young woman with blonde hair and blue eyes, the mortarboard cap cocked rakishly on her head, the tassel draped symbolically to one side. Beside it on the nightstand was a heavy black phone, its long cord coiled on the carpet.

"Kara's room," I said, and Darcy pulled me to the bed where we tumbled on the shadows of leaves. The frilly white pillowcase smelled like Darcy's hair, as did the sheets, the bedspread and fuzzy brown bear. Glancing at a window where our breathing fogged the glass, I made out the shape of a fish, the smile on its face like the curve of a hook, drawn with the tip of a finger.

"I thought we were going to your room, the Van Gogh room," I said. "I still haven't seen it, you know."

She was kissing me then, climbing atop me, her tongue in my mouth when she said, "No, I can't deal with this … this hair."

Leading me down the hallway to the master bath, she bade me to sit on a stool, pulled off my shirt—as well as her own—and brushed shaving cream on my face with an actual shaving brush, dipping it in a ceramic shaving mug she'd fished from beneath the sink. Wielding an old-fashioned, pearl-handled razor, she raked it on her belly, making sure it was as sharp as it looked.

"I'm Zooey," she said, "from your favorite book. "You can be Bessie, his mom."

"What's gonna happen if your parents come home? Is that your father's razor?"

Letting hot water run in the sink, she tipped my head back with her finger, the sound of the ocean in the palm of her hand as she dragged the blade down my cheek, slowly, carefully, as I watched her every move in the mirror. A stripe of smooth skin appeared on my chin, bold as a brush stroke in her sure, artist's hand. I watched too the elegant outline of her breast as she bent to consider her work, its pointy tip jiggling like strawberry Jell-o, her tongue in the corner of her mouth.

Gripping her waist, I kneaded the flesh that contoured her slender rib cage, cupping the rounds of her perfect breasts, her nipples as cool as hard candy. She'd shave a clean line then give me a kiss, shave more, then kiss me again. Straddling my knee she rocked easy in the saddle, as much cream on her own face as mine. She smiled at our reflection in the oval mirror, lips curled in the grin of a fox. Dropping the razor, she wrapped me in her arms and pressed herself hard against my chest, twisting, wiggling as she bounced atop me until I felt myself explode in my jeans. Supple as a seal, she laughed with her head back, her spine describing a Romanesque arch as steam breathed a mist on the mirror.

"I'm sorry," I said, a minute later. "I can't believe I did that."

"Don't be. I haven't come that hard in months."

"Really? I didn't sleep with anyone. Did you?"

"No," she said, and then more forcefully, "*No!* I just went out a couple of times."

"You did? With who?"

"With Erik. We're friends, is all."

"Erik? You went out with Neumann? Where'd you go?"

"Into the city. To hook up with some friends. Erik's in jail, you know. His hearing was in August, but it got postponed, and then he sold pills to a narc."

"Acid?"

"I don't think so. It was reds, probably. Seconal."

"Downers? That's what he's into?"

I should have asked then about Antoine Jones and the curious nature of their relationship, both of them wasted, or appearing to be, nodding off on Darcy's porch.

"You're all I have," she whispered. "You're all I want. You and the Yankee cap," she giggled, snatching it from the rumpled pile of our clothes, tugging it on her head. Glancing at her torso in the foggy mirror, she was beautiful to behold, her hair steamed in ringlets, stuck to her cheek, naked, except for the ball cap.

"What?" she said, watching me watch her, "you want to shave me now?"

I nodded that I did, too anxious to speak, and stropped her damp skin like a razor.

Some time later I awoke on Kara's bed, my heart pounding loudly as footsteps mounted the stairs. A minute passed while I held my breath, wondering if I was dreaming, hoping that I was, then just as fervently wishing I wasn't, resolved to finally confront the Doctor and end the ridiculous charade. But when one minute passed, and then another and no one appeared at the door, I heard myself exhale, released from the scrutiny of a dozen glass eyes that peeked from the mountain of blankets. The frog and the Teddy Bear leaned by the window where we'd shoved them away in our ardor, the first glow of sunset infusing the leaves, Darcy's back dappled in shadows. Easing stealthily out of the blankets, I peeked down the hallway before striding boldly to the bathroom, where I hopped around on one bare foot as I struggled to pull on my jeans, observing the razor where it lay on the tile, its blade gleaming close to my heel.

Intending to return to Kara's room, I paused by a narrow, almost hidden stairwell that rose into total darkness. This was my chance, I told myself, to finally see Darcy's room, painted in orange and sunflower yellow like Vincent's room at Arles. The worn treads creaked as I made my way up, the air growing cooler as I climbed. A landing at the top revealed a small bath with an old-fashioned clawfoot tub, the dangling pull chain of a ceiling lamp reflected in the cloudy mirror. At the end of the corridor a single door beckoned, the wall sconce useless, missing its bulb.

Traversing its length with a hand on each wall it seemed to take minutes to get there, my eyes slow to focus in the musty gloom as I felt ahead for the door jamb. Drawing a breath before turning the knob, preparing myself for the scene, the hinges squeaked as the door swung wide like tearing a hole in my chest.

There was no yellow chair, no crimson blanket, the walls weren't cerulean blue. The space before me was blank as a canvas, sterile as an operating room, a white-painted cube of raked walls and high ceiling, its lone window obscured by a blind. A white-shaded lamp leaned cockeyed by the bed, angled like a lance in the hardwood floor. The sheets were white, the quilt was white, as was the one pillow at the headboard. The only real proof that the room was Darcy's was her red coat hanging on a doorknob, so bright in the absence of all other hues it shouted like blood on white sand.

Backing down the hall, then the stairs to the landing, I glanced into Kara's room, Darcy still curled in the fetal position, adrift in wisteria dreams. I left without waking her and tiptoed down the stairs past the picture frames lining the wall: pig tails, horse tails, patent leather shoes, babies grinning toothless at the camera … a gallery of memories, or photographic lies? Diabolical, or misunderstood? The most truthful photos were the missing ones of Lena, more honest in their absence than the others. Tossed out, hidden, their whereabouts suspect, at least the motivation was clear.

All the way home I could smell Darcy's scent, her hair, our sweat, our cum. Something had changed when I entered her bedroom, like entering another person's mind, a room like a thought, a thought like a life, a landscape of lies and illusion.

Welcome home, Teal, I said to myself, far from the promise of mountains.

Chapter 27

DARCY CALLED THE NEXT DAY at the crack of noon, catching me still in bed. She'd been shopping all morning at Saks in White Plains and had run into Mary Ann. "She works there," she told me, "at least for a while before starting at Brown next semester."

The Westchester store wasn't as fancy as the one in Manhattan, but the clothes were just as expensive. Darcy had purchased a new pair of shoes—"Like Alice in Wonderland's," she said. For me she'd bought slacks, a turtleneck sweater, and a scarf I'd never wear, anything that tickled her fancy.

Tickling her fancy was all I could think of, recalling our moment with the razor.

"Dinner at eight, at DeLindos," she said, explaining the plan she'd made with Mouse. "Dionne's the hostess—isn't that cool—so Bosco will probably be there!"

She'd done it for me, the date with the gang. Hanging out with "old friends" just wasn't Darcy's thing; I doubt she believed she had any.

"Great," I said, "and sorry about yesterday, leaving without saying goodbye."

"No sweat," she laughed, and I felt it again, remembering her glistening skin. She talked for an hour, and it felt like old times, just lying there listening to her voice reading me the horoscopes and Sunday comics until I almost fell back to sleep. "Teal," she said, "that night on the roof … nothing I told you was true."

I wanted to ask what else was a lie and confess that I'd visited her room. "I figured as much," I said instead. "Your dad is a fucking prince."

"I mean Carter Mason," she was quick to correct. "Nothing ever happened between us."

Greeted by Dionne as we entered the restaurant, she gave us each a big hug. In a form-fitting dress and platform heels she suddenly looked much older, her hair in an Afro that haloed her face, as pretty as Angela Davis. Leading us to a table that overlooked the river, she lit the white candle in its center, and we sat for a minute catching up on the news—who'd gone to what school, who planned to get married, who was keeping the baby. The walls were hung with fishnets and wine bottles, posters of Venice and Rome. A tank full of lobsters glowed green by a window, close to the kitchen doors. Half listening, half dreaming, I observed the doomed creatures through the membrane of tinted glass, the lights of the Tappan Zee Bridge shining through, like part of its undersea world.

Darcy ordered wine, and I a beer, anything they had on tap. Dionne supplyed an extra menu when we told her that Mary Ann was coming. She pointed to the lounge before scurrying away, where Bosco's broad shoulders, squeezed into a sports jacket, took up one end of the bar.

"I gotta say hi," I leaned to tell Darcy, and left her reading the menu.

Sneaking up behind Bosco, I tapped his right shoulder then leaned to the left like the idiot grammar school prank. He fell for the ruse and both of us laughed, giving each other a manly abrazo, Bosco's touch surprisingly tender for an hombre his size.

"Yo, man," he said, "you lookin' good, all tanned an' shit. Almost like a brother."

"Speaking of which," I said, not bothering with small talk, "I saw Antoine yesterday. What's his story?"

Bosco sighed. "Twon's story kinda fucked up."

"How's that?"

"I told you he got in some trouble with the army. Well, it was pretty big trouble." Bosco paused to eyeball me, bro to bro. "Thing is," he said, "Twon killed a guy."

I was shocked, then confused. "So?" I said. "He was in Vietnam."

Bosco shook his head. "Nah, it ain't like that. Antoine, he killed a good guy, he fragged the dude."

I'd heard the term. Everybody had. It was when an enlisted man, a grunt, killed an officer—often in combat—with a fragmentation grenade. "Holy fuck!" I said. "Why is he still walking?"

"The dude was ARVN, man—the officer he capped. He was South Vietnamese. That cat was *cold*, Antoine said. He did bad, evil things, and one day he just did something *too* bad, *too* evil, and Antoine stopped him. He wasted the motherfucker."

"And they didn't arrest him? Antoine?"

"Oh yeah, they tossed him right in the brig. Thing is, it got all political, see? After all the protests and shit, the brass didn't want the bad press. They ain't above bullshitting, and it would have looked bad if a GI got busted for offing a gook Major. So they quashed it, shut people up. Twon did some time over there, then got booted with a dishonorable discharge."

"Wow, that's heavy."

Bosco nodded. "Only good thing," he said, "Antoine got straight in the brig. He was strung-out bad over there. There's beau-coup dope in the Nam."

"You sure?" I asked.

"Oh yeah, they got poppies growing every-fucking-where."

"No, I mean, are you sure he's straight now?"

Bosco frowned. "Why, he say something to you?"

"No, he didn't say anything."

"You ain't into that shit, are ya?" said Bosco.

"Hell no. How can you ask?"

Bosco chuckled, reached out to flick my long hair. "No reason," he said, flashing a grin that reminded me of his brother.

Through the bamboo partition that divided the rooms, I watched Mary Ann breeze through the door, and at first I couldn't believe it was her, dressed up like a salesgirl at Saks. She was wearing green eye shade and startling pink lipstick, her hair swept high on her head. Sparkling earrings trailed down her neck, a gold chain disappearing between her breasts. I was stunned by the depth of her transformation from mousy to all-out babe, released like a butterfly from its drab cocoon through the magic of make-up and jewelry.

Darcy rose to greet her in the center of the room, and they hugged in a genuine embrace. When Bosco and I strode out of the bar, Mary Ann looked almost startled. She broke into tears, threw her arms around my neck, and pulled me hard to her chest. "He's getting on a plane this very minute!" she cried. "Todd's on his way to Vietnam!"

We moved to the table and circled our chairs, Darcy huddled close by her side. Dionne brought wine, more beer, and more bread sticks while Mary Ann slowly recovered. "I'm sorry," she said. "I knew this was coming. I shouldn't be so upset."

"It's alright," Darcy soothed. "Nothing a trip to the powder room can't cure."

Bosco and I ordered while they were gone: Caesar's, steaks, and a couple of the unfortunate lobsters. When the ladies returned, they were arm in arm, freshly made up and giggling like school girls. We dined, chugging wine from a wicker-wrapped bottle, the red juice staining our chins, then shared a dessert of rich, dark chocolate from which Bosco was obliged to abstain, observing a strict diet before beginning football camp in Florida.

Once the table was cleared, Darcy plucked a pack of cigarettes from her mirrored handbag and lit one. Sliding her chair away from the table, she rubbed her tummy and exhaled a long plume of smoke.

"What are you doing?" I said.

"What? Smoking?"

"Yeah. When did you start doing that?"

"I haven't *started*. I just bought a pack, is all."

"Hey," said Bosco, "gimme one a them. They ain't got my fat ass yet!"

Darcy laughed, and the two of them sat puffing Kools together, Mary Ann glancing across the table at me, sneaking a smile, like, What's up with these guys?

Minutes later Darcy's eyelids began to droop, her long lashes fluttering like butterfly wings, flitting once, twice, then closing, dreaming, before opening again. When she saw me looking, she blew me a kiss and reached to cover my hand, her fingernails brushing the flat of my palm, cold as the claws of a lobster.

"So what's up with you, Darce?" Bosco asked, releasing the perfect smoke ring. "You going to school or something?"

Darcy smiled glamorously, slumped in her chair with her stockinged legs crossed, her high heels kicked to the floor. She was wearing the proverbial *little black dress*, slung low on her shoulders, tight at the hips, and she looked simply gorgeous in repose. "I'll be doing some modeling," she said. "I already started, at an agency in the City."

"You are?" I said, completely surprised. Bosco and Mary Ann visibly stiffened, reflecting my sudden discomfort. "Why didn't you tell me?"

Darcy shrugged. "You weren't here, how could I?"

"Yeah, but why wait until now?"

"I didn't wait, it just came up."

I let it go, sensing a potential scene. When Dionne crooked a finger at her tipsy boyfriend, he excused himself and left. With Bosco gone, Mary Ann stood and thanked us for dinner, Darcy having paid in cash. The girls hugged, and Darcy told Mary Ann to call her. Mouse and I smiled and nodded at each other, too awkward to hazard a hug.

"Why didn't you say something?" I asked Darcy, once we were alone.

"I did," she replied with an exhale of smoke. "We talked in the restroom. She's just upset about Todd."

"I mean about the modeling."

"Why? What's the big deal?"

"Nothing, I guess. It's just that we talked so much about what you'd do after school, and then—you didn't even mention it."

"You don't approve?"

"Of course I do, if that's what you want! I'm surprised is all, with your thing about beauty."

"My thing?"

"Yes! Are you gonna pretend—"

"It's not about *beauty*, Teal. It's clothes, and photos in magazines. It's just another game, like baseball. Can't you be happy for me?"

"I am happy."

"Then shut up, and kiss me, okay?"

I did, but apparently poorly, because she pushed from the table and hustled out into the drizzling night. I said goodbye to Bosco and Dionne, then headed for my mom's borrowed car. Darcy sat slumped in the passenger seat, her bare shoulder pressed to the window. Halfway to her house she scooted over and cuddled herself against me, her knees drawn up so they touched my thigh, her head beneath my chin. The smell of her hair was intoxicating, and a wave of arousal rushed through me.

She didn't move when I pulled to the curb half a block from her house. We kissed very slowly, with the tips of our tongues, our fingers at work in our clothes. When I slipped my hand beneath her dress, she squeezed it between her thighs. "I'm having my period," she whispered in my ear, reaching for the zipper of my brand-new slacks. Dipping her head, she blew me like a whistle, the rain on the roof keeping cadence with her head, my hand at the back of her neck. When finally I came, I felt only shame, like I'd somehow betrayed my only lover, who leaped from the car before I could speak and dashed off into the night, crossing the lawn with a shoe in each hand until swallowed by the darkness of her porch.

Chapter 28

Darcy called a couple of days later, cheerful as ever, to discuss going down to my orientation for SVA. It was being held at a theater on Forty-Second Street, and she wanted to come along. I thought that was a great idea because I was nervous, and because I still missed her so much, even when we were together.

That Friday, the big day, we met on the train, Darcy getting on at the Manor station, me at Tarrytown because it was closer. She looked incredible gliding down the aisle, coming to greet me where I stood between cars. She was dressed in spiked heels and a calf-length dress with a neckline that flattered her throat, pearl earrings dangling from thin, gold chains, swaying with the tilt of her head.

"Look at you," I said, smiling. "You really are a model!"

She laughed, genuinely, the warmth of it more becoming than any jewel or lip gloss.

The train lurched ahead and we grabbed each other, fumbling with a kiss. Taking a seat, we huddled together and watched the river go by, hip to hip and hand in hand, Darcy's head on my shoulder. It was a gray day, Indian summer on hold, or perhaps over. The river was leaden and the Palisades austere—carved by glaciers, I knew, recalling my lessons from Earth science class where my passion for mountains was inspired.

"Darce," I said, "I'm sorry if I've done anything to hurt you. Have I?"

"Of course not."

"I knew you'd say that, but really, are we okay?"

She raised my hand and tenderly kissed it, kissing hers by mistake, then kissed them both with the imprint of lipstick, her giggle the perfect reply.

"So how does it work, your modeling job?" I asked.

"Pretty simple. They call me up, I go down to the shoot. I've only done one, but the client was pleased, and I'm scheduled for a couple more."

"You like it, huh?"

"It's a job."

"C'mon," I laughed. "Most girls would kill for a job like that. Aren't you excited?"

"Yeah," she said, but I saw in her eyes that she meant it only for me.

Walking down Forty-Second Street, Darcy with her gray cape flapping, me in my new turtleneck and slacks, people turned to watch us pass, and I knew why she'd bought me the clothes, so we'd look like a couple whose destinies merged, worthy of the streets of New York.

I was nervous, and Darcy knew it, so she made us stop at Horn & Hardart for a cup of coffee and pecan pie. I didn't really want the pie, my stomach was so upset, but Darcy got hers ala mode, with chocolate ice cream and vanilla syrup.

I sipped at my coffee, tapping the counter as we perched on tall stools by the windows. "Stop that," she said, "you're making *me* nervous. Why are you so uptight?"

"We're gonna be late."

"So? Relax, Teal, it's like any appointment. No matter what time you arrive, you're gonna have to wait. Are you having second thoughts?"

"No," I lied, "I'm *here*, Dar, with you. Just like you wanted."

"I mean about school."

"Of course not," I said, gulping hot coffee, forcing a huge bite of pie.

The theater was old and funky beautiful with tin panels stamped on the sloping ceiling, once-plush carpeting worn in the center, bordered by intricate tiles. Old-fashioned sconces adorned the walls, their lightbulbs flickering like candle's flames. A crystal chandelier dominated the lobby where long, narrow mirrors reflecting its glow; Darcy leaned toward one and freshened her lipstick, ruined at Horn & Hardart. Impatient, listless, I stared around, self-conscious in my brand-new clothes. There were hundreds of students and a smattering of adults, many of them long-haired artist types, a stereotype difficult to avoid. Darcy was digging it, intrigued by all the people, while I was inexplicably anxious. Once we were seated, holding hands as a spotlight scanned the stage, she turned to me and whispered, "Teal, you're trembling." Squeezing my hand in both of hers, she leaned to catch my eye. "Are you okay?" she asked. "Is there something I can do?"

She fished around in the pocket of her cape and I heard the soft rattle of a pill vile. "Take one," she instructed, and held out her palm where a small pile of capsules were nestled.

"What is it," I asked, thinking of Erik Neumann, "Seconal?"

Shaking her head, she appeared annoyed. "Do these look red? They're yellow, see? It's Nembutal. It'll help calm you down."

We each took one and sat there in silence as an older man wandered on stage. Dressed in jeans and a tie-dye shirt, he welcomed us all to the New York School of Visual Arts, a banner with the school colors—purple and orange—draped behind him, and a recording of the Mothers of Invention blaring from loudspeakers: "We are the other people, We are the other people, You are the other people too!"

Ten minutes into the program I began to relax. The featured speaker, Berne Hogarth, author of *Dynamic Anatomy*—the book I'd given to Darcy—proved genuinely humorous and sincere, the students laughing, the school president smiling, the whole thing feeling warm and welcoming, eliciting the same kind of freak camaraderie I'd felt in the streets of the Haight. Darcy squeezed my arm, pleased to see me smiling, then laughing, enjoying my enjoyment of it all. I felt better about everything: school, Darcy, the promise of our future together. New York was a cool place after all, a mindscape of peaks and riverine canyons every bit as alluring as mountains.

After the ceremony we bought slices at a tiny pizza joint, all dressed up and standing at a counter where an old black guy snored and a couple of drunk kids burned holes in their napkins with cigarette butts. It was dark by then, and the plate glass windows reflected all that went on inside, the drunk kids making obscene gestures behind Darcy's back, a fat lady slapping her little boy for sucking his ice with a straw. We ignored it all, me telling Darcy how there was no real pizza west of the Mississippi, where delicatessens were as fabled and non-existent as Shangri La. She told me about the outfits she'd worn at her shoot, extravagant clothing you'd never see in stores, or at least not yet. Once outside, Darcy knocked a Kool from a brand-new pack and I lit it for her. It smelled so good I plucked it from her fingers and took a drag myself, the taste reminding me of the long drive home from the Pentagon, the night of her father's heart attack.

Stuffed as we were after pecan pie and pizza, Darcy made us stop at the chocolatiers in Grand Central. We ate from the little white bag on the train, Darcy displaying our sugary choices on the bumps of her nyloned knees. When the bag was empty, she held up her hand with two yellow capsules in her palm. Without even thinking I popped one in my mouth, and Darcy did the same.

Cuddling my arm with her head on my shoulder, she instantly fell asleep. Train wheels clacked, black branches whipped past as I slipped into something like dreams, the lights across the Hudson floating like stars, like candles in the current of the Ganges.

I got off at the Tarrytown station and Darcy stayed on for the Manor. Walking up Cortlandt, it struck me as strange that I hadn't remained on the train, escorting Darcy home down the cool blue streets for a last, long kiss at her corner. But that night she hadn't ask me to, and I never thought to offer.

Heading toward the projects I saw Antoine Jones leaning on the fender of a car, his long legs crossed, heels cocked on the sidewalk, his pointy shoes aimed at the sky. He kept one hand in his leather coat's pocket, the tip of a cigarette slicing the night. Exhaling a trembling plume of smoke, it turned pink in the glow of the streetlight. "Yo, Teal," he grinned. "What's happenin', bro?"

Holding out his hand I tried to shake it, immediately lost in a series of moves I didn't know fuck-all about. He chuckled at my ignorance, very cool and practiced, and slapped my shoulder instead. "You cool, man, don't sweat it. I just figger you for a brother, is all."

"Yeah? Thanks."

He laughed again. "Ain't nothin'," he said, and offered me a Kool from his pack. He lit it from his own and handed it to me. "So, whatchoo up to, T?"

"Big thing at my school today. Orientation. Darcy went down with me."

"Way cool. How she doin'?"

"Good. She's … fine."

"Hey, bro," he said, "about that girl. We just friends, you dig? Ain't nothing else, just so you know. We friends too, I figger. You an' me. I ain't never forgot your pop, Little League an' shit. He was cool, your dad. And you too, s'all I'm saying."

"Thanks," I said. "I remember, too. You were great. A fucking great pitcher."

Antoine held up his hand and I grabbed it again—he shook it, once, and let go. "Maybe someday I teach you," he laughed. "The shake, not my fast ball."

Walking away I was thinking of Bosco, what he'd told me about his brother. What kind of shit had Antoine seen that led him to do what he'd done? And what was he doing on Darcy's porch? How had they come to be friends?

The thing about questions, the thing about drugs, is that one negates the other. The more you take, the less you wonder, and the farther you get from the truth.

Chapter 29

My FIRST DAY OF SCHOOL I was massively nervous, everything being so new. But once we got started, the familiar smells soothed me, the Gesso, varnish, and turpentine like a calming form of incense, like sandalwood was for the Krishnas.

There were two buildings, one on East Twenty-Third Street where there was also a gallery, and another on Twenty-First, with three full stories of studio space, but no cafeteria. From the big rear windows on the top floor of the Twenty-First Street building, you could look down on the adjacent rooftop of the Police Academy where New York's Finest drilled, white gloves on their hands, black shoes in the sun, marching in cadence to whistles. Art students lined the opened windows and shouted mindless insults, squashing their faces to the sooty glass, taunting the oblivious rookies. I didn't join in for personal reasons, never explaining why.

Some of the artists were better than me, and lots were a great deal worse. But none were as good as Darcy, and I struggled with that knowledge whenever I saw her, which was often, almost every day, when our schedules coincided and we arranged to commute together. Jonah Gold was going to Lehman College in the Bronx, and sometimes I saw him on the train. We hadn't spoken for quite a while, and he caught me up on things: Seth Gold had postponed graduate school and was seeking a second degree in numerology, or alchemy, anything to keep him from the draft. Their oldest brother Levi was in a hospital in Bonn, suffering from gonorrhea, or syphilis. "I hope they cut off his dick," Jonah said, "purge the ethnic gene pool. What's a Jew doing in Germany, anyway?"

He told me about Neumann, still incarcerated, how his minister dad had given up on him, declaring that maybe a little jail time was exactly what his son needed. PH3 was shacked up with Belinda Cake, no longer just gooey inside. They'd finally decided to keep the baby, which I thought was cool, but which Jonah thought was absurd, pronouncing the word with a z—"Abzurd," repeating it over and over.

The craziest news was about Steve Railsbeck. Due to the dearth of LSD—a direct result of Neumann's absence—his second attempt to fool the draft board had failed, and he'd received his orders to report to Texas, or North Carolina, or somewhere down south. The week before he was scheduled to leave, he lopped off his finger in a fan belt accident and had to go to the ER. I was surprised that Mom never told me, but hospital business was deemed confidential, or maybe Steve's dad was protecting his son, having failed to prove he was psycho.

A few weeks into school I'd relaxed enough to feel excited about it, doing pen and ink drawings after Albrecht Durer, oils after Homer and Turner, all of them landscapes, mountains in the mist, scaling great peaks with my paintbrush. Our instructors were all professional artists and they took us to visit their studios, one of them as big as the Twenty-First Street building, sandwiched between brownstones uptown. Darcy and I museum-hopped together, going to the Whitney, the Guggenheim, the Frick Galleries. One day we met for lunch at the MOMA where I found her sitting out in the courtyard, smoking a cigarette with her stockinged legs crossed, a plum-colored waistcoat unbuttoned at the neck, revealing the valley of her breasts. "Hi," she said, remaining seated, offering me her cheek.

"Lipstick," she mouthed, by way of explanation, her sunglasses slipping down her nose.

"Sorry I'm late," I said, pulling my chair closer.

"You're not."

"What, sorry?"

"Late," she laughed, smiling behind the dark lenses.

"Have you eaten?" I asked.

She shook her head. "I'm not very hungry."

I was about to say something funny again, to mention her usual equine appetite, but I let it go and bummed a cigarette instead—Gauloises, now—and coughed away the first puff. "I'm not that hungry either," I said, glancing at the paleness of the city sun eclipsed by adjacent buildings. "Shall we go in? It's kind of chilly out here."

Stubbing out our cigarettes, Darcy slung her mirrored bag over her shoulder. She was wearing high heels that clicked across the patio in front of me, her ass swaying smartly in a clingy black skirt, her carriage perfected at the agency. We wandered the wings looking at the new shows, then at the permanent collection, *Guernica* looming large and powerful on one entire wall, a bizarre Picassan geometry of sharp angles and blocky gray shapes. Squeezing my arm, Darcy whispered, "We finally made it, The Modern!" Her made-up face was lit with excitement, a bit of my old girlfriend shining through. Her spiked heels echoed through the halls as we strolled, both of us moved and stunned to silence by the masterful works we saw. We stood before a canvas of a massive head, a self-portrait of the artist, a balding man with a bushy red moustache, his horn-rimmed glasses framing frank, staring eyes. Painted in a million tiny dots, it was almost pointillistic, but not, too photographic to evoke emotion, too real to be called Impressionistic.

"That's my drawing instructor, Chuck Close," I confided.

"Really?" said Darcy, truly impressed. I was impressed, too. I'd seen his work, but not here, not at the Modern with the likes of Picasso, Oldenberg, Rothko. "What's he like?" she asked.

"He's nice, you know. A normal guy. He had us buy these jigsaw puzzles and copy them piece by piece, side by side, scribbling away until the puzzle—the drawing—was finished, and you could finally see what you'd done. Mine was a montage of musical instruments—trumpets, oboes, clarinets. It took forever with its squiggly little lines, but he told me he really liked it."

"Fantastic!" said Darcy. "What's he look like?"

Both of us stood there staring at the portrait, and after a moment I said, "Like that!"

We burst out laughing in the high-ceilinged room, the happy sound bouncing around us. Darcy threw her arms around my neck and gave a sloppy kiss. "Hey," I whispered, as the other patrons watched, "you're messing up your lipstick."

"That's okay," she whispered back, "I have lots more in my purse." She peppered me then with plum-colored kisses, pecking both sides of my face, carefully pressing her lips to the cheeks I'd so carefully shaved that morning. "There," she said, leaning back to observe her work, "Portrait of Teal Conover, by Darcy Saint James."

By late afternoon on the second floor, the light had grown dusky through the walls of plate glass, pink clouds rouging the sky. Seated together on a long narrow bench we were finally alone, surrounded on three sides by the huge, angled panels of Monet's *Water Lilies.* Darcy relaxed with her back against mine and her legs stretched out on the cushions, one foot dangling over its edge, her heels tumbled off on the carpet. The colors of the water lilies—pink, violet, cerulean, teal—seemed to drift from the canvas like mist into the room, the oil-painted evening in the Provence countryside magically transposed to West Fifty-Third Street in Manhattan. The fecund scent of it was heady as perfume, pungent and rich as plowed earth. Bull frogs croaked and sand pipers piped, blue turtles poked their snouts from the water where Darcy's toes dangled near the surface.

"Are you happy?" she asked me.

"Yeah," I said, mechanically, without real thought. "Are you?"

Darcy fell silent, never one to mince words, or employ them by way of an answer. I turned on the bench and she fell against me, curled across my lap. She said, "I once read this thing about Eskimos in the Arctic, where this guy is half frozen on the ice. He kills his trusty reindeer, cuts open its belly, and curls up inside where it's warm. He saves himself that way. That's what I feel like," she said at length. "Like I just want to crawl up inside you, where it's warm, and safe, and you love me."

"Don't you think it would hurt?" I said. "You know, for me?"

She pinched my leg, but I knew she was smiling, a dimple on the plane of her cheek.

"I'll save you, Darce," I whispered softly, my lips just brushing her hair. "You will always be inside me. You will never be gone from my life."

Chapter 30

ON HALLOWEEN WE HAD A PARTY AT SCHOOL and I invited Darcy. She had a shoot that day and said she'd be late and wouldn't have time for a costume. True minimalist that I am— or maybe just lazy—I painted my face like the bull in Picasso's *Guernica*. It was pretty easy, black and white, a few quick strokes like a cow's square nose—only sideways—and I was done. It took maybe two minutes.

We had the party at Twenty-Third Street, downstairs in the gallery. There were plenty of freaky, imaginative costumes, as you'd expect from a bunch of artists. One chick was made up like the fetus in *2001, A Space Odyssey*. Another guy dressed as a rookie cop with a mask from *Planet Of The Apes*, marching around the gallery floor, occasionally blowing a whistle.

People palmed joints behind their back, tipped flasks behind vampire capes. At some point in the festivities, I spotted Darcy standing in the center of the gallery, looking for me, turning slowly on a spiked heel to scan the crowd. I hung back a moment and watched my classmates and instructors watch her, dressed as she was in some outfit from the shoot, a crazy, aluminum foil-looking sheath with no back to speak of and a long slit that merged with her crotch. Her platinum hair twisted up like a Frisbee, like a hat from the forties, cocked at an angle and shading one turquoise eye.

When I stepped into view she smiled brilliantly, obviously relieved to find me, and kissed me with lips that matched her blue eye shadow. "Darce," I said, "You look … silver."

She smiled. "And you are a handsome cow. Moo!"

Introducing her to some of my friends, Darcy held out her hand, her nail polish aqua, a small silver purse dangling from her wrist. When she asked for the restroom and excused herself, Maxwell Hempler, a speedy little sleep-deprived guy from Long Island said, "Holy shit, Conover, is that your girlfriend? I thought she was Nico at first, or some other Warhol protégé."

"That's not how she usually looks," I explained. "She's a model. She only wears that stuff when—"

"We know what a model is," groaned Meighyn Welch, spelled with an I, and an H, and a Y. She'd been listening in, as were a number of other bystanders interested in Darcy's ass. "Does that slit ever end," she asked, speaking of the dress, "or does she have a cleft palate?"

"Look who's jealous," laughed Rufus, whose nickname was of course Dufus. It was hard to take anyone seriously, dressed as they were. Rufus had a big red button taped to his forehead, plastic, like the lens of a taillight. It must have had a small battery attached, because he could light it up and say, "Open the pod door, Hal," *2001* being a big hit that year.

Meighyn was one of those black-hatted witches with the massive cleavage. "Fuck off, you little perve," she told Rufus. "You'd tit-fuck me in a New York minute!"

"A Long Island minute!" joked Hempler, also from Leavittown, the subject of the Pete Seeger song about ticky-tacky boxes.

When after five minutes Darcy hadn't returned, I decided to go have a look. I needed to piss anyway, having sucked so much wine from crappy bota bags, my mouth dried out from bumming cigarettes. The SVA bathrooms were unisex, a relatively new concept if you discounted the middle ages, so I stood at the urinal and relieved myself, craning my neck to look at the row of stalls where I spotted Darcy's mirrored bag on the tiled floor.

"Hey Dar," I said, "everything all right?"

I heard her sniffle like she was crying, and I shook my head in silence, weary of those scenes wherein I talked her down from some quiet form of hysteria. After shaking off and washing my hands, Darcy had yet to answer, so when I heard her sigh and sniffle again, I strode over and opened the door of the stall. She sat on the john with a dot of white powder on her knuckle, an equal amount rimming one nostril, her peacock eyelids barely open.

Kneeling, I placed my hands on her knees and leaned to look in her eyes. "What are you doing?" I asked. "What's this stuff you're taking, huh? Are you feeling all right?"

"Yes," she whispered, nodding. "I'm fine. Just … give me a minute."

"What is this stuff?"

"It's smack, Teal," she said, without hesitation.

"Heroin?" She nodded again, her eyes drooping shut.

I pawed through her bag, then the little silver purse. "Is this all of it?" I asked, holding a waxy packet between my fingers. "Darcy? Is this all you've got?" She nodded just a little harder, struggling to hold up her head.

"Ten minutes," I said. "I'll be right outside the door. Then we're getting out of here." Heading toward the exit I saw my face in the mirror and bent at the sink to wash off the paint. "Eight minutes," I called, and left her in the bathroom. It was fifteen minutes before she came out. She'd washed up, the powder gone from her nose, her lipstick freshly applied. She smiled when she saw me and tugged at the neckline of her dress. "Ready?" she asked.

We didn't bother to say goodbye, slipping out a fire door in the corner of the gallery. It was cool on the street, and Darcy seemed to perk up. "You hungry?" I asked. "Wanna get something to eat?"

"No," she said, "that doesn't sound very good."

"You should eat, Darce. I really think you should eat something." Stopping to assess her as she teetered on the sidewalk: her eyeliner was running, her lipstick smeared, and I took her in my arms in a crushing embrace until I heard her groan. "Jesus, Dar, why are you doing this to yourself?"

We were both crying when she pushed me away, bent convulsively and vomited into the gutter where a couple of pigeons hopped nimbly to the curb. Leaning beside her, I held her forehead, my other arm looped around her waist. Once she'd finished, she forced a weak smile but refused to look me in the eye, wiping repeatedly at her chin.

"I'm sorry," she said, "that was stupid of me. I took too much. I … I was so nervous about meeting your friends, all those artists, wondering what they'd think of me."

"Are you kidding? You were the talk of the party! The belle of the ball! What did you think they'd think of you?"

"I'm just so pathetic!" she cried. "Look what I did! Why do you love me, Teal? How can you even stand me?"

I pulled her against me to stop her crying, the negligent weight of her hanging in my arms. There was of course a pizza shop handy, so I got some napkins and a cup of water and made her sip from its flexible straw to rinse the taste from her mouth. She was freezing in the backless dress, and I held her close and rubbed her spine as she drank. "C'mon," I said, ushering her down the street.

"Where are we going?" she asked.

"A friend of mine lives just down the block. He's a student. His parents rent an apartment. I'm sure he'll let us stay there tonight."

Kelly was no fool. Soon as he saw us standing at the door he pulled us inside, tossed a blanket and a couple of pillows on the couch and whispered, "She'll be okay. Just keep her awake for a while. Make coffee or something. There ain't much on TV."

"You going to the party?" I asked.

"I'm going to *a* party, but not at school. I might not be back, so make yourselves comfortable. That your girlfriend?" he said. "Phew, do *you* got good karma."

Kelly split, so I made the coffee, and we drank it on the couch by the blue light of the TV screen. "Hey," I'd say, when Darcy began to drift, "you with me? You with me or not?"

"I'm with you," she'd whisper, and press her lips to mine. I pulled all the bobby pins from her space-age coif and let her hair tumble to her shoulders.

We watched *Barney Miller*, which was always pretty funny, Abe Vigoda the quintessential New Yorker. Then *Casablanca* appeared on channel nine, an old movie, but a good one. Darcy started fading just when the charming inspector showed up. It had been a couple hours, so I figured it was cool to let her sleep. I'd taken off her silver dress and she was naked under the covers, and I lay beside her with the blanket peeled back just looking at her body, feeling the warmth rise from her skin, seeing for the first time the tiny freckles and moles I'd never noticed before. Part of it was her vulnerability, her sleepy innocence and childlike expression that made me start to cry, to kiss ever so tenderly her pale white shoulder, her forehead, and empty hand. Ingrid Bergman's beautiful eyes filled the TV screen, and even in fuzzy black and white you knew they were blue, knew it was real the way she looked at Humphrey Bogart, the same way I looked at Darcy, as if she, as if I, would never see love's face again.

Rising from the couch, easing her head to the pillow, I headed to the bathroom for some water and a piss. I peeled off the T-shirt I'd worn for two days and studied myself in the mirror, my pale white body not as muscled as I'd like, not nearly as sculpted as

Darcy's. And I wondered what the fuck she saw in me, besides my being a semi-nice guy, a semi-good artist, and half-ass philosopher. Stripping down to my jockey shorts, I wiggled my jeans to the floor and noticed the glassine envelope when it tumbled out on the tiles. Picking it up, I turned it in my fingers, flicked its folded edge with my nail. Finally, I opened it, slowly, carefully, the fine white powder collected in the creases, pressed there flat as a razor. Wetting my pinky, I dipped it in and touched the finger to my tongue. It had a sharp, metallic taste that my tongue soon failed to notice, going numb in an instant, like a shot at the dentist's, feeling too large for my mouth.

Glancing at my image in the mirror again, I looked boney and gaunt in my baggy briefs, the residue of grease paint smeared in my pores making a mask of my face. In the garish light of the dangling bulb, I appeared old, tired, wrinkled around the edges, and I frowned at my reflection, so honestly portrayed, rendered from my palette of mixed emotions since deciding to return to New York. In shocked detachment I observed my eyes widen as a sad epiphany overtook me: Is this how Darcy saw herself? Was this the lens that distorted her image in the Funhouse mirror of her mind?

Tossing the envelope toward the rim of the toilet it teetered there, but didn't fall in, refusing, it seemed, to be flushed. I stood for some moments turned from the mirror, afraid I might recognize the thought in my head, creeping on legs like a spider's. From out in the living room, I could hear canned laughter, the tinkling notes of a ragtime piano in prelude to *All In The Family*, old Archie Bunker chewing his cigar as the dingbat reached for the high note. A narrow window above the tub admitted no light into the room. Neither could I see what lay beyond it, and yet I was glad it was there, if only to suggest some means of escape from the life to which I'd returned.

Snatching the packet, I turned toward the tub and stepped up on its rim. An arm's length away was a red clay flowerpot abandoned too long on the sill, geranium petals flaking like paint when I hooked my thumb on its lip. Sliding the envelope safely beneath it, I let it drop back with a clunk, assured of its presence for centuries to come, like pennies slipped under a headstone.

Chapter 31

IN NOVEMBER THEY ELECTED Richard Nixon president. It seemed so twisted, after all that had happened—the shootings, the protests, the riots in the streets. Cheering Republicans dominated the TV screens amidst flotillas of colored balloons, along with more body bags and trumped up conspiracy charges in the trial of the Chicago Eight. Sirhan Sirhan had acted alone, and James Earl Ray recanted his plea, all to the amusement of string-tied congressmen who began each sentence with *y'all.*

One day at school we were sitting in the cafeteria, Kelly, Hempler, Rufus and I, and Meighyn, of course, who we'd begun calling *M*, as if the spelling of her name made it too onerous to pronounce. The previous Sunday the Jets and Raiders game had been preempted in the final minute to allow for an airing of *Heidi*, and Jets fans never got to see Oakland come from behind, score two touchdowns in less than sixty seconds, and win the game. A week later, Hempler and Rufus—the Long Island boys—were still incensed, reading aloud the venomous editorials in the Daily News, and even the Times, from angry New York sports fans.

"You two are fucking idiots," M declared. "Listen to this if you want to be pissed about something."

She read us an article about the Paris Peace Talks, LBJ's decision to halt the bombing of North Vietnam in a "bold" bid to end the war. A second story, buried on another page, announced the commencement of a new bombing campaign in Laos, a three hundred percent increase over Operation Rolling Thunder, the subject of the aforementioned token peace offering. The next weekend, sitting in the cafeteria, there wasn't a single letter about the sleight-of-hand escalation of the war, but the Jets had a shot at the Super Bowl!

Just before Thanksgiving I got a call from Mary Ann. She'd just received a letter from Todd, the first since he'd left the States.

"He's in Da Nang," she said.

"Are they fighting there?"

"If they are, he didn't mention it."

"Of course not. They could be holding a gun to his head, and he'd ask how you were doing."

"Teal, please."

"Right. That was stupid. So how are you doing?"

"I'm still at Saks. I won't start Brown until February. How's school?

"Great. Cool. I'm working on a portrait, something I started a long time ago. It's a painting of Darcy," I added, the omission too conspicuous to ignore.

"How is she?"

"She's … fine. I don't know. Maybe I'm worried about her."

"I saw her at P's party. Did she tell you?"

"No. PH3 had a party? Was she with anyone?"

"I don't think so. Listen, I didn't mean to—"

"That's okay. How's Three doing?"

"Great. He's engaged to Belinda, you know."

"He is? How long's that been going on?"

Mary Ann laughed. "Since they got pregnant. About a year, I guess. Where have you been?"

Her words chilled me. Where the hell *had* I been, all wrapped up in myself, and Darcy, lost in our private world. "That's right," I said, "I remember now. Jonah said something about it."

"Teal, if I give you his address, will you write to Todd?"

"Of course, why wouldn't I? I've been waiting for a letter myself."

"Great," she said.

"Seriously, why wouldn't I? He's not still mad at me, is he?"

"No, but he thinks maybe you are. Like maybe you disapprove of him."

"Disapprove? Jesus, Mary Ann, he's my best friend. How could he think that?"

"You're just so distant sometimes."

"I'm distant? Like when? When was I distant?"

"You're just … aloof, like you've already made up your mind, and anything else is wrong."

"C'mon, Mary Ann, I'm not that way. Am I?"

"I love you, Teal, you know that. And don't take that the wrong way. Or take it any way you want. This is all just so crazy. I miss him so much!" She was crying then, and there was nothing I could do about it, staring at my poster of Guernica.

"Look, let's talk," I finally said, "in person, not on the phone. Where are you now?"

"I'm at work. Just about to start my shift."

I was ashamed how relieved I was to hear it, that she wasn't just down the street, calling from the basement of her parent's house. "I'll call you," I said. "Soon. We'll have a beer down at George's."

"Really, you'd go back there?"

"Sure. Football season's over."

After we hung up I moped around the house, fidgety, feeling uptight. I thought of calling Darcy and was surprised how easily I talked myself out of it. Instead, I lay back on my bed and jerked off, scanning the wall for the picture of Darcy in her skimpy yellow bikini. Not finding it there, I was puzzled, then shocked, recalling what Mouse had said, how distant I was, self- absorbed, not even noticing that the picture was gone. So I thought about Mary Ann instead, recalling that night she'd rushed into Delindos, how her necklace disappeared between her breasts … I felt kind of creepy after that, shame fast becoming my premier emotion.

Pulling on my funky old blue hooded sweatshirt, I walked down the hill to George's, maybe looking to get my ass kicked, or kick some ass myself. The same old guys were sitting at the bar, and when George saw me enter he just stood there, one hand on the counter, the other on what once had been his hip.

When I sat on a stool he waddled down and pinned me with a glare. "You gonna behave?" he asked.

"I behaved last time," I said. "Those jocks started it."

"You're lucky Mason finished it. He ain't here now, so try keeping your mouth shut. You need a beer?" I nodded, and he made a big show of appraising my hair, pulled back in a ponytail. "You a cheerleader now?" he asked. "You looked better with your face smashed in."

Swiveling on my stool as he shuffled away, I spotted Steve Railsbeck sprawled at a table in the darkened rear of the tavern. I wasn't sure if he'd seen me, and I was tempted to slip away without waiting for my beer. But then I figured fuck it, and sauntering over I dragged back a chair, rousing him from his stupor.

It took him a second to recognize me, but when he did he actually smiled and swept a hand across the table, missing its mark by a good two feet.

"Teal fucking Conover," he said. "Holy shit!"

"Steve fucking Railsbeck," I echoed. "That *is* your Christian name?"

"It is now, buddy," he slurred, never having called me buddy before, or even friend. "How the fuck are you? Did you go to California? Of course you did," he said, answering his own question, "look at that shit!" He meant my hair, the ponytail, and I sighed with resignation. Just then George floated up with my beer. "Yeah, right," he said, "I shoulda known. You and Steve are buds."

"Fuck that fat piece a' shit," said Steve, once George had gone. He held up his right hand, minus the trigger finger, a wad of adhesive tape wound around its stump. "You heard about my accident, I guess. I don't even know what happened. I was working on that Mustang, and bam! The fucking fan blade cut it clean off!"

"Bummer," I said. "Does it hurt?"

"Not so much anymore. I got some pills. You want some?"

"Nah, no thanks."

"For sure?" he said, giving me a sly smile.

"Yeah, for sure. And what's with the shit-eating grin?"

"Oh, nothin'. I just figured, you know, the company you keep …."

"What's that supposed to mean?"

"Nothin', man. Really. I'm just trying to be friendly, righteous. We go back a long way, you and me. Know what I'm saying?"

I didn't, but I took a swig of beer and let it go.

Steve said, "So, what, you back now? You living here?"

"I'm going to school. Commuting to the city."

"Oh yeah, where at?"

I figured he'd never heard of SVA, so I just said, "Art school."

"Yeah, that's right. You were good at art. Real good."

Embarrassed by his patronizing, I turned uncomfortably in my chair. It was hardly busy in the tavern, only one booth occupied, a middle-aged couple holding hands across the table, the guy actually wearing a letter jacket, reliving their high school love affair when they were both too timid to fuck. "Hey, Steve," I said, "so what's the deal? Did you cut off your finger to avoid the draft?"

A bird could have flown from the oval of his mouth, then back again, it hung open so long. "What?" he finally said.

"You know, did you mutilate yourself to get out of Vietnam?"

Steve just sat there shaking his head while I waited for his reply. Out of patience, I said, "No? Is that what you're trying to say? Steve? Hello? How many missing fingers am I holding up?"

"Fuck you, Conover," he spat across the table. "You're so high and mighty! You can buy your way out of that shit! Going to fucking art school! You and that rich bitch Darcy! The fucking whore! The fucking junkie!"

So, I hit him pretty hard, but not hard enough to knock him out of his chair. To my great surprise Steve just sat there, wiping a thread of blood from his mouth. If he was gonna say something he didn't have time, because George hustled over with surprising speed and grabbed me by my pony tail.

"Okay, kid," he said, the cigar bobbing in his mouth, "you're outta here. And I mean eighty-sixed. Forever! You dig?"

I don't know why, but something Steve said occurred to me then, and I pulled away, turning back toward the table. "What fucking Mustang?" I asked.

Steve glared up at me. "Why? You believe me now?"

"*What* Mustang?"

"Deloit's."

"You mean Carter's?"

"I mean mine, actually."

"What are you saying? Deloit ain't—"

"No, he ain't dead. But he might as well be. He'll never drive that car again."

I kept staring at Railsbeck, too afraid to ask, and so he said, "Blew *both* his legs off, beating his crazy-ass brother. He's down there now at Walter Reed, and he ain't coming back."

Hopping the fence at the Restoration, I wandered around in the dark, freaking out the geese and ducks that nested around the lake. I'd once read about some guy who went crazy on the swans with a golf club. I don't know why I thought of that, or about the Indians who'd lived here for centuries before my ancestors killed them, probably whacking their heads off like some fucker with a nine iron.

I cut through the woods along the marsh pond, a stupid decision in the dark, falling down a bunch of times, feeling my way toward the glow of porch lights on the desolate streets of the Manor. I walked across lawns, through backyards, staying away from the sidewalks where someone might see me, maybe an old friend cruising by, wanting to shoot the shit. Autumn had been non-existent that year and I was freezing in my sweatshirt, the grass all wet and frosted beneath my sneakers. But it hadn't snowed, and I missed that, dredging up a fondness for Erik Neumann, for last Christmas when we'd walked these streets in prelude to his naked Santa act. On the dead-end street above the train station I loitered at the abandoned playground where Darcy had played as a kid. It wasn't a big place, long and narrow and comprised of the skeletons of a swing set and slide, its ramp missing, a metal ladder ascending into nothing but air. I took a piss, relieving myself of my half glass of beer, realizing in midstream that I was pissing on the spot where Darcy and I had once made love, chastising myself for doing absolutely nothing right, seeing ominous symbolism in every stupid thing I did.

At the end of the street was a stone stairway that led down to the train station, and I stood at the top and listened for bag pipes. All I could hear was the slapping of waves on the riprap across the tracks, the Hudson a vast black plane in the dark, the lights of the bridge like a beacon. But then I did hear something, the tapping of footsteps ascending the stairs that rose from the north bound platform. When a figure passed under the yellow lamp, I saw it was Antoine Jones, hands tucked in the pockets of his leather coat, a cigarette stubbed in his mouth. His head was bent to the buckled asphalt as he hoofed it up the street.

I waited out the slapping of his pointy-toed shoes then hurried down the stairs. Slowing as I descended to the boiler room, I saw that the door was cracked open, the buttery stripe of guttering candles slashed like chalk on the concrete. The wood frame creaked as I gave it a shove and Darcy reared back in panic, hunkered on a stool with her arm across the table, a necktie clenched in her teeth. There were tears in her eyes and blood on her skin where the point of the needle poked through. The tie fell away as she started to speak, pleading, "Help! I can't do this alone!"

"Antoine," I said, "I just saw him—"

"He wouldn't do it."

"He sells you the dope, but he won't—"

"Help me!" she cried. "I'm butchering myself. I'm making this huge abscess—"

"Okay!" I shouted. "O-fucking-kay!"

She really started crying then, her forehead pressed to her outstretched arm, her cupped hand poised as if asking for alms, begging for someone to fill it. I patted her head, smoothed her silk hair and knelt to take up the syringe. "I don't know how to do this, Dar. You're gonna have to tell me."

She nodded anxiously. "I have small veins," she explained. "You can hardly see them, but … right *here*," she said, directing my eyes to the crook of her arm. "See? Don't go straight in, kind of at an angle. Just lay the point along the vein, then—Ouch," she said. "That's okay, keep going. You'll see the flag when it's in."

"The flag?" I said, my voice, my hand trembling.

"The blood," she said, "you'll see it in the dropper."

It wasn't a real syringe, but something fashioned from an eye dropper and a baby pacifier, a rubber band looped around its neck. "There," she said, "now squeeze the bulb, slow, slowly." I could see it register in the pools of her eyes, her lashes fluttering, the orbs rolling back. It freaked me out, and when I removed the needle her head swiveled back on her neck, a beatific look on her candlelit face as she drifted away into dreams.

A minute later I'd made my decision, and wrapping the tie around my bicep, cinching it tight as though I'd done it for years, I felt my arm for a vein. "What are you doing?" I heard her mumble, struggling to focus her eyes. "No!" she said, "you can't do that!"

"Why not? I'm sure you have plenty."

"No, Teal, please! Don't let me do this to you!"

"You're not," I said, "how could you? You can't even stick yourself." I felt angry, mean, convinced of my righteousness, exactly as Mouse had described me.

"Don't!" Darcy shouted, but I waved her away, swatting her hand like a fly.

I was good with a needle, a true artist at heart, and as the dregs in the dropper coursed through my veins, I understood well why she did it, anxiety jettisoned like bombs from an airplane, shrinking ever smaller over distant fields, cottony poofs like dandelion heads blotting out the surface of the Earth. I stood, staggered, spun on a heel and let myself fall into the arm chair. With eyes barely closed and mouth hanging open, I watched scarlet ripples cross the velvet of my eyelids, felt Darcy slide down in the cushions beside me, her skin smooth as satin on my cheek. Trains rumbled by, alone or in convoy, and at first, I tried to keep count, eventually lost in a soporific landscape devoid of all need or intent.

A week or so later, we were still there, or there again, in the same green chair, with the same red velvet and small drops of blood on our arms. I never called Mary Ann, and I didn't write to Todd. I noticed the orange Mustang on Beekman Avenue one day, but I didn't wave, or even bother to look. I thought I saw Damian

White riding shotgun, but it could have been anyone, the Angel of Death, who seemed to favor the sleek Ford muscle car.

At school I worked on the portrait of Darcy but was never satisfied with its progress, if you could call it that, always going back and painting over, painting over, going back. Kelly asked me to move into the apartment with him; I didn't have to sweat the rent, his folks were fucking rich. One night in the green chair, dreaming of Darcy, though she lay right there in my lap, I said, "You know that Antoine murdered a guy, fragged him with a grenade." She barely moved when finally she spoke, the faintest breath on my neck.

"No," she said.

"Oh yes," said I.

Stifling a yawn, she spoke again, "*No*, he slit his throat."

Chapter 32

I MOVED INTO KELLY'S a couple of weeks before Christmas. I didn't have a lot of stuff, everything fitting into the same crappy knapsack I'd taken to San Francisco. There was only one bedroom, and Kelly said I could have it, that he actually preferred the couch. "Besides," he reminded me, "you have a girlfriend." The room wasn't much, postage-stamp size, one dirty window with a splendid view of the brick wall across the alley. Darcy helped me decorate, putting up a single poster, a print of Van Gogh's *Sunflowers* that truly brightened the meager space. My mom was bummed, and she cried when I left. "Why?" I asked. "You didn't cry when I went to California."

"That was different," she said, "I knew you'd be back. And besides, I cried at home."

Darcy and I saw less of each other, which hurt but was probably for the best. We seemed to feed off each other, devour each other, the sweet tooth gone wild. I'd meet her at the movies, matinees in the city where we'd buy Milk Duds and wine, Mateus in the oval bottle. Sitting in the dark we'd grope and make out, Darcy falling asleep or nodding out, I could never tell which.

We met one evening at Saint Pat's Cathedral, went in and lit a candle. "What did you wish for?" I asked.

"It's not like a birthday cake," she said, "you don't ask God for something, then blow it out."

"Why not, isn't that what prayer is?"

Crossing the street to Rockefeller Center, a crowd had gathered for the lighting of the Christmas tree. You couldn't get close to the skating rink, people packed tight to the windows of stores, squashed against the median where the trumpet-playing angels glittered in tiny white lights. Darcy and I stood on the granite wall, a couple of feet above the crowd, the office-lit facade of the NBC building rising precipitously above us. It was cold enough that you could see your breath, and we hugged each other for warmth, Darcy's green mittens smelling of cigarettes, her red coat lit by the angels. She rocked very slowly as the clock ran down, twitching like an infant in sleep.

"Everything okay?" I asked, and she raised her chin to mine. Just as we kissed the crowd went wild and the plaza turned luminous with light, the tree a Rorschach of colorful bulbs, reminiscent of *The Night Cafe*. Somewhere below a band struck up and a joyous chorale filled the canyon. I felt a hard tapping on the back of my leg and glanced down at a cop with his night stick extended, his raw face tilted and chapped lips moving as words tumbled out in a cloud. "Get offa there, you two," he said, slapping the palm of his glove.

We'd missed the actual lighting of the tree, and later Darcy missed her train, so we sat in a hotel across from Grand Central and drank gin and tonics at the bar, our drinks lit blue in the neon glow, smoking Galoises until they closed. Taking the subway to my crappy apartment, we crashed fully clothed on my bed. Darcy woke up frantic in the morning and called her mom from the phone booth on the corner. I didn't go with her, so I don't know what happened, and later I didn't ask. She never came back, and I guessed she'd gone home, but really I just never knew what she did when she wasn't hanging with me.

One time at Orange Julius, or Nathan's in the Village, I asked how she first got into modeling, or why she got into it, considering.

"Considering what? Not the beauty thing again?"

"You don't have to tell me."

"It was Patty," she said, her patience tapped. "Patty does it. Models."

"Who's Patty?"

"A friend of mine. From the agency."

"So you knew her before she got you the gig?"

"She gave me the number. *I* got the gig."

"You visit her a lot. Canal Street, is it? Does she do heroin, too?"

"Are you mad at me, Teal? Are you trying to hurt me?"

"No."

"Then why are you asking me this?"

"Because you won't tell me."

"Tell you what? And why should I tell you?"

"No reason," I said, walking out the door, and didn't see her again for two days.

She showed up at ten on a rainy morning when I was still asleep. She'd bought one of those cheap plastic Christmas trees in Chinatown. It stood less than three feet tall, and you could fold it up, like an umbrella. "It's a mobile holiday!" she laughed.

"A moveable feast," I smirked, grumpy as Hemingway. "The spirit of Christmas is borne—with an *e*—in the heart. Which thanks to modern science can be easily replaced."

"When did you become such a cynic, Teal?"

"Same time I lost my virginity, I guess."

Standing in the doorway she looked down at my bed, my hair a swallow's nest of errant strands from the rubber band wadded in back. "If you're gonna be mean, I'm leaving," she said.

"Wait, please stay. I'll even make breakfast."

Breakfast was two packets of instant oatmeal, fortified with raisins and the remnants of a bag of M&Ms. I made coffee, the freeze-dried shit, and killed the taste with sugar. We sat at the wobbly kitchen table, four feet from the giant Philco TV, maybe eight from Kelly's unmade couch where his knotted bed sheets lay strewn on the floor, underwear hanging for all to see where he'd tossed it on the radiator to dry.

"What are you doing for Christmas?" I asked. "Shall we go to the Old Dutch Church?"

Her mouth was full, so I waited while she chewed. "I can't," she finally said. "My father has a stick up his butt about going to Saint Teresa's this year."

"He goes to church?"

"Not for years. Do you want to go? It'll just be Mom and me."

"He gives the order and you two jump? It's like you're in the army."

"Into the Valley of Death," she said, smiling, trying to keep me from ruining things.

"You're missing the point, Dar. I don't go to church to be close to God. I go because it's a cool old building my ancient ancestors built, and because I like sitting there thinking about that, especially if you're with me."

"Saint Teresa's isn't so bad. It's pretty at night, and there's incense. But they don't sing."

She fingering a crucifix looped around her neck, gold in the morning light. She'd just started wearing it a few weeks back, an old confirmation gift from her mom, lost since her time in parochial school, and somehow discovered again

"I don't know, Darce. All that kneeling and shit. How does your mom do it?"

"She's not that old. She works in the garden all the time."

"Where she fell and broke her wrist—both of them? Or was it on the stairs?"

"What does that have to do with anything?"

"She's pretty *broke* into kneeling, I suppose. The Japs made prisoners squat for hours with bamboo sticks behind their knees. I read that in one of my dad's old letters."

When Darcy sprang up I grabbed her wrist, instantly reminded of the Doctor. "I'm sorry, Dar. I'm such an asshole. I don't know why I do it."

"Well, I do," she said, yanking her arm away, heading for the door.

"I'll go!" I called after her. "I'll go to your church!"

"Forget it! I don't want you there now."

"C'mon," I said, grabbing her again. "Don't do this."

"Me? Like *I'm* always fucking things up?"

"Like you're *not*?"

I felt her let go, begin to collapse, and caught her in my arms.

"Whoa!" I said. "What was that about?"

She didn't answer, and I maneuvered us the short distant to my bed. "Are you okay?" I asked.

"I'm just so tired, Teal. I feel exhausted."

Feeling her forehead like my mom always did, I checked to see if she had a fever. "You're not hot. You feel sick?"

She shook her head, rolling it on the pillow. "I gotta go," she said, and tried to get up.

"Hold on thar, Queeks-draw," I said, in lousy imitation of the cartoon. Plopping down on the bed beside her, I pinned her there with my knee. "Take 'er easy now. The fashion world can survive another minute without you. Let me be nice for a sec, the way I used to be."

Then I was crying, a real switcheroo, and Darcy was stroking my ratty hair, pecking my stubbled cheek. "You're still nice," she whispered. "You're still my Teal."

We lay without talking, just stroking, soothing. Traffic

rumbled down in the street, the constant drone of the mega city like a monstrous, idling machine. People shouted, sirens whooped, Darcy's heart thumped in my ear. Slipping her hand beneath my T-shirt she smoothed it over my ribs, licking my finger like a push pop. "Are we gonna make love in an actual bed?" I asked. "In it, not on it?"

"We've never fucked in a bed?"

"Must you use that word, dahhling?"

She giggled, and I reached and pulled up her shirt, fumbled at the buttons on her jeans. Kicking her shoe off, the sock came with it, exposing half her foot. Bending to massage it I heard her sigh, and I lavished tiny kisses on its delicate arch. She relaxed as I fondled, groaned as I squeezed, her body gone limp as a won ton noodle. "Is this the foot?" I asked, studying her heel, "the one with the evil scar?"

She was up like a shot, snatching her shoe, fumbling with the buttons on her jeans.

"Lighten up," I said, "I was only kidding."

"A joke?" she said, heading for the door. "My life is so funny to you?"

"Come on, Dar. I'm sorry—again. I'll go to Saint Teresa's if you want."

"It's too late now. I have to go."

"Where, to Patty's?"

"Jesus, Teal, is this the Inquisition?"

"Are you the Little Prince?"

Chapter 33

School let out the day before Christmas. I took Darcy's portrait home on the train, covered with newspaper so no one would gawk at it or make some critical comment. I read the newsprint as the train rattled up the Hudson, the Daily News, not the Times, so mostly tabloid stuff, yet more or less true. One was the story of a little girl killed in the Bronx, struck by stray bullets as she decorated her Christmas tree. Not to be upstaged, some crazy fuck in Trenton New Jersey cut off his mother's head, stabbed the shaft of Old Glory in its stump and tossed it in a crèche on somebody's lawn. The crèche, in my mind, looked just like the one I'd seen at Darcy's house, and the head, of course, resembled her mom. Guess who the crazy fuck was.

Mom had set up the tree in my absence, a chore that had once been mine, and before that my father's. I recognized every ornament on it, the elves and angels and chubby Santas, a couple of which I'd made out of pie dough in old Mrs. Hopstaedder's class. Mom made us hot chocolate with baby marshmallows floating in it, and I watched them melt as she watched Dick Cavett. When the telephone rang at 11:15, we both knew it was Darcy.

I took the call in my room, not bothering to flip the lamp on, laying in bed with one hand on the head board, a toe on the lathe-turned post. "Hey," I said, "I knew it was you."

"Am I that predictable?"

"Thank God. At least there's something I can count on."

"My, what angst."

I laughed. "You got me," I said.

She invited me to Christmas dinner at her house. On Christmas Eve, actually. Kara would be there, and Kevin and the kids—Lily and baby Lilah. Plans for Mass had been duly canceled when Kara refused to go. They'd even booked a hotel room so as not to disturb the Doctor.

"He wants to meet you," said Darcy.

"Get the fuck out! Now I know you're kidding."

"Will you come?" she asked.

"You want me to, after all this time? Sure," I said, "why not."

Darcy squealed, and it was a beautiful sound, something I hadn't heard for too long. "I love you, Dar," I added, "in case you wondered."

"I know you do. And I know it's hard for you, staying here with me."

"Stop it. That's not why I'm here. I'm going to school, you may have noticed."

"I love you, too. Like you can't believe."

"Sure I can."

The TV was silent when we finally hung up, so I knew Mom had gone to bed. I lay on the sheets staring up at the ceiling, at the shadows I'd known all of my life, three flat planes that met in a corner, the light from a streetlamp striping the wall. I should have felt anxious about meeting Darcy's father, the Headless Hessian himself, demonic sire of Rosemary's Baby, the black-hooded countenance of Christmas Yet to Come.

Driven by a sudden, senseless urge, I picked up the phone and dialed Mary Ann's number. It rang a bunch of times before she picked up. "Hello?" she said, sounding sleepy, or on edge.

"Hey," I said, "it's me."

"Teal?"

"How's it going?"

"Is everything alright? It's … after midnight."

She was silent a moment, maybe waking up, maybe not so happy to hear from me.

"You never called," she said.

"I believe I'm calling now."

"It's too late to be funny."

"You're pissed."

"I mean its 12:30, Teal. Did you call to make jokes?"

"No, but its Christmas. Stuff like that."

"Is that a joke, too?"

"What?"

"That flippant thing, how you can't be serious."

"So you are pissed. I'm sorry, Mary Ann. I really am."

She didn't say anything, so I knew it was all up to me, like I was just calling to hear myself talk, which maybe I was. "So what's up with Todd? Have you heard from him again? And no, I never wrote. But I will, I mean it."

"I got another letter," she said, "just one. He's in some special unit, the Tigers, like it's some kind of football team. He sent me a picture of him and some other guys wearing those jungle hats. They don't even make them wear helmets, Teal! He could get shot in the head! Sorry, I don't mean to sound so mad."

"That's cool."

"No, it's not! It's not *cool!* And I *am* mad! At you and him both! What the fuck is wrong with you guys? You think you can just throw people away? Like they're shit paper or something? Something you wipe your ass with?"

I'd never heard Mary Ann use language like that, Mouse saying words like shit, or even ass.

"I'm sorry—"

"You're always fucking sorry, have you noticed that? When's it gonna dawn on you to stop doing things to be sorry for?"

"Look, Mary Ann—"

"Look at what, Teal? I've been *looking* all my life. Look, but don't touch! Hands off the merchandise! I just want what you have, Teal. I want to *have* somebody. I want … Oh, God!" she wailed, "Who cares what I want. The whole world *wants*! Doesn't mean we'll ever get it."

"Sure you will, Mary Ann."

"Yeah, right."

"C'mon."

"Listen, I gotta hang. I have to work tomorrow."

"Maybe I'll see you?"

"Sure."

"Great. Goodnight then. Merry Christmas."

I bought wine to bring to the Saint James's dinner, a bottle of red with a shiny green bow. The guy at the store said it was good stuff, though all wine tasted the same to me. You gotta drink a lot of it to develop a taste, and then of course you're supposed to spit it out. That always seemed *abzurd* to me, like not inhaling pot. It cost me ten bucks.

I loafed around the house watching TV all afternoon, also watching the clock, my bravado of the previous night pretty much evaporated. The Yankees had had a bad year and were shopping around for pitchers, but Joe Namath and the Jets were on their way to the Super Bowl! Giant fans like me weren't supposed to care, but I was happy for them, the sports nuts from Queens and Long Island, though I really didn't give a shit about football. Apollo Eight was the really big news, three astronauts about to orbit the moon in the same kind of dinky space capsule that fried

Gus Grissom the year before.

I was nervous about meeting Mrs. Saint James. She'd kind of read me the riot act when I'd last spoken to her from the phone booth at Cala Foods. I'd said some things that were pretty rude, maybe stepping over the line. There were certain things that adults did not discuss with kids, and vice versa, thank God. *Read me the riot act*, I thought; another of those meaningless things people say, like *once in a blue moon*. If there really was a riot act, we sure would have heard of it by now.

I took a shower and shaved. I only shaved because of Darcy, because she hated to kiss my scratchy face, which was cool, because I loved to kiss her perfect ass. I put on a blue blazer, and the old maroon tie I'd last worn when I spoke at the church, right after my father died. I'd lied to Darcy about the Japanese torture. I hadn't read that in my father's letters; he would never have said that to my mom.

Looking in the mirror, I thought of Jonah Gold, how navy blue and maroon were his signature colors, his pathetic attempt at Ivy League cachet. He was still flying that flag last time I saw him, sitting way up at the front of the train, while I slumped down in the rear. But here I was now, all prepped out, except for my ponytail, which I'd playfully tied back with Darcy's gold ribbon, part of her gift from the previous Christmas.

I'd planned on taking Darcy's gift—her portrait—down there with me but walking out the door I decided it was too big to carry, even though I'd humped it all the way from the City. Besides, I told myself, I didn't want a big audience the first time she saw it. I wanted it to be *our* moment, something we'd remember years from now, when the painting hung above the grand old fireplace, in our grand old home, as I, with suede patches on my elbows and pipe in hand—

I truly was a cynic, and really, when the hell had that happened?

My mom needed the car, so I had to walk down there, but

that was cool because I always enjoyed the stroll. It was one of those damp, chilly afternoons, the sky turning purple through Pieter Breugel trees, Christmas lights on lawns and porches just beginning to wink on. It hadn't snowed yet, but like a little kid perched by his bedroom window, I still hadn't given up hope, expecting that at any moment the air would fill with snowflakes, that sleigh bells would tinkle and carolers sing and Erik Neumann run crazy-naked, dashing through the snow.

None of those things had happened by the time I reached Darcy's corner, my one hand frozen—the one holding the wine bottle—my teeth chattering from cold and fear. *God dammit*, I thought, I'd never even met the Doctor and he has me shitting bricks. How must Darcy have felt all those years, living in the same house with him, hating him so, enduring his wrist snapping cruelty. But that, of course, was my own interpretation based on Darcy's stories, a portrait painted by her own artist's hand as surely as I'd painted hers.

A blue Volvo station wagon with Vermont plates sat in the driveway, Big Bird from Sesame Street straddling the suitcases stacked in the rear. Mrs. Saint James's Caddy was parked beside it, the windows frosted, icicles hanging from the tail pipe. Standing on the porch before the Charles Dickens door knocker, I took a deep breath and clanked it once, twice, three times, waiting for Jacob Marley to appear. To my surprise and great relief, the door was opened by a little girl in red tights and pink tutu, maybe three years old, who rushed at me without thinking twice and wrapped her arms around my knees. With equal abandon I swept her up and settled her on my hip, careful to avoid her bare arm with the cold bottle, my new friend absorbed in its shiny green bow, poking it with her finger.

Her daddy appeared and held out his arms, saying, "Here, I'll relieve you of that," meaning the little girl, not the bottle.

"That's cool," I said, "I love kids," thinking of Little Angel and her baby soft skin, Twig and his big brown eyes.

"Come in," said Daddy, which I did, closing the door behind me. "I'm Kevin," he said, smiling, "and the ballerina is Lily, my daughter."

"Hi, Lily," I said, ducking my head to peer into her eyes. She glanced up to study my frozen face, fondling the bow as she appraised me, and when I plucked it from the bottle's neck, making her a present of it, she wiggled down from my arms and ran into the dining room.

Kevin and I shook hands. "You must be Teal," he said.

"That's me. Pleased to meet you."

When I stepped around the corner into the dining room the women were all standing there, Darcy and a woman I assumed to be Kara, Mrs. Saint James just rising from the table. It was like seeing three generations instead of two, Kara being a decade older than Darcy. There was a strong family resemblance, each with the same kind of blondish hair, Kara's darker than Darcy's, Mrs. Saint James' gone pewter with age. Kara was a little plump, or wide, from being a mommy. She was pretty in a different way than Darcy, more wholesome than exotic, cute rather than glamorous. Mrs. Saint James wore a gold dress, gold jewelry and diamond earrings. Her hair was as perfectly coiffed as I'd recalled, and she was truly stunning, so different in countenance and demeanor than when I'd last seen her in the garden.

Darcy danced over and gave me a hug and a chaste kiss on the cheek. Kara watched it happen, standing with her hands clasped before her, smiling non-stop like a gameshow host. She extended her hand for me to shake. "I'm Kara," she said.

Darcy bobbed nervously on the toes of her feet. She was wearing pink slippers and pajama bottoms, and the sweater I remembered from our hike to Swan Lake. Lily, I noticed, was sitting on a blanket on the floor, surrounded by a legion of expensive toys, playing with the silly green bow. "You know my mom," Darcy said, nodding at her, as if I needed assistance.

"Mrs. Saint James," I smiled, "Merry Christmas."

"Merry Christmas to you, Teal."

We were all smiling then, so much that my jaw was beginning to ache.

"The Doctor is anxious to meet you," she said. "You'll have to excuse him, he's on the phone at the moment."

Probably calling the cops, I thought, thinking also, *she actually calls her husband "The Doctor"*.

Taking my arm, prancing on tip toe, Darcy hurried me into the living room where a fire was burning in the grate, and an infant— *dressed in swaddling clothes*—lay sleeping on the sofa. "This is Lilah," she said, bending over the child, her hands clasped between her knees. Darcy cooed at the baby, whose milky blue eyes opened and closed in transient sleep, then she sprang up and wrapped her arms around my neck. "I'm *sooo* glad you're here!" she squealed, delighting me again with the happy sound. "Oh! Wait a sec!" she added, and ran away and up the stairs, leaving me standing there with limbs akimbo—another of those phrases— and the beginnings of an erection.

Stepping toward the sofa I looked down at baby Lilah, her tiny hands pink, her even tinier fingernails a miracle of miniaturization, like something the Chinese might accomplish in a spare century or two. I wanted to pick her up but feared she'd start crying, precipitating a scene wherein Kara or Kevin would intervene, inviting frowns and silent accusations, and so I turned away to find the Good Doctor standing in the doorway, nattily dressed in a suit and vest with a kerchief in one pocket, a watch fob like Dewey's looped at his waist, though undoubtedly much more expensive.

He was tall, dark, and broad shouldered, though his stomach was oddly paunched, a protrusion the size and shape of a bowling ball lifting his gold belt buckle, revealing its shiny hasp between the flared vee of his matching vest. There was no resemblance to Darcy, or to Kara. Perhaps Lena, I thought, who I knew from the yearbook was brunette. The Doctor's hair was black as ink, even at his advanced age, thinning perhaps at the temples, exaggerating a widow's peak, and surprisingly long in back, like an old-fashioned villain or snake oil salesman; a fitting allusion, I considered. He wore a mustache like the one in the wedding picture, only smaller, trimmed tighter to his lip and slightly yellowed, perhaps from smoking a pipe.

He might have been good looking once, but he wasn't now, his skin gone sallow, sagging at his chin, jaw and cheekbones indistinguishable. His long nose seemed an edifice of its former self, too hooked or flaccid near its tip, the nostrils arched, cavernously deep, revealing too much nose hair. His thin lips pursed of their own accord, as if having just tasted a lemon or lime, and when he spoke his tongue flicked like a frog, or a snake, a creature that slithers on its belly. "Mr. Conover," he said grandly, "we finally meet."

"Hello, Doctor," I said, offering my hand, "or Mister Saint James."

"Doctor is fine," he said, smiling, "the other is too long." His handshake was limp, "like a fish," my mother would say.

"Admiring my granddaughter, are you?"

"Yeah. Yes. She's beautiful. I love babies."

"Intending to have any of your own?" he asked, coming straight to one of many points.

I shrugged. "Someday, I guess. No immediate plans."

"A planner, eh? That's reassuring. So many young people have no idea what they want. You don't strike me as one of those. Am I right?"

"Partly," I said.

"How so?"

I shrugged again, making a mental note to quit doing that. "I know what I like, and what I don't. Sometimes I don't know what to do about it."

"Honest of you. Very forthright. Let me be frank—Do you love my daughter?"

I nodded this time, as opposed to shrugging. "Yes, I do."

The Doctor smiled, glanced away, raised both fists to his watch-fobbed waist and arched his pinstriped back. Stepping toward the fire, he rested one arm on the mantle, placed a wing-tipped shoe on the hearth. "I see," he said. "My wife believes you do, though it's difficult to say why, knowing you about as well as I do, which is to say, not at all."

"Then I guess it's good we finally meet," I said. "Thank you for inviting me."

The Doctor laughed. "I did not invite you, boy. That was my daughter's idea, and her mother's. I merely acquiesced."

I really didn't know what to say, but then I didn't need to, because Darcy bounded noisily down the stairs and burst into the room. She was gripping a smallish, rectangular Christmas present in both hands, wrapped in cheerful gift paper. Speaking even before she entered, she said, "Sorry, but I'd forgotten to wrap—"

She stopped when she saw the two of us posed there, the awkwardness of the tableau translated instantly on her face where her smile quickly melted. "Dad," she said, "I didn't know you were off the phone. I would have introduced you."

"No need to apologize. As you can see, it's too late for that."

"Sorry," she said again, and we both winced.

The Doctor seemed to enjoy it. "Is that gift for me?" he said, knowing full well that it wasn't.

"It's for Teal," she said, "I couldn't wait to give it to him."

"Well, that's nice of you dear, such a thoughtful girl. And impetuous."

Kara rescued us, stepping into the room with an apron over her Christmas dress. "How's my baby?" she said, allowing me to step back and break the spell, the circle of tension that was causing my neck to cramp.

"Still asleep," I said. "She's beautiful."

Kara smiled. "She is," she agreed. "Dinner's almost ready. Daddy, will you slice the turkey?"

"Of course!" said the Doctor, his smile generous, his hand sweeping from the mantle, every move a grandiose flourish, an act of casual chivalry. "Excuse me," he said, nodding at Darcy and me, and sashayed out of the room.

When Kara departed, Darcy apologized. "I should have been here. That must have been weird."

"Pretty much," I said. "He is weird. I can't say that I like him."

"You're not supposed to. No one is."

"What are you supposed to feel?"

"Afraid," she said, and winked. "But here, this is for you."

She handed me the gift, and I knew right away it was a photograph. Tearing at the paper she'd so carefully applied just minutes before, the last striped shred revealed a picture of my parents, the negative from the solar eclipse, now developed and framed in gold, and held in my trembling hands.

Tears ran down my freshly shaved face, and I was glad that it was just Darcy in the room, she and Baby Lilah, who would someday suffer the same sweet pain and unexpected joy. "Thanks," I sniffled. "How did you do this? Where did you get the negative?"

"Your house. At Thanksgiving breakfast. It was tucked like a bookmark in *Franny and Zooey*."

I wondered how she'd even noticed their image when no one

else had, not Todd, or Mary Ann at Laughing Hill. Some saw the elephant inside the snake, while others were too old to see.

"Now I wish I'd brought your present."

"Having you here is all I want. Gift enough for a lifetime."

Mrs. Saint James then issued a cough, standing in the doorway, the sudden appearances of Darcy's parents becoming unnerving, like a scene from Scrooge's bedroom. "Dear," she said, "it's time to put on some clothes. Or did you plan on wearing pajamas to dinner?"

Without a word Darcy ran up the stairs, the sound of her two-tread-at-a-time ascent continuing all the way to the third floor. The echoing vacuum of her sudden departure left Mrs. Saint James and I alone in the room, she with her white gloves folded like doves, nestled in the crook of her arms, me with my hands hanging limp at my sides, legs spread in an outfielder's stance.

"Mr. Conover—Teal," she began, "I believe one of us is owed an apology."

"Sorry, ma'am," I stammered, realizing she was speaking of the phone call from San Francisco. "I guess I was prying to say those things, totally out of line. Not really prying, but—"

"I'm trying to apologize to *you*," she said. "I spoke rudely, as one would to a child, and you and my daughter aren't children anymore. My husband disagrees. He considers you too immature to have a lasting relationship, or any relationship at all. The Doctor is a man of convictions, and not shy, or even diplomatic about stating them. Please forgive his obstinacy. He's a good man who's used to getting his way. We're a family of mostly women here, and Father has always held court, so to speak, always wielded the scepter, or whatever it is that kings wave." She smiled nervously, realizing perhaps that her words registered nothing defensible (*I command you to yawn!*) or even comprehensible to me.

"I'm sorry, too," I said. "I'd never say anything to hurt you, not on purpose. I *do* love Darcy, and if I said anything stupid it was because I wanted to help her."

Stepping forward, she extended her hand as if to touch my cheek, but stopped with her damaged wrist poised between us, cocked at a curious angle. Without even thinking I reached for her hand and kissed it, briefly, impulsively, immediately seized by a swelling fear of gross miscalculation.

Tears welled in her eyes, the bizarre reality of what I'd done dawning on us both in embarrassment and wonder, the palpable spirit of Darcy and all our feelings for her allowing our defenses to crumble and pretensions to evaporate.

We released each other simultaneously, and when Mrs. Saint James turned on her spiked heel to leave the room, Baby Lilah began to cry. We both looked toward the sofa where a pair of tiny, pleading hands stirred the smoke-scented air. Mrs. Saint James then glanced at me and offered a pained but genuine smile. "She wants to be held," she said, and vanished into the foyer.

I was holding Lilah, her pale eyes struggling to remain open, when Kara entered the room. "Thanks," she said, content to watch me cradle her daughter, her pretty smile no longer forced. "You're used to babies?" she asked.

"Not really. I've only known one."

"That's all it takes to get hooked," she grinned. "Here, I'll take her. She'll be hungry, and I'm afraid you're ill-equipped to handle that. Come into the dining room, we're almost ready."

Kevin was seated at the table, his chair turned toward Lily, still playing on the floor. Lily looked up when I entered; she appeared almost to glare at me, her lower lip turned down, blue eyes narrowed in shameless scrutiny. But quickly enough she returned her attention to a nearly naked doll, whose misshapen hair she tugged at with a miniature comb. The doll's hair was blonde, as was Lily's, as were all the Saint James women but Lena.

Kevin snagged Lilah and arranged her in the highchair, the baby fully awake now, a look of stunned curiosity about her. "Sit down, please," he bade me. "Would you like some water? Or wine? Is this yours?" he asked, squinting at a bottle.

I squinted at the label as well. "Honestly," I said, "I don't know. I color-code them by bow."

Kevin had the aura of *a really nice guy*. Baby faced and smooth of skin, his plump cheeks almost sparkled. He wore his brown hair in the Kennedy style, a wing across his forehead, slightly too long for convention, but short enough to run for office.

Kara must have heard us talking because she floated through the kitchen door with a crystal pitcher of water and filled my drinking glass, leaving the pitcher on the table. "The chardonnay is Teal's. We brought the burgundy," she said and disappeared back into the kitchen. No sooner had she gone than the door opened again, and Doctor Saint James strode out, tugging at his vest with hands still pink from washing, and lowered himself into the armchair at the head of the table. Beaming at Kevin and me, he said, "The only advantage in carving the turkey is nibbling the crispy skin." His red lips testified to the verity of his statement, gleaming with a greasy halo in the light of the crystal chandelier.

Amused by his own wit, he laughed and slid his chair back, threw one long leg across the other and said, "So, what shall we men talk about before dinner? Kevin, how goes the battle in Burlington?"

Kevin smiled too eagerly, and said with a jaunty nod of his head, "Excellent. No complaints. Too much snow, perhaps. Difficult driving to work at times."

"What do you do?" I asked.

"Grin and bear it," he said, and smiled again, as if to illustrate his point.

"I mean, what do you do for work?"

He laughed nervously, and the Doctor smiled, delighted by Kevin's high-pitched bray. "Oh!" said Kevin. "I teach!"

"At the college?"

"No, no! We live in Burlington, but I teach sixth graders at a public school about five miles away."

"Cool," I said, for lack of anything more patronizing to say.

"Oh, yes, *cool!*" said the Doctor, re-crossing his legs, delighted at himself again.

"How about you?" Kevin asked. "You're going to art school, I hear."

"SVA, in the City."

"I've heard of it. Pretty avant garde?"

"Compared to some."

The Doctor interjected, "You couldn't have gone to Cooper Union? I've heard that's a very good school."

"I didn't apply. It's a good school, I guess, but different than SVA. Cooper has accredited teachers, licensed by the state."

"And that's a bad thing?"

"No, I just thought it was cooler to learn from professional artists, the doers, as opposed to—"

"It's *cool*, I see. The *cool* factor always applying."

It was obvious where this was going, so I clammed up, and the three of us sat in awkward silence until Kevin said, "Darcy says one of your instructors is famous?"

"Yeah. You probably never heard of him, but he has stuff at the Modern. Chuck Close."

Kevin made a face, shook his head. "Nope," he said, "doesn't ring a bell."

"He's well known in the art world, so I guess he is kind of famous, in an esoteric sense."

"Ahh!" said the Doctor, "the esoteric sense! A splendid word! A *cool* word, in fact! Though I must confess I've always confused its meaning with *eclectic*, another cool word, yet nearly its opposite, meaning all inclusive, rather than merely exclusive."

The Doctor's humorous moment was spoiled when Lily suddenly climbed into my lap, pretty much scaring the crap out of me, and she nestled comfortably against my chest while staring up at the ceiling. "Look, Daddy," she said, pointing her small finger at the glittering chandelier. Kevin smiled, his love for his daughter apparent, overtaking any consideration for his pompous father-in-law, now forgotten at the end of the table.

"Heads up!" sang Kara, rushing through the door with a huge and apparently heavy turkey platter held before her. She fairly dropped it on the table, saying, "Whew! That's a lot of turkey!"

Mrs. Saint James came in behind her wearing oven mitts, holding two steaming dishes aloft.

"Here," said Kevin, "let me help."

"Me too," I said, but Kara glanced at Lily in my lap and said, "Please, sit tight. You're already helping!"

"Where is Darcy?" the Doctor asked.

"Getting dressed, dear," said Mrs. Saint James, "let her be."

"She should be helping," he objected.

"She's making herself beautiful, Father. Her beau is here." Mrs. Saint James winked at me then, and smiled. Lily noticed her do it, and craning around she winked at me too, several times, until I winked back, prompting her to smile gorgeously, looking very much like her mother. Kevin rose to go to the kitchen, snatched the green Christmas bow from the floor and tossed it on the table for Lily. The little girl turned it over in her hands, poking a finger in its various cavities, inspecting its looped assemblage with a focused curiosity. I chose to watch her, knowing the Doctor was watching me, and passed the several minutes required to lay the table before the aprons came off and the family was ready to be seated.

Kevin lifted Lily from my lap and lowered her into a highchair beside her little sister, both girls seated at one end of the table, flanked by their mom and dad. The Doctor sat enthroned at the head, Mrs. Saint James at his elbow, across from the empty chair beside me.

The Doctor repeated, "Where is our daughter?"

Just at that moment Darcy appeared, having slipped down the stairs in stockinged feet, and stood in the doorway like a debutante keenly aware of her posture, her shoulders squared and bare back arched, her smile radiant, anxious, aimed directly at me.

Her burgundy dress fit tight as a glove from chest to hardwood floor, hugging her hips, flattering a waistline that needed no assistance. Her shoulders were bare and creamy white, the wide, low neckline allowing just a hint of cleavage, revealing the waxen architecture of her throat where a sage-green choker encircled it, the ivory cameo at it center depicting a woman's face in profile. Her platinum hair was drawn back from her temples and woven in braids at the back of her head, the few errant strands incandescent as a lightbulb, spiraling down the pedestal of her neck. A glittering comb retained the braid's integrity, providing all the regal bearing of a diamond encrusted tiara.

Standing, I extended my paint-stained hand, my chair squeaking painfully in the silence. Kevin stood, then Mrs. Saint James, clapping her gloves approvingly, beaming at her daughter. Kara remained seated with the little girls, as did the Good Doctor. "You look lovely, dear," said Darcy's mom, breaking the princess spell.

Darcy floated across the floor, the luxuriant nap of the velvet dress smoldering like coals as she moved, arriving at my side to kiss my cheek and take her seat beside me. "Doesn't she look beautiful, Philip?" said Mrs. Saint James.

The Doctor grunted his assent, and said, "That cameo looks familiar, doesn't it Mother?"

"Of course it does. It belonged to your mother. You gave it to me at her passing."

"And you are still alive, last I checked."

"It seemed the right time, dear. I don't want to die before seeing her wear it. She looks much prettier than I."

"You've just made Kara jealous."

"Nonsense, Dad," said Kara, "it takes the perfect throat to wear that choker, and that kind of elegance is all Darcy." She smiled at her sister. "You nailed it, sweetheart."

"Good! Now let's eat!" said Darcy, lunging at her silverware.

"One minute!" the Doctor commanded. "Who would like to say grace?"

"C'mon, Dad, we haven't—"

"Mr. Conover, perhaps you'd like to offer thanks?"

I'd never said grace in my life, my family not big on it, being Protestant and all. "Thanks," I said, "but I really don't know what to say."

The Doctor smiled good-naturedly, enduring my ignorance. He said, "One simply acknowledges the provenance of the Lord, offers some simple words of gratitude, thanks him for the bounty—"

"Splendid!" I said. "Shall we eat?"

Darcy squealed and dug right in, spearing the turkey platter with her fork. The Doctor was obviously miffed, but everyone smiled and began serving, feigning to look at him, Kevin fixing Lily a small plate, Lilah engrossed in the carnival of movement around her.

"It's great, Mom," said Darcy, making a second pass with the gravy boat.

"Thank Kara. It's all her doing."

"Everything's great," I agreed.

The Doctor was mercifully consumed by consumption, eating

voraciously, food visible on his lips when I shot a glance his way.

"You're not hungry, Mom?" Kara asked.

"I've been picking at things all day, saving some room for dessert."

"Wine, she means," said the Doctor, an orange piece of sweet potato ejected as he spoke.

Everyone looked down at their plates, myself included, the *bounty* becoming less palatable by the second. Minutes later, everyone seemed to have had their fill, Lily having eaten only her cranberries, betrayed by the stains on her face.

The Doctor tossed his napkin on his empty plate and pushed back from the table with a satisfied burp.

"Well done, Mother," he said, "and daughter, of course. One of you, anyway. Too bad your older sister isn't here. What is Lena up to these days? Does anyone hear?"

A vacuum of silence enveloped the room, so acute it made my ears pop.

"She's still in Miami," Kara said. "I heard from her at Thanksgiving."

"Still single, I trust. She shies from the males. We'll never see grandkids from her."

Darcy sat glaring with a fork in her fist, a look of pure hatred in her eyes. It was there for a second, then smoldered away, doused like the coals of a fire.

"You have grandchildren here you never see," said Kara, "and we live a just a few hours north."

"I'm a busy man, daughter, and don't be flip. She could at least send us a card."

No one responded, not wanting to join the game, contrived for my benefit alone.

I thought I heard the Doctor fart then summarily re-cross his legs, fingering the bottom button of his vest, letting it out an inch.

"Where's the cake, Mommy?" Lily whined, getting squirmy in the highchair.

"Ask Aunt Darcy, dear."

"Right here!" chirped Darcy, springing from her chair, her spirits miraculously recovered.

Heading for the kitchen, the tightness of her dress demanded she take short, choppy steps like a geisha, and passing through the door her back was revealed from neck to dimpled spine, the velvet material puckered at the bottom, exposing the curve of her hips. I noticed Kevin sneak a peek, and much less timidly, her father.

She returned with a platter held high in both hands which she swung around over my head, placing it on the table before me as I slid my plate away. It was a chocolate cake shaped like the Old Dutch Church, the roof and arched windows outlined with green and red M&Ms, the steeple rising to a frosted point made of cherry-filled chocolates from Grand Central station.

Leaning beside me, she whispered in my ear, "Can you hear them singing inside?"

"Ahh!" said the Doctor, "our youngest has contributed after all! And a church, no less! Albeit the wrong one."

"Philip!" said Mrs. Saint James. "They are all the Lord's House, especially at Christmas."

Bah humbug! I expected him to say, but he held his reptile's tongue.

Darcy cut the first piece, the steeple, and lay it on a plate for me, then handed me the knife so I could finish slicing. "Lily," I said, "would you like a window?"

The little girl nodded, and Kevin prompted, "What do you say?"

"Yes, please," she recited, causing almost everyone to smile.

"Shall we open Teal's wine?" Kara asked. "Daddy, would you do the honors?" She placed the bottle in front of him, along with a fancy corkscrew.

"Of course," he said, holding the bottle like a trophy. "It's a fine weight," he said. "Now to see if it's worth a damn."

"Ten bucks," I said, no longer caring what the Doctor thought of me. "It's worth ten bucks."

"And a red," said the Doctor, "though who knows what goes with chocolate?" He was staring at the bottle's label, squinting, making a show of it. "I can't read without my glasses," he said, fishing around for someone to fetch them, but no one did. "Pinot Noir, perhaps? A cabernet? Can't be Manischewitz," he laughed, "no square bottle! Besides, Christmas is hardly a Jewish tradition. Even the Protestants know that!"

"I'll open it, Daddy," said Darcy, clearly annoyed.

"No, dear, I've got it." Twisting the screw into the cork, he wiggled it a few times until it released with a subtle pop. "Smells excellent. Darling?" he said to his wife, tipping the bottle toward the rim of her glass. Mrs. Saint James placed two fingers over its throat. "No thank you, dear."

"Oh, come now, you're not still sensitive about my little joke? Please, I insist."

"Really, Philip, no," she said, but the Doctor fenced at her fingers with the bottle and filled her glass to the brim.

He filled my glass, then Darcy's, then passed the bottle to Kara. Kevin declined and Kara proffered the bottle back to her father, "Daddy?" she said.

"No thank you, dear, I believe I'd like a whiskey. Don't get up," he said, as he stood and fingered a tumbler from the hutch, and a bottle of single malt.

"Would you care for some ice?" asked Mrs. Saint James.

The Doctor sat down. "Thank you," he said, whereupon his wife rose and went into the kitchen. We could hear the refrigerator door open, water run in the sink, then the sound of ice cubes tumbling into a bowl. She returned with a small ice bucket traditionally used for that purpose and placed it before the Doctor; extracting two cubes with a set of tongs, she plopped them into the empty glass.

"One more, please," said the Doctor. When his wife complied, he poured the whiskey, saying, "One never puts ice in the whiskey, one only pours whiskey over ice."

No one had spoken the entire time, and the Doctor raised his glass and said, "Cheers!"

And Mrs. Saint James, raising her own glass, added, "*Merry Christmas!*"

We ate the cake and sipped the wine, except for Mrs. Saint James, who did neither. I had no idea whether it was kosher—excuse the expression—to eat dessert and drink vino simultaneously, but no one objected, and Darcy and I had two pieces. Smiling at me with a fork full of devil's food, she announced without looking away, "Teal and I have quite the sweet tooth, don't we?" At which point I blushed, red as the Cabernet in my glass, and choked on a mouthful of the Old Dutch Church. I couldn't say if anyone noticed because I didn't look up, and then the Doctor said, "So, Mr. Conover, what exactly do your parents do?"

My father pushes up daisies, I almost said, but offered instead, "My dad passed away four years ago. My mother is a nurse."

"I'm sorry," he said. "About your father, that is. Nursing is a noble profession."

"Almost as noble as being a doctor," said I.

"I may have known your father. I'm involved with the Police Benevolent Association, so perhaps our paths had crossed. Another noble profession, law enforcement. Your parents are the salt of the earth young man, the unsung heroes of society. Poorly paid, largely unheralded, yet where would we be without them?"

"I suppose there'd be riots in the streets, racial inequity, the poor sacrificed while the rich profit. I can't imagine."

"You're quite insolent for a policeman's son," he said. "Arrogant."

"Daddy, please," said Darcy.

"Your father was in the war, wasn't he?" the Doctor asked. "The real war, I mean, World War Two."

"He was. You weren't, I heard."

"So well informed," he said, and glared at Darcy.

"Like you didn't know my dad was dead."

"I wonder how he'd feel to know his son was a war protester, hating his own country, waving the flag of the enemy."

"I don't hate my country, and I don't wave flags."

"But you think our government is wrong? You think they lied—"

"Please, Philip," said Mrs. Saint James, "can't we talk about something else?"

"Would you muzzle our free speech, dear? Mr. Conover doesn't offend me, as I'm sure my humor doesn't offend him."

"Humor, Daddy?" Darcy spat, "is that what you call it?"

"It's a form of debate, dear, like any discussion. A bit of verbal jousting."

"Well, I don't like it!" she shouted.

"But I'm not speaking to you, dear."

"Stop calling me *dear!*"

"Ouch! I don't know who offended who."

"You are offensive! Everything about you is offensive!"

Kevin rose from the table, lifted Lily from her highchair and said, "Excuse us, will you? We have to go potty." Tucking the little girl on his hip, he disappeared up the stairs. Lilah had fallen asleep again, and Kara sat stroking her baby-soft hair.

"Well," said the Doctor, "you may speak freely now!"

"Leave us alone!" said Darcy. "Don't say another word!"

"Philip," her mom implored.

"Oh, do shut up, dear!"

I said, "It's okay, Mrs. Saint James. No need to get upset."

"I'm so sorry," she apologized, "and please, call me Constance."

"He'll do no such thing!" the Doctor shouted. "He's just a pup! He has no right to address his elders by their first name! Who do you think you are, young man, speaking to me like that, as if you know anything about the world?"

"And you do?" I said, struggling to remain calm, or at least coherent. "Why, because you're old?"

"Of course, you mutt! How else does one accrue wisdom?"

"Wisdom? More like vanity, I'd say."

"You would say that, would you? You with your long, effeminate hair, and that ridiculous ribbon! What is that, some cheap memento from high school sports—your highest level of education? Except for art school, of course, which is to say *no* school!"

"Philip! I insist that you—"

"Sit down, Constance! No more of your interruptions! This young man—if he is a man—comes here pretending to love our daughter, both of them all of eighteen years old, and you are defending his arrogance, his self-righteous nihilism? I don't want him near her! I don't want any of his pedestrian, back-street parenting rubbing off on our—"

"Teal can *rub* me as much as he wants!" Darcy shouted, exploding to her feet, her chair screeching back behind her. "Because he does, Daddy, he rubs me all over, and I like it! Is that what really bothers you, the touching, the kissing, the part where you imagine us fucking!"

"Darcy!" shouted Kara, standing, shooting out her arm. "You come with me! Right now!"

To my further amazement Darcy did, but only after Kara came around the table and took her sister's elbow, escorting her from the room.

"Leave now," the Doctor told me.

"Philip—"

"Constance!"

"Thank you, Mrs. Saint James," I said, "you're very kind. Now I know why Darcy loves you so much."

The Doctor guffawed, and said, "Thereby implying that she doesn't love me?"

Standing, leaning, I looked down at him in his chair. "In all your wisdom, Doctor Mengele, how can you not see that?"

"Get out!" he shouted, jumping to his feet, a string of saliva webbing his chin.

"When I've said goodbye to Darcy."

"You'll leave now!"

I walked into the living room where Darcy stood hugging her sister, her French-braided head buried on Kara's shoulder as she rocked with each muffled sob.

Seeing me enter, she rushed to my side and pressed her wet cheek to mine. "I'm *sooo* sorry," she cried. "Honestly, Teal, I truly believed that just this once … I wanted for us to be normal, like a *real* family! I should have known it was impossible!"

When I glanced at Kara she was looking right at me, her blue eyes glistening with tears.

"Wait here!" said Darcy, "I'm leaving with you!"

"Please, Dar, don't. He'll do something stupid. He'll probably call the cops."

Kara squeezed her sister's shoulder. "C'mon, sweetie," she said. "I'll run you a bath. We'll stay for a while. We'll all relax, and calm down."

Darcy only shook her head and pressed herself closer against me. "Please," said Kara, "you can take a bath with Lily. You know how she loves that."

"I should go," I said, "it's better this way. I'll call you tomorrow, or you call me. We'll go for a walk, have a picnic at the falls. Turkey sandwiches on chocolate cake."

Looking down at her face I could see her smile, a single tear caught in her eyelashes. "Okay," she said, wincing, hugging me harder.

"I love you," I said.

"I love you," she said back, "and I'm sorry."

"That you love me?"

"Noo!"she cried. "And don't do that! Don't ever kid about love!"

Kara walked me to the door, slipping Darcy's present, the framed photograph, beneath my arm. She kissed me on the cheek, her hand on my wrist. "You're a very nice boy," she said. "I hope you treat her well. I know you will."

I wondered about that on the long walk home, how well I might treat her, how nice I really was.

It was close to eight and bitter cold, the Christmas lights seeming to make it even chillier, dressed as I was in my light cotton blazer, its collar turned up, to zero effect. *The Doctor is fucking psycho*, I thought, *every bit as Darcy had described him*. I expected that any minute a patrol car would roll up and a cop invite me inside, so when that happened, I was hardly surprised, the window sliding down and the driver asking, "Need a lift?"

It seemed inappropriate to refuse, and when I got in, I saw it was the same cop who'd picked up Darcy that Halloween morning. "Thanks," I said, as we pulled away, "it's getting cold out there."

"Just out for a stroll?"

"I had dinner with friends."

"The Saint Jameses?"

I didn't answer, waiting for the denouement, the coup de grace, or some other French-sounding end.

We drove in silence for several minutes before he said, "A word to the wise, son. The Doctor's daughter, the youngest one, she's your girlfriend, right?"

I nodded.

"You know a kid named Antoine Jones?"

I nodded again. "Yeah," I mumbled.

"We got our eye on him. Him and the girl, you understand? You *understand?*" he repeated.

"Yeah, I got it."

He let me off in front of the Van Tassel. Shuffling up the stairs, I considered what a fucked night it had been, except for Darcy, of course, in the incredible burgundy dress. I loved her so much, despite the craziness, or maybe even because of it. But try as I might I just couldn't picture the classic, fairy tale ending; even the Little Prince got snake bit.

Alone in the house I lay on the couch with the Christmas tree lit and the TV turned low. The Apollo Eight astronauts had circled the moon, sending back truly awesome pictures of the Earth, a black and white orb floating in space, the backdrop for their reading of Genesis: "In the beginning, God created heaven and earth, and the earth was without form, and darkness was upon the face of the deep …"

Crossing the room in my Jockey shorts, I turned off the volume and stood looking at our planet, the swirls of white cloud like smoke from a fire, the Earth a delicate, fragile bulb on the cosmic Christmas tree. 1968, the year that Todd—the *Tiger*—had a good feeling about, was almost over. Lots of innocent people had died and many more had been born.

"He slit his throat," I heard Darcy murmur.

"We've made peace with the fact," Hannah said.

"Peace," I whispered, flashing two fingers at the TV screen in the cosmos of our darkened apartment. I set Darcy's present—

the photo of my parents—on the coffee table, and we stared at each other in silence. On the walls of my room were pictures of a monk in flames, a young Vietnamese girl screaming, a VC suspect being shot in the head. These were the images, the baseball cards of that time. People collected them as such, like gathering the pieces of a jigsaw puzzle with which to assemble the bigger picture, an image of a planet in space, attempting to arrive at some greater, more intuitive understanding of life, of our lives, even those only eighteen years in the making.

Chapter 34

Four hours later, I was asleep when the phone rang. It was after 2 a.m., and the tree was still lit, so I thought maybe Mom was calling from work.

"Teal," said Mrs. Saint James, not bothering with introductions, "you have to come. Something is wrong with Darcy!"

She was freaking out, a frantic edge to her voice, all proprieties dispensed with.

"What's wrong?" I asked, instantly absorbed in her fear.

"She won't wake up! I've been shaking her, shouting at her. I even poured water on her. She's unconscious, Teal."

"Call the hospital," I said, "have them send an ambulance."

I could hear her panting, as if she'd run around the house. "I don't know," she said.

"They'll know. You have to call them."

She was slow in answering, clearly hesitant to act. "I can't," she finally said.

"Why not?"

"I just can't. He won't let me."

"The Doctor?"

"They'll call the police."

It was my turn to hesitate, and I remembered what the cop had said just hours before about Darcy and Antoine being watched. If Darcy was fucked up on drugs, which I was pretty sure she was, she could get in big trouble, maybe go to jail, especially if there was heroin in her possession.

"Please," Mrs. Saint James pleaded, "come help me. Help *her*."

"Where's the Doctor?" I said, then, "Never mind. I'll be there fast as I can."

I threw on some clothes, wearing my heavy corduroy coat this time, and jogged down there, leery of seeing a cop car, having no good excuse if I did. It took me about fifteen minutes to reach her corner where I finally stopped running, my lungs and throat in agony from the cold, and walked the rest of the way to the house so I'd be able to speak when I got there.

Kara and Kevin's blue Volvo was gone, a rectangle of bare asphalt remaining on the frosted driveway. I saw the living room curtain move and Mrs. Saint James appeared at the door, motioning me inside with rapid flicks of her damaged wrist. "Thank you so much," she said. "I know it's a lot to ask, especially after this evening, but I didn't know what else to do. Please forgive me. I know it's not your business—"

"Of course it is! What are you saying?"

"I don't know what I'm saying," she sobbed. "I don't know anything anymore!"

I couldn't tell if she was drunk, or had been, but at that moment she was completely disoriented, an emotional mess. "Let me take your coat," she said, which she did, tossing it at a chair, and missing. "Upstairs, "she said, "she's in her room."

The Chamber, I thought, the barren plain, the place where dreams go to die.

I followed her up there, the carpeted treads squeaking, the raked geometry of stair rail and lightbulb casting crazy black stripes on the wall. Constance was wearing an old pink robe and floppy slippers, her unkempt hair like a tumbleweed in silhouette. There was something strange and creepy about it all, the prison cell shadows, the darkness at the top of the stairs, the apparent falseness of the photo gallery making a mockery of even the concept of a family. Ascending to the second floor, we turned to negotiate the final flight, the light even poorer there, the feeling spookier. *Where is the Doctor*, I thought. *Why am I here, and not him?*

At the top of the stairs Constance touched my arm. "There," she said, pointing down the corridor to where a rectangle of light spilled from Darcy's bedroom door. She froze with that finger aimed like a pistol, crooked as a witch's broom. I could see that she was afraid to enter, hesitant to learn what might have happened in her absence, and the feeling passed directly into me as I eased down the hall, leery of even the groan of a floorboard until, gripping the doorjamb, I leaned to peer inside. There in the negative space of the room, Darcy lay stretched on her bed, her skin even paler, translucent as tallow, naked except for a pair of red panties, the mate of the sexy bra she had worn our very first day at the Met.

Turned on one hip, her legs were drawn up, her red painted toes barely touching. Her torso lay twisted at her narrow waist, her shoulders pressed flat to the mattress, one arm crooked and tucked to her side like a folding pocketknife, the other tossed over her head. In the light of the lamp, her silver hair swirled in a galaxy across her face, strands of it moving with the ebb of each breath, as slow as the wilting of flowers.

"Darce," I called, afraid to move any closer.

"What the hell are you doing here!" the Doctor roared behind me.

Standing like a golem at the end of the hall, he still wore his starched white shirt, the rest of him clownish in pajama bottoms and patterned argyle socks. He glared at me, then at Mrs. Saint James where she cowered against the wall. "You fool!" he shouted, and she raised her hands in a posture of self-defense. Traversing the length of the darkened hall, the Doctor continued to shout as he ran, his footsteps thudding on the hardwood. "How dare you enter my daughter's room!" he bellowed, closing the distance between us. To my surprise he did not stop but collided with me like a train. Raising my hand to cushion the impact, he palmed it with true expertise, bending it downward then pushing it back as he slammed me into the wall. The pain was intense as I spun around, employing his manic inertia, and jammed my forearm under his chin, crushing his Adam's apple. I could hear him gasp as he struggled to breathe, and that only made me push harder.

"Stop!" Constance called, "remember his heart!"

Pulling a phrase out of Charles Dicken's ass, in keeping with the spirit of Christmas, I said, "I should fucking *kill* you, old man, and decrease the surplus population!"

"Please!" said Constance, pleading for the sick bastard's life. So I let him go, shoved him away and he slid down the wall with a groan. Crossing the threshold of Darcy's room, I knelt beside her bed. "Darcy," I whispered just inches from her ear.

I thought I detected a vague response but couldn't really be sure. Sweeping the hair from her beautiful face I opened one eye with my thumb. The sapphire orb rolled back in her head, a half moon of iris revealed. I smacked her cheek, softly, then a little harder, then shook her, shouting, "Darcy! Darcy, wake up!"

I heard someone—the Doctor—stumble down the stairs, and then Constance appeared at the door.

"I need water," I told her, "cold water!"

Nodding emphatically, she rushed away, and I heard the tap running in the tiny bath, then the hurried slap of her slippers returning with a plastic cup and damp face cloth. Placing the cup on the window sill, I used the cloth to bathe Darcy's face, her neck, her entire torso, pouring water over her from the cup, daubing it around with the cloth. "I don't know what else to do," I said, as Constance looked on from the doorway, her one hand pinching the point of her chin, the other clutching her robe. "I think we should call for an ambulance."

Raising both hands, Constance covered her face as though trying to hide behind them, removing herself from the scene. Recalling what she'd said about the cops—and the drugs—I asked, "Could you please go downstairs and get me some ice?"

Once she was gone I looked under the bed where I found Darcy's pj's and the sweater she'd worn earlier. There were few pockets, and no drugs in any of them. Rushing to the closet, I opened its door and found the burgundy dress, and an orderly row of familiar blouses and skirts. I searched through them quickly, even fingering the linings of her red wool coat, but found nothing. When Mrs. Saint James returned with the ice—in the same bucket she'd used at dinner—I was sitting on the edge of the bed again and quickly began the process of washing her daughter's body with ice, and expecting no reaction, got none.

"I'm gonna try to walk her around," I said, "get her blood running." So I did, the task not as easy as I'd thought, her dead weight considerably more cumbersome than a lively Darcy wrestling atop me. I was dragging her mostly, her legs, her bare feet not assisting in the effort. After five minutes I laid her back down and, turning to Constance, said, "I'm sorry. That's all I can think to do. I'm scared, Mrs. Saint James. I'm gonna call the hospital."

There was real fear in her eyes, and she didn't object.

"My mom works in the emergency room," I explained. "She'll know what to do. Is there a phone I can use?"

She led me downstairs to Kara's old room, where the big black phone sat on the night stand. Across the hall a door was closed, and a pale bar of light shone beneath it: the Doctor's crypt, the mummy sealed within, waiting with a scimitar to attack.

"Mom?" I said when the operator paged her. "It's Darcy, she took something. She OD'd."

"What? Where are you?"

"At her house."

"Are her parents there?" she asked. "Why haven't they called an ambulance?"

"They're afraid, Mom. There might be drugs here. She could be arrested."

"Where is the Doctor?"

"He's crazy, Mom. I had a fight with him. He attacked me!"

"My God, Teal—"

"Please, Mom. You have to help her! You have to come!"

As I headed back to Darcy's room, the Doctor's door burst open. He was wearing his suit with the vest unbuttoned, unlaced shoes on his feet. "Mr. Conover," he growled, "if you don't leave this very second I will call the police!"

"Go ahead," I said.

"You think I'm bluffing?"

"You're all bluff, you phony bastard! From your dyed fucking hair to your contact lenses! I can't believe I was afraid of you!"

Finally back at Darcy's side, her skin had turned blue, the cool color of slate.

"To the bathroom," I told Constance. "Can you help me?"

We carried her down the hall to the bath where I threw open the shower curtain and stepped into the tub with Darcy in my arms. Fumbling with the valves, holding us both under the nozzle, the water was freezing, then warmed up until I turned it to cold again for as long as I could stand. Pretty soon I was shivering, hoping that Darcy would shiver too, but she didn't, and just hung there heavy in my arms, my back muscles aching, screaming in pain.

Then Mom walked in with Constance trailing, her black bag dangling from her shoulder. She slung it to the floor and reached behind me to turn the shower off. "My God, you're freezing!" she said, squeezing my arm.

We settled Darcy into the tub and filled it with warm water, Mom lifting her eyelids, feeling her pulse. "What did she take?" she asked.

"I don't know, Mom, I—"

"Don't fuck with me, Teal! Tell me what she took!" My mom rarely swore, at least not at me, and it served to frighten me even more.

"Heroin, I think. I'm pretty sure."

I heard Mrs. Saint James gasp, standing by the door in an awkward pose, clutching the front of her robe. She looked at me with renewed suspicion in her red rimmed, ice-colored eyes. Down in the driveway a car started up and quickly backed out of the driveway.

"Find me a basin, a waste basket or something," said Mom. "Never mind, she's in the tub. Just get out. Leave us alone now."

We stood together in the hall for a while, Mrs. Saint James and I. She didn't choose to speak to me, nor I to her—I didn't know what to say. There was nowhere to sit, and after ten minutes of pacing, Constance said, "I'll make some tea," and disappeared down the stairs.

The car had been the Doctor escaping, departing the scene of a crime. I pictured him stranded just down the block, having tried and failed to scrape ice from the windshield, waiting for the defroster to work before repeating the process and driving a bit farther in his bid to deny complicity. Walking down the hall to Darcy's room, I stood staring at the blankness of its walls, a negative moonscape revealing nothing of her soul, nothing young, or girlish, or pretty, an empty arena like the Roman Coliseum where the faithful were devoured by lions.

"Teal," I heard my mother call, "give me a hand."

When I got to the bathroom the tub had been drained and Mom was removing Darcy's wet panties, lifting each foot to slip them off. She was pink again, Darcy was, and the room smelled of vomit, a small mountain of bath towels piled in the sink. "Help me get her to her room," said Mom.

Laying Darcy on the bed, as naked and helpless as Lily—with whom she'd just bathed in the same porcelain tub—I tucked the sheet around her, combed the hair off her forehead with my fingers. Her eyes fluttered open, her pupils still tiny, yet focused directly at me. "Teal," she whispered, her lips shaping the word before her blue eyes closed again.

"She'll be okay," said Mom, "this time. Where is her mother?"

Mrs. Saint James had never returned with the tea, as I hadn't expected she would. "Downstairs," I said.

"Meet me down there. Five minutes."

"I'm gonna stay with her," I said.

"No, you're not. Her mother can sit with her. You're coming home with me."

Alone with Darcy, I squeezed her hand, raised it to my lips and kissed it. "Forgive me," I whispered, "I shouldn't have left you. I'll never leave you again." Glancing around once more at the room, I studied the white-painted walls, a vacuous space, an empty shell, a darkness on the face of the deep.

I guess I stayed longer than five minutes, and when I got downstairs, Mom and Mrs. Saint James were sitting across from each other at the dining room table, their hands folded on its surface, in absolute silence. Mom reached out and patted Constance's gold ringed fingers. "You'll call me if anything happens? Nothing should. I think she's fine now."

"Thank you, Mrs. Conover. I can't express how grateful I am."

I half expected her to thank me as well, but she didn't, and how could I blame her? There was nothing to say, and so I left it like that, heading out into the chilly morning just an hour or so before dawn.

The Cadillac was nowhere to be seen, and Mom didn't ask about the Doctor. What she said was, "You knew she was taking heroin, and you didn't tell me?"

"Tell you?"

"Yes! I could have helped the poor girl! Someone had to know! Someone responsible!"

"An adult, you mean? Come on."

"Come on? Teal, honey, you're just a boy. You … you've behaved deplorably! Foolishly! You're not taking narcotics, are you? Oh, God, Teal, you'd tell me—"

"Mom, I'm not taking that stuff."

"Is that the truth? Are you lying to me?"

"Of course not," I said, shriveling inside.

"Honestly, Teal, I don't know whether to believe you."

Nearing the apartment Mom pulled to the curb, shifted the car into park. The radio was tuned to a Christmas station, chipmunks singing about fun and cheer. She was shaking her head as if negating her thoughts before she even spoke them. "Teal," she said, "you know that I love you. I'm your mother— you're my only child. Doesn't that mean anything to you? Do you ever, in a blue moon, think of me?"

Chapter 35

I WASN'T AFRAID OF THE DOCTOR anymore, but I was afraid of the cops, so when Darcy didn't call the next day, I didn't call her or go down there. When three days passed, I was getting frantic, thinking the worst, when Constance called. She was polite, but formal, explaining how Darcy had requested I be informed that she was well and voluntarily enrolled in a month-long "retreat" in Armonk, highly recommended by Dr. Deveroux.

I was relieved, but conflicted, because that meant I wouldn't see her for a long time. Yet another part of me realized it was a good thing, a necessary thing, and maybe even a kind of vacation for me, from the Saint James family, including Darcy, whose love was sometimes overwhelming. I was trying to be extra nice to Mom, cooking her dinner, which was mostly disastrous, or washing her car, which was more my style. She kept Darcy's framed photo of Dad and herself on the coffee table where I'd left it, and I saw her staring at it sometimes during *Ed Sullivan*, or *Bonanza*. Mom was as sweet and considerate as ever, but I sensed her suspicion, a cautious reserve when I told her I was going out, headed down to George's for a beer. I wasn't going to George's, of course, just walking around in the cemetery, or down at the river, waiting out the holiday recess. I didn't want her to think I was moping, feeling depressed, like I was. I thought of calling Mary Ann. I'd always intended to, but I still hadn't written that letter to Todd and I felt guilty about it, about both of them.

Just before New Year's I decided to go to back to the City, leaving early to avoid potential invites to someone's pathetic party. My last night home I took a walk down Cortland Street, where I found Antoine in almost the same spot as last time, leaning against a wall instead of a fender, still looking sharp and smoking a Kool. I bummed one after we fumbled through the handshake, Twon laughing, saying I was white as ever. I told him about Darcy, and he seemed truly bummed.

"That chick," he said, "I dig her, you know? You know how I mean. She's fine, she's hip, but fucked up, man. I feel for her, you dig? I feel for you, too, 'cause you love her so much, and she loves you, man, she really does."

I told him about the cop, what he'd said about Darcy and him being watched.

Twon laughed, he said, "Nothin' new there, my man. They always watchin' me. Watchin' you, too, if you're standing here."

"Think so?" I said.

"Don't sweat it, bro. Let 'em watch. I ain't holdin'".

"I want to ask you a favor."

"Shoot, bro," he said, pointing his finger like a gun.

"Don't sell dope to Darcy anymore."

Antoine made a face. "I ain't sold her nothin' for a long time. She got herself another source, you dig?" Knocking another Kool from his pack, he offered it to me. I took it and lit it from his.

"I'll put the word out," he said, "but no promises. Her money's green as the next chick's."

"Hey, Antoine," I said, "you ever heard of the Tigers?"

"Detroit?" he said. "Where you been, bro, they took the series. It's the Super Bowl now. Go Jets!"

"Not baseball," I said. "In the army, you know, the Tigers."

"Oh, hell yeah. Everyone heard a them. Why you ask?"

"Todd, he's in the Tigers."

"The fuck," he said, "you kiddin' me? Straight ol', white hat Todd?"

"Yeah. He's in Vietnam."

"Well, that's fucked up, bro. A motherfuckin' bummer."

"How come?"

"Them dudes are crazy, man. They a whole different breed."

"They wear those floppy hats," I said.

"That ain't all they wear. Those cats high on speed all the time, government issue, USP. Methamphetamine, man. They get it straight from the commissary, like ammo, like MREs. Those are the dudes with the ears, you dig? Them guys be wearin' the necklace."

I walked back up Cortland with my hands in my pockets, wishing for another Kool, a whole pack to chain-smoke by myself. I figured Antoine hadn't made that stuff up, though I couldn't imagine Todd doing those things, or being friends with anyone who did. I was pretty sure Darcy was getting her dope from Patty, who I'd never met and almost didn't want to. I'd have gotten on a train right then if it wasn't for Mom, if I wasn't obliged to say goodbye. Walking up past Saint Teresa's the bells began to toll, and I thought of how Todd, Bosco and I—and sometimes even Railsbeck—used to break into the gym at night and shoot baskets in the dark. Mouse said you could hear us from up on the sidewalk, the sound of the bouncing balls. But we didn't care, we didn't stop; we knew we'd never get caught.

Now Todd was in the Tigers, first string starter, headed for the gook Super Bowl. Glancing up at the steeple, at the crucifix on top, I blessed myself with the sign of the cross and prayed for Heidi's intervention.

I spent Super Bowl Sunday drinking skunky beer in a place called Mo Lee's in Chinatown, right on the border of Little Italy where you could hear Italian mandolin music playing through the walls. The Tsing Tao ale was tasteless, the fortune cookies stale, the little strips of colored paper written in Chinese. Kelly was with me, one of the few New Yorkers not interested in watching the Jets get their ass kicked. His portfolio of photographs was spread across the table, black and white images of actual dog shit taken in Thompson Square Park, part of a series he was putting together from various sites around the city.

"Whaddya think of this one?" he'd ask.

"Kinda shitty," I'd reply.

"How about this?"

"Total crap," I'd say, and so on and so forth through "It stinks," "Pee-ew," and "Get a load of that!"

"Kelly, why do you take pictures of excrement? Like, what's the poop on that?"

"No one else is doing it, and some of them are really interesting, don't you think?"

He was holding one up for my perusal, turning it this way and that, until I reached out and flipped it upside down. "Aha," I said, "I see it now. There's a definite kinetic energy here, kind of like a swirling tornado."

"You think?"

"No, it just feels better upside down, an e. e. cummings-type thing. Did you hear about the slashings at The Metropolitan?"

"No. What?"

"Some asshole carved the letter *H* in a bunch of Old Masters paintings, a protest of that photo show about Harlem."

"Really? Intellectual vandalism? How stupid are smart people?"

It was the ultimate absurdity, I thought, with a capital *Z*, artists defacing art over the definition of what art is. It was Dewey's thing twisted beyond all recognition, intent turned in upon itself to arrive at the unintended. There seemed little hope for the world.

"Hey," said Kelly, "some weird chick came looking for you yesterday."

"Darcy?"

"Hell no. I said *weird*, not erotic."

"She give a name?"

"M talked to her. Ask her, she's right behind you."

I turned to see big M coming through the door. She waved to us, her version of a greeting with the fuck-you finger slightly pronounced. "Is she coming over here?" I asked.

"I invited her," said Kelly.

"What for? Are you guys fucking?"

"No! I just like her, she's cool."

"M?"

Approaching our table, she was dressed in what appeared to be a black parachute that concealed her wide ass yet exposed her cleavage like a fault line. She was wearing tons of jewelry: bracelets, beads, Medusa rings, and they jangled with the authority of a plow truck. "Hey," she said, slumping into the chair across from us. "You already ate? I thought I was invited to dinner."

"You're late," said Kelly.

"There's a statute of limitations on courtesy?"

"It was for drinks, actually," Kelly said, instantly backpedaling, as was always the case when conversing with Meighyn.

"You call this piss alcohol?" she said, picking up my beer bottle and examining the label. "And you, Grasshopper, you never seen tits before?"

I guess I was staring at them, but just out of curiosity, as one would gaze at a geologic wonder. "It's like a crevasse," I said.

"You think I don't know what a crevasse is, Mountain Boy? I got another one you can lick when you're done drooling."

"Teal wants to know what's up with that weird chick," said Kelly, "the one who came to the studio."

"Which weird chick?" said M. "It's SVA, for fuck's sake."

"The one with the purple tights and peacock feathers."

"Oh, her," said M, and smiled at me. "What about her?"

"What did she want?" I said. "I heard she was asking for me."

"She *asked* for you, but she was looking for that girl you fuck, the one who likes to vomit."

"What was her name?" I asked.

"You're sleeping with her, you don't know her name?"

"Not Darcy," I groaned, tiring of Meighyn's game, "the weird chick!"

"Calm down there, Charles Whitman, don't get all homicidal. Her name's Patty. She just wanted to ask about Miss Perfect, said she hadn't seen her for awhile."

"She leave a phone number, an address?"

"No, why would she? You're the competition, asshole."

"What's that mean?"

"Patty's hot, in that sleazy way. I can't blame your little blonde for going for it."

"Darcy isn't gay," I said.

"Doesn't have to be to dabble, and dabbling seems to be that girl's thing."

"How do you know Patty's gay? She's a model, they all look like that."

"They don't all kiss like that," said Meighyn, proud of herself, strutting her stuff. "Takes one to know one, and I know dyke when I see it, you dumb bastard. Obviously you don't, you and the Mapplethorpe of dog doo here, or you wouldn't waste time gawking at my tits."

"We wouldn't gawk at them if you didn't shove them down our throats!" said Kelly, also reaching the boiling point.

"And wouldn't you just love that!"

"No, I hate fast food!"

"Touche!" said Meighyn. "I'm glad to get some kind of rise out of you."

"I don't get a rise from chicks!" Kelly shouted, realizing too late that he'd blown his cover.

"I see," said M, as she stood to go. "Guess I'll leave you two alone. It's been interesting. Revealing," she added, tugging at her neckline.

"Wait!" said Kelly.

Meighyn stopped, placed a hand on his shoulder and said, "Don't sweat it, Ziggy. I got a big mouth, but I know how to keep a secret."

"What the fuck?" I said when she was gone. "Are you serious? You're gay? What about my *erotic* girlfriend, how lucky I am to have her?"

"She *is* erotic. And you *are* lucky! Don't worry, man, I don't have the hots for you. Why does every straight guy think the queers are after him?"

"Is that why you like M?"

"I don't like her, I just feel sorry for her. She won't even let people like her. She's just as lonely as the rest of us."

After Mo Lee's, Kelly spent less time at the apartment, presumably out taking pictures of shit. "What a waste," I told him, on one of the few nights he came home. I hadn't heard anything from Darcy in weeks, the call from her mother being the only communication since Christmas. I figured that wherever she was—at the retreat, as Mrs. Saint James had called it—they wouldn't let her write or call outside. That's what I hoped, anyway. The thing about Patty gnawed at me, not that I believed anything strange or bi about Darcy. But if Patty was gay and Darcy wasn't, what else did they have in common, besides the job?

The Jets beat the Colts 16 to 7 to win the Super Bowl in the most boring game in its short history, and the *Visions of Harlem* show opened at the Met without further incident. I brought Darcy's birthday/Christmas present back to school where I finally finished it, *really* finished it, such that I could hang it on my bedroom wall and feel her looking at me, feel her love smiling down. Darcy's smile was all it needed. That's when the girl in the portrait began to look like my girlfriend, when I quit trying to make her beautiful and made her happy instead.

Chapter 36

IT WAS WARM AT THE BEGINNING of February, and I sat out on the fire escape smoking cigarettes in my T-shirt. Kelly didn't care if I smoked inside, and he wasn't home anyway, but it was sixty degrees and I was doodling in my sketch pad, enjoying the view of other fire escapes and the underwear that fluttered from clotheslines. There was no such thing as silence in Manhattan, and whatever thoughts one chose to ponder were strained through a sieve of distraction. It was an editorial process, necessarily performed if one was to have a coherent conversation with himself, or perhaps write a letter, as was the case when I finished my final Kool and grew tired of doodling, wondering how Jake and Hannah might be doing out there in the Haight.

Dear J and H, I wrote, scribbling over the sketch I'd been doodling on my pad, a charcoal rendering of nimbus clouds that looked a lot like dog feces. *I hope you're not too surprised to hear from me. I hope you are doing well and can forgive me for waiting so long to write. I guess I've been busy, lots of stuff happening here, some good, some not. The Jets won the Super Bowl, I guess you heard. I guess maybe Mary Ann has written to you, so you know all the new stuff at home ....*

I knew after the first sentence that I was writing a letter to Todd, that I'd actually tricked myself into doing it, finally, after so many months of procrastination.

She said you were mad at me. I know she is, and I don't blame her. I always believed I was a good friend, but maybe I'm not, not as good as you were, as you are, I mean. Cause I'm still your friend, or hope I am, whether you know it or not.

If I said anything stupid about you joining the army, I'm sorry. I can't pretend to understand what makes people want to be soldiers, but I guess you do. If you truly believe you're serving your country, then who am I to say different. What I am allowed to say is whether I believe you're serving me, whether I believe my country is served by war. Remember how you freaked out about the people waving VC flags? That's how I feel when soldiers insist that they're killing for me, for my freedom. You take away that freedom when you question my conscience, call me a coward for not doing what I'm told.

Antoine Jones told me about the Tigers. He said some really bad shit, and I hope it isn't true. But if it is, then I hope you're the person I think you are, that I know you are, and will come through all this safe and intact. I met a lady in San Francisco whose son was killed in the war. I told her I was against the war, and for peace, but didn't really know what peace was. We were working in her garden, pulling out weeds, and she handed me this big red tomato. Later, I asked her husband what it meant as he sliced it up for a salad. Jake laughed and said peace was just everyday life that you nurtured with love and compassion. I don't even know what that really means, but if I had a tomato, I'd give it to you so you might make some sense of it, or at least make a sauce of it. Do they even have pizza over there?

There are other things I could tell you about, stuff about Darcy, and my mom. But I don't imagine it's anything worse than what you're going through, so I'll just say Medic! and you'll know what I mean. So please be careful, and please be kind—Go Yanks! Teal

That evening I went down to the booth on the corner and called Darcy's house. I had about two dollars in quarters, and I figured if no one answered, or if the Doctor hung up, I could still get a couple of slices for dinner. But Constance answered, and when I said hello there was a telling silence, which I broke by saying, "I just want to know what's going on. It's been so long, and I haven't heard anything. Can't you just tell me how she's doing?"

"She's well," she said, not unkindly. "I saw her this weekend."

"When's she getting out?"

"It's not a prison, Teal."

"I know, but … when do think she'll come home?"

"Whenever she wants. She misses you. You're all she ever talks about."

"Really?"

"I just don't know that you're the best thing for her right now."

And I felt like shouting, *So who is, the fucking Doctor?*

"I know," I said, "but I can't help wanting to be with her," thinking, admitting, *We're like each other's drug.*

"Why doesn't she write to me?" I asked.

"She's not supposed to. They're very strict."

But it's not a prison. "Will you tell her I called? Tell her I miss her?"

"I will, dear," she said, and I felt a little of the sadness, the sympathy I'd felt for her when she thought her daughter was dying, when she'd believed I'd helped it happen.

I'd used up most of my money in the booth, and with the remaining quarter bought half a dozen breads sticks to bring back to the apartment for dinner. I had some peanut butter up there, and I could dip them in the jar ….

When I got to the landing on the fourth floor, I knew someone was waiting on the stairs, their shadow long and skinny on the graffiti painted wall. It was Mary Ann, long and skinny personified, and I was mortified and ecstatic all at once, glad to see her, but ashamed that she'd had to track me down after all my broken promises. She smiled when she saw me, holding a greasy paper bag with both hands. "Thank God it's you," she sighed, "this place gives me the creeps." I walked up to within a couple of treads and hugged her narrow hips, my face crushed against her silky jacket, infused with her perfume. "It's good to see you," I said.

"Me too," she whispered into the part of my hair. "Is that a gun, or are you really just happy to see me?"

She was talking about the bag of bread sticks jammed in the small of her back. I took a bite of one, to show her they were harmless. "Have you eaten yet?" she asked.

We laughed about my dinner plans, the peanut butter dip and a carton of hardened chow mein noodles from Mo Lee's.

"Are you broke?" she asked. "Do you need money?"

"I have money at home. I just haven't gone back for a while."

"I know," she said, "I called your mom."

"She filled you in?"

"Sort of. Not really. C'mon, I bought calzones and a couple of cannolis."

We grabbed two plates and Kelly's jug of purple wine, the kind that doesn't age as much as get old, and went up to the roof with a blanket and a flashlight with dead batteries. We didn't really need the flashlight, the sky perpetually orange in Manhattan, and we spread the blanket by the roof vent where hot, stinky air spewed forth. We drank from a couple of jelly jars with Howdy Doody on them, nibbling at the edges of the calzones, still hot enough to burn our mouths. I drank most of the wine and ate half of Mary Ann's cannoli, surpassing myself in the appetite department, usurping Darcy's role as human waste disposal. I pulled a flattened cigarette from my pocket and smoked it, looking up at where stars might have been in any place other than New York.

"I wrote a letter to Todd today," I said, proud of myself, expecting she'd be pleased. But Mary Ann just looked away and stuffed her hands in her pockets, pretending to star gaze as I was. "Heard anything from him?"

She shook her head. "Nope," was all she'd say.

"He's okay," I assured her, "he's all right." *He wears ears around his neck, a psychotic kind of flower child.* "He probably can't write. They're very strict about that."

"Who is?"

"I don't know. Them, the generals, the powers that be. You haven't heard anything since we last talked?"

"Not a word."

"Jeez, I'm sorry, Mare."

She smiled at me then. "You said it," she said, "you called me *Mare*."

"Yeah? So what?"

Her smile turned melancholy. "You don't remember," she sighed. "Back when we were little, and everyone called me Mouse …. You didn't. You called me *Mare*. You were the only one."

"Really? I'm sorry. I mean, I'm sorry I don't remember. I guess I did something right for a change."

Her smile shriveled instantly, fighting back tears.

"Hey, C'mon, don't spoil my big moment."

Just as quickly she was smiling again, her snivel turned into a laugh. "You're right," she said. "Enough of all that!"

"C'mere," I said, "I wanna show you something."

I took her downstairs, leading her by the hand through the myriad clothes lines. I'd left the apartment door wide open, and anyone could have ripped us off. Anyone into peanut butter, that is, and pictures of dog shit.

I took her to my tiny bedroom where we stood in the gap between the bed and the wall. "What do you think?" I said, nodding at my portrait of Darcy.

"It's beautiful, Teal. She's beautiful. I wish I looked like that."

"C'mon, Mary Ann, you're beautiful too."

She shook it off. "Where is she now?" she asked.

I sighed and plopped down on the unmade bed. "She's in treatment. Some place in Armonk, a volunteer prison of sorts." Mary Ann sat down beside me, her weight barely squeaking the springs. We both slid back against the wall, looking up at the painting. "She almost died, Mare. My mom was really scared. Did she tell you?"

"Not in so many words."

"It was the weirdest fucking thing. Her father is insane. A criminal, is what he is. I'll fucking kill him if he hurts her!"

I was glaring at Mary Ann when I said it, and she looked shocked, and a little afraid. "Hey," I said, touching her arm, "I'm only kidding. Not kidding, but … just not as crazy as he is."

"She looks happy," said Mary Ann.

"She is happy."

"No, she isn't. You are her happiness. You make her smile, just like you did in that painting."

"Me? No way, I fuck up everything. I'm the Fifth Horseman, the fourth Stooge, the third idiot waiting for Godot. What the hell are you smiling about?"

"See?" she said, "See how you do it?"

"That's bullshit, Mary Ann. How the hell would you know?"

"How would *I* know?"

Darcy watched as Mary Ann's hand crept across the blanket, so slow and stealthy I jumped when our fingers touched. She was fighting back tears again, a soft, silent struggle she was destined to lose. "I'm leaving, Teal," she said, "it's time I went to school. I can't wait anymore, not for Todd, or for you. I need to make myself happy, and so does she," she whispered, nodding toward the painting. "So does a girl as magically, as tragically beautiful as Darcy Saint James."

"Mare," I said, and she squeezed my fingers, tears running down her cheeks. When I slid up against her, she raised her hand but I pushed it away as I kissed her, her thin lips trembling, salty with tears. She didn't resist as our tongues intertwined, stifling a groan in her throat, and the last coherent thought I recall was how one girl's sadness tasted much like another's.

I awoke to the whiteness of Mary Ann's back, her freckled shoulder and skinny arm, her hair so much darker and thicker than Darcy's, its scent so familiar to Todd. I knew she wasn't sleeping by the cords in her neck, a tension rising off her like heat. She jumped when I touched her, a full-body shiver that coursed down the bumps of her spine. Squeezing her arm I pulled her to me, one breast revealed in the window's light, its aureole dark against the sheets. Her eyes welled with moisture as she pulled away, hiding her face in the pillow.

"I'm so tired of crying," she said. "Please don't look at me."

"I shouldn't have kissed you."

"It's not your fault! Do you know how long I've dreamed about this? And now … now we wake up and I leave, and it's over, what I've waited for all my life!"

"No, it's not—"

"Of course it is! You're so … stupid, Teal. Stupid sweet, but … you just never knew, and you never will! So shut up. Go pee, or brush your teeth. Leave me alone to get dressed."

I did all that, even jumping in and out of a freezing cold shower, and when I stepped from the bathroom she was dressed and combed and standing by the door with a note in her hand. "This is my address at school," she said. "Write and I'll give you a phone number. You don't have to call, that's not why I'm giving it to you. I don't *need* you, understand? But if you ever need me, then call, or write, or shout from the top of the monkey bars.

"I know you love *her*, but it's true what I said about making her happy, and someday you'll have to make a choice, just like I am. And please, if you hear from Todd, tell him I love him, but don't give him my address. I just can't take the waiting anymore."

She opened the door and I leaned and gave her a clumsy hug. "No," she said, when I tried to kiss her, "I'll keep the one from last night. The first one, before all the fumbling began."

I couldn't do anything after she left. I felt lonely, empty, hollow inside. Crawling back into bed I stared out the window and away from my portrait of Darcy, Mary Ann's perfume still on the pillow, the wet spot damp on my hip. My sketch pad was tossed on a pile of dirty laundry, folded over to my letter, my epistle to Todd. I'd never mail it now, I knew, another false promise inscribed in the clouds, my artistry reeking of dog shit. I thought of what Mary Ann had said about Darcy, how she wasn't happy unless someone made her that way. It's like we were too close to see one another, always together, just inches apart, every pore and blemish revealed.

Darcy's yellow flip flop floating in a pool, bobbing on the surface of memory. That was the image that eased me to sleep, drifting away like Blynken and Nod in Wynken's stolen shoe. I don't know if I dreamed or not, or would choose to remember if I did, but I awoke to a hesitant knock on the door, a soft and timid tapping sound like pecking through an eggshell. I thought perhaps it was Mary Ann returned to inflict even more revelations. Or maybe Kelly had lost his key, or the will to photograph feces.

I sat up warily when I heard the door open, the creak of a floorboard announcing her presence, and there stood Darcy in her brilliant red coat and Alice in Wonderland shoes. The look on her face held both dread and excitement, as easy to read as a headline, and I blanched to think what my own face revealed as the shame rushed up like a wave, my bed, my dreams still perfumed with Mary Ann and the betrayal of my best friend. But when Darcy smiled and fell into my arms, all thoughts of guilt were forgotten, cast off like a booster rocket jettisoned in space, a vapor trail twinkling like stars in its wake as it faded away into heaven.

"Please don't be mad," she said. "I missed you so much!"

Tossing her coat, I pulled us to the couch where we curled up on Kelly's snarled blankets. I should have felt terrible lying beside her so soon after Mary Ann. Sleeping with Mouse had been awkward, foreign, like putting a T-shirt on backwards. But Darcy and I were the perfect fit, as cozy as a pair of old slippers.

"I wanted to talk to you so bad," she said, "but I couldn't. You're not supposed to communicate with anyone besides your parents, and sometimes not even them."

"Shh. Don't talk about it now."

"But I want to, Teal. I feel so stupid for what I did! And your mom, what must she think of me?"

"She loves you. It's me she's mad at, and your psycho fucking dad."

"It's not just him," she insisted. "It's me too. I have to stop blaming other people, using them as an excuse."

"C'mon. You think you're using your dad? You think you're using me?"

"Yes! Look what I've done! You'll do anything I say."

"Whoa. Wait a minute."

"We have to stop seeing each other, Teal, at least for a little while. Until I stop hurting you. Until I stop hurting everyone!"

"Wait a fucking minute. Are you breaking up with me? Again?"

"No! Not breaking up, just … healing a bit."

"You're dumping me?"

"Don't say that! That's not what I mean. I need time to think, to go to clinic—"

"No, you don't need that! You need to get the fuck out of that house, away from your father, *and* your mom, and start a new life with me, the guy you supposedly love so much, the guy you want to be with forever!"

"I do want to be with you forever!"

"Then do it! Hang your red fucking coat on the fucking doorknob and move in with me right now! I'll paint the place red—or white, if you want—and you can pretend that you've got us all fooled, that the poor Little Prince didn't die in the end and is off growing roses with Tiny Tim—"

"I'm leaving," she said, and jumped up quickly, pushing me away as she did. "Fiona said this was gonna be hard, and I don't blame you for being mad. But I'll come back in a couple of days and then we can try this—"

"Where are you going, home? Back to that nightmare?"

"I'm going to Patty's."

"Fucking Patty's?"

"You don't even know her!"

"I know she's a dyke! Why do you have to go there?"

"To see if I still have a job! Please, Teal, don't do this."

"I'm not doing anything! I'm your puppet, remember? Wait!" I shouted when she moved toward the door. Dashing into my bedroom I returned with her portrait, holding it backwards against my chest. "Merry Christmas," I said, leaning to kiss her. "And Happy Birthday, Happy Valentine's Day, and Happy Easter, too."

I watched her face as I turned the portrait, her eyes growing wide with stunned fascination. She was the mirror image of the girl in the painting, her tears in the light that shone through the window like brush strokes defining her eyes. "Is that how I look?" she asked. "Is that how you see me?"

When I nodded yes, she said, "You're making this too hard. What do you want from me?"

"The same thing I've always wanted—you, the way you really are, not always hiding the truth."

"That's what I'm trying to do here, Teal. I'm not leaving, I'm moving forward."

"That sounds like something from rehab," I said. "That doesn't sound like you."

"But I want it to sound like me. I want to be the person you want, but I'm not that person yet."

When she turned and tried to leave again, I said, "Don't you dare fucking go. I know what you want. I know what you need. Wait, just one more second."

Running to the bathroom I stepped up on the tub and lifted the dead geranium from the sill. It was still there, hidden beneath the flowerpot, the little glassine envelope from Halloween.

Palming it quickly I returned to Darcy and held my fists before her, in cynical parody of the old guessing game. She rolled her damp eyes, refusing to choose one, so I opened the hand with the heroin in it and held it up to her face. "Is this what you're after?" I asked. "Is this why you're going to Patty's?"

Her eyes grew as wide as when I'd shown her the portrait, but in a totally different way, a terrified way that revealed her confusion, her panic at what I had done. "You don't have to go there now," I smiled. "Everything you need is right here."

She tried to shove past me, but I grabbed her wrist, cognizant of all it implied. "C'mon," I said, "I got the sweet tooth bad. Still got your works in your purse?" Tugging the mirrored bag from her shoulder, I turned away and pawed through its contents: lipsticks, eyeliner, an old pack of Gauloises … and the shiny silver purse. Squeezing the fabric, I felt for the fit, for the narrow, compact shape of it, and drawing it out I waved it like a wand, grinning with satisfaction.

"No, Teal! Please don't!"

"Why not?" I said, "I got a turn coming. You took yours without me."

Seated at the tiny kitchen table I took out the dropper and cigarette lighter, fumbled through the dish rack for a semi-clean spoon and mixed in the fine white powder.

"Why are you doing this?" Darcy pleaded, leaning anxiously above me. "Do you hate me this much? Are you getting back at me? Why, because I hurt you, like you know so much about pain!"

"All I wanted was to see the mountains, but you made me come back to *this!* Now sit the fuck down at the table you set, and for once let me do what *I* want!"

The smack bubbled up then cooled in the spoon. I tied off with the belt of Kelly's plaid bathrobe, tore off a chunk of cigarette filter and drew the dope up in the dropper.

Darcy fell into the chair beside me and placed her hand on my arm. "If you do this, Teal, I will too!"

"Is that like a threat, your big sacrifice? Like you weren't gonna do this at Patty's?"

"Honest Teal, I didn't know about the fit! I forgot it was in my bag!"

She watched me slide the needle in, move it around, register the flag. I booted the blood up and down in the dropper, watching it get darker, a deeper red each time. Touching my arm, she smoothed her fingers over my skin, just inches away from the needle. It was good stuff, I suppose, and leaning back in the chair I soon lost track of Darcy's hand, of all sensation save the rushing of my blood, the center of my being bathed in golden light, a child of the sun, a victim of its beneficence.

When I thought to open my eyes again, Darcy was staring at me, through me, the warming rays now passing through us both, spearing us like needles through the carcass of a butterfly, desiccated husks with multi-colored wings. Sliding off her chair, she approached me on her knees, laid herself across my lap and let me stroke her silver hair. Decades later we moved to the couch where she tucked herself against me, a leg across my thigh, her lips pressed wet against my neck as she breathed into my ear. We lay melted together like a grilled cheese sandwich, the same blood oozing the same thick warmth, our hearts beating softly in counterpoint, so slow they felt like echoes of each other.

Eventually I became aware of the ceiling, the cracks in it radiating like spider's webs, flakes of paint and plaster curling like dry skin. I could feel Darcy's fingers stroking my soul, tracing out the hollow of my jaw. Dropping my eyes to the plane of her forehead, I observed the curl of her eyelash, the fuzzy down on her cheek. The gold chain of her crucifix lay pooled on her chest, and as if at some divine prompting she whispered, "Teal, do you believe in God?"

I shook my head, too complacent to speak.

"Is that a silly question?"

"No," I whispered.

"Are you going to answer?"

We were silent again for what seemed a long time, our pulse coming slower than our breathing. I thought she'd nodded off again when she said, "I don't mean the old man with a beard, but *God*, the spirit, whatever makes something out of nothing."

"A Supreme Being?"

"That's what I'm asking."

I tried to shrug but could only blink. "They say God is love, but no one believes it. God can't be a feeling, something you share, only a being to fear."

"How can God be a feeling?"

"An emotion, like energy, like light from the sun. God is the power, we are the filament, together we illuminate the world."

"And the world is just out there, waiting in the dark?"

"No," I said, making a fist, tapping it once to my chest, "inside us, within us—*the Kingdom of Heaven*—biding its time to be noticed. Satori, enlightenment, a feeling of rapture, whatever the old books call it. And all of us waiting, like tigers in a cage, consumed by insatiable yearning."

Dust motes hovered in the light from the window, suspended and golden in the silence of the room. Like rays from heaven, it spread across the ceiling, and I lifted my arm, so heavy in its sleeve, and immersed my hand within it. "Michelangelo," said Darcy, staring at the silhouette, at the dance of atoms so convincingly portrayed. "They say he poured layers of milk in a mold, then chiseled the shape he saw there ... first a finger, then a hand, then the beautiful face of Jesus."

Her crucifix lay tumbled in the hollow of her throat and I fished it out with a finger. "You're no sinner, if that's what you're thinking. And neither is Lilah, or Little Angel."

"Little Angel?"

"Children, people, aren't born that way; they learn to sin, like your father did. I'm glad he believes in the devil."

"Please don't say that. You're just being angry."

"And you're not, and that's what I don't understand. You have so much to be angry about."

"No, I don't."

"Of course you do! Look at your arm! Look what I did to you!"

"I stumbled, we stumbled. We made a mistake. There will always be a next time—"

"Fuck the next time!" I managed to shout. "Leave with me now and we'll go to the mountains, live like *I* want for a change! We'll build a log cabin and float on a lake, have ducks and dogs and silver-haired kids—"

Snatching the crucifix she wobbled to her feet. "I have to do this," she said. "I have to get straight, and Fiona will help me."

"I'll help you!"

"How, like this? Is this how you help? We can't always be together, Teal! We can't be *inside* each other!"

"But you wanted to be! You were my Eskimo!"

"You can't have all of me!"

"I can't have half of you either!" I shouted, lurching erect. "I'm leaving, Dar, I'm walking away, and if you really love me, if you want to be with me, you'll follow me right now! Because I'm out of this city, out of this state, out of this fucked-up life! Yours, too, if that's how you want it!"

Pulling on my coat I rushed out the door. "Teal!" she called, "please don't go! This isn't what I meant!"

Stomping down the stairwell, I turned on the landing and looked up to see if she'd followed. Darcy stood at the top of the stairs with her hands clenched in fists at her sides, her black shoes aligned as though clicking her heels, wishing us over the rainbow. "No, Teal!" she cried, her face gleaming with tears, the golden light filling the doorway. But I kept on running, my footsteps resounding, down the four flights to the lobby. I could still hear her calling as I burst out the door, my broken heart pounding, the single word echoing—"No! No! No! No!"

No.

PART
THREE

MY MOTHER JUST SIGHED when I told her I was leaving, as though she'd known all along that I would. From the hindsight of age and its teardrop of wisdom, it must have been easy to foresee. It's mostly those struggling in the heart of the maelstrom who are blind to the path of the storm.

I'd been vicious, duplicitous in the way I behaved, the act of a vengeful child. I'd swung out at Darcy in the only way I could, extracting my pound of soft flesh. She'd crushed my dreams and so I crushed hers, destroying us both in the process. How often I see that, now that I'm able, the maimed striking out at the wounded, enjoined in impassioned, combative embrace while writhing in each other's arms.

It was never her intention to send me away—I'd made that decision for us both. But how could I have helped had I chosen to stay, struggling with demons of my own, first blaming my father, then the Doctor, then the times, finally descending on Darcy. Such is the province of youth and its folly, its penchant for leaps of blind faith. Or faithlessness, which is just as myopic, the result of my being unfaithful. I'm happy now but was devastated then at the tender age of eighteen, as lost as ever in the Leather Man's woods, revealed in my buckskins of sorrow.

As to who suffered more, it had always been Darcy, surviving on wishes like candy, like prayers, always lighting one candle from another. I knew in my heart I would see her again but could not exist just for that moment. The moment was now, the past only gone—there was no life at all in between. Seen from this distance, through eyes like my mother's, I'm amazed at how obvious it was:

the artful deceptions, the stained glass lies transparent of all but their warmth.

Candles and crosses are not symbols of faith but tokens of wonder and awe, a lifetime quest for meaning, or truths, much higher than the summits of mountains. Most of my questions have long since been answered, all but the last one resolved: Who was the Eskimo, and who was the saint? Whose soul was saved by the other?

Chapter 37

I CAUGHT A BUS CALLED the Grey Rabbit out of Manhattan, a hippie version of its namesake with all the seats torn out and mattresses spread on the floor. It was cheaper than Greyhound, and far more comfortable, chock full of people much stranger than myself. I tried not to think about Darcy, wishing I had a copy of Franny Glass's pea-green book so I could recite the Pilgrim's Prayer over and over, blocking all thought from my mind. I settled for Freedom's version of the Hare Krishna mantra, the one he kept mumbling as he sleep-walked down Haight Street—"Hum, Manny-Patty, hum. Hum, Manny-Patty, hum"—the gospel of Manny and Patty my longtime favorite.

When I got to San Francisco I went straight to Jake and Hannah's, but no one was there. The Krishnas still danced on the corner of Ashbury, but Captain America was gone, and Crystal's wheelchair was missing from its spot beneath the theater marquee. Running down to Stanyan, Sunshine wasn't sitting by the park entrance throwing the I Ching, and Beau's sleeping bag was absent from the woods above Hippie Hill.

The only person I recognized was BeBop, standing in the doorway of the clinic, singing yet another dislocated tune, shouting "War! What is it good for—Absolutely Nothin'! Say it again!"

Jake had passed on, Doctor Dave told me, and Hannah had taken him to be buried with their son, on a hill above the ocean where you could hear the breakers, smell the salt air on the breeze. I was numb more than shocked, reduced more than crushed, and the panhandling street kids who wandered the sidewalks were poorer for not having known him. The Haight now felt like a ghost town to me, or a spirit town, as Jake might have joked. I spent the night at Beau's favorite tree with the candle wax melted on its roots, and the next morning hitched over Golden Gate Bridge, then north along Highway One.

Seeking the solace of the infinite sea, I spent many days wandering the beaches, sleeping in the redwoods that towered along the shore. Sitting by tide pools in the salty spray, my legs folded like Sunshine had taught me, I read from the only book I'd brought with me, John Muir's account of ascending Mount Rainier. I'd memorized its every exhilarating passage, committing them all to heart, the prospect of mountains assuaging my grief with their promise of deathless beauty.

Standing with my thumb out in the eucalyptus groves, I knew which cars would stop and which would drive past without looking. Volkswagens, pickups, and old school buses were always a guaranteed ride, while Buicks or Oldsmobiles—American sedans—sped up at the sight of long hair. It appeared that the freaks had moved out of the cities and into the countryside. Living in teepees, campers, and yurts, they hacked at the soil with shovels and hoes, living on lettuce, carrots, and onions, growing pot way back in the woods. I got rides from Mistrella, Pony and Jubal, Lilac, Sun Bear and Gail. They invited me to their homes, where we sang around campfires, passed around joints in the moonlight. But I never stayed long, put off by their closeness and all of its tender reminders.

I finally called Mom from a phone booth in Portland, within sight of the Columbia River. She was happy, then mad that I'd waited so long, making her sick with worry. "Darcy has called every night since you left. She wants you to call her, collect."

Responding with silence I heard her sigh, pressing the phone to her cheek. "You're so much like your father," she finally said, "stubborn, sensitive to a fault."

"I didn't think that was possible."

"It's hard to avoid pain, but you don't have to nurture it."

"That's what artists do, Mom. If it isn't real, it isn't art."

"If it doesn't *hurt*, is that what you mean? Could you please stop being an artist for a minute? Be a boy, Teal, that's what you are. Will you call her?"

"You know I can't. Darcy is right. I do whatever she tells me."

"But is this the right time to leave?"

"It's the only time, Mom. There never will be a right one."

Reaching Tacoma, the rain fell in curtains, blocking my view of the mountains. Hitchhiking east I crossed over a pass where it rained a bit less but was colder, living for a time in an open shelter at a trail head no one visited. At night I'd build bonfires and dance around them to dampen the bite of the cold, or sit in the center of a frozen lake and gaze at the peaks all around, sparkling like sugar cubes—minus the acid—but just as psychedelic after three weeks of Slim Jims and Mrs. Wagner's pies.

I thought about Kelly and how I'd run out on him and the apartment, leaving behind a cardboard box full of paperback novels, my Huckleberry Hound toothbrush, and a quart of sour chocolate milk. Hard as I tried not to think about Darcy, I couldn't stop seeing the tears in her eyes as she leaned at the top of the stairs, repeating her singular mantra of denial, lingering as long in the echoing hallway as it did every night in my dreams.

The days grew longer and with them my beard, and when the dirty snow melted, I stuck out my thumb and headed for Mount Rainier, following a lonely, tar patched road through farmland and logged off hills, stopping at a store in the last little town to buy raisins and M&Ms, the healthy kind with peanuts in them.

Picked up by a ranger in a Smokey the Bear hat, we wound uphill on a sinuous road through massive trees called *old growth*, the biggest, most ancient trees in the forest. It was damp and foggy, and crossing over bridges on hairpin turns he told me that a clear day would reveal the mountain towering above us, framed like a snapshot at the head of a creek or river drainage.

Dropping me off at a fern-tufted trailhead, saying I'd like where it led, he gave me a couple of oilskin sacks that were used to package tree seedlings. "In case it rains," he drawled, giving me a wink, his tongue at work in his cheek. I walked all day on a muddy track that switch-backed forever upward, the forest mystical, draped in green moss, thrusting in angled geometries. Curved at their base, the trees hooked from the hillside to rise like the stem of a wine glass, merging in a canopy that blocked out the sun, dark and mysterious as a cave.

I had no idea how long I'd been walking, enthralled by the soughing of wind, the sawing of tree limbs. Blowdowns lay scattered like pickup sticks on the inclined forest floor, pierced by the mandibles of rotting red stumps as ancient as dinosaur jawbones. My legs were aching and my sneakers soaked through as I dunked my head in a creek, pushing ever upward until the timber thinned and sunlight bled through the mist.

In a bonsai garden of miniature trees, I found a spot just flat enough to roll out my sleeping bag. With my ears ringing and mind abuzz, I snuggled inside it with my sneakers on, the mist coalescing in tiny white dots like electrons encircling an atom. Pulling the Yankee cap down on my face, the dots swirled on in the darkness, spiraling out to the edge of awareness where Darcy leaned over its rim, posed like a princess by a looking-glass pool as the scent of her hair filled my dreams.

I woke in the morning to a buzzing in my head, the literal hum of a bee, and opened my eyes to a slender red flower with a chaliced throat and dangling collar of hollow, yellow chambers. Inside those chambers were a great many bees, buzzing and bumbling their way from one to another, more insects humming, hopping, whizzing all around me. Sitting up straight when the humming grew louder, an iridescent hummingbird zipped into being just inches from my nose. We looked at each for what seemed like minutes, its invisible wings describing a circle until it darted away with sudden, stunning velocity. Following its erratic, transparent trajectory, my eyes locked upon the biggest individual entity I had ever in my brief life beheld. A leviathan of nature, a colossus of the Earth, the mammoth white flanks of an active volcano rose in neck-breaking perspective directly above me, gleaming like crystal, like polished silver in the rising sun. "Out of the forest at last," Muir had said, "there stood the mountain, wholly unveiled, awful in bulk and majesty, filling all the view like a separate, newborn world. "

It was well into morning and the heat off the hillside caused *Tahoma's* visage to shimmer like a reflection, like a hallucination—only real, beyond real, supra-real in its impact and austere, radiant presence. Haphazardly stuffing my bag in my pack, clutching its straps as I ran, I threaded the trail through precipitous hillsides of red, yellow, purple wildflowers, the echo of waterfalls funneled by the wind, rising from the folds of the blue-green forest bristling with silvery snags. Down in the flatlands from which I'd come, the bends of a river lay tossed like a necklace on the sloping valley floor, pewter in the shadows, platinum in the sun, braided in strands through the sandbars.

The shoulders of the volcano broadened with my ascent, taking on ever greater proportions as a mile and then two fell away and I was standing on a rocky spine, looking out across a jagged ravine at the whole of Mount Rainer, no different than John Muir had described it a century before, no different than any sentient creature might have seen it for a thousand years. It wavered in my vision like a furling flag, like nothing I could have imagined before, that I presently found difficult to believe.

But with great exaltation I did believe it. I beheld it, I dug it, I grokked it deep within me. It flooded my consciousness like the rising wind, lifting all winged creatures in its path, flocks of small birds brocaded in spirals, diaphanous insects spun golden in the light as they rose from the cleft of the valley. With a tilt of my head, I captured time in the wind-burned cup of my ear, modulating its sound with the slightest movement, lifting my spirit on raven's wings to soar toward the towering summit, where at that very moment, I had no doubt, the Little Prince labored at breakfast.

I walked all day, stopping many times to gaze about and fill my belly with blueberries. I felt nourished enough without food but figured my body needed to eat, to replenish the energy that arced like a spark between my mind and the mountain. Puffing a roach that I found in my pack, I smeared purple berries on my sunburned face and thought of Darcy, wishing she was here, if only to witness this mastery of nature where all composition took root. The entire mountain seemed the work of a gardener, a robe-swaddled Japanese monk, and I looked for him everywhere, scanning the sculpted meadows, searching through tapestries of lichened rock for the furrows of a wooden rake, the impression of a clogged shoe.

There were plenty of boot prints, and I followed them high above the meadows onto crumbling rock, then snow, then onto the shining glaciers themselves. My sneakers were soaked and slipped easily on the polished ice. There was nowhere to sit, so I threw down my pack and sat on it, at least keeping my butt dry, and removed my sneakers and ratty socks to massage my frozen feet. The wind moaned louder and the sun shone brighter, forcing me to squint across the blinding snow. Still, I went on with a hand to my face, peering through slotted fingers.

I came upon a cluster of stacked stone huts and leaned against them in the shade, resting my eyes and my wobbly legs, trembling from exertion. Unrolling my sleeping bag, I lay down upon it and shielded my face with one arm, the sound of the wind like a mighty breath sucked from the lungs of the earth. Falling asleep in the pleasant shade, I dreamed that I was flying, soaring in place at a spot above the mountain where winds intersected and pinned me to the sky, my mind looking down like a feathered wing held cupped in the current of dreams, revisiting the sights, the sounds, the perfumed scents of everything I'd experienced that day.

I woke up shivering sometime in the night and crawled into my soggy sleeping bag, too exhausted to reach for the oilskin sacks. Curled in a ball, leaving only my face exposed, I gazed up at the heavens, filled beyond comprehension with stars. The vastness of the universe made me feel small and huge at the same time, part of me feeling divorced from it all, another part lending it meaning.

Whatever I'd once believed about mountains—that they would deliver me from thought and introspection—was replaced by an understanding that those were the things that made life vital, that without the quest and the promise of knowing, life would be one dimensional, literally flat as a canvas, reduced to existence or nothing at all without the capacity for awe. If there was ever a lightbulb, I told myself, Tesla's own, drawing power from the thinnest of air, the embodiment of energy illuminating itself, the Creator made manifest in all creation. Chicken or egg like a motherfucker—hum, Manny-Patty, hum.

I visited myself on the side of the volcano like the Little Prince might visit another planet, with just that much perspective, just enough remove to not rationalize what I saw or how I felt. I was angry, selfish, a bullying coward, blinded to and by myself, incapable of knowing whether I ran toward or away from the things I loved. Yet people loved me just the same, loved me perhaps for the things I wasn't, or the person I wished to be. Mostly I was confused, and I accepted that confusion and did not judge myself or others for it, or because of it. That was the thing I saw in the stars. It wasn't bliss, and it wasn't satori, but it was true and honest, and it filled me with peace, the kind I'd hoped to learn from mountains, the kind that saw no end.

Dawn broke without my notice, without my being aware of time and the elements that suggested its passage. I bathed with snow in the chill morning breeze, watching the sky brighten to the east, standing naked atop my frosted sleeping bag until the sun rose huge and fiery over mountains and painted my body a rich, burnt orange. I took a toke of pot, ate a handful of snow encrusted with raisins and glissaded down the ice the way I had come, my heart running wild with the adrenaline of a new day, a fresh page, a very first breath of an eternal present that was neither held for the future nor exhaled toward the past, filling only the *now* with its cool mountain air, inflating the soul like the wind in my sleeves.

I hiked what must have been many miles, eating berries as I went, lapping water like a dog from alpine ponds, the reflection of the volcano framed within their wild-flowered ovals. Wandering from the beaten path, I explored other ridges, narrow fingers of alpine perfection that led into meadows where marmots peeped and raptors soared, their ancient voices echoing off the walls of sudden canyons, waterfalls cascading in transient rainbows existing at the behest of the wind, whimsical proof of some vast, invisible imagination, the womb of experience, the well-spring of art. I found a ridge where many small pools dotted the landscape, nestled in copes of speckled rock, frilled at their edges with blue and magenta wildflowers. I dove naked from precipitous, lichened ledges a dozen feet above the surface, the water bracing in the brilliance of midday, the chill of it licking every part of my body, the wind drying me instantly where I dripped on the shore. The sundial of my shadow spun in circles like a wheel, and the intervening hours became mornings, then nights as the days slipped by without my knowing. My hair turned the color of tiger lilies, my skin as russet as cedar. Floating on the surface of a private pool, my face and toes barely breaking the surface, the sun a red-hot coal on my eyelids, I dreamed a dream of Darcy.

For the very first time in that mountain lake, I imagined never seeing her again, that everything we'd shared and touched and felt would vanish like the Cordilleran ice sheets, leaving only this chalice of icy water and an artist devoid of intent, who had traded his past for an everlasting present where everything stayed the same, an unchanging landscape where beauty prevailed, and death was absorbed by the seasons.

Standing one morning by a purple defile, gazing at the blue cloisonné of crevasses, a sudden wind nearly swept me off my feet and into the thousand-foot chasm. Sparing me, it took my hat, lifting it as deftly as a pick pocket, the Yankee cap flying up over my head before I knew what had happened, my outstretched arms closing only on air as love tumbled down into shadow.

Chapter 38

Skinny, tired, and out of food, I descended into the foothills, waving my thumb at the first passing truck, falling asleep in its cab. In a funky old tavern called the Hoot Owl Cafe I sat by a window watching log trucks roll past, reading the weeks of news I'd missed from old newspapers stacked by the woodstove. A rock concert in Woodstock, just north of my home, had attracted a million freaks; a crazed cult of "hippies" went nuts in LA and butchered a Hollywood starlet; the Chicago Eight trial of Abbie Hoffman and friends had turned into a three-ring circus.

Devouring a Logger Burger, I studied a photo of Hamburger Hill and thought of Todd, read a story about the Stonewall Riots in Manhattan and thought of Kelly and M, wondering if they were there. John Lennon and Yoko Ono held a *bed-in for peace* in Montreal, wearing pajamas beneath the sheets, singing the chorus of "Give Peace a Chance" while flashing the peace sign at the camera. *Peace*, I thought, recalling the night I had lain half frozen on the glacier, the millions of stars like the millions of people surviving on the surface of the planet. Was peace only knowable when no one was there to distract from its rumored existence, cunningly contoured to look like a cloud, hidden somehow in plain sight?

I bathed in a sink at a Mobil station where the hot water valve was broken, barefoot and shivering on the crumbling tiles, patting myself dry with paper napkins. A heavy-set woman in a hair net and curlers told me about an old-timer who'd recently broken his ankle and who just might need some help chopping firewood. Turned out old Gustav had about ten cords to cut and split, and more logs to yard with his big yellow bulldozer, and how the hell did anyone expect him to all that with a stove-up leg and a bad case of white finger?

Gustav owned any number of worn out Homelite chainsaws, and he showed me how to use them, filing their teeth to bright crescents of sharpness, easing the dogs into the log, allowing them to provide the fulcrum while the two-stroke engine did the work. When the logs were bucked and the rounds stood on end, he taught me to find the check in the wood and let fly with the heavy maul, aligning the head toward the heart of the round, using the natural fault to pop a chunk free. It was hard work, but I found that I liked it, relishing the feel of wood calving from the blow, the saw cutting through the log, saw dust flying, using the tricks that allowed gravity to work *for* and not against you.

"Never run a saw half throttle."

"No sir."

"Never do nothin' half ass."

Gustav offered me a room in the old house he'd built himself, but I choose to crash in a little shack by the river where he said the horse loggers used to camp. I swept the place out, raked up the deadfall, and built a big fire outside. Sitting beside it on an old folding chair, I finally wrote a letter, a postcard to Todd. It was a glossy picture of Mt. Rainier with one penciled arrow that said "*ME*," and another pointing to the volcano that said "*IT*." On the back I wrote "Meet ya at the top" and left it at that.

There were other small cabins not far away, in similar states of dishevelment. Most were empty, but a few were rented or squatted in by longhairs who offered me weed and hospitality in the manner of Jake and Hannah. Down at the Hoot Owl we'd sit on tail gates in the parking lot, smoking doobs and swapping stories of where we were from, where we going. Some of the chicks were cute, and I knew I could be with them, but I just couldn't try, and so I spent most nights down at the river, sitting by a fire with Gustav's old dog for company, Coot sleeping with his warm body snuggled against me, his gray head resting on my thigh.

Gustav didn't agree with my politics, nor I with his, and so we didn't speak of it when the Weathermen's Days of Rage exploded amidst the trial of the Chicago Eight, or a week later when hundreds of thousands of protesters staged demonstrations across the country. He was cool when the Miracle Mets won the World Series, beating Baltimore four games to one, grumbling that at least it wasn't the damn Yankees! He cursed the Indians when they seized Alcatraz, but when sergeant William Calley was convicted for the massacre at My Lai, he was humbled to silence, and when a few days later half a million people staged a March Against Death in the Capital he had nothing to say, not even jokingly as President Nixon hid in the White House, angry Americans chanting at the gates.

At the beginning of December, with fresh snow on the ground, the earth turned to slop and the Cat work came to a halt. On the tavern's old Zenith bolted above the bar, I watched in amazement as Richard Weaver, a kid I knew in high school, drew the second number of the newly established draft lottery. The first number, previously drawn, coincided with Richard's birthday, and thus he'd been chosen to seal the fate of thousands of other young men on nationwide TV. My birthday, as it turned out, was in the two hundreds, and well above those the army intended to induct. I called Mom immediately from the phone booth by the gas pumps. It was late in New York, but I wanted to tell her the news so she'd stop worrying about me. She answered on the third ring, so I knew she'd been sitting dozed off in her chair with Johnny Carson on

TV. "Mom," I said, "did you hear about the draft? Richard Weaver was on television! We were in Cub Scouts together!"

Mom was still sleepy but glad that I'd called, saying she remembered little Richie. She hadn't heard anything new about Todd but had bumped into Mary Ann at Thanksgiving recess. She looked great, Mom said, and she even had a tan. "She met a boy, a transfer student from Italy. His name is Luciano. Lucky for short."

He has no idea, I thought.

I asked her what else was new, and she told me Erik Neumann had beaten his rap, only to be arrested again on his way to Woodstock, pulled over on the Thruway for a busted taillight. They found marijuana in the trunk of his Audi, and he was right back in jail, waiting to learn his sentence. PH3 and Belinda Cake had a baby they named Four and had moved to Boston where Three was enrolled at MIT. Bosco and Dionne were engaged to be married, Bosco having torn an ACL and destined to lose his scholarship.

"How about those Mets?" I said, realizing then how long it had been since I'd called. "First the Jets, now the Mets. They must be going crazy in Queens."

"Teal," said Mom, "Darcy is in treatment. She finally quit calling, but I received a short note on this cute little stationery. Listen, hon, do you want her address?"

"I don't know, Mom. What would I say?"

"Anything, dear, she just wants to hear from you. Have you written her at all since you left?"

When I didn't answer, she said, "Oh, hon, I'm sorry it hurts so much. Reach out to her, Teal, don't hold it in. That's what your father did, and I don't want that for you."

"Wait a sec," I said, fishing through my corduroy coat for a pen. I found a nub of pastel crayon in a pocket, the tiniest remnant of my former life buried amidst the saw dust. Writing the address on the glass of the booth, I later borrowed a pen from Tiny, the bartender, and copied it on my hand. That night in the shack, I sat on my beach chair staring at that hand, writing a letter to Darcy in my head, searching for an opening line. When I woke after midnight the fire had gone out and a sickle of moon lit the window. Washing my face in a metal bucket, I was careful to keep my hand dry, and I crawled into my bag on the folding cot with one arm draped to the floor. I spared that same hand washing up in the morning, and even the following day, but by midweek the numbers had all worn away and I hadn't transferred them to paper. I bathed outside with fresh snow on the ground and ice on the rim of the tub, scrubbing myself with a bar of lye soap that smelled nothing at all like Darcy.

Chapter 39

THERE WAS THIS GIRL WHO WORKED at the Hoot Owl on weekdays, the breakfast shift only, never after dark. Her name was Aurora but she wasn't a hippie—far from it. She was the daughter of a mill owner and great-granddaughter of Aurora McMillan, the widowed lady who'd once run the old trading post long since flooded by the dam. Aurora had thick black hair, gray eyes, and a rosy blush to her apple cheeks. Friendly, pretty, she was bright as a sunflower, the favorite of the old timers who came in every morning to sip black coffee and listen to her laugh. With no work available, I spent my mornings there as well, reading the paper, eating poached eggs, peeking at her from behind the pages of the Seattle Post-Intelligencer.

One morning she plopped herself down at my table and topped off my coffee without even asking. "So," she said, "your name is Teal, you're from New York, and you put way too much sugar in your coffee. What else do I need to know about you?"

Folding the paper, smoothing it across the red-checked tablecloth, I said, "I like mountains. I like this town, and books, and chocolate."

"You ever read that *Zen and Motorcycle Maintenance?*" she asked. "I own a motorcycle, and I just don't know what that book was about!"

"Anything Zen is that way," I explained. "You're not supposed to get it."

"You like movies?" she asked. "I wanna see that *Midnight Cowboy*. When do you want to go?"

We went that weekend, driving forty miles to the nearest theater in a town of about 50,000 people; i.e. the big city. We ate dinner at a Mexican restaurant owned by real Mexicans, not Puerto Ricans like in New York. Aurora was funny. She stole a plastic flower from the vase on the table and stuck it behind her ear, telling me all about growing up in the country, her high school class of a dozen seniors, a double-wide trailer with a potbelly stove transformed into a science lab. Every other guy in town was her cousin, and not the kissing kind. She asked me what New York was like and I tried to tell her, but a picture was worth several thousand words, and later, as we sat in the theater watching Dustin Hoffman fend off traffic and the Midnight Cowboy smile through despair, all I could think of was Darcy, recalling us kissing by the Christmas tree at Rockefeller Center, strolling through pigeons in Central Park, lighting candles in the darkness of Saint Pat's Cathedral while sparrows chirped high in the ceiling. When Ratso Rizzo died on the bus and Jon Voight cried in the window, I cried along with him, fighting back tears, and though Aurora said nothing, she squeezed my hand as the soulful harmonica wailed, and I slumped in my chair as if riding that bus, New York just a dot in the rear view.

One day I got a letter within a letter, reminding me of Darcy and the elephant in the hat. So, I wasn't too surprised that the letter was from her, my name on the envelope, minus an address, mailed to me by my mom. Tearing it open, a fortune fluttered out, a narrow strip of pink colored paper from a Chinese fortune cookie: *Hope is just Love awaiting its turn, Peace is the Joy of arrival.*

"Dearest Teal," Darcy wrote. "This is the fortune I saved from that day we spent at Laughing Hill, wrapped in a blanket, eating cookies until I got sick. There must have been dozens and we read them aloud, using a lighter when it got too dark. I ate all your cookies as well as mine, so no wonder my stomach ached. You held me in your arms and stroked my hair, rocking us both till it stopped. But now you're gone and I'm all out of cookies, and there's no one left to ask—am I still waiting for love to arrive? Will the Yankee hat ever return?"

I remembered that day and the twilight evening, the pink slips of paper blown over the grass as the stars winked on overhead. Darcy moaned, laughed, then moaned again as I gently rubbed her tummy. "This is like watching the world spin around," she said gazing up at Orion, "the satellites and falling stars trying so hard to keep up."

"Teal," she had asked, "do you still love me, even the times when I'm weird?"

"Especially then," I said with a smile, my hand sliding under her sweater.

"But really, I mean … I know sometimes you get angry at me, upset by the things I do."

"Or don't do," I said.

"What's that mean?"

"The drama, the secrets that border on lies, all of the things you won't tell me."

She'd sulked for a moment, but my hand kept moving, warm from the heat of her skin. She said, "Not all secrets are mine to tell. And besides, you'd eventually hate me."

"Never," I'd said as my fingers slid down and found their way inside her. She'd moaned again, but not in pain, and her wet lips tasted like sugar.

The letter stopped then began again in a different color ink.

"I'm in this big room full of speed freaks and junkies that reminds me of Mrs. I's class. Detention was the best time ever for me, being with you, sneaking off to the woods, feeding green apples to horses. I wish so much we could both go back to those lazy, wildflower days, you showing me the headstones by the Old Dutch Church, reciting the names of your family. You never caught on how nervous I was, afraid you'd see right through me. That day at the zoo you said I was beautiful and I thought I had already blown it, that I'd never be able to make someone want me for more than the way I looked. We stood in the dark by the tiger's cage waiting for our eyes to adjust, for the tiger's magnificent face to resolve, to see if I still had a chance. Sometimes I wish we had stayed in the dark where no one could know who we were, just the sound of our breathing, the warmth of your hand where I held it behind my back.

"It's funny to write this 'cause I sound just like you when I try to express how I feel, the way you talk, the look on your face as you're trying to choose the right words. Sitting in the basement in the old green chair, the freight trains rumbling outside, you told me that I was a really good artist, even better than you. But that's not true because I'm no artist, not like Dewey described. I draw what I see in exacting terms like copying pictures from a book, tracing the outline of life all around me because I don't have one of my own. And now I'm still waiting for beauty to find me, for my stripes to emerge from the darkness. But I only felt beautiful when you were around, the real me hidden away in my room like the portrait of Dorian Gray."

I remembered what Mouse had said about Darcy—how *I* made her happy, how I'd made her smile with a flourish of pigment and brush. "I'm just some old painting you hang on your wall, a book you make up as you read." That's what Darcy had told me on the roof of the station the first time we broke up, when I tried to force her to tell me the truth about what went on with her father. "Not all secrets are mine to tell," she'd explained at Laughing Hill, as if reading the words of a fortune cookie written expressly for her.

Slipping the letter back its envelope, careful to tuck in its folds, I figured I'd finish reading it in the morning in the brilliant light of day, in the generous warmth of the rising sun and not the pale glow of a candle, when Darcy's words weren't fuzzy and blurred by the quake of my trembling hand.

I spent Christmas Day alone, hiking along the river in the National Forest. A skiff of fresh powder filigreed the peaks, the valley floor crusted with ice. The wet brush soaked my old corduroy coat, now reduced to near rags from working in the woods. There were deer tracks pressed in the virgin snow and I wondered how they survived through the winter, and when I found some old antlers and a knuckled spine, I realized that sometimes they didn't. The rush of the river was a constant drone that diminished as I wandered from its banks. But it never vanished, never ceased to exist, Siddhartha's voice fading to a mumbled chant, then a whisper, then a vibrating *ohmmm*.

Toward evening, after washing outside in the cold, there came a knock on the cabin door. It was Gustav, inviting me over for Christmas pie and ice cream. He waited impatiently while I got dressed, my soaking wet coat still dripping from a nail, creating a puddle on the floor. "I got you something," he said. "You damn well better like it."

"Yes sir," I replied.

Sitting in his kitchen, we ate rhubarb pie with vanilla ice cream—two scoops for me, one for Gustav—my wet coat and boots drying by the woodstove. Kerosene lamps lit the corners of the house, the old man not accounting for electricity when he built the place after returning from the First World War. Gustav shoved his plate away, tamped tobacco in his pipe and lit it. Watching the smoke as it twirled toward the ceiling in perfect, trembling rings, he told me a story from his childhood about coming downstairs one Christmas morning to find a horse eating popcorn off the Christmas tree. "It was my present from Mom," Gus chuckled. "Pop thought I was too young for a horse, so he got Mom's goat by bringing the scrawny colt into the house, gettin' it damn near under the tree!"

He smiled for a moment, then gestured with his pipe. "Go over to that closet and tell me what you find."

I did exactly as I was told and opened the creaking door. There on a peg hung a fine woolen coat, green-and-black plaid with a pocket in back for the storage of ducks while hunting. I pointed that out, which precipitated another of Gustav's tales about his older brother Hugh, now deceased, who once shot a squirrel and stuffed it in the game pocket of his coat, only to have it miraculously revive. Hugh leaped and danced in manic circles, trying to keep the resurrected rodent from biting his backside. "Ended up shootin' the damn thing twice," Gus laughed, "coat and all!"

I thanked him for the gift and wished him a Merry Christmas, saying I was sorry I had nothing for him. He told me a gift was hardly necessary, but fellowship was a requirement. "You read the Bible, boy?" he asked.

"No sir. Not anymore."

"You read books, though?"

"I love reading."

"Fine habit," said Gus, "soothes the mind. I take you for a thinker, a believer. And I don't mean the Bible," he added, reaching for the Book where it sat on the sill, cradling it in his lap like a favorite old cat. "You believe in something, I can see it plain as day."

"I guess."

"You guess?" he replied, reminding me of Todd.

Without really thinking, or just thinking out loud, I said, "I believe that we create the world, paint it like a picture, play it like a song … to make something beautiful. To make something art."

Gustav puffed his pipe to life, blew another smoke ring toward the ceiling. "There's plenty I'd never have chose to see," he sighed, "much less make it happen. Weren't nothin' beautiful about it."

"Not like pretty," I tried to explain, "or happy, or even good. But *full of beauty*, like a song on the radio, the colors of autumn, the honking of geese overhead. It's sad, but still, you have to look up, you touch the red leaves, you turn up the volume because … it's beautiful."

"So we're all like God?" Gustav asked.

"We're all creators, if that's what you mean, though I don't quite know how it works. If art is intent, then the world is *intended*, a stained-glass window of all we believe, inspired by all we desire." And I thought of the tiger and his guttural growl, his green eyes piercing the darkness.

"Like you and that pie," Gustav joked. "Your God's got a sweet tooth for rhubarb."

"For something," I laughed. "Maybe just ice cream." Or maybe not sweets at all.

On the way home I walked past the Hoot Owl where I could see someone cleaning up inside. It was dark, and pressing my forehead to the glass, I saw it was only Tiny, a Christmas carol playing on the eight-track tape deck, colored lights blinking around the bar. Crunching through slush I headed for the phone booth, toasty warm in my new wool coat that smelled like Gustav's pipe. I called Mom collect and she answered on the first ring, sitting by the telephone, waiting for my call. "Merry Christmas!" she enthused, interrupted by the operator asking if she'd accept the charges.

"How was your day, hon?"

"Great," I said, trying to sound cheery, giving her the images I knew she needed, of me surrounded by happy people, sharing the day with those who loved me, or at least liked me. I'd mailed her a present, a turquoise pendant I bought at the railroad car tourist shop in the next town down the mountain.

"I loved your gift," she said. "I hope you didn't spend a lot of money."

"Mom, I'm not broke. I work when I can, so please stop sending me checks."

"Sweetheart," she said, "I have some troubling news for you. Darcy has disappeared. She ran away from the treatment center. There were legal charges involved, and her enrollment was compulsory. She called her sister in Vermont—"

"Kara."

"She was headed there, but never arrived. Or if she did, Kara's not saying. Teal," said Mom, "did you ever write? Did you let her know how you feel?"

Surrounded by snow in the telephone booth, I stared at my reflection in the glass, reminded of my very first day with Darcy on the train ride home from New York. All that was missing was the Yankee cap, her gift to me on my seventeenth birthday—our best day together, though far from the last, with many dark pages between. Darcy was the candle atop my cake, my prayer to the Eskimo Saints, the whickering flame on the brim of my hat in a field full of Van Gogh stars. "Art is in the eye of the beholder," she once told me, and I had been quick to correct her—"I believe the word is beauty, Dar," not knowing how wrong I might be.

"I'm coming home, Mom," I heard myself say, surprised by my sudden resolve. "It's all my fault. I've been so selfish. I should never have left her like that."

"But Teal, honey, you're just a young—"

"No," I insisted. "I'm not all that young. And there's nothing that people just *are*."

Chapter 40

I LEFT THE NEXT DAY, stopping at the Hoot Owl in the morning to tell Aurora. She asked me if I was coming back, and I didn't know what to say. "I want to," I told her, "but I just don't know. I can't ever tell what I'm doing." I stopped at Gustav's to tell him, too, and thank him again for the coat. He tried to give me money, but I wouldn't take it, then insisted on driving me to the Interstate where I hitch-hiked across the Canadian border and hopped on a train for Montreal.

I'd hoped to see the Canadian Rockies, but the train passed through them at night. We stopped at one place long enough to get out and stretch, walk away from the lights of the station. A three-quarter moon embellished the sky, bright enough to see by, and a dark bone of mountains trailed north into the night like a sinuous dragon's tail. It was flat and lonely where I stood on the plain, the land all blue in the distance, fading into nowhere, into literal nothingness toward glittering stars and the Arctic, which I knew to be everywhere, everything wild beneath the surface of things.

Montreal was cold and windy, and I thanked Gus again for my warm wool coat. Most people spoke French, and they scowled when I asked questions in English. It was a beautiful city, old and grand and full of cathedral-like buildings. I took a bus to the border and, passing over, received a glare from the uniformed agents, most of whom were used to seeing American longhairs heading the other way, into Canada, and not out. Once in the States, I held out my thumb and was picked up almost immediately by some freaks in a van with Jersey plates. They'd just delivered a *gift* to Quebec, and we smoked a bit of it before they dropped me off just south of Lake Champlain, where I headed east into clouds that soon delivered a maelstrom of snow, thick cords and curtains of it blowing around me in perfect semblance of the wind.

A tractor-trailer pulled over on the shoulder and I raced toward it, the driver just stopping to put on his chains. I helped him chain up, then hopped in the cab and we lumbered over ice rimed roads through what passed for mountains in Vermont. Night came on and we drove even slower, the truck's bright headlights so filled with snowflakes the road became a swirling white cave. We stopped at a café where other semis sat idling in the parking lot, mercury vapor lamps casting lacy cones of winter over everything, delicate reminders of the cold and wind to those who sipped coffee by the steamy café windows, cupping their mugs with both hands.

The driver's name was Ted and he reminded me a little of Jake in that he called me Pilgrim. He was more John Wayne than John Lennon, but kind and friendly just the same. "Well, Pilgrim," he said, his thick finger barely fitting through the loop of the ceramic mug, "I'm afraid our paths are about to part. I'm headed to Boston, and Burlington's north of here. You got family up there?"

"Kind of."

"I hope so. You don't want to get stranded in this. You got a hat?"

"I used to."

"Used to? That damn sure don't help." Sweeping the cap off his balding scalp, he reached across the table and tucked it on my head. A bright red *B* was emblazoned on its crest—*Boston Red Sox*—and I couldn't in good conscience turn it down. The waitress came and we ordered breakfast: eggs, bacon, sausage, and home fries at nine o'clock at night. "Breakfast's all I ever eat," said Ted, who even looked a bit like Ted Williams. "Driving so damn much, it's best to pretend it's always morning!"

An hour later I was glad for the cap, my last ride dropping me off at a lonely fork in the road where she went left and a battered sign advised me to stay right. The silent storm would come and go, and through the swirls of falling snow I saw the outline of hills and sugarcoated timber, humming to myself the familiar tune that ran in a loop through my mind, how *the Berkshires seemed dream-like on account of that frosting, with ten miles behind me and ten thousand more to go.*

I hopped and paced and did everything I could to keep warm, and when finally I lost the feeling in my toes and my nose developed an icicle, I stood there and took it, posed like a statue as the snow piled up—one, two, three inches tall on my Sox cap and green plaid shoulders.

With nothing else to do and nothing left to lose, I did what I'd been putting off since dawn of Christmas day. Reaching in the pocket of my soaking wet coat, I pulled out Darcy's letter. In yet another shade of ink her words, her voice, began anew, flickered to life by the glow of my lighter, like we'd done reading fortunes on Laughing Hill.

"The people here are pretty nice, but I don't really talk to them much. Not unless they ask me a question, and then I don't know what to say. I know what you're thinking, how that's so much so much like me, the girl whose whole life is a secret. But it's only a secret to other people who think they're entitled to know it. White lies and dark truths all look the same when seen from the distance of time, all squashed together in memory's eye they're parts of a much bigger picture, like the guy from the Modern, your drawing instructor who paints with a million small dots.

"I saved the portrait you painted of me. It's hanging on the wall of my room. And no, I'm not lying, it's actually there, or it was before I came here. I'm trying so hard to be that girl, even if you don't want me. It's who I *should* be, the person you made me, the one who deserved to be loved. If you just came back I could be her again, or maybe just for the first time. I'll tell you whatever you want to know and then you can hate me some more. You said that you couldn't have half of me, though half was all I had left, and I gave it to you with all my heart and am willing to give it again. You just have to want it, so please, please do! I'll try to be different, I promise—"

The writing just stopped, the letter concluded, no goodbye, no love Darcy, no more shades of blue ink. When a fierce wind gusted and the pages caught fire I dropped the lighter in the snow, fanning the letter as if to save it, only causing the flames to grow brighter. Burned down to my fingers, I finally released it to tumble away on the wind, a pinwheel of light on a background of gray, receding at length out of sight. For an insane moment I thought of just quitting, of turning around and walking away, returning to the solace of mountains. But after two steps in no real direction, I stopped and laughed at myself, posed by the road sign with shoulders hunched, at a literal fork in the road.

I was looking and feeling like an arctic snowman when an old Ford Galaxie pulled up beside me with snow chains tinkling and emergency lights flashing. It was moving so slow I couldn't tell if it had actually stopped until the passenger window rolled down and an old woman called out, "Hello? Are you all right?" Before I could answer she turned to the driver and I heard her say, "Yes, he's real. I told you he was real, Drew. I know a real person when I see one." Returning to me she repeated again, as if to test her theory, "Hello there?"

The old man got out and brushed snow from my coat with

a plastic windshield scraper. Satisfied, he then helped fold me into the back seat of the car. The heater was blasting hot, dry air, the whir of its fan a hymn to my frozen ears. Dressed in a wool knit cap and scarf— even in the car—the old woman introduced herself as Doris and her husband as Drew, then poured me a cup of Salada tea from a battered metal thermos. I held it to my lips for a while before sipping, letting the warm steam thaw my nose, hearing a crackling sound in my head as my sinuses slowly melted. "Here, doll," said Doris, folding down a cushion that divided the bucket seats, "Take off those shoes and stick your feet up here by the heater."

"Yer lucky we came along," said Drew, craning his neck to peer in the mirror. "State police closed the road down south due to a pile-up. We live just this side a' things, headed up ta Dottie's place to babysit the grandkids. Matt and Dottie, they drive plow for the State. You'd a froze straight through out there. Dottie might a plowed you come mornin'."

Dottie lived in Burlington, a ninety-minute journey at twenty miles an hour. Stopping at a gas station, the only place still open in the storm, Drew and Doris waited in the car while I looked up Kara's address in a phone booth. I thought of calling first but was afraid that maybe they hated me and wouldn't tell me where Darcy was. Better to just show up, I figured, and knock on their door unannounced. I told Drew the address and he drove over there at the speed of dark, the only traffic being State vehicles and the local police. Kara's was a quiet street at the edge of town, a few porch lights describing the length of the block, the flickering blue of a solitary television screen prompting me to ask the time. Doris squinted at her watch, made a face and thrust her arm at Drew so violently he flinched in alarm. "What the heck time does that say?" she asked. "The hands on this watch get smaller every day!"

"'Leven thirty, said Drew, "and wear the dang glasses."

I was surprised at the hour, and disheartened, destined to add rudeness to the list of my shortcomings. It was either wake up Kev and Kara or freeze on their porch until morning.

I'd given Drew an address just down the street from theirs, not wanting to explain my situation, or cause a commotion outside the house. Drew shook my hand as I clambered from the car, the door left hanging open. Doris said, "You give us a call if you need to. It's under Kearns, Dottie Kearns."

"No it's not," Drew sighed, carefully spacing the words, letting his exasperation be known. "It's under *Matt* Kearns. Ain't no *Dottie* in the book."

Doris said, "You get yourself a hot tub, hear? Get some soup in you. Doesn't that sound good," she said, turning to Drew and smiling, "some nice, hot chicken soup?"

"Let the boy go, Dor. You'll freeze him all over again."

I promised to call if I had to and walked half a block to the house that bore the correct address, a modest white rambler with blue or gray trim, difficult to discern through the snow. One light shone in a lace-curtained window, and I stepped up onto the tiny porch and peeked in. The living room was empty, but I could hear a TV or radio playing, so I figured that someone was up, unless they'd left it on for security, for strange guys like me who came creeping in the night. I paced a little, careful not to make any noise, hoping I didn't step on a squeaky floorboard. Briefly sitting on the snowy porch rail, I jumped back up and pressed my forehead to the window again, the clock on the wall showing midnight. I was leaning on the wall between the window and the rail, screwing up the courage to knock, when the door squeaked opened and Kevin stepped out in bare feet and pajama bottoms, a cardigan sweater with suede patches on the elbows pulled tight across his chest.

We stared at each other for several long seconds, he squinting thoughtfully, me inviting his recognition by removing the soaking wet Sox cap. "Teal?" he said, mentally erasing my scruffy beard.

"Kevin. Hi. Sorry to bother you." *I was just passing through New England.*

"Geez," he said, "look at you, you're frozen. Come in, please. Let me get you something hot."

He led me into the living room, led me also through the process of removing my coat and boots. Once relieved of them, exposed to the warmth of the room, I began to shiver, and shiver so hard that I couldn't speak, my teeth clacking uncontrollably. Standing there like that, incapacitated by tremors, I barely registered Kara's entrance in a pair of long-eared bunny slippers and a pink robe much like her mom's. Clutching a hard cover book to her chest, an index finger keeping her place, she slid a pair of reading glasses down the length of her nose.

"Teal?" she said. "My god, what happened? Are you—Kevin, go run a bath. And put the kettle on."

Taking my arm, she led me down the hall to where Kevin had flipped on the bathroom light. Stopping at the door, she told him, "Forget the bath, just turn on the shower. Here," she said, addressing me, shrugging the robe from her shoulders, revealing gray thermal underwear beneath. "Get out of those pants and socks. You're almost blue, you know that?"

The shower was so hot I yelped stepping in. Turning the valve to freezing cold I let my body adjust, slowly making it hotter and hotter as every inch of my flesh complained. It reminded me of Darcy on Christmas Eve just the year before, how frightened I'd been that she might die while hanging limp in my arms. Shoving the thought from my pounding head, I chose instead to focus on the pain, recalling again her letter. Five minutes later I was still shivering, my toes screaming, my nose apt to shatter on my face. I stayed in the shower at least twenty minutes, maybe longer, until the pipes began to whistle like I'd run the hot water tank dry.

Tiptoeing back to the living room in Kara's too-small robe, there was a fire roaring in the fireplace, and bowls of soup—*had Doris been here?*—on the coffee table. Kara grabbed a pillow from the overstuffed sofa and tossed it on the stoop of the hearth, unfurled a puffy goose down quilt and held it up before me. "Out of that robe," she ordered, and when I hesitated, naked underneath, added, "Don't be silly. They're all the same, you know." I did as instructed, then sat on the pillow, and Kara gave me a wink. "Besides," she said, "you're in love with my sister."

Just like that I began to cry, my face buried in my hands, my sinuses draining with the tears.

"She's not here," said Kara. "It's like I told the police, Darcy hasn't been here, and I don't know where she is."

I blew my nose for several minutes, tissues magically appearing from whatever place women like Kara hid them. Kevin passed me a steaming bowl of corn chowder, and one to Kara, then drew up a chair beside his wife and we all slurped hot soup for a while, the fire crackling, popping in the grate, the glow of a green lampshade spreading an arboreal warmth over everything. Kevin said, "We heard you were out west somewhere, California, or Oregon."

"Washington," Kara confirmed. "My god, Teal, did you come all this way looking for Darcy? Why, that's wonderful!"

I shook my head, offered my sardonic grin. "There's stuff you don't know. Otherwise, you wouldn't say that."

"I wish I could tell you where she is. She's not at home, that's for sure. I think Daddy would have her arrested. The longer she's gone the worse it gets—with the cops, and her chances of returning to rehab."

"Was she … pretty bad?"

"She was caught with drugs on her, that's all we know. I'm so worried about her. She thinks she's so worldly, so mature, but … she's just a kid. No offense."

"None taken."

"You can't take the blame for her. No one can."

"Someone sure can," I sneered.

Kara set her bowl on the hardwood floor, the spoon clinking loudly in the pensive silence. "I know what you think," she said, "and I'm not making excuses for Daddy, but Darcy has to grow up and live for herself. She has to get out of that house."

"But she won't," came a voice from the dark of the hallway, eerie as wind in a cave. Looking up from my place on the hearth, a diminutive woman stepped into the light, thin like Darcy, dark like her dad, and I knew right away it was Lena. Dwarfed in a pair of Kevin's pajamas that hung like a tent from her shoulders, she tiptoed barefoot across the room and knelt beside me, her hands folded stiffly in her lap. She said, "If you thought I was dead, this is quite a surprise. I don't know what Darcy has told you."

I was more than surprised, and at first, I couldn't speak in the presence of this eldest sister, a fabled, ghost-like, Dickensian figure in the annals of family lore. "She said you're alive, or that you are now," I finally managed to utter. "She explained the story behind it."

"I doubt it," said Lena. "If she's anything like me, she's told you as little as possible."

Crouched on her haunches, she was posed like a cat, her sloe eyes as feline as Darcy's. "So you've come here to find her, to take her back? To where? Some commune in the mountains?"

"No," I snapped, instantly defensive, then just as quickly confused. "But I agree with Kara, she has to leave. She has to get out of that house."

"And that will change everything, hiding in the woods?"

"Lena," said Kara, compelled to interrupt, "you took her yourself for the very same reason. Surely you can't object."

"And how well did that work? She ran away after one month!"

"Shh," shushed Kevin, "you'll wake the kids."

"What are you saying?" I whispered. "The Doctor didn't *send* her to Miami?"

"She kidnapped our sister," Kara said. "She took her without discussion."

"But why?" I asked, staring at Lena. "How did you convince her to leave?"

Folding her arms across her chest, she spoke with an air of defiance, "I didn't convince her—you did it for me … I threatened to tell you her secrets."

"You blackmailed Darcy into leaving me? You coerced her to run away?"

"This is not about a teenager's broken heart. It's about broken bones! Broken lives!"

Lily appeared suddenly from the dark foyer, winding a finger in her sleep-tangled hair. "Mommy," she whispered, surprising her mother, Kara caught wiping a tear. Running to the safety of her mama's arms, she appraised me with one blue eye, her bottom lip glistening in the light of the lamp, curled in a petulant pout.

"Aren't you sleepy?" Kara cooed to her daughter.

"I woke up."

"Sure you did. And that's all right. We're all gonna go to bed now, okay? Mommy and Daddy, and Auntie Lena. You remember Teal, don't you, hon? Aunt Darcy's friend?"

Lily shook her head—no, she didn't remember me. Sliding into her father's arms, he swept her to his hip as he rose to his feet, and they disappeared down the dark hallway. Kara gave her sister a short, pained smile before wishing us both goodnight, tousling the curls of my still damp hair before following her husband to bed.

We sat in silence, Lena and I, her arm almost touching my knee, she seemingly engrossed by the crackling fire while I studied the plane of the ceiling. "Let's start again," she said at length. "I don't make a great first impression."

The Saint was her nickname in the high school yearbook, and she seemed every bit that austere, armored in pajamas that should have seemed clownish, yet stoic as Joan of Arc.

"You just flew up from Miami?" I asked.

"You hitchhiked here in this storm?"

Silent again, we gathered our thoughts, recalling what we knew of each other, which wasn't much in light of the secrets that shrouded the Saint James family.

"I know that you love her," Lena said, "and that you're just trying to help. But I just don't believe that escaping reality is the answer to Darcy's problems."

Before I could speak, she held up a hand, demanding I hear her out.

"That's what I did when I was her age, and you see what it's done to my life."

She paused for a moment, as if inviting my appraisal, my assessment of the woman she'd become.

"You can't see, of course," she chastised herself, a nervous tic in one eye. "How could you know the girl I once was … if ever I'd truly been young."

"But you ran away, so why not Darcy?"

"They sent me away, I just never came back. A part of me, anyway."

Peering at me sideways, she narrowed her eyes in a look of vague recognition. "It was you on the phone a year ago. I thought at the time it was Darcy."

"No," I answered, surprised by my lie. "I would never intrude like that."

"Why not," she said, "if you love her so much? How can you say you're trying to help when you don't even know what's wrong?" Sensing my anxiety, she backed off a bit, allowing her shoulders to slump. "I just don't want her to end up like me, alone in a cottage by the sea."

Smiling at the image, I recalled how Darcy had first described her *dead* sister. "She called you the widow with a shawl."

Lena grinned, but only for second. "It's true," she admitted, "I'm not much for company, alone with my cats all these years." Regaining composure, she straightened her back and returned to the business at hand. "Darcy told me about your father."

Shocked again, I recovered quickly and mumbled, "He died five years ago."

"I'm sorry," she said, "but not surprised. About why she chose you, I mean. Surely you must have wondered why, what gave you that special allure. Not that his death was the only reason. Darcy is starved for love."

My pain, my confusion at hearing those words must have shown on my face, as Lena appeared to pause for a moment, but then as quickly continued.

"We were good for a while down there in Miami, swimming in the ocean, playing with pancakes, laughing like little girls. I'd disabled the phone and poached all her letters—you can't take chances with my father. But she found the postcards stuffed in the trash and it caused a terrible scene. She ran off down the beach in her yellow bikini, not even wearing her flip flops. When I woke the next morning Darcy was gone, returned to you, to your arms."

"To Constance," I corrected. "I'm not the one she can't leave."

"You seem to object to her loving my mother, like that means she must love you less."

"Everyone has to make a decision. You can't stay a kid all your life."

By the look in her eyes, I could see I'd hurt her, had poked a nerve of some kind, and she said, "But you're always a child in a mother's eyes, no matter how old you get."

Letting it go for another time, as if there might actually be one, I decided to pursue a different tack in learning what Lena was up to. "I was there that morning you took her away. I saw your car hidden in the garage."

"I didn't hide anything. I had not come in secret. And I never intended to *kidnap* Darcy—that's Kara's word, not mine."

"Then why were you there—to be with your father, a man who considered you dead?"

Cornered by the tone of my accusation, she tugged at her overlong sleeves, bunching them up in the balls of her fists, chewing her lower lip. "I was there for my mother in a time of need. She still loves him, though God knows why."

"And you don't?"

She shook her head violently as though shedding the thought, a tumor infecting her brain. "My father is evil," she nearly spat. "You have no idea what he's like."

"Oh, but I do," I replied with some relish. "And that's why it's odd that you came when you did. If you hadn't returned to save your sister, then why had you come back at all?"

Suddenly crying, she hid her face with the blue striped flags of her sleeves, her dark head bent and body swaying like a girl on a rocking horse. Crouched on her haunches with her legs tucked beneath her, the soles of her feet were aligned side by side … The scar formed a hook on the flat of her heel like the curve of a question mark, half of a whole that had now come full circle, as patient as the hands of a clock.

Lena jumped when I reached for her foot, her head snapping up to follow my eyes and read the confusion on my face. Her mind worked quickly, collecting her thoughts, collating the facts as she saw them. "She told you," she said, "what happened on the beach. What I've never told anyone else."

"I … don't understand."

"Of course you don't, how could you?" she said, her voice reduced to a whisper, her emotions constrained by years of seclusion and a lifetime of well-kept secrets. "There's things you don't know," she added at length, repeating verbatim what I had said less than an hour before. "My own sister Kara, she doesn't know. She was spared somehow, for some strange reason, or was just too young to remember. But I'm going to tell her—that's why I'm here. Then they can all wish me dead."

"But it's not your fault!"

"I've wanted to believe that was true for so long … I just never had the courage to prove it. But now I must, and you can't stop me—promise you won't interfere." Swiveling on her hips she reached for my hand where I still gripped the heel of her foot. "I have no intention of taking Darcy," she said. "This time, I'm after my father."

A truck rumbled past on the street outside, its tire chains tinkling, a plow scraping ice. *Dottie*, I thought, my thoughts all a swirl, seeing Matt's name in the phone book.

Lena rose from the fire and kissed my head, combed my hair with her fingers. Walking away in the baggy pajamas, her heel punctuating each step, she stopped when I spoke and glanced over her shoulder, a shiny green tear in her eye.

"Darcy …" I said, "that terrible room. Was it violent, or was it—"

"Honestly, Teal," she sighed before leaving, "do you really think there's a difference?"

Making my way to the overstuffed couch, I curled on my side in the puffy blue quilt, watching the fire as it burned down to embers, crumbled to smoking coals. Somewhere in the house a clock struck two and the furnace kicked on in the basement. There were no more sounds from out on the street and I thought I could hear the snow fall, flakes elbow to elbow, colliding with the porch rail, whispering politely as they struck—*excuse me, forgive me, sorry about that. I'm sorry, I'm sorry, I'm sorry ....*

Just before dawn I was drifting through dreams of deer spines and Ratso Rizzo's raincoat, when the tiniest sound bade me open my eyes to find Lily standing just inches away, leaning into my face. Dressed in pink pj's with booties on the bottom and Pooh stitched over her heart, she placed a misshapen green bow on the pillow and waited for my reaction. It took me a second to recognize the bow from the ill-fated Christmas dinner, but once she felt assured that I did, she climbed unceremoniously onto the sofa where I scooted over to make room, folding the comforter over us both, the green bow crushed beneath her. Five minutes later she was snoring like a logger, the cooling grate in the fireplace ticking along with the clock, the smell of the smoke mixed with baby shampoo as dawn drew pink crescents on the windows.

Chapter 41

THE NEXT MORNING, Kevin drove me to the bus depot in brilliant sunshine, the world beyond the frosted windshield gleaming white, the sky above it sapphire. The day continued clear and bright well into afternoon, and the bus ride south was hot with slanted sunlight pouring through the tinted windows. Moving to the shaded side of the nearly empty Greyhound, I twisted in fretful snatches of sleep, my forehead pressed to the freezing glass, eventually giving me a headache. Clouds closed in as we entered New York, a gray shroud of foreboding as cold and cutting as the wind on Forty-Second Street. It was way too late to start looking for Darcy, to go to SVA and find Meighyn, who I hoped might have an address or a number for Patty.

On the train, sitting on the river side looking out, the Palisades appeared miniature after the Cascades. The cloud ceiling sank as daylight faded, and soon the Hudson was lost to dense snow that streaked by the window at fifty miles an hour. It was dark when I got off at the Tarrytown station, the sidewalks salted and gray snow plowed like breakers along the curbs.

Walking up Cortlandt Street, my shoulders hunched against the wind, I wondered if anyone would recognize me in the Red Sox cap. I kept my eyes peeled for Antoine Jones, half expecting to find him leaning on a fender, smoking a Kool in the midst of the storm. Just the memory of him made me crave a cigarette, though

I'd quit smoking since leaving New York and until that moment hadn't even thought of one.

Being in town again, being *home*, was like looking at the world through the wrong end of a telescope, everywhere seeming small yet intimately detailed, distantly familiar like a movie I hadn't seen for years. Looking in the window of Rose's Corner Store, Ollie sat hunched behind the counter doing a crossword puzzle or rubbing a nickel on a twenty-dollar scratch-out. The neon sign in Malandrino's deli shone pink through the drifting snow, winking erratically, shorting out like it always did. A cop car cruised by on Beekman Avenue, its wheel wells hung with lobes of frozen slush. The driver observed me with no sign of recognition, just another hippie with a beard.

The key was in the wreath on the door of our apartment, its silver bell tinkling when I pushed it open. I'd called Mom from Kara's and she'd explained that she'd be at work when I got home. There was a note about a meat loaf in the oven, but I wasn't hungry. After hanging my coat on the closet door, I walked around the house just looking at stuff, lighting the Christmas tree she'd left up for me, standing in the middle of my bedroom that hadn't been changed—except for the sheets—since the day I left.

I flopped on the couch with the tree lights blinking and the television on, listening to the same old laugh tracks and sit-com jingles as last year. Tommy Smothers made me laugh, Henry Kissinger made me swear, so I turned off the tube and sat at the kitchen table looking out the window at the dark, at the rare passing car and the personal snowstorm raging in its headlights. Teacups dangled from a rack above the table, our names printed on them in gold: *Mom, Dad, Teal.* Dad's cup had been broken and glued back together; no one had used it for years. Lifting it carefully, I washed it in the sink, feeling the cracks with my soapy fingers like a blind man reading braille. I put water on to boil, grabbed the cream from the fridge, sugar, and a tea bag from the counter. When the whistle blew, I poured boiling hot water into Dad's mended cup, thought better of it, and added some cold from the tap. With the string around my finger like a fishing line, I dunked the tea bag and watched the stain swirl, studying its vortex as my father had all those years before.

Might I someday be someone's father, I thought, my name wrought in gold on a teacup, married to Darcy and her imaginary family of *kids who don't like me and a husband I hate?* Spilling a dollop of cream in the cup, I heaped in two spoonfuls of sugar. Endlessly stirring, I tried to be angry, or sad, or simply self-righteous. But I couldn't feel anything but empty inside, just a dusty old cup on a hook. I was all of those things and always had been, never knowing when things got worse, like a lobster slow-boiled from tepid water, barely noticing when things grew hot, then scalding, then unbearable.

A tower of mail was piled on the table: bills, solicitations, more bills. One near the top had red and blue stripes along its edges, like the letters from my father at war. Slipping the envelope from the tidy stack, I studied the hand-scrawled print, addressed to me with a government posting, mailed from somewhere overseas. I looked for Todd's name on the return address and instead found one I didn't recognize, staff sergeant somebody at an airbase in Da Nang.

Staring at the letter for several long minutes, the tea cup grown cold in my hand, the words on the envelope turned cryptic as hieroglyphs, like runes from a pharaoh's tomb. Holding what felt like Todd's life in my hands, I struggled with what to do: open the letter and seal his fate, or suspend all knowledge to the closet of the past, resigned to the shoebox of history. Lost in these thoughts, the letter unopened, I barely heard Darcy's knock on the door, and marched down the hall like a Nutcracker soldier obliged to take part in a play.

She was looking right at me when the holly wreath tinkled, snow piled high on her crimson hood, big black galoshes on her feet. As she took a step toward me, the boot buckles jingled, a funny little reindeer sound, and she paused to glance down at her man-sized boots, charmed by their musical notes. When she looked up again, there were tears in her eyes and a single word on her lips. "Teal," she whispered and fell into my arms, her wool coat electric with cold. We squeezed each other like toothpaste, like lemons, bittersweet and minty cool, prisms of dampness freckling her cheeks, her skin the cool texture of satin.

"I can't believe I'm touching you," she said. "It's like that dream when you finally wake up and realize it isn't true. But this time it is, and you're actually here … Am I getting you wet?" she asked, stepping back quickly, her fingers ice cold on my wrists.

"Come in," I said, "take off that coat. I'll make you a hot cup of tea." Reaching out with both hands, I flipped back her hood, my thumbs left framing her face. She'd taken scissors to her beautiful hair and barely an inch remained, a snow-speckled halo of silver-blonde curls as sparkly as Tinkerbelle's wand. Absent all makeup, perfume, or jewelry, no hint of her old self survived, her skin drawn pale across her cheekbones, shadowed beneath her brows, where tiny blue veins cast a lavender blush like a bruise or the stroke of a brush. It served only to make her eyes more alluring, even bluer than I recalled, more ice now than turquoise, more bottomless than deep, twin wells to the depths of her soul.

"Come in," I repeated when she hadn't moved.

"No," she said, "let's go out."

"It's a blizzard, Dar. You're soaking wet."

"But it's beautiful, Teal. Soo beautiful out there. Please come out. It'll be like that night. Like Christmas Eve at the Old Dutch Church."

"My mom's not home, if that's what you're thinking."

"That's not it. I love your mom. I just want us, alone, together, out in the mystical night."

She stood in the hall while I got dressed, resurrecting my old blue sweater from a drawer, pulling on my new wool coat, showing her the game pocket in back. "No!" she cried, "not ducks!" I assured her that I'd never shoot one, but that's what it was for. When I put on the Sox cap her mouth dropped open. "Dar," I stammered, "about the hat—"

But she raised her hand and covered my lips, rose on her toes, and kissed my nose. "Not now," she said. "Maybe not ever. Let's just make everything new!"

Out on the street it was still snowing heavily, though elegantly, silently, instantly magical with Darcy by my side. She was already dancing in the clumsy rubber boots, chasing down snowflakes to melt on her tongue. Her face appeared elfin in the cavern of her hood, her skin the same color as the drifting snow, pale and translucent as vellum. From the unseen steeple of Saint Teresa's, the bells began to peal, their clarion tolling muffled by the snow, though resonant in my heart, a timeless sound I'd once heard every day, every hour of my life. "Listen!" said Darcy, letting a snowball drop from her hand. "They remind me of you. They remind me of me."

Pulling a Kool from the pocket of her coat, we shared it as we walked. It was broken in the middle just above the filter, and we pinched it there as we passed it between us, careful to keep it alive. The sidewalks were shoveled, but no wider than the blade, the pavement still buried beneath packed snow and ice. Huddled together, we negotiated the trench, Darcy's arm looped in mine, keeping each other upright as we descended the steep hill of Pocantico Street. The gate to the Restoration was padlocked, the entrance bereft of tire tracks, and across 9A the neon lights of George's tavern glowed, a tiny Christmas tree winking in its window, barely visible through the snow.

"How did you know I was here?" I asked.

"Kara told me."

"Kara told *me* she didn't know where you were."

"She didn't. I just happened to call."

"Just happened?" I said. "After all these weeks, everyone looking for you, and you just happened to call when I left?"

"Yes," she said, pausing to look at me, to make me look at her. "*Yes*," she repeated.

"What else did she tell you?"

"Nothing. Why?"

We walked a bit farther, neither of us speaking, then she stopped and said, "Don't spoil this, Teal. Give me this night, this final chance. Then you can say whatever you want."

I nodded, and she smiled and squeezed my arm, tugging me across the deserted road and under the blinking stoplight toward the cemetery. The iron gates were drawn and locked and behind them the old road hadn't been plowed. The trees beyond the entrance were monstrous and gnarly, legendary, even in the Land of Legends. The halo of the moon shone bright through the storm, through the branches of those trees, like the beacon of a ship far out at sea plotting a course through the fog. Stepping off into thigh-deep snow, into the Hollow itself, a silence descended like snowflakes falling, buffering the world outside, like putting on ear muffs, like turning off the volume when Astronauts circle the moon.

"To the Church!" said Darcy, still tugging at my arm.

"We could have gone the other way," I argued. "The front's easier."

"Don't be a grump. This way's prettier, more magical."

She was right, of course, the cemetery being the perfect scepter for all seasons, this one no less beautifully so. The older headstones were buried almost to their corniced tops, only the round wings of angels revealed, the names now lost to the winter. We waded through it toward the church above, the snow squeaking beneath our boots, clouds of our breath trailing like scarves as we negotiated the terraced hillside, careful to avoid the rusty chains now hidden in sculpted drifts.

Reaching the church, Darcy knelt before those very first headstones and brushed snow from their faces with her bare hand. The sweep of her palm etched my family's names in white, the church-building, Indian-killing Van Couenhovens of Sleepy Hollow. She smiled up at me then, her own face an angel's.

Pulling a candle from her red coat pocket, she lit it with a match, the wind no stronger than her frosted breath, and we walked around the church with the tiny flame cupped in her hand, watching ourselves, our fluttering reflections portrayed in each passing window. The flat, smooth plane of the séance crypt was mantled in undisturbed snow. Darcy swept it away with the sleeve of her coat, packed up a mound of what remained and stuck the candle upright in its center. Turning to me she leaned back against the crypt and pulled me to her. "I have a present for you," she said with a smile, a bit of the candlelight shining in her eyes. I held my breath as she rummaged through her pockets, fearing she was about to do to me what I had done to her not a year ago at Kelly's apartment. Withdrawing her hand, she held not a needle but a bag of M&Ms. "Merry Christmas," she said, and leaning to kiss me, balked at the look on my face. "What's the matter?" she asked.

"Nothing."

"Nothing? Really? Then kiss me, please. Let's make out."

She kissed me awkwardly, self-consciously, then quickly turned away. "You don't love me anymore," she said.

"Of course I do. That's why I'm here."

"To save me? Again?"

"Maybe," I said.

She asked me where I had been for a year, and I told her. "I live in a cabin, but it's kind of crappy. No waterfall, but there's a river out back."

"Is it beautiful?"

"Yeah," I conceded, "it is. It's simple, and quiet. Peaceful, like *real* peace, the kind you feel inside you."

I could feel my excitement mounting as I spoke, allowing myself to believe that maybe she would come back with me, that everything might end as I'd dreamed.

"Are you painting?" she asked.

I smirked, shrugged, the bright moment gone. "Not really."

"What's that mean?"

"No. I'm not painting."

"But what about art?"

"What about it? Art is everywhere. You should see what people do out there, they like … make their own lives, build their own homes, create entire worlds."

"And that's what you want?"

"I guess."

"Dammit, Teal," she said. "If only Todd was here."

"What? Why did you say that?" I asked, my face suddenly burning, reminded of the red-striped envelope.

"*You guess?* Is that what they'll carve on your tombstone: 'Teal Conover—He Guessed'."

"Then yes, that's what I want! What's more creative than staying alive?"

"Staying in love maybe."

It hurt to hear it, and I had to look away, craving another cigarette.

"Are you seeing anyone?" she asked.

I shook my head, feeling suddenly tired, like fighting the onset of a cold. "I don't know how to be with girls."

"You know how to be with me."

"I *only* know how to be with you."

"So, you're not saving *me?*" she asked.

A moment passed, neither of us looking at the other.

"Why'd you cut your hair?" I asked. "Looks like you did it with a knife."

I could see I'd hurt her, amazed how easy it was.

"I just… had to change something," she said. "You don't like it?"

"What's to like? There's nothing left."

She stiffened, actually stomped her booted foot. "Is there anything left of me you like?"

"What about him," I asked, "the Doctor?"

"My father?"

"And your mom. How's that working out for you, protecting her and all? Tough job when you can't live at home. Where exactly is your hideout? Down in the train station basement?"

"God, you must just hate me!"

"I don't, Dar! Can't you see that? It's just … fuck, this is so strange. Strange as ever."

"I thought you'd like it here. It's one of your favorite places."

"It is, but—"

"I thought you'd like *me* here, *love* me here. Please, Teal, don't be mad. Hold me, kiss me, make love to me right here! Right now!"

She tore at the toggles of her scarlet coat, her fingers fumbling at the little football shapes of them. Her hood fell back as she pulled it open, revealing a man's overlarge dress shirt beneath. Soft and faded, it was patterned with pinstripes, its sleeves still missing the cufflinks. Impatient with the buttons, she tore them off and the shirttails flapped in the wind. Pale and skinny, she was naked underneath, the arch of her rib cage distinctly pronounced, the ridge of her hips concave. "Touch me, please," she begged, "don't just leave me standing here."

"No, Darce, this is crazy. You don't want this."

"*I do!*" she cried, "I want it more than anything!" Grabbing my coat, she pulled me closer, struggling to wrap my arms around her.

"Then why did you leave me?" I had to ask.

"I didn't leave you! I *released* you from feeling that you had to love me! That you always had to be there to save me!"

She was crying then, and I hugged her back, trying to stop her shivering.

"Come with me, Darcy, leave with me now! I have some money, I have a place—you can't stay here with *him!*"

"Who, my father? And what about yours?"

"What's my dad got to do with this?"

"Everything, Teal. You see everything through him, like looking through a photo at the sun."

"Bullshit," I snapped, "you're just afraid. The sister who can't leave her mother."

"Like you left yours?" she shouted back.

Closing my eyes, I tried to escape, ashamed at hearing the truth.

The half-moon bruises beneath her eyes turned mother-of-pearl in the light, reflecting the glow of the candle's flame, as opaque and purple as seashells. "Please stay!" she pleaded. "I promise I'll change. I'll never do drugs again. We'll paint, and read, and have little babies—"

"Don't!" I shouted, my anger returned. "You said in your letter you'd tell me the truth, but I'm just hearing more of your lies!"

Stunned for a moment, she started to speak but I waved her off with my hand. "Lena was there at Kara's house. She told me what really happened. It wasn't you that day on the beach … Will you *ever* be honest with me?"

A moment passed as I felt the snow falling, grazing my cheeks and nose, white feathers clinging to the ruff of my beard, perched at the edge of my vision. I watched it fall too on Darcy's face, her eyes now closed, her head thrown back, snowflakes starring the tips of her eyelashes, kissing her parted lips. She exhaled a terrible cloud of despair that hovered in the air like a wreath, her last hope of love leaking out in a sigh as she let herself crumble against me.

Limp as a baby, she hung in my arms, sobbing in the collar of my coat. With her wet hair tucked beneath my chin I smelled the old shampoo, and my heart nearly burst with the love I felt, recalling each day, each moment we'd shared, every laugh, every smile she'd fought to maintain in perfecting the grand illusion.

"So … what?" she whispered. "Like you know something now? You've figured the whole thing out?"

"Come with me, Darcy, we'll leave right now—to hell with Lena's plan!"

"Plan?"

Suddenly conflicted, recalling my promise, I decided in that moment to reveal it all, to act in my own self-interest. "She's putting an end to this lifetime of lies. She's telling the truth about your father."

Darcy's eyes flooded as her face screwed up and her lips curled back in a snarl. Raising her fists, she swung them like hammers, cuffing my ear, grazing my shoulder as I struggled to hold her against me. She was wailing something I could barely hear much less understand, until I realized it wasn't words at all but a desperate, animal mewling. She only stopped when her arms grew weak and her voice too hoarse to continue. Curling her fingers in the collar of my coat, she pulled my face so close to hers I could see snot glisten on her lip. Eye to eye and breath to cheek, her words tumbled out in a cloud, "Lena is my sister … She's my mother, too. The truth is I'm everyone's daughter."

Even as she said it, I could hear Lena's voice, the look in her eyes when she'd whispered, "There's things you don't know," she had all but confessed, one secret wrapped in another. It all made sense, it all came together as I watched our reflection in the window: the false confession at Yankee Stadium, her panic on the roof of the train station, her breakdown in the basement of Mary Ann's house the night she lay curled in the afghan, the bitter pill of the ultimate truth the only drug she had taken.

Darcy leaned back so far on the crypt my arms were strained to support her, her mouth opened wide as if catching the snowflakes, incapable of making a sound. Like the woman in Edvard Munch's *The Scream*, like the young girl running from the flames of My Lai, every part of her secret, tortured life, every wound she'd ever endured, every dream of escape she'd ever resisted came out as nothing but air, barren of content, stark as her bedroom, silent as falling snow.

When I pulled her against me, she struck out again, gouging my neck with her blunted nails, kicking out with the clunky boots. The candle fell and was lost in the drifts, the bag of M&Ms with it. She hit me so hard I had to let go, and she posed there a moment in a warrior's stance, her red coat open, shirt tails flapping, tears in her glistening eyes.

Rising from a crouch, she fumbled at her clothes, ashamed to be naked before me. Her hand brushed the pocket of my birthday shirt, and she fingered the shape inside it. Withdrawing an old snapshot, she held it out, her thumb pinched tight to a corner. Leaning to see it, I had to squint, the snowflakes obscuring its surface. "Take it," she said, "I saved it for you, to hang in your mountain museum."

It was the picture of Darcy on Miami Beach, retrieved with my shirt when she'd tossed it on the tracks the night that Carter died. She was smiling and tanned in the lemon bikini, posed on one foot at the water's edge, her other leg raised with arms splayed wide, as if swimming underwater, or reaching for a star.

When I took the photo, when Darcy released it, she sprang and snatched the cap from my head in a single, blinding swipe. When I stammered, "Hey, that's not the—" she looked me straight in the eye.

"You were my team, my favorite Yankee. It was always and only you."

Stomping off through the mounting drifts, her boots made the tiny tinkling sound that faded away as she went. I watched her vanish around the corner of the church, saw her reappear briefly through a window on the other side. Then there was just my own dark reflection and the outline of wintry trees, each pane glazed at its own distinct angle, uniquely distorted and dimpled with age. Memories eddied in the warped planes of glass, floating like lily pads on the surface of a dream, pastel and perfumed with shampoo and lilac, impressions like teeth marks tattooed on the skin. In collage-like reflections of mirror and mind, I watched Darcy slip daisies through the fingers of angels, draw peace signs on berry-brown skin. Smoking Kools, lighting candles, holding matches to a spoon, licking snowballs, reading fortunes, kicking flip flops down the tracks … I could hear her dress rustle through the lightning bug fields, taste the salt tears on her chin, her hair in the moonlight an eclipse of the sun, her panties blood red on white sheets.

How like me to betray her, I thought, and how like her to forgive. After all my suspicions, all my jealousy and doubt, I was the source of the one true deception, while she remained faithful, even to herself. Darcy's past was not so dark she couldn't attempt to escape it; her present was simply the darker place from which she refused to run. She disguised more than hid the awful truth, dressing it up like a doll or a model in the semblance of beauty she denied in herself, her greatest lie the sin of omission, while I omitted all my sins, admitting only to those that served me.

I turned and plunged after her through the falling snow, following her boot prints to the narrow stone stairway, squinting down the length of deserted 9A toward the pink light winking in the distance. Stepping backward, retracing my tracks, I followed her trail to the headstones of the Van Couenhoven's where I spied her struggling up the white mantled hillside, headed ever deeper into the graveyard.

"Darcy!" I shouted, raising a hand. "Wait!"

She faltered a second and fell to one knee, her red hood obscuring her face. "Don't try to follow me. Please!" she called and plunged ahead again. Then she stopped, and turned, and shouted something I struggled to hear in the storm, her words sucked away in a fierce rush of wind, a cowl of the winter cloaking her departure.

Standing there on the graves of my ancestors, searching for a glimpse of her scarlet coat, I was swept by a spiraling gust of emotion as voluminous and silent as the snow, and I caught my breath at the beauty of the moment, its hint of a kōan, the haiku's perfection, a flourish of ink upon linen. In all that I'd read or believed of such things, nothing could have prepared me, the puzzle parts falling in place from the sky revealed as a swirling self-portrait. Painted in the tiniest, most painstaking dots by a deft, Michelangelan hand, I saw through its eyes the man I'd become, the child I had been now departed. The ghosts of my past trembled out on my breath, heedless of snow passing through them, released to discover a truth of their own on a trail through great beauty like mountains, reduced to mere legends, to letters in closets, forbidden from haunting my life.

Fading away there remained only snowflakes, great robes of chaotic design, the most delicate fabric, the whitest of lace from the shawl of an Eskimo Saint. It was all I could do to surrender the dream, to lower my arm and just let her go. When my heart beat again, the world was transformed, life become art in the mind's sleight of hand, and it stunned me how fitting our poem came to end, how exquisitely crafted the turn, that hope should survive in the last, lost words of the mysterious Darcy Saint James, my blonde Madonna, God's own sweet tooth, the only girl I would ever love if I lived for a thousand years.

About the Author

SCOTT SWANSON grew up in the New York suburbs, attended the New York School of Visual Arts in Manhattan, and moved to Washington State in the early 70's. He's been a logger, construction worker, and oil refinery hand. He is currently a semi-retired building contractor living in the shadow of the North Cascades.

www.ingramcontent.com/pod-product-compliance
Lightning Source LLC
Chambersburg PA
CBHW030910300726
48970CB00001B/94